D0253064

SMILE BEACH MURDER

SMILE BEACH MURDER

Alicia Bessette

BERKLEY PRIME CRIME
NEW YORK

BERKLEY PRIME CRIME
Published by Berkley
An imprint of Penguin Random House LLC
penguinrandomhouse.com

Library of Congress Cataloging-in-Publication Data

Names: Bessette, Alicia, author.
Title: Smile Beach murder / Alicia Bessette.
Description: New York: Berkley Prime Crime, [2022] |
Series: Outer Banks bookshop mysteries
Identifiers: LCCN 2021047548 (print) | LCCN 2021047549 (ebook) |
ISBN 9780593336885 (hardcover) | ISBN 9780593336892 (ebook)
Subjects: LCGFT: Novels.
Classification: LCC PS3602.E783 S65 2022 (print) | LCC PS3602.E783 (ebook) |
DDC 813/.6—dc23
LC record available at https://lccn.loc.gov/2021047548
LC ebook record available at https://lccn.loc.gov/2021047549

Printed in the United States of America
1st Printing

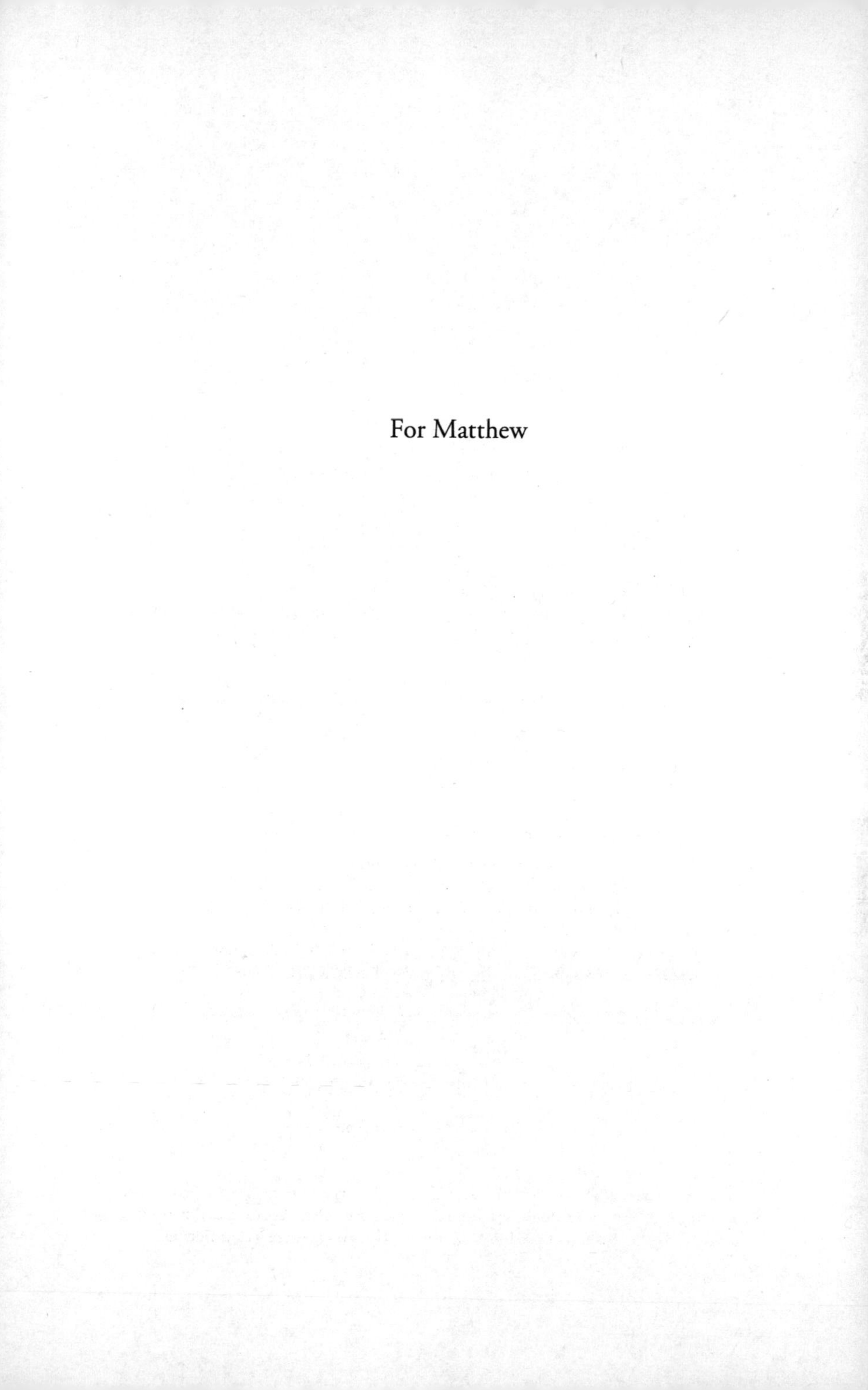

For Matthew

SMILE BEACH MURDER

1

I ran for Smile Beach with the tangs of summer in my nose and an ache in my heart. The parking lot smelled like sunscreen and cedar trees and French fries. I breathed it all in, trotting past the burger truck parked in the shade, past the rows of cars steaming in the sun, and onto the sand-strewn ramp. Overhead, purple martins somersaulted against an impossibly blue sky. I heard the *tling-tling* of a bicycle and, farther south, the bellow of the ferry as it bumped the rubber-edged dock in the harbor.

Cattail Island.

My mother had loved it.

I wanted to love it too.

"Hey, ma'am!" A dad was passing me on the ramp, leading his cute family to the burger truck. "It's called *Smile* Beach," he said to me as he pulled a T-shirt over his furred belly. "Not Frown Beach!"

His kid's floppy hat cast a pink glow on her single enormous front tooth. She erupted in giggles when the mom tickled her. The mom then shot me a smile like the one I'd seen on many a summertime visitor over the years. A smile brought on by chilled wine and vitamin D absorption. "Is this place paradise or what?" she asked.

"Paradise," I said.

"It's just like that old chamber of commerce slogan. What was it? *Cattail—the isle worth your while.*"

"Something like that." It was actually *the down-home isle that's worth your while*, but I didn't feel like getting into it, so I gave the woman a friendly little wave before turning onto Smile Beach. The gentle curve of it suggested a half-moon or a crescent—or a smile, which is what the founding Cattailers went with. I slowed to a walk so I wouldn't kick sand onto the families as they sprawled on towels and reclined in beach chairs. Parents held tablets above their faces. Teens took selfies. Kids became entirely encrusted in sand.

Cattail Island is known for its beaches. The east-side ones evoke the covers of summer escape novels—windswept dunes sloping to fine sand and, beyond, the vast gray Atlantic. The west-side beaches, including Smile Beach, feature the shallow, gentle waves of the Pamlico Sound. Unless, of course, there's a storm.

It wasn't the first time I'd wondered what it would have been like to go on a beach vacation with my parents. To have rubbed sunscreen onto my mom's shoulders. To have tossed a football with my dad, whoever he was. To have dozed so hard I forgot my name, then galloped for the water like a wild Outer Banks mustang.

I walked toward the old Smile Beach fishing pier, which sagged ten feet above the Pamlico. The sad old thing had missing railings and crooked pilings and looked as though the next stiff breeze would send it toppling into the chop. That didn't stop anglers from casting out, trying their luck for speckled trout or bluefish or flounder.

Past the pier, the Elder Tree came into view, its branches beckoning as if wind had blown them into that shape. And wind had, over the centuries. At the northernmost point of Cattail Island, the live oak's trunk measured fifty feet around. Shade engulfed me as I followed the path curling from the beach into the woods.

I could still climb like a local. Scaling the queenliest tree on Cattail involved making use of a rotten fence remnant. Hopping,

I grabbed the pickets and crept up until I could hook an arm around the giant branch paralleling the ground. My fingertips caught the lip of a teardrop-shaped cavity. I wriggled and grunted and heaved and soon was seated, legs dangling. Sweat trickled down my temples, my back, my shins. I must have sweated away my sunscreen, because my skin felt like rugburn.

If heat had a sound it would be waves crashing and insects clicking and leaves stirring in undetectable breezes and, from someone's portable speaker, Carrie Underwood snarling about taking a Louisville Slugger to both headlights.

This barrier island, nine miles long, is shaped like a cattail, whip thin except for the wide part, three miles across. The wide part's where most of the dwellings are, bungalow-style rental cottages and modest cedar-shake stilt homes. The southern end of Cattail Island curves slightly westward, allowing a glimpse of the lighthouse even from where I sat in the Elder Tree. All these years later and the sight of that hometown landmark poking above the treetops still made my chest hollow, as if someone had taken an icy scoop and cored out my heart.

I shifted so that a clutch of Spanish moss blocked the lighthouse from view.

In addition to its beaches, Cattail Island is also known for being difficult to access. No bridges touch its shores—which means a long drive no matter what direction you're coming from, followed by a long wait for the ferry.

Whenever I visited home, I felt marooned.

"How's the job search going?" a voice boomed.

My uncle appeared on the path. He peered up at me, his beard like pine shavings springing out in all directions, his sea-green eyes twinkling.

I took him in—his dusty overalls, his cannonball belly, the water bottle in his big hand. A nugget of confusion knocked around inside my chest. I wanted to throw my arms around him *and* hightail it back to Charlotte. Back to my old life. My adult life. My real life.

"How'd you find me?" I asked him.

"Drove around for miles looking for the only person crazy enough to go for a run at high noon." Hudson was one of the hundred or so remaining Cattailers who still spoke what was known as the Outer Banks brogue, in which *miles* sounded like *moiles* and *high* came out *hoi*. It was strange and charming, a southern drawl lilting with an English accent.

"I needed to get outside," I said. "I might be in a tree right now, but the past couple days I've been all over this glorified sandbar, looking for work. I won't be living in your loft for the rest of my life. And I won't be staying on-island very long either. That, I can guarantee."

"Cattail really is a prison sentence to you, isn't it?"

"Please don't take it personally." I slid down from the branch and landed hard, knees crackling.

"You do realize it's two-thirds of the way through June. Seasonal work's been arranged for months. What's your plan? Go back to waiting tables at the diner? Vacuuming rental cottages on change-over days?"

"What do I look like, a college student?" That was who got those jobs. Not thirty-eight-year-old laid-off newspaper reporters with crackling knees. "I'll find something," I said.

"Obviously the *Cattail Crier* isn't an option."

"Obviously." My complicated history with the editor in chief made working for the local weekly an impossibility.

"What about the MotherVine?" my uncle asked.

"The bookshop?" I pictured it. The tall windows and pine-plank floors. My mother, curled in her favorite armchair, an open book in her lap . . . "Not my speed," I said.

Hudson stepped closer. His hair stuck up in tufts as if he hadn't bothered brushing. Because he hadn't. He smelled like lumber and Irish Spring soap. "Your mother loved that bookshop. You did too, at one time."

The air was suddenly too thick, like paste in my lungs. He handed me the bottled water, and I took a few ice-cold sips. Then I squeezed some water over my head, yelping from relief and shock.

"It's been twenty-five years, Callie," he said.

"Twenty-six."

"The way I see it, your only other alternative is shelling crabs at Cattail Seafood."

"I'd literally rather *be* a crab at Cattail Seafood."

"City made you special? Above selling books to the good people of Cattail? The people who raised you up? The tourists who put food on our tables?"

I looked away. When he worded it that way . . .

2

The MotherVine Bookshop's front door shined a candy-apple red. A sign taped to the jamb read: PLEASE MIND THE WET PAINT!

It was annual Paint Your Door Day. Red paint doesn't last on Cattail Island. In less than a year, the sun and gritty wind tag-team to beat all reds into pinks. But many owners of the downtown waterfront businesses had a thing for red front doors. And at the start of every summer, those doors were painted en masse.

Standing on the sidewalk, I took a few deep breaths. The breeze wasn't oceany here on the west side but instead smelled like brine and honeysuckle and whatever enticing specials the bistros were preparing. These few tree-lined blocks comprised the commercial section of Queen Street, which ran the whole length of Cattail Island, from the lighthouse in the south to Smile Beach in the north.

Tourists buzzed around me, ducking in and out of shops. Some paused to lick the ice cream dribbling down their wrists, to greet passengers streaming off the ferry, or to snap photos of the rows of glistening red doors. Across the street, the replica pirate ship was a favorite attraction, docked in the harbor and accessible by a gangplank. Kids climbed the rigging and waged air-sword fights on the main deck.

Before me, the brick bookshop looked enticing. A chalkboard out front promised a visit from a local author later in the week, and inside, shoppers browsed. Every now and then they'd pick up a book and turn it over, or run fingertips across the jacket. Their expressions ranged from delight to curiosity to sheer flight of fancy.

I steeled myself for more rejection. So far, I'd been turned down by just about every on-island employer that hired literature-major types, including Cattail Heritage Garden, which deemed me overqualified to scribble its press releases. Hudson had been right: the MotherVine was my last shot at somewhat-professional temporary employment.

I was about to enter when a passing car slowed, then swerved. It was avoiding a barrel-shaped silver tabby cat, hunched in the middle of the crosswalk, nibbling the remnants of what looked to have been a delicious fish taco. The food must have tumbled from some sorry pedestrian's takeout carton.

I crouched and made a kissy noise, trying to lure the cat out of harm's way. But I was no match for the fish taco. Another vehicle rounded the corner, a vintage Jeep Grand Wagoneer, mint green with a strip of wood paneling, the ultimate surf-mobile. The driver gave no indication that he was going to avoid the cat.

Meanwhile, the silver tabby was fully taco committed and didn't flinch at the oncoming vehicle.

"Hey." I stepped into the street, waving my arms. "Watch it. Look out!"

The Wagoneer still showed no signs of yielding. Neither did the cat.

I shot into the crosswalk, scooped up the tabby, pivoted, and leapt for the sidewalk. The Wagoneer braked, laying rubber and sending out a screech. It came to a stop in the crosswalk, front tires straddling the taco.

A few shopkeepers scurried out onto the sidewalks. "Slow down, mister!" yelled a mother pushing a stroller.

The driver stuck his head out the window. I couldn't see much of him; the sun was dazzlingly bright. But I did see him wave in my direction. "Sure am sorry about that," he called. "You okay?"

"Fine," I said. The trembling cat was so heavy it started slipping, and I had to jiggle it to get a better grip.

"My bad," he said before slowly driving off.

The cat—TIN MAN, according to his collar's name tag—squirmed in my arms. But when I scratched his chin, he stopped trembling and pressed into my fingers, purring like a boat motor. "You've got eight lives left, big guy," I told him.

A trim woman darted from the MotherVine, arms outstretched. Antoinette Redfield was the owner of the bookshop and, apparently, the cat. "Tinnakeet Man!" she said. "Oh, my dear sweet Tinnakeet Man."

I passed the cat into her arms, and she cradled him. "Callie," she said, her eyes shining. "I was out back but a customer told me what happened. He saw everything." She kissed Tin Man's head. "Thank you."

"Right place, right time."

"He was a stray. I started feeding him."

"Looks like you haven't stopped."

"He refused to go away, so I had to make him a proper bookshop cat. He usually isn't tempted by the outdoors. Except when it's filled with the scent of fresh, hot mahi-mahi from the taco joint."

"I can relate. Those tacos are narcotizing."

She canoodled Tin Man some more, picking a piece of cilantro from his whiskers. "He seems no worse for wear. What about you? Are you all right? Did you hurt yourself? Are you shook up at all?"

"I'm fine, Ant. Really."

As always, she was dressed sensibly. Plaid button-down shirt, walking shorts, sandals. Her chin-length silver curls retained hints of strawberry. She was still nimble thanks to all the surfing she'd done in her youth, when she would even brave winter's wind-tossed, thirty-degree waves. Her voice had a ringing-bell quality.

She went over to the bookshop's entrance and placed the cat inside. Turning back to me, she asked, "How can I thank you?"

"Oh, you don't have to—"

"I most certainly do."

"Well, actually, I came here looking for work. Did Hudson mention it?" My uncle and Antoinette had been friends for years.

"The island rumor mill mentioned it," she said. "Shame about the big buyout in the city."

"Right. Thanks." I looked down at my feet. Flip-flops were perfectly acceptable for job hunting on Cattail, but I couldn't help feeling suddenly self-conscious—about my chipped toenail polish, hasty ponytail, and dress from several seasons ago, which had started to resemble a large dishrag. But it was practical, cotton with hidden pockets sewn into bias seams, a dress my mom would have approved. And at the moment, it was the best I could do.

The truth was, the *Charlotte Times* hadn't laid off everybody. Only the sixty-two worker bees who had failed to make themselves indispensable.

Callie Padget, Worker Bee Number Sixty-Two, at your service.

"My high-school helper quit high and dry last week when she realized lifeguarding was more lucrative than slinging books," Antoinette said. "That gives you an idea of my pay scale."

Shading my eyes, I peered straight into her face. "I'm prepared."

"What do you know about working in a bookshop?"

About as much as I knew about quantum mechanics. Newspaper work was my true vocation.

And it was a dying vocation. As was working in a bookshop.

Temporary measure, I reminded myself. My plan, hatched during my post-run shower thirty minutes earlier, was to keep publishing independent articles on my online portfolio in the hopes of attracting a daily newspaper job. I was going to get back to being a reporter ASAP. If not in Charlotte, then in any other city that would have me. "I promise to make myself useful for as long as I'm on-island," I said.

"You know your way around a coffeepot?"

"Like a pro."

"Wheels?"

I gestured to a Honda Civic, my trusty two-door steed, parked in one of the coveted spots along Queen Street. The front and rear tires had caught the curb.

Whoops.

"My on-island delivery service is a big hit," Antoinette said. "Locals put a high value on face-to-face interaction. You can drive, or walk, if you have the time and inclination. I don't care, as long as people get their books."

"I'm hired? Just like that?"

She glanced at the bookshop's front bay window, where Tin Man was sitting, swishing his tail and training his amber eyes on the seagull that had descended upon the abandoned taco. "You earned this job, as far as I'm concerned," she said. "Work whenever you want. My hours of operation are somewhat sporadic, as you probably remember. But we'll figure it out. Just don't rack up more than twenty-five hours a week."

Something like relief washed through me. Was this the job I really wanted? No. Was it better than no job? Yes. "Thank you," I said.

"Tin Man isn't the only new thing around the MotherVine

since you were home for Christmas. I've made a big change. Did your uncle tell you?"

"You know how he is."

She spread her arms before the red door. "Come on in and see for yourself."

3

The shop's front corner still hosted a reading area, though the magnolia-patterned armchair where my mother spent so much time had been replaced by two microfiber papasan chairs. Many afternoons growing up, I'd walked straight from school to here, to find Mom taking a break from work. Sometimes thimbles still adorned her fingertips as she turned the pages of the latest book by Mary Higgins Clark. If I had a nickel for every time I'd heard Antoinette laughingly say, "This is a bookshop, Teri. Not a library," or every time my mother declared, "Good old MHC never lets you down."

I turned down the main aisle, aware of Antoinette watching me. The floor creaked as sunlight slanted and dust motes hovered. I inhaled the aromas of coffee and paper and ink. As far as layout went, the MotherVine hadn't changed. The cookbooks faced the coffee station. The children's titles were still in the vicinity of the off-limits staircase, which led to second-floor storage. Pots of lavender graced every windowsill.

"What's different?" I asked. That was when I noticed the fruit-scented breeze, and the back door, flung wide. "You opened the mother vine to the public?"

She grinned.

Out back, a sun-bleached pergola shaded wrought-iron tables and chairs. A few tourists—their too-pink cheeks and fanny packs were dead giveaways—sat quietly, sipping beverages and browsing through books they had selected from the shop. Beyond the tables, stone pavers transitioned into soft dirt, and the pergola became a living ceiling: the tendrils of the mother vine, which gnarled up from the rear of the yard. Serrated leaves and bunches of bronze grapes twisted over the trellises, stretching all the way to the surrounding privacy fence, slatted to allow the breeze.

Each table featured a copper platter full of grapes and a placard that read:

> The world's oldest known progenitor of Tinnakeet grapes grows here, in this small patch of land. Five centuries ago, Native Americans and the earliest European visitors might have plucked grapes from this very spot. The vine has survived countless hurricanes as well as permanent settlement. Like books, with proper care, the vine will survive long after we are gone. Thank you for not picking the grapes or disturbing the vine in any way.
>
> —The Mgmt.

Antoinette had never allowed customers out back, for fear they'd tamper with the vine. So it was always a special treat come August, when she asked my mother and me to help with the main harvest. The rest of the year, the most we saw of the vine was whatever we glimpsed through the back window.

"Nowadays, people want more than books," Antoinette said as we stepped outside. "For one thing, they want selfies with Tin Man. He's sort of internet famous."

"A social media sensation?"

"He's got Instagram flair. Good thing, since it's the only advertising I can afford these days. So far, I've been able to avoid selling puzzles and games and a lot of other novelties because I have this little piece of natural history to offer."

"It's beautiful," I said. "Like an oasis."

"The grapes are free, y'all," she announced to her customers. "The books are not." We'd reached the vine. From it, she plucked a perfect orb and popped it between my lips. Flavors crashed over my tongue. Wine and jam and spindrift. "Welcome home," she said.

Back inside, before a seashell-bordered mirror, Antoinette fluffed her curls. Then, reaching behind the checkout counter, she grabbed her phone and wristlet-style wallet. "Now that your little orientation's over, I've got to run some errands."

"But I don't know how to do anything," I said. "I can't even open the register. Let me run errands for you."

"What's the point of hiring an assistant if I don't get to soak up the sun every now and then? I'll be back in ten. Maybe fifteen. Possibly twenty."

"But—"

"If anyone comes in, greet them. They'll browse without encouragement, believe me."

"What if they want to buy something?"

"Stall. Turn on that Callie Padget charm."

"*Charm?*"

"What's the worst that could happen?" My new boss was out the door like a blur.

4

Tin Man, sitting nearby, looked up at me and meowed. "Guess this makes us coworkers," I said.

He turned and strutted away, tail high.

The spinnable tower of new releases stood in the same old spot. I gave it a twirl, admiring the variety of book covers. Sweeping gowns, soaring vistas, a dog brimming with humanity. The typography enchanted me too, romantic cursives and cold-edged sans serifs and everything in between.

I hadn't read a new release in quite some time. In fact, I couldn't remember the last book I'd read. I suddenly wanted to remedy that, to read every book in sight.

I was devouring the first page of *Cottage by the Sea* by Debbie Macomber when a woman barreled into the shop, gauzy blond hair flying. She bolted for the far wall, the Local Interest section. Scanning the shelves, she collapsed onto the floor and started picking off the lowest books one by one. "No," she muttered, stacking them beside her. "No, no, no . . ."

Eva Meeks. Older sister of Georgia Meeks, the only friend from high school I'd bothered keeping up with. I'd kept up with Eva too, by extension. She wore a lightweight Meeks Hardware sweatshirt, cutoff denim shorts, and low-top magenta Chuck Taylors that looked so old, I wondered if they were the same pair she'd rocked back in 1995.

I stepped closer. Eva's head whipped up, and a thousand-watt smile lit her face. "Callie Padget! Come on over. I'm on to something."

I knelt beside her. "What's up?"

"The historical society wasn't much help, and neither was the library, so I came here. Figured the MotherVine might point me in the right direction." She paused to catch her breath. "Of course, I've already studied most of these books. And the ones I haven't read don't seem relevant."

"Relevant to what, exactly?" I asked.

She glanced around, then leaned closer. "A treasure hunt."

"Ah. Of course."

Eva was the island's foremost treasure hunt junkie. Blackbeard, the notorious pirate, was rumored to have hidden from authorities here in Cattail back in the day, and was definitely beheaded by them a couple of islands south. Many enthusiasts like Eva believed in his buried treasure—actual chests long-ago forgotten on the Outer Banks, waiting to be recovered.

I slipped a volume from the shelf. The cover showed a pirate ship pitching against an ominous sky.

"That's a new one to me," she said.

Opening to the index, I scanned until I reached the *T*s. "Nothing about a treasure *hunt*, per se, but lots of references to treasure. See?"

"I'll take it." She snatched the book from my hands, then gave a self-aware laugh. "Wait—what are you doing here? You know how I get with stuff like this. I didn't even ask about you! Last time I checked you were killing it in Charlotte. Miss Bigtime Reporter."

"Taking a short break from the rat race."

"Good for you." As she got to her feet, she seemed weaker than I'd known her to be, as if the burst of activity had exhausted her. Maybe she'd had a rough night of sleep, tossing and turning as her mind waltzed with visions of rubies and sapphires the size of babies' fists.

"Hey," I said. "You okay?"

"I'll call you. Girls' night out at Salty Edward's? Beers for you and me, chardonnay for my sister."

"Definitely."

Winking, she slid a twenty-dollar bill from her back pocket and tossed it onto the checkout counter. "In the meantime, I'm gearing up for adventure."

Later that night, I had just fallen asleep in my old Murphy bed in Hudson's loft. The humidity combined with the running and job begging had pounded me into an exhausted lump. But I'd forgotten to silence my phone, and it rang.

It was Eva, spewing words with the ferocity of a tornado. "Want to meet me? I know it's last-minute. But I just had a big break. And it seemed like you could use some fun."

"What?" I rubbed my eyes. "Meet you where?"

"The lighthouse." There was a short, stabbing silence. "Oh my God," she blurted. "I'm such an idiot. I'm so excited I just—"

"Don't sweat it," I said.

"I'm sorry."

I sat up. Hudson's little terrier, Scupper, was curled next to me. I massaged his neck. "I'm over it," I told Eva.

"You sure you don't want to join me?"

"Rain check. Tell me all about it tomorrow, okay?"

5

The next morning, Antoinette gave me the task of sorting books that had been dropped off in the MotherVine's donation bin. The shop sold mostly new books, but to customers who didn't mind stooping and riffling, wooden crates on the floor offered deeply discounted used books.

She set me up out back, where the scent of grapes wafted on the gentle breeze. The donation bin—an outsize plastic storage container—took up most of the table. Extra-musty or dog-eared books went into a box labeled FREE! while books in better condition were set aside for resale. I worked with a cup of coffee steaming at my elbow. Tin Man used the edges of the bin and box to scratch his chin, alternating between them.

Antoinette was strolling under the grapevine's tendrils. She was just short enough to fit. Red half-moon reading glasses perched on her nose as she scrolled on her phone. "Listen to this review that just popped up. 'Decent book selection, crap coffee. Their tea isn't all that great either.' Three stars. It's like, excuse me, the MotherVine is a bookshop. And what about the free grapes? Doesn't that count for anything?" She tossed her head, curls glinting in the sunlight that peeked through the grape leaves.

"I think the coffee here's decent," I said. "But maybe we could up our hot beverage game."

"That didn't take long."

I tossed an abused copy of *Death on the Nile* into the free box. "What didn't take long?"

"You said *we.*" Antoinette nodded at the bin. Tin Man had jumped inside, and his tail was flicking to and fro. "Watch him," she said. "He's prone to the munchies."

I looked in. The cat was nibbling the corner of a like-new paperback. Grunting at his heft, I set him on the pavers. Then I reached back in to rescue the book he'd been chewing—and my jaw hung open. The cover showed a far-off woman huddled underneath an umbrella, pushing against a rainstorm. It was a copy of my mom's favorite book, *While My Pretty One Sleeps*, by Mary Higgins Clark.

"Wow," Antoinette said, wandering over. The scent of grapes clung to her. "That's one of MHC's lesser-known books. But your mother sure did love it. Did you ever read it?"

"Once." Right after Mom had died. Up until that point I'd pretty much stuck to murder mysteries, the cozier the better. I'd refused to wear the sundresses my mother sewed for me, and I'd refused to read her books.

It took her death to make me curious: Why did she love *this* particular tale?

I soon found out. The main character was a fashion designer in New York City, Neeve Kearny, whose life of snacking on caviar and gliding through city streets in the back of a Lincoln Town Car was about as far away from my mother's as I could imagine. Mom never complained about hemming housedresses or patching the occasional hole in a boat sail. But had she secretly dreamed of running her own Madison Avenue boutique, like Neeve in *While My Pretty One Sleeps*?

I examined the paperback, which would have been in great used condition if it weren't for Tin Man's teeth marks. "Do you still have . . ."

"The Mary Higgins Clark shelf? Didn't you notice it yesterday? Let's pay a visit."

Just inside the back door was the MotherVine's large selection of mysteries. Agatha Christie's detective novels got prime, eye-level placement. Antoinette had a soft spot for Agatha because she was reportedly the first European woman to stand on a surfboard. In the shark-infested waters off South Africa, no less.

The classic mysteries gave way to hard-edged moderns starring down-and-out private eyes or unreliable narrators. On the other side of a tall window were the softies—mysteries that involved knitting and antiques and teashops and every other sweet theme you could think of. The cozies had been my favorites—but when my mother died, I'd picked up the book on her nightstand, and my adoration of Mary Higgins Clark began. Just like in the cozies, MHC's heroines were professional, independent, and nervy. But they occupied a darker world, which mine had suddenly become.

Opposite the cozies was a shelf devoted entirely to MHC's books. Antoinette stocked them partly because they were perennial sellers, but also as a tribute to my mother. The shelf was painted bright foliage green like all the other shelves in the MotherVine, but a small sign set this one apart.

> Good old MHC never lets you down.
>
> —Teri Padget

I ran my fingers along the spines. *Where Are the Children?*, *A Stranger Is Watching*, *A Cry in the Night*.

"Did I mention the employee discount here is a hundred percent?" Antoinette asked.

I looked up. "Are you serious?"

"Not at all. But just this one time, why don't you take that copy of *Pretty One* home. On the house. Tin Man picked it out for you, after all."

Maybe she was right. Perhaps a little Neeve Kearny would do me some good.

An hour later I was behind the counter, about to learn the Mother-Vine computer system. For all the after-school time I'd spent in this bookshop, I'd never seen it from this perspective. And I had to admit, I liked it. I liked watching customers stroll in, blink away the sun, and sigh as the cool—but not too cool—air-conditioning embraced them. Then they'd look around at all the books, each one offering them a chance to lose themselves, find themselves, or both.

It was also fun to discover what Antoinette had tucked away behind the counter: a bowl of peppermint candies, a felted mouse stuffed with catnip, and random supplies such as glitter, construction paper, and chalk.

I'd freshened our coffees, and she was giving an encouraging speech. "Remember. The many quirks of the computer system are part and parcel of the MotherVine's charm. Ready?"

"As I'll ever be," I said.

And then a man rushed in. He was in his fifties, and his face was sunburnt except for the white shape of sunglasses around his eyes. He scurried over to a woman of similar age who was perusing the Local Interest titles, right where Eva had been kneeling a little more than twelve hours earlier. "Honey," the man said, placing a hand on her shoulder. "I thought I'd find you here. Guess what I just heard? You aren't going believe it."

Antoinette and I exchanged a surprised glance. Then we both leaned forward ever so slightly, trying to be discreet about our eavesdropping.

"A woman jumped off Cattail Lighthouse last night," he said. "They say it's been almost twenty-six years to the day since this other woman jumped."

With a sharp intake of breath, the woman clutched the book she'd been holding. "How horrible."

"I know," he said. "I didn't think things like that happened here."

Everything seemed to tilt and tip. Like all the books were about to slide right off the shelves.

Antoinette laid a hand on my arm. "You know how this island gossips, Callie," she said quietly. "I'm sure it's nothing."

But dread had hooked a net around my heart and was tugging it down, down. If something had happened to Eva, and I could have prevented it . . . "Eva was in here yesterday, talking about an adventure," I said to Antoinette. "And last night, she called me. She was rambling. About the lighthouse." Tears brimmed in my eyes, but I wasn't a weeper, so I blinked them back.

Then I grabbed my cross-body bag and said, "I have to go."

6

The shadow of Cattail Lighthouse sliced across the marsh like a blade.

A blade pointing to a body. A woman, a gauzy blonde, lying facedown. The back of her sweatshirt declared MEEKS HARDWARE. Her cutoff shorts and low-top magenta Chuck Taylors were splattered with mud and blood. Her impact had bent the cattails; their cigar-like tips now pointed horizontally.

I didn't need to see her heart-shaped face, her feathery eyebrows, to know it was Eva Meeks. My chest seized with an icy, hollow feeling. If you'd punched me in the heart, I'd have shattered.

A moment ago, I'd elbowed past the crowd of silent onlookers, ducked under the police tape, and walked the boardwalk until . . .

Not ten feet from the ends of Eva's sprawled hair, a white cross stood, crooked. The cattails around it were encroaching, obscuring my mother's name. *Teri Padget.* Something papery and chestnut-shaped hung from the crossbar. A wasp nest, just getting started.

I swallowed hard. My bag suddenly felt like it weighed as much as I did. I tried not to picture Eva in free fall, arms flailing, scream piercing. Tried not to picture my mother, celery-green dress billowing.

Last night was when I should have come here. Last night. Not now.

Now I was too late.

Calm, Padget. Calm. I forced myself to take a few deep breaths, inhaling the sharp tang of the marsh and the sweet aroma of cattails, which smelled to me like earth and ocean combined. I exhaled deliberately, blowing air through my lips. *Calm.*

Footsteps clattered on the boardwalk. A large man with bushy cinnamon-and-sugar eyebrows and a face like a potato was hotfooting it from the lighthouse.

Drew Jurecki, chief of Cattail police. "What are you—hey, aren't you . . ."

"Callie Padget, sir."

He glanced at the white cross. "How'd you get here so fast from Charlotte? I don't need any big-city reporters—"

"I'm here as a concerned citizen. Maybe I can help."

"I'm not one to mince words, Callie. So here goes. *She*"—he pointed to Eva's body, then to my mother's cross—"has nothing to do with *her*."

"Of course not."

He stepped to the opposite side of the boardwalk, motioning for me to come along. As I joined him, his face softened. "This looks to have been a suicide."

"What? No. Eva Meeks called me last night. See?" I showed him my phone, Eva's 9:32 call. "She asked me to meet her here. Why would she invite me along if her plan was to end her own life?"

"Cry for help? Or maybe it was a spur-of-the-moment decision."

"She didn't jump. There's no way." In high school, she'd had the leads in all the musicals. She'd been Little Orphan Annie and Peter Pan and Dolly Gallagher Levi. People who could harness that kind of life-affirming positivity didn't . . . Or maybe they did. When they tired from all the harnessing. "She came into the bookshop yesterday—"

"The MotherVine?" Chief Jurecki said. "You working there now or something?"

"Temporary setup."

"You were friendly, you and Eva?"

"With her sister, Georgia, who was my grade. Eva was a few years older than us."

"All the more reason you shouldn't be here."

"But, Chief, she was talking a mile a minute about a—"

"Not to be harsh, but I can't deal with emotions right now. There'll be enough of that when I inform the next of kin."

Next of kin.

Georgia. And Summer, Eva's daughter. Eva had been forty-one years old, I knew. Which meant Summer was . . . twelve.

Just like my mom had been forty-one when she died, and I'd been twelve.

Jurecki hadn't been chief back then. He'd been a beat cop, and he'd spent the ensuing years climbing the ranks. No doubt he was thinking about his legacy now. He needed this situation to be cut-and-dried. Tidily wrapped up.

We stood in silence for a moment. The breeze churned. Overhead, clouds like battleships rolled. I glanced at the tourists gathered in the parking lot. Some wore cameras or binoculars around their necks. A few sipped from Tervis tumblers, ice cubes rattling, as if they were at a backyard barbecue and not the scene of a tragedy.

Two police cruisers were parked, along with my rusted Civic and a dozen sedans and SUVs topped with kayaks. More tape fluttered around a red SUV boasting Meeks Hardware decals. Beyond the lot, nestled among scrubby trees, was the lighthouse keeper's cottage.

"Couldn't it have been just a crazy accident?" I asked. "Like what happened with my mother."

"We'll try and rule that out," Jurecki said. "But I doubt it." He gave me a sad but severe look. "My wife had gotten to know Eva from her volunteer work at Cattail Heritage Garden. And Eva had received some bad news recently. About her health."

"Oh." So she'd killed herself to avoid illness? That was his theory?

An ambulance crunched into the lot. No siren, no rush, as two EMTs unloaded a gurney. A tourist took advantage of the distraction to separate from the crowd, duck under the tape, and aim his smartphone toward the body. "Sir!" Jurecki bellowed. "Stop it right there, buddy." He thundered toward the man.

Leaving just me and Eva, embedded in a starfish shape at my feet.

Trembling, I gazed up at the lighthouse. Navy bricks on the bottom half, white bricks on top. This close, it seemed gargantuan, like some sort of obelisk-monster looming up from the marsh.

Eva Meeks, found dead. Twenty-six years, almost to the day, after my mother. At the base of the lighthouse, just a few feet from where my mother had landed.

What if I had met Eva last night, like she asked? I might have prevented . . . whatever happened.

A lump like a sharp-edged seed pinched the inside of my throat. Part of me wanted to lose it, to drop to my knees on the boardwalk and burst into tears.

But this was no time for falling apart.

7

A cinder block propped open the lighthouse door. Stepping onto the harlequin marble floor, I let my eyes adjust to the gloom, taking in the old nautical maps and a bronze plaque dated 1883.

Eighteen eighty-three. Blackbeard predated the lighthouse by a century and a half, so whatever treasure hunt Eva'd been after couldn't have had anything to do with him. But something must have pointed her here, and she'd decided to investigate nonetheless. *I'm gearing up for adventure*, she'd said.

The hallway opened into the main area, where an iron staircase helixed. A lanky beat cop leaned against the railing, scrolling on her phone. "You press?" she asked. "Press only."

"In that case . . ." I reached into my bag and flashed my old pass from the *Charlotte Times.*

"What paper was that?" she asked.

"I'm independent." It wasn't *exactly* a lie. The slick feel of my old press pass made me realize that a responsible, nuanced article about what had really happened here, posted to my online portfolio, could set straight the public record *and* impress hiring city-desk editors. I fished out a pen and notepad, hoping they made me look more official, less dazed. "The chief knows me, Officer . . ." Her name tag glinted in the dim light. "Officer Fusco," I said.

Fusco was younger than me by ten years at least. She had wrangled her carroty hair into a French braid and a few strands escaped her cap, clawing her ears.

"Did you know her?" I asked.

"The deceased? Only from the ads. *Everything* and *the kitchen sink.*"

"Right." Eva had been the star of a series of local television commercials. My personal favorite featured her dressed as a pirate, complete with an eye patch and plastic sword. Another popular variation showed her on her surfboard off Cattail Beach, dropping into a barrel. Each commercial ended the same: Eva spreading her arms as the cash register chimed open. *At Meeks Hardware, we've got everything* and *the kitchen sink!* "You know Cattail Volunteers Month?" I asked Fusco. "She started it. Eva. Back when we were in high school."

"You're from here?"

"Born and raised. Sounds like you're from Bertie County." I'd spent some time there. Did a big feature on an experimental agricultural school. Fusco's accent was gooey, like theirs had been.

The officer glared down her slender nose. I must have nailed her accent, and she didn't like being outed as a country bumpkin.

"Can I show you something?" I presented my phone, the call history. "If Eva had suicide in mind, why would she request my company?"

"You should tell the chief."

"I did."

Footfalls rang from above. On the spiral steps, a formidable woman in her late forties appeared. Her dark eyes were deep-set, giving her a fierce look.

The bottom of my stomach dropped away.

In my rush to get here, amid the bombshell of taking in Eva Meeks's lifeless body, I'd forgotten whose journalistic territory I was invading. Trish freaking Berryman's. Editor in chief of the *Cattail Crier*, and my former neighbor.

Take away her harried newspaperwoman facade, and she

looked much the same as she had on the front porch of the funeral home, the day of my mother's calling hours. In fact, it was all too easy to picture her retching over a yaupon hedge while my uncle Hudson patted her back.

Trish reached me and Fusco and said hello, pleasantly enough.

"Hi," I managed, my quavering voice echoing off the bricks. I must have had a look on my face like I wanted to say a hundred complicated things at once. The tension between us made the air thrum. Were Trish's eyes warming with sympathy, or was I imagining it?

Fusco looked from Trish to me, back to Trish. No doubt the officer was wondering just what had happened between us.

Trish finally broke the awkward silence. "Terrible, terrible circumstances," she said. "But it's nice to see you, Callie. The *Charlotte Times* sent you all the way out here?"

"Oh, no. I'm on summer hiatus." I mashed my lips. She would have heard about the buyout. There's no way she'd believe they'd granted me leave.

"Well, I wish I could put you on the *Crier* masthead," she said, calling my bluff. "But we've been shoestringing it for years." She nodded at Fusco and stepped through the hallway, out into the morning.

"Bad blood?" Fusco asked me.

"Long story." Encountering Trish reinforced my resolve to ask good, reporterly questions. As a soft news source, the *Crier* was serviceable, but not many readers relied on it for the hard-hitting stuff. I could fulfill that need. "How'd Eva get in here, anyway?" I asked. "I know for a fact that extra precautions have been in place since the early nineties, when . . . when a woman fell, and—"

"You'll have to ask the chief about that." The officer's shoulder-mounted radio squawked. She twisted it off.

"Who discovered the body?"

"Chief told me to handle any press. I know the *Crier* lady, but I don't know you. You said you were an independent journalist?"

"That's right. Just gathering some basics." I slipped pen and notepad back into my bag. I hadn't written a word anyway, and maybe Fusco would open up if I didn't appear to be chomping at the bit.

Sure enough, she nodded. "The new lighthouse keeper, Gwen Montgomery, discovered the body. Chief will have more questions for her, once she's pulled herself together."

"Oh?"

"She was a bit wound up. She'd been performing a routine check of the grounds when she made the 911 call. Miss Montgomery did lock up, per protocol, at sundown last evening. We believe Eva gained access sometime after lockup."

More footsteps sang out from the spiral stairs. A statuesque woman descended and stood beside Fusco. I introduced myself as a freelance reporter, which brought order to the chaos clashing inside me. False order, maybe. But it was better than feeling helpless.

The stately woman turned out to be the medical examiner, Rasheeda Scarboro. "How long has Eva been there, Dr. Scarboro?" I asked.

"I'd estimate between eight and twelve hours, based on rigor."

"The autopsy will tell you for certain?"

"No autopsy for a lot of suicides these days. Budget constraints. If the family indicates the victim had been depressed or under a lot of undue pressure?" She shrugged.

"Are the railings safe up top?" I asked.

"Provided you stay on the proper side of them," Fusco said. "We have recovered positively no evidence to suggest this death was suspicious in nature. And I think you've asked enough questions."

"But how did Eva get inside the lighthouse? If that main door was locked."

Fusco gave me another down-the-nose glare.

"You don't know, do you?" I said. "You don't know how Eva got inside."

"Off the record," Dr. Scarboro said, pointing to the door, "there's supposed to be a big padlock. But apparently, it's nowhere to be found."

8

Eva didn't kill herself," I said out loud as I walked toward the lighthouse keeper's cottage. It was something I knew instinctually, the way a pelican knows to twist a certain way when it dives, to protect its fragile throat. If I was going to write anything accurate about her death, I needed facts. More than the ones I currently had.

I climbed the cottage's rickety porch steps and rapped my knuckles on the door. No answer.

Peering through threadbare curtains, I made out a couch, where a woman lay dozing, curled up like a child. I rapped again and she shot up as if triggered by an ejecting spring.

The door cracked open, revealing a pair of sunglasses, frazzled hair, and a mouth that looked too tired for a face little more than a quarter century old. Gwen Montgomery, I presumed.

It was strange to see her standing in this doorway. The previous resident—the curmudgeonly lighthouse keeper who'd preceded her—had sported a legit wooden leg and a Lincolnesque, curtain-style chin beard.

I told her my name. She opened the door wider. An odor of mildew escaped the entryway. "You with the *Crier*?" she asked. "They're supposed to interview me for a feature. Introduce me to the community. The new era of Cattail Lighthouse."

"Actually, I'm—"

"Been thinking of offering moonlight tours, on nights when there's a full moon. They do that at the lighthouse down in Hatteras and the public loves it. Brings in revenue."

I searched Gwen Montgomery's sunglasses but saw only smears behind the lenses. She seemed to be rambling. She must have been in shock, as they say. I knew something about shock. "You've had a difficult morning, I'm sure," I said.

"Up until an hour ago I thought I had the coolest job in the world." She chewed her vowels like natives of Delaware and the Philadelphia area. A lot of them had landed on the Outer Banks and in Charlotte too.

"I don't want to take up too much of your time," I said. "You see, I'm—"

"Before I got this job, I'd never stepped foot on Cattail Island. To this day I still haven't been north of the sound-side shops. And now I've got the police interrogating me. The police! And—" Gwen's jaw dropped. I spun around. A Virginia-based news van had pulled up to the boardwalk. The reporter hopped out, a pastel swirl. She began preening in the van's side mirror.

The news crew would be disappointed. The ninety-minute drive plus the ferry ride might have been worth it to cover a prominent death. A celebrity who had surreptitiously rented a sleepy cottage, perhaps. But the co-owner of a mom-and-pop store? Not splashy enough.

I don't know whether Gwen realized the major media wouldn't be gunning for her. But evidently, she'd had her fill of nosy people, including me. "I'm not here," she said. And the door slammed shut in my face.

9

A great blue heron winged over my car as I drove north through waving cattails. Beyond them on either side, water stretched. The Pamlico Sound to my left, the Atlantic Ocean to my right.

Ten minutes later I was mid-island, west of Queen Street, steering through a middle-class neighborhood. This was where the locals lived. Their homes were simple, their yards well-kept. I parked down the street from Georgia Meeks's house at the end of Loblolly Lane. Counterarguments clamored in my head. Would I have liked it if someone came knocking on my door mere hours after my loved one died?

If that someone was an old friend who was going to do some digging until she struck truth, I might have liked it very much.

I watched from behind the wheel as cars pulled up. From them staggered women and men followed by uncomprehending children, who all made their way to the front door. The scene reminded me of a similar one from twenty-six years ago. After the news broke about my mother, the house she and I shared had been overtaken by great-aunts and elderly second cousins. They'd brought extra coffeepots, made quiches and cobblers, and opened the door to stricken friends and neighbors. I'd stayed in my tree house, which Hudson had built. I'd curled up on the floor underneath the curtains my mother had sewn, listening to car doors opening and closing, plates clattering, the air-conditioning unit rumbling on.

What was I doing outside Georgia Meeks's home? What was

I doing in Cattail? I didn't belong there. I missed Charlotte. My dim apartment, my musty tub.

Eyes on the house, I sank lower behind the wheel.

A tall woman exited the side door. She had flowing hair. A lightweight, duster-length sweater rolled behind her.

Georgia Meeks. Sister to Eva, aunt to Summer.

Georgia and I had shared flag duty one year. Every dry weekday morning, we'd gotten the Stars and Stripes flying in front of Cattail High. Pole buddies, we'd called ourselves.

Since then I'd felt a kinship toward Georgia. She'd become primarily a careerwoman, like me.

Now she kept glancing behind her—she'd made a surreptitious escape from her own home. She scooted to a pink-painted shed in the side yard and let herself in.

I ripped the key from the ignition. *Now or never, Padget.*

10

Inside the shed, an old card table served as a work surface. A glue gun clicked as it heated. Georgia stuffed a packet of marigold seeds into a small pot. Her face was blotchy. "Heard you were in town," she said.

I pressed my back against the shed door. "I'm so sorry."

The pot Georgia was holding slipped and clunked onto the table. She covered her face with her hands. "I don't feel like talking."

I waited. Georgia was like her sister: she always felt like talking. I knew she'd add more words, if only to kill the silence.

"My family's all inside the house crying and carrying on," she said. "At least out here, I'm getting things done. The things Eva would want done. Pass me that box?"

A box at my feet contained pairs of gardening gloves, new, the tags still on. I picked up the box and set it on the table. "This all for the Cattaillion?" The Cattaillion was the island's biggest celebration-cum-fundraiser, and the unofficial summer kickoff, originally called the Cattail Cotillion until some thoughtful founding parent decided to combine the two words and save everybody some syllables.

"Free giveaways," Georgia said, nodding. "They're like honey to flies. That's what Eva always says. She mans the Meeks Hardware table every year. She loves the Cattaillion."

Manned, I thought. *Loved.*

"You know why my sister and I made such good business partners?" she asked. "Because we *weren't* the best of friends." She shoved a pair of gloves into the pot along with another seed packet. Zinnias. She grabbed the glue gun, dotted the tip against a length of ribbon, pressed the ribbon to the flower pot. Crooked. Cursing, she ripped it away, scissored off another section of ribbon, and attacked it with the gun.

This, then, was Georgia's running. Her tree climbing. When life engulfed her, she retreated to her she shed and busied her hands in the glow of little mermaid-shaped lights festooning the walls. The whale-patterned floor pillows were just for show; relaxing didn't help Georgia relax. *Not* relaxing did.

The last time I'd seen her was Christmas, during my annual visit home. She, Eva, and I had met at Salty Edward's. Georgia sipped white wine while Eva and I split a pitcher of light beer. The three of us had thrown darts and talked about ex-boyfriends and laughed at my horrendous aim.

Georgia smoothed the newly glued ribbon against the pot, lining it to the edge. "Eva got the diagnosis a while back. She'd been having ups and downs. This past week, she was mostly up. *So* up, it was easy to forget she was sick. But the one-year prognosis was grim. Only a nineteen percent survival rate. She'd been so stoic. It must have been a show, and she ultimately came to the decision that she didn't want to go through with the chemo and the surgeries and everything else. Didn't want to make Summer go through it. I can't decide if my sister did the brave thing or the cowardly thing. I'm leaning toward cowardly."

I picked up the scissors, snipped a few lengths of ribbon, and placed them in a pile. "Is there anything I can do?"

"Is this even real? Every word we're saying seems . . ."

Massive.

Bizarre.

Part of me wished Georgia and I were back at the flagpole

together. I'd clip up the heavy nylon, she'd keep it from touching the ground while chattering about how hot Mr. Eckstrom was.

I took a pot from the stacks and handed it to her. "Eva wasn't much of a partier, was she?" I asked. "I mean, she wasn't in high school. But what about lately?"

"Drugs? Come on. She got high on treasure hunt lore."

"Any exes in the picture? What about enemies?"

"Chief Jurecki asked me all this."

"Did he give you Eva's things?"

"You mean her 'effects'?" She made air quotes. "That's what he called them. He was here earlier. I was about to call Eva. She and Summer were supposed to come over for brunch."

"Special occasion?"

"Just something we do every now and then. For Summer, mostly. She likes to see Eva and me together. Friendly. All week Eva had been experimenting with a new recipe. A green bean casserole, of all things. Fresh green beans from her garden. She was so *random* sometimes." Georgia's hands again flew to her face. This time, her narrow shoulders quaked.

I fought the urge to bolt from the shed. And yet I knew a substantial part of Georgia wanted me to do just that: leave.

"All Eva had on her was her phone," she said after she'd pulled herself together. "Nothing unusual there. A million photos of Summer, a lot of them duck-face selfies. Summer liked to steal her mom's phone when she wasn't looking and goof around on it." Georgia rubbed her eyes with the heels of her hands. Then she looked at me, weary. "Eva called you last night."

I nodded. "She asked me to meet her at the lighthouse. I didn't go. That's why I'm here, now, asking you these questions. Something's not adding up."

Georgia stared out the window. It was like she couldn't take in my words. They opened too many doors. "Eva didn't have a will," she said. "I'm going to raise Summer."

"Here?"

"Of course here. The family business is here. All Summer's friends. Her school. Where else would we go?"

There was nowhere else.

Like my own father, Summer's father had never been in the picture. Thirteen years ago, Eva had found herself infatuated with a vacationer. A summer guy. She'd hoped a baby might make him a full-timer.

But as my mother knew well, summer guys rarely stuck around.

I heard a distant gasoline-fueled buzz, perhaps a neighbor's weed whacker. "You don't think Eva climbed over the railing for some reason?" I asked. "For a reason other than—"

"This isn't about my sister, is it? How old were we? When your mother . . ."

Heat rushed to my face. I put down the scissors with more force than I intended. "I just don't believe Eva jumped. And I want to do the right thing by your family."

She picked up the glue gun, clenching it with two hands, as if she might wrench it in half. But her face was soft. "You asked if there was anything you could do."

"Anything at all."

"Go home, pole buddy," she said.

11

Rain spattered the windshield. I had just cued up some bluegrass—my favorite kind of music, as it helped focus my galloping brain—when there was a tap on the passenger-side window.

A twelve-year-old girl slid into my car.

Summer Meeks. She wore a spaghetti-strap top and short-shorts. I couldn't read her expression, couldn't see her face beyond the spilled-lemonade hair. A pencil was tucked behind her ear. She stared at the dashboard.

The words were on my lips: *I'm sorry for your loss.* But I knew all about being twelve and wanting to bash in the face of every person who'd addressed me that way. Especially if I didn't really know the individual. "Hey," I said.

"You're Aunt Georgia's friend, right?" Her voice had that monotone, ragged-edged quality of just-shed tears. "You're the one who lives in Charlotte and writes for the big newspaper."

Lived. Wrote. I gripped the steering wheel and said, "I'm on-island for a few weeks."

"My mom and I were supposed to make a green bean casserole today."

"Is that your favorite dish? Green bean casserole?"

Summer turned to me. The family resemblance was striking. Feathery eyebrows, heart-shaped face. I remembered her as a little girl, zooming up and down Meeks Hardware's aisles on her kick scooter.

"I heard them all whispering just now," she said. "In the kitchen. About what happened to your mother. A long time ago."

My grip on the wheel turned white-knuckle.

Summer slid something out of her pocket.

A vial, no bigger than the average adult female index finger. Bits of burgundy wax dotted the rim, as if at one point it had been sealed. Mildew blotched the inside of the glass.

She pried off the cork stopper and tapped out the contents: a scroll several inches wide. Its edges were blackened and flaking, like someone had held them to a lit match for effect.

She passed me the scroll. It was light on my palm, as detailed as an insect. The paper was a buttery stock, flecked with dried petals, and retained a vaguely burnt odor.

With my fingertips, I spread apart the ends, revealing calligraphy. Someone had taken pains to pen each loopy letter by hand, in still-shiny midnight-blue ink.

Congrats on finding the very first clue.
Now I'll tell you what to do.
Spiral upward toward the light.
Pass through blue and into white.
Then hold on. Hold on tight
and you'll spy the hidden sight.

A shiver spidered the back of my neck. "What is this, Summer?"

"Yesterday, Mom was planting flowers along our walkway. She loved gardening and yard work and stuff. But she only got halfway with the flowers."

"Why's that?"

Summer shrugged. "She came running inside the house without even rinsing off her hands at the hose. She would have killed me if I ever did that."

This riddle was what Eva had found. What had sent her to the MotherVine to rifle through books, searching for clues. She must have realized the artifact was not centuries old, that it wasn't going to lead her to life-altering fortune and fame. The scroll was not antique; it had only been made to appear so. It was intended to be a bit of fun. Something Eva couldn't resist. "You think your mother dug up this vial while she was planting flowers?" I asked. "Then what'd she do?"

"Sat down at her desk in the kitchen. Just sat there and stared. A couple times I came in and asked what was going on. But she shushed me. Said she was thinking. A while later I rode my bike to a friend's house for a sleepover. When I left, Mom was still sitting there."

"She was thinking about this riddle? Trying to puzzle it out?"

"That big policeman that came to the house? He said my mom was trying to think up a note. Like a suicide note, I guess."

"He knows about this riddle? Chief Jurecki?"

"I showed it to him."

"And?"

"He said 'very helpful,' then gave it back to me."

Anger—a spiky heat—crept up my throat. "What else did he say?"

"Nothing. He thinks I'm stupid. Right?"

"He thinks you're a twelve-year-old girl."

"I *am* a twelve-year-old girl."

I had a second look at the riddle. *Spiral upward toward the light / Pass through blue and into white. / Then hold on. Hold on tight / and you'll spy the hidden sight.*

"I know what it means," Summer said.

"The lighthouse?"

"My mom must have figured it out before too long."

"The bottom half of the lighthouse is painted blue. And the top half is white."

She spiraled a finger upward. "When you climb it, you pass through blue, and into white. Aunt Georgia couldn't figure it out. I had to explain it to her."

"Your aunt Georgia knows about this too?"

"She doesn't think it's important. She said it's just another one of my mom's wild-goose chases."

"Your mom was big into stuff like this, huh? Treasure hunts and things."

"She went to the beaches with her metal detector every chance she got."

"Did she ever take you?"

Summer shook her head in a way that didn't invite further questioning, which made me wonder if treasure hunting was Eva's me-time activity. While other moms unwound from a long day by nursing a glass of wine, Eva swept an electronic wand over the sand.

Rain pattered the windshield, the windows.

I had a pretty good idea how Summer was feeling. Desperate to change the narrative, and like something around her heart had erected a fortress to keep that desperation at bay. But instead, it got walled in.

She gestured to the scroll, still unfurled in my hands. "The fifth line," she said. "You'd have to *hold on tight* once you reached the top of the lighthouse. Right?"

"That part is straightforward."

"But what does *and you'll spy the hidden sight* mean?"

I had no idea. Had Eva deciphered it? Driven like a bat out of hell, straight for the lighthouse the second it dawned on her? She'd have found the thrill of the chase irresistible, no matter what sort of chase it was—serious treasure hunt or frivolous amusement.

This delicate thing in my hands was proof that Eva Meeks really had climbed the lighthouse with no intention of killing herself. Instead, she was searching for something. *The hidden sight.*

Whatever that meant.

"Did your mom take this scroll with her when she climbed?" I asked.

"I found it in her desk drawer when I got back to our house this morning. She had a crazy-good memory, my mom."

"She sure did." I remembered sitting in the high school auditorium, marveling at the lines that flew from Eva's mouth as she lit up the stage. She never stumbled. Never hesitated. She'd probably left the scroll behind because she'd wanted to keep it safe. "Who would your mother have told about this riddle?" I asked. "Who were her friends?"

"Everybody, I guess. And nobody. She didn't have a lot of *close* friends, you know?"

"What about your grandparents? Can they help you?"

"They just got here from Kitty Hawk. I can't talk to them."

I took that to mean they were too overwhelmed to converse. They'd retired a while back, leaving the business to Eva and Georgia. "You think your mother found something at the top of the lighthouse," I said. "And you think . . ."

"It killed her. Somehow. That's about the size of things, Miss Callie."

"Could I look after this riddle for a while?"

"Don't tell my aunt Georgia?"

I made a gesture—locking my lips, tossing the key. Then she handed me the vial, and I carefully tapped the scroll back home.

There was a feeling inside that car. Like Summer and I, two people who'd known each other only peripherally until that point, were now bonded.

"Why me?" I asked. But I already knew the answer.

"No one else is listening," she said.

12

My running shoes slapped the wet Queen Street sidewalks, keeping beat with the bluegrass jigging from my earbuds—Dobros and dulcimers and fiddles. Rain pelted my skin. Cattail's waterfront shops were open, but there wasn't a tourist in sight. All the cute vacationing families were holed up, huddled together watching Netflix, flipping grilled cheese sandwiches, or playing Monopoly, substituting paper clips and matchsticks for the missing game pieces.

After speaking with Georgia and Summer, I'd gone back to the MotherVine and spent the afternoon behind the counter, trying to learn how to work the computer system, the credit card system, and the cash register. They were every bit as temperamental as Antoinette claimed, and I'd had a hard time focusing.

And now I was hoping some time outside would cure that.

I turned north, into a leafy neighborhood. Rental cottages were buttoned up, flags inside, windows shut. Two miles became four miles and all the while the rain needled, along with Eva Meeks, a storm unto herself inside my mind. Her long tan legs, her hands that seemed to be reaching, grasping.

I'm on to something, she'd said in the bookshop.

On to what?

I took a sand path that snaked through maritime forest. The trees became dense, the pine air coating my lungs. Quite the contrast to Charlotte, which smelled of car exhaust and belching sewer grates. Slowing to a walk, I passed a vernal pool covered with slime. A frog plopped into it, undulating the whole green carpet.

In my mind, Eva Meeks tumbled through the dark sky. Her hair streaked like the tail of a comet.

And then I was thinking about my mother and all the hours she spent working in the small sunroom off our kitchen, surrounded by the tools of her trade. Sewing machines and pin cushions and thread spools. I envisioned fabric stretched taut between her fingers—mother-of-the-bride gowns, prom dresses, christening smocks.

The sand path dumped me into the Smile Beach parking lot, devoid of cars. With the rain gentling, I strolled the empty beach. As much as I loved Smile Beach when it was full of people—kids splashing in the shallows, adults pretending like they didn't want to be buried in the sand—I also loved it when no one was here. There was something magical about the solitude.

I walked all the way to the old fishing pier. Many of the railings were crooked or missing altogether, and some of the pilings leaned at precarious angles. Two purple martins swooped over the water and came to rest in the pier's undergirding. Only a few dozen of the dark-winged swallows roosted now, but in a few weeks, there'd be many more. Those birds loved the fishing pier as much as Cattailers did.

I remembered one summer evening when I was eight years old or so, my mother and uncle and I walked halfway onto the pier and sat on one of the built-in concrete benches. At dusk, the purple martins came. One or two at first, then dozens, then hundreds. Cheeping, midnight-colored, fist-size birds streaming toward the bridge, looping over the waves.

"Ain't they somethin'," Uncle Hudson had said, his head tipped back, a cigarette burning between his lips.

Mom had put her arm around my shoulders and said, "Appreciate the small things, princess."

Now I climbed the little hill that led to the pier access and stood there with the toes of my shoes lined against the edge. The pier stretched before me, ten feet above the water, its planks buckling and dipping. A sign flapped from the gate, puckering in the rain. It declared the old Smile Beach fishing pier the official beneficiary of this year's annual Cattaillion. The event was like a sidewalk sale on steroids. The shops on Queen Street threw open their red doors. Tourists and locals alike bid on items—everything from kites to bicycles to weeklong stays at rental cottages. It all culminated in fireworks, shot over the water from the pirate ship.

The thought of this Saturday's Cattaillion cheered me. I hadn't been in years. And maybe it would raise enough money to return this old derelict of a pier to its former glory.

I almost walked out onto it. I wanted to sit on the bench that my mom and uncle and I had shared all those years ago. But the pier looked so decrepit, I decided it wasn't worth the risk.

13

"Any chance I can get you to put these away?" My uncle Hudson stood in his garage turned woodshop among the suitcases and boxes that crowded the floor.

So far, I'd unpacked only the essentials: laptop, blender. "I'll take care of it," I said. I hadn't seen him all day; earlier, when I was here for a change of clothes, he'd been out. "Have you heard what happened?" I asked.

"Eva Meeks. It's all over the island. I can't believe it."

"I know." Words gushed out of me. I told him about Eva landing in the cattails near Mom's cross. About how Eva'd been forty-one and her daughter was twelve, and those ages—the cruel coincidence of them—had been pinging against the inside of my skull all day.

"Why were you there?" he asked. "At the scene?"

"Because I might have been the last person to speak with Eva before she died."

"She jumped?"

"That's what everyone seems all too ready to accept."

"I just don't understand. They made it so that sort of thing would never happen again. After Teri." His voice cracked on his sister's name.

Behind him on his workbench, a nearly complete surfboard lay drying. Nobody surfed on wooden boards anymore, but this one would command attention above a fireplace or marking the entrance to a poolside cabana. He'd auction it off at Saturday's Cattaillion.

I got a clean rag from the cabinet. Sitting on an old metal stool, I dragged the rag over my face, my ponytail, my arms. The day was catching up to me. The lighthouse, the new job, and my six-mile on-foot adventure, half running, half walking. My limbs felt as heavy as sandbags.

Scupper trotted over and licked the rain and sweat off my ankles. He was squat and bearded, with protruding eyebrows. His tongue was a rose petal against black fur. I scooped him in my arms and he wiggled, crabby breath on my neck. "Beer me," I said.

"I only stock up when you're on-island for Christmas. Decaf?"

"Does it have sawdust in it?"

"More than likely." He went over to the coffeepot, poured a steaming mug, dumped sugar from a shaker studded through with uncooked rice, and didn't stir. We liked it the same way: acrid start, with a sludgy, sweet finish.

He handed me the mug. I traded Scupper for it.

The rainstorm had passed. The barn-style doors were open to the backyard, where the air hung thick. Gulls jockeyed for position on the pilings of Hudson's dock. A pontoon boat transporting several boozy couples sailed by in the canal. Two of the women toasted me with Koozie-wrapped drinks. I toasted back.

"Eva's the one from the commercials, right?" my uncle asked. "The older sister."

"Not that much older."

"Her daughter's always reading behind the counter at the hardware store. Always got a pencil tucked behind her ear."

"Summer. Wait here. I have something to show you." I slid off my stool. Between the jigsaw and the band saw, a ladder was mounted against the wall. I climbed it, into my loft.

Returning with the vial, I tapped out the scroll and spread the edges with a thumb and forefinger. I told Hudson about Summer getting into my car outside Georgia's house. About Eva's obsession with some treasure hunt. How she'd called me last night. Said she'd had a big break.

My uncle ran a hand through his hair, making it stick up even more crazily. "This riddle means Eva climbed the lighthouse with a purpose," he said. "A purpose other than jumping. Somebody's got to set the record straight."

The record.

My plan to write up Eva's death suddenly seemed ill-conceived, despite my honorable intentions. How could I even think about advancing my career while Georgia and Summer's loss was clinging to me like smoke from a campfire, permeating my pores?

No. In no way did I want to risk exploiting or upsetting the Meeks family by writing about them. I couldn't. I wouldn't.

But—as Hudson had just reminded me—the record.

"I agree," I told him. "Somebody needs to set the record straight. And that somebody is me."

"Good." He nodded approvingly. "Where do you start?"

I had no idea.

14

It took almost an hour to haul my things up the ladder. Hudson helped, handing me a box or bag or suitcase, then steadying me, his hand on my back as I prepared for each ascent.

Now it was midnight. The loft's single window was shut to keep in the air-conditioning, but I heard crickets chirping outside. A nightjar crying.

After my mom died, Hudson had taken me in. Here, in his one-bedroom house. There was nowhere else. He'd offered his bedroom, said he'd sleep on the couch. But when I spied the loft in his woodshop and begged to sleep there, saying it reminded me of my old tree house, my uncle couldn't refuse. He cleared out all the scrap wood and busted equipment. Within a couple of weeks, the loft had a fresh coat of paint, a Berber carpet, a dormer window, and a shower curtain to keep out the dust and provide privacy.

Now I pulled down the custom Murphy bed and flopped onto the mattress. Next to the bed, a cardboard chest doubled as a nightstand. I rolled over and opened the bottom drawer. The crown was there, right where I'd left it six months ago, when I'd been home for Christmas.

Some mothers bequeathed heirloom crystal or summer homes or vinyl record collections. My mother left behind two cheap sewing machines prone to seizing, which Hudson eventually donated to the churches, after he was satisfied that I truly had no interest in them.

She also left behind this: a crown of woven cattail leaves. The design was simple. Peaks and valleys, level all the way around. The weave had aged into a stony tan, like the hues of some of the island's wild mustangs, though in the darkness the crown now took on the color of a shadow.

I'd been about five years old when my mother made the crown. It was summertime, a dazzlingly bright day. She'd led me to the edge of our property and selected a few tall plants. The grasshopper-green hue meant they were at their most pliable, she said.

"What's pliable?" I asked.

"You'll see." With a sharp knife, she hacked the cattails at the base and started weaving right there, on the lawn.

Mesmerized, I'd watched her fingers dipping into the leaves. "What are you making?"

"Something for my princess."

15

The next day, I walked to work, a six-minute trip from Hudson's house on the residential portion of Queen Street. The air was heavy with the scents of gardenia and roses.

At the MotherVine, Antoinette hadn't yet flipped the OPEN sign. She was behind the counter, squinting at the computer through her reading glasses.

"Good morning." Joining her, I stuffed my bag into a storage cubby.

She placed a gentle hand on my shoulder and said, "Yesterday."

"How about we just focus on work? Eva would want that."

"I think you're right." She was quiet for a moment. Then she gestured to the front window, where she'd spread some supplies. "Well, can you whip up a display while I answer a few emails? We really need one—foot traffic's picking up, and summer's getting going. Plus we have a signing in a few days, and then the Cattaillion of course. We need some window candy." She began tapping away at the computer.

I wasn't exactly the crafty type, but I headed over to the window. Tin Man was dozing, curled up in one of the papasan chairs. "Anything specific in mind?" I asked.

"You'll figure it out. I want it to look . . . you know."

"Cute?"

"Exactly."

The bay window was a prominent feature of the bookshop, and typical of the century-old brick buildings that lined the waterfront section of Queen Street. On the deep ledge, she'd piled green and blue swaths of satin, squares of sandpaper, and cocktail umbrellas—the kind you'd find sticking out of a mai tai.

"Who's the author?" I asked, smoothing a hand over the fabrics. They reminded me so much of my mother and her seamstress work.

Antoinette didn't look away from the computer. "Hm?"

"There's going to be a signing here in a few days?"

"Oh, yes. Daisy Kapur. Shark expert. She's a peach. We just got a shipment of forty copies of her first-ever book. I'll have you unpack those later."

Thinking, I ran my fingertips over the sandpaper. "You want a little beach scene?"

Antoinette scowled at the computer. "You just try to freeze up on me. Go ahead. See what happens."

I decided to let her concentrate. Selecting a square of sandpaper, I tore it into strips, then spread the strips along the window. I shook out some light green satin and arranged it in gentle sweeps, festooning the middle portion of the ledge. I did the same with the darker green, then transitioned to the blues—light blue into dark, out toward the edge of the sill. The activity had a relaxing effect.

I stood back, admiring my work. The sandpaper was sand, and the fabric was ocean.

"It's lovely." Antoinette was standing beside me.

"Yeah?" I said. "I'm glad you like it. Now I need to figure out a way to get the umbrellas involved."

She had a secret little smile on her face.

"What?" I asked.

"Nothing. Don't forget those." She pointed to a nearby stack of hardbacks. One by one, I stood the just-released beach reads on the ledge, nestling them into the fabric. The books were crisp and had that brand-new paper-and-ink smell. The covers showed bare-shouldered women in sun hats, and cottages huddled in dunes. Just looking at them made me want to go to the beach. "Oh, and before I forget," Antoinette said, "you have deliveries to make today. I'll show you where I keep them."

I followed her behind the checkout counter. Inside one of the storage cubbies, three books leaned against one another, all with vine-patterned bookmarks sticking from the pages. On the back of the top bookmark she'd written *Trish Berryman. Crier office okay.*

Aversion twisted my insides.

Trish and I had volleyed a mutual silent treatment for the better part of two decades. Yet there we were, about to have our second face-to-face in two days.

I loaded Trish's book, along with the others, into my bag.

Antoinette was studying me, reading me. "The Berrymans are good customers," she said. "Big readers. Can you play nice?"

I forced a smile.

I could certainly try.

How in the world had my mother been friends with this woman? Then again, maybe Trish was different back then. Maybe my very presence in this office made her as uncomfortable as I was. And demeaning me was her way of coping.

Trish fanned through *Riding Lessons,* then set it aside and leaned back in her chair, which squeaked like a protesting mouse. "I'm confused," she said, "because I ordered two books. This one and the sequel, *Flying Changes.*"

"Oh." I shrugged. "Sorry. It must not have come in yet."

A smile played at her mouth, taking years off her appearance. "Want to see something?" she asked, hitting a key on her laptop. The screen filled with a photograph of her holding a lamb, fuzzy legs hooked over her forearm. "Is that not the cutest thing you've ever seen?"

Though Trish's presence in the photograph brought down its cuteness quota, the lamb was adorable, all cottony and bewildered. I tried to summon some appreciation for her attempt at normalizing our interaction, diffusing the strain with a bit of small talk. "Where'd you see a lamb?" I asked.

"Cattail Stables. I've taken up horseback riding. There's a summer camp for adults this week. You learn all about caring for horses. Also goats, chickens, ducks—you name it. They've got all kinds of animals there."

Cattail Stables. It was on the northern end, ocean side, the only place on the island to take riding lessons or go on trail rides.

"Cool." I looked around. I'd never been inside the *Crier* office. On the wall, the word *Hoover* was legible under layers of paint; decades ago, the space had been a vacuum repair joint, and it still smelled like dust and lubricant. A framed citation from the North Carolina Press Association hung slightly crooked.

No one sat at the other desk, but the camera revealed it was Trish's husband's workstation. Jeff Berryman was the *Crier*'s pho-

16

The *Cattail Crier* office was a short walk down the waterfront, past a clothing boutique and a jewelry shop. Its glass door stood out among the red doors. The newspaper logo featured ocean waves curling into capital *C*s.

Inside, Trish Berryman sat at a desk, typing. I watched her for a second, wondering what she was working on and staving off pinpricks of envy. A part of me missed that mental state of being absorbed by writing, laser focused on words.

Trish had evidently committed to growing out her roots and had reached the halfway point; just above her chin, gray streaks transitioned into milk-chocolate waves that skimmed her collarbones. She wore wide-legged trousers and low-rise pumps. Aerosoles, or some other brand that marketed to women with aging joints.

I was headed for Aerosoles soon enough. But I wasn't there yet.

I stepped inside the *Crier* office.

Turning away from her laptop, Trish eyed me. Any softness I might have detected at Eva's death scene was gone. This was the Trish I remembered: the hard one. "I thought I mentioned it," she said. "I'm not hiring."

"Yeah. I know." I handed over the paperback she'd ordered. *Riding Lessons* by Sara Gruen.

"I'm confused."

"Cattail gossip hasn't reached you yet? I'm working at the MotherVine. Just for the summer. Not even the whole summer."

"Bit of a demotion, isn't it?"

tographer as well as the official adman. Aside from a few stringers and the occasional intern, the island's local weekly was a husband-and-wife tag-team operation.

"How's Mr. Jeff?" I asked. Growing up, that was how I'd addressed him. The Berrymans had lived next door to my mother and me. I remembered them as pudgy young newlyweds. Trish never paid me much attention, but Jeff assumed an older brother kind of attitude and often engaged me in chitchat.

"He's late," Trish said with an annoyed sigh. "I'm due at the stables. Just waiting for Jeff to get back with my crop. I forgot it at the house. Sent him back to fetch it for me."

"Your crop?"

"You know. My riding crop." She made a whipping motion, along with a sound effect. "I wonder what's taking him so long. Probably lost his car keys again. Guy would lose his head if it wasn't screwed to his neck."

I indicated her computer screen, which still showed the lamb. "Were you working on your Eva story when I came in?"

"Trying to get to the heart of who she was, and what she meant to this community. Everyone in Cattail knew her. If you shop at Meeks Hardware—and who doesn't?—then you know the Meeks sisters. A comment on the continued success of their business is in order too. It's hung in there even with all the box stores and big chains popping up on the other islands. That was Eva's doing, as I understand. But my biggest thrust, I think, will be Eva's mental health."

"You really believe she killed herself?"

"That's what Jurecki said."

I ran a hand through my hair. The thought of Georgia and especially Summer reading some dishy article about the circumstances that led to Eva ending her own life—I couldn't let that happen. Not if there was a possibility she'd died some other way.

"There's another angle I could give you," I said. "Eva came into the bookshop just yesterday and was totally aflutter about a treasure hunt she'd stumbled upon."

"*Aflutter?* Bless her heart, but that woman freaking out about pirates' long-lost loot isn't exactly news."

"What I'm trying to say is, everyone's buying into this tale about Eva taking her own life. But what if she didn't?"

"Oh, Callie. This isn't the *Washington Post*, you know?" Trish gazed out the window, where her silver Buick was parked. A fresh I ♥ HORSES bumper sticker camouflaged the dented rear fender. Someone was tucking a flyer underneath the back windshield wiper. I could read the large font—an advertisement for the Cattaillion. *This Saturday on the waterfront! Don't miss it! Let's save the old Smile Beach fishing pier!*

Trish turned back to her laptop and resumed typing. "And I'm not Woodward and Bernstein," she muttered. "Thank goodness."

17

Walking, I crossed Queen Street. The how-to book in my hands, *Making Pottery You Can Use*, was my next delivery. The back of the bookmark read, *Reedley Anderson, Cattail Pottery.*

Reedley Anderson must be a practical guy. He wasn't available, so I left the volume for him with the owner of the pottery shop, who explained that Reedley was her summer intern.

Back on the sidewalk, I checked out the third bookmark, my last delivery. *Pearleen Standish, Cattail Heritage Garden, 11–1.*

Pearleen Standish. Someone I hadn't thought of in ages. She was Cattail's wealthiest resident, heiress to a furniture empire that was founded on the island. The furniture was all constructed on the mainland now, had been for years. But the family still oversaw operations.

I walked back to the MotherVine to get some details. Antoinette had flipped the OPEN sign, and a lone shopper perused the cozies. She had an armful of books by Kate Carlisle and appeared to be agonizing over which one to buy.

"Pearleen Standish is alive?" I asked Antoinette. She was behind the counter reading *Glass Houses* by Louise Penny, one of her favorite contemporary authors.

"Pearleen's more alive than most teenagers I know," she said, removing her glasses. "And more temperamental. Her eightieth birthday bash is today, at the Heritage Garden."

"But shouldn't it have been rescheduled? In light of Eva."

“This is Pearleen Standish we’re talking about. Cattail’s answer to Cruella de Vil.”

“I’ll need to get my car for that delivery. Couldn’t I just drop off the book at her home?”

“Again—Pearleen Standish. Have you ever known her to turn down an opportunity to show the world how special she is? Even though we deliver books to anyone, anywhere on-island, *she’ll* make it seem like we’re personally catering just to her. But no matter. It’ll be good visibility for the MotherVine. And you can snap some pics of the festivities while you’re there. For Tin Man’s Instagram. He likes to get out and shoot the town every once in a while.”

I laughed. “Is that right?”

“He’s an excellent photographer,” Antoinette said with a wink.

Outside Hudson’s house, I hopped into my rust bucket. I had some time to kill before Pearleen’s party began, so I headed south, to the lighthouse. I didn’t want to go there. My palms grew slick on the wheel as I thought of Eva’s body lying in the cattails. But Summer Meeks was counting on me.

When I hit the marsh, the speed limit increased, and I drove with the windows down, taking big gulps of billowing warm air. Brown signs on the roadside pointed the way to the southern beaches. On the ocean side sat Mustang Beach and Starry Beach. Love Beach, Pretty Beach, and Wonder Beach were on the sound side.

At the lighthouse, the police tape was gone. Benches near the shady end of the parking lot were occupied by some overly curious tourists. As I got out of my car, I felt anxiety prickling the atmosphere. Whereas yesterday’s onlookers had been mostly quiet and respectful, today they were buzzing. Snippets of conversation hummed on the breeze, some of the same questions uttered twenty-six years ago. *Why'd she do it? I wonder how high it is . . .*

A woman tapped my shoulder. She wore a visor and her coppery hair poked out the top. "You must be local," she said.

I glanced down at my outfit, wondering what had given me away. My heather-gray dress was casual but not summery. I was hardly tan, having spent most of my time inside an office building for the past fifteen years. And I was far from a sun kissed blonde, with my straight black hair. I wanted to protest, to proclaim that I'd been living in Charlotte most of my adult life, but it didn't seem worth it.

"I live here," I said.

"What do you know about this curse everyone's going on about?"

"A curse?"

"The lighthouse curse. My son heard some surfer boys talking about it in the water yesterday, and now that's *all* he can talk about. It's driving me nuts. I came here to see if I could get some *real* information." She pointed down the boardwalk. There were now two white crosses—someone had erected one for Eva, right next to my mother's.

"There's no curse," I said. "Tell your son it's complete nonsense."

"It *is* just nonsense, isn't it? That's what I kept telling him. He just got caught up in things."

"That's understandable. Enjoy your vacation."

"Oh, we love Cattail. It's our fourteenth summer in a row here. Wish we could live here year-round. How lucky you are. What was that old slogan? *The isle that's worth your while*?"

I gave her a quick smile before continuing toward the boardwalk. But a watermelon-shaped man of retirement age was blocking my path. I recognized him—the hair flattened against his head, the fuzzy neck in need of a shave. Ralph Burrus, head of the Cattail Conservationists, the nonprofit group that oversaw the lighthouse.

He probably hadn't seen me since my mother's calling hours. There'd been much scrutinous whispering that day. About how Ralph Burrus should have realized the safety hazard. Teri Padget had gotten up there unsupervised, after hours? How had the top door been allowed to lock behind her? And what about the bottom door being unlocked in the first place?

"Hi, Mr. Burrus," I said, approaching.

"Guided tours every half hour, Callie," he said. "Twenty minutes until the next group departs. Only halfway today."

"The top's closed?" I had mixed feelings about that. On the one hand, I'd come here with the riddle in mind. I thought maybe I'd *spiral upward toward the light* and see if that got me anywhere. On the other hand, the fact that even partial tours were already up and running struck me as pretty distasteful.

"We're awaiting a safety inspection from the brass," Mr. Burrus was saying. "Hate to think how many people that's discouraging from buying tickets. We're losing money here."

"Is Gwen Montgomery around?" I asked, trying to swallow my aversion toward this man.

"Who do you think's leading the tours?"

"Right."

Out came my phone.

Wandering away from Ralph Burrus and the crowd, I dialed Gwen, whose number was listed on the lighthouse's website. Voicemail. "Callie Padget here," I said. "We met yesterday? I hope things are getting back to normal for you. I didn't get a chance to tell you that I'm a bookseller here in town, and I'm friendly with the Meeks family, and they've asked me to do some additional investigating. Nothing formal. Anyway, it would be great to speak with you and check out the lighthouse as soon as the top's accessible to the public once again."

I tapped *Gwen Montgomery* into my phone's search window. Turned out to be a fairly common name. But this particular Gwen Montgomery didn't have any social media accounts. She did show up in a newsletter put out by Virginia Beach College. A photograph of her posing with graduate-level classmates at a start-of-the-semester meet-and-greet a couple of years back. Gwen stood apart from the rest of the group, as if she didn't quite fit in, or didn't want to. I'd been right about her accent. Her hometown was listed as Mullica Hill, New Jersey, in the southern part of that state.

My next searches combined various words. *Riddle, Outer Banks, lighthouse, hidden sight, Cattail, scroll.* Those results were even less fruitful.

Sighing, I glanced up. Just a hundred feet away, the lighthouse keeper's cottage sat in the shade. Something about the salt-obscured windows and sagging front porch reminded me of a rheumy old face.

Most likely, nobody was inside.

18

I mounted the steps leading up to the cottage and knocked on the front door.

Nothing.

I tested the knob. Unlocked. Cattail Island had retained its fisherman roots in addition to a widespread habit of not locking doors. Maybe Mullica Hill, New Jersey, was a similar sort of place. Or Gwen just wanted to adopt the local customs.

With the lightest of taps, the cottage door swung open.

"Hello?" I stood there, my skin electrified. Was I going to step inside? Snoop around a stranger's digs?

A glance over my shoulder confirmed that almost everyone awaiting a partial tour of Cattail's favorite phallic symbol was hunched over their phones, including Ralph Burrus, who stood at his post at the start of the boardwalk.

The things we'd notice if we only paid more attention to our surroundings instead of an eleven-square-inch screen. For example, me, Callie Padget, entering a home uninvited, in broad daylight. I couldn't believe how easy it was. On a surface level, anyway. On the inside, I was a quivering, guilt-laden mess.

But Eva was dead. And Gwen had acted so squirrelly. And Summer had looked so lost . . .

"Hello?" I called again. Closing the door behind me, I was officially a trespasser. Might as well go for it.

The kitchen was straight out of 1940. It was cute enough to make even me wish for a frilly apron and a fistful of flour to slap onto a wooden rolling pin. A bulbous refrigerator stood shorter than me, which was saying something. I yanked up the old-fashioned fridge handle. Orange juice, veggie burgers and buns, a plastic container of soon-to-be moldy strawberries. Inside the trash can, two used teabags.

Opposite the kitchen, the living room was cramped. The couch had suffered at least ten million butt crashes during its abused existence. Same with the red armchair brightening the corner. The television on the floor must have weighed a half ton.

Two at a time, I mounted the staircase, slanted with age. The bathroom was so tiny you could spit out your toothpaste while sitting on the toilet. In the bedroom, the only personal touch was a framed photograph. Gwen with a handsome, sharp-jawed, silver-templed man, their arms wrapped around each other at some sort of picnic. I picked up the photo and smiled back at the pair. Who were they to each other?

A wavy-glassed window framed the lighthouse. I imagined what it might be like to wake up to that view every morning, to a literal and figurative beacon of history surrounded by unmarred wetlands and, beyond them, the Atlantic.

If your mother hadn't slipped, alone and intoxicated, from the top of the lighthouse, waking up to it every morning might well be a marvel.

A second window looked out onto a parked car plastered in bumper stickers. Back downstairs, inside a partially opened kitchen cabinet, I found a set of keys. Among them, a Volkswagen fob. Aiming it toward the driveway, I hit UNLOCK—but the car was already unlocked. I went outside, up to the older-model Jetta, where a fresh stirring of guilt made me pause. I'd helped myself to Gwen's private living quarters. Did I really want to inspect the trunk of her car too?

Yeah. I did.

~

I shoved it open, wincing as the hinge let out a groan. Sunlight glinted off three empty handles of rum. Rotgut. Either by choice or by necessity, Gwen was a bottom-shelf girl. I checked the fine print. Fifty-nine fluid ounces per bottle. Had all of it ended up in the bloodstream of petite Gwen Montgomery?

The rum bottles put a new spin on the OJ in her fridge. Maybe her sunglasses and swooning hadn't resulted from the trauma of discovering a dead body. What if she'd been hammered? Or suffering a banging hangover?

Then again, just because someone drank wasn't reason to distrust her. It certainly didn't criminalize her, or even mean she'd blundered on the job.

Still, the empty rum bottles felt relevant. Why put them in your trunk?

And why put them in your trunk alongside a concrete tray, the kind you'd find underneath a downspout, containing what appeared to be hardened plops of metal? The hot bronze burned my fingertips.

A voice drifted on the breeze. It was Gwen, wearing her traffic-cone-orange Cattail Conservationists shirt, three-quarters of the way down the boardwalk. Her face was mostly sunglasses. "Thank you . . . do come again . . . *so* appreciate your support . . . tell your friends." Meanwhile, the bench sitters got to their feet.

I had to hurry if I was going to make the next tour. I was about to shut the trunk when I noticed a nozzled item lodged behind the tray. I pulled it out.

A baking blowtorch. Hot-pink letters spelled out BONBLOW! My fingers fit the grooves, invitingly ergonomic. I thumbed the red button. A hiss elicited from the nozzle, followed by a blue-gold flame rocketing outward. "Holy sh—" With my free hand, I steadied my arm. The thing actually had kickback.

A couple of thousand degrees of heat shooting from my hand produced an odd sense of satisfaction.

Then it hit me—the melted lumps of metal. Were they what remained of the lighthouse's old padlock? Had Eva, or Gwen, melted it off with the blowtorch?

I released the red button and placed the BonBlow! where I'd found it, behind the tray. I latched the trunk and made my way back along the parking lot. Gwen was already departing with the next group of eight. Her voice carried over the cattails: "One million one hundred seventy-two thousand bricks were used in its construction . . ."

By the time I reached the boardwalk—still blocked by Mr. Burrus—they were entering the lighthouse. "Looks like you just missed another one," he said.

19

I pulled into the lot of Cattail Heritage Garden, which graced a treed area on the opposite end of the island, a few miles past downtown.

Gleaming diagonally across two parking spaces was a black convertible sportscar, curvy yet lean. The tires sparkled as if they'd driven on nothing but showroom carpets. I recognized the hood emblem: rearing horse, yellow background. The new-car scent reached me from several spaces away.

"What the . . ." I exited my rattletrap as a retirement-aged couple—he in a sports coat, she in a beflowered hat—admired the Ferrari's sleek lines. "Looks like Whitman got himself a new toy," drawled the woman as they headed toward the grand iron gates.

She meant Pearleen's grandson, Whitman Standish. Sole heir to Standish Furniture International and, after Pearleen herself and now Eva Meeks, the closest thing Cattail had to a local celebrity. A couple of generations ago, if Cattailers didn't make their livings from the sea, they worked for Thornton Standish, Pearleen's father, producing internationally renowned dining room sets. Tables and chairs sought after by the famously rich, from household-name movie stars to Arabian royals.

Speaking of the birthday girl, the book in my hands was a delivery for Pearleen. It was a straight-up bodice ripper complete with a stone castle looming in the background. In the foreground, a Fabio-looking dude, nude except for a kilt, clutched a maiden's heaving, half-covered boobs. I had to admit, part of me was impressed that a serious-minded eighty-year-old businesswoman had no problem ordering *Very Hot Scot* from her local independent bookshop.

The paperback would have made an eye-catching Instagram post propped against the Ferrari's windshield. But I was fresh from invading Gwen Montgomery's private property and wasn't sure I could muster the gall to invade Whitman Standish's.

I strolled through the main gates into full octogenarian swing. Guests clustered in twos and threes and fours, jabbering away. Men in golf shirts and chinos, women in cheaply made but new sundresses, the best they could find at Belk for thirty-nine bucks or less.

And then there was me, wearing the Callie Padget standard: ratty dress from three seasons ago, and even rattier flip-flops.

A wood-chip path threaded through labeled bushes and trees. Sweet gum, magnolia, partridgeberry. The garden was the kind of place for art classes and weddings and senior portraits. Benches circled fountains. Statues posed demurely in the shade. I made my way toward the most celebrated statue: a monstrous likeness of Queen Elizabeth, namesake of Cattail's Queen Street, starched up to the neck in sixteenth-century-style lace. Standing on tiptoes, I tucked the bawdy book in the crook of her tire-size arm, snapped a shot, and posted it on Instagram, adopting the gossip columnist persona Antoinette had established for Tin Man.

> Good Queen Bess knows how to get her kicks! Get yours at the MotherVine Bookshop, where I, Tin Man, will be your purrsonal guide.

"Looks like Tin Man's secret is out."

I spun around.

There stood Dr. Rasheeda Scarboro, silver braids gathered neatly over one shoulder.

"I thought that sweet cat was the clever photographer," said the medical examiner. "But it looks like he has a minion doing the heavy lifting."

"Guilty," I said, retrieving *Very Hot Scot*. I explained my temporary MotherVine employment, then added, "This isn't my book."

"No judgment here. *Outlander*'s the most action I get these days." I laughed as she asked, "Was that too much information?"

"What's your relationship to our gracious hostess?"

Dr. Scarboro leaned in conspiratorially. "Miss Pearleen's far from a pleasant old gal, wouldn't you say?"

"She's a character."

"That's one word for it. You know, her heart's not made entirely of stone. My late husband served on the board of Standish Furniture International, and one Christmas she gave all the trustees exquisite Elizabethan-style chairs made from responsibly harvested timber. And word on the street is, her annual bonuses are astronomically generous." Dr. Scarboro had mastered the garden-party trick of munching from a floppy plate, sipping sweet tea, and conversing, all at the same time. There was a placid elegance about her. She struck me as the type to call in requests to the classical music radio station. Hard to believe she was an expert on decaying human flesh.

"Would you mind if we talked about something a lot more somber?" I asked.

"Let me guess. Eva Meeks." She led me a few steps from the speakers playing yacht rock.

I felt tacky but determined. These types of conversations were de rigueur for medical examiners. And everyone around us was probably whispering about Eva anyway. "You didn't perform an autopsy, I'm aware," I said. "But you did have a look at the body. At the scene."

"Of course. A good look."

"And just for my own edification—there were no signs of a struggle? Scratches or bruises that she might have gotten before she fell?"

"If there were, I would have autopsied."

"Right. But what about—" My throat went hot at the thought of that blowtorch hissing in my hand. "What about burns?"

"Burns? Goodness, no." Dr. Scarboro slanted toward me. "Callie, this is as basic as they come. Eva jumped. It's a difficult thing to understand. Especially when there's a child involved. Twelve is quite a vulnerable age."

I fiddled with the book. I suddenly wanted out of the very conversation I'd initiated.

"I know this is all very hard to accept," she was saying. "But all signs point to—"

"Thank you, Dr. Scarboro." I held out my hand and she shook it. "I appreciate it," I said. "I'll stop pestering you. This is a party, after all."

"It's no problem. So, whose book is that?"

"The MotherVine upholds the privacy of its patrons."

"Good to know."

20

I wove through the partygoers toward a self-serve refreshment table. The day was warming, and a sip or two of cold water seemed like just the thing. I accepted a paper cup from a gawky middle-aged man. Glasses topped a beaky nose, and his pouch-chin was prematurely quivery.

I realized with a jolt that this pelican man who was now filling my cup with water from a pitcher was Jeff Berryman. He was probably thirty pounds lighter than he'd been in the nineties, when he lived next door to my mother and me. *Dingbatters*, my mother used to call Trish and Jeff, our newlywed neighbors. It was Cattail speak, part of the dying Outer Banks brogue. *Dingbatter* was a somewhat pejorative word for someone not born here.

"Hi, Mr. Jeff," I said.

I expected him to call me chum and ruffle my hair like he used to when I was a kid. But his easygoing manner seemed to have vanished. He reminded me of a balloon that had leaked helium, going from plump to lifeless.

"Heard you were back in town," he said. No greeting, no grin.

Wow. Trying for the teasing banter he used to employ on me, I gestured with my cup at our surroundings. "Guess you pulled the short straw at the *Crier*."

He didn't respond. His camera hung from his neck, protruding like some sort of extra midriff beak.

"I know *I* wouldn't want to miss an afternoon of old-lady perfume and limp crudités," I added.

He scoffed. "Yeah." The word was biting. Bitter.

I remembered one evening, before my mom died, watching from the window of my tree house as Mr. Jeff came strolling down the road. "Hiya," he'd called, waving a slim stack of envelopes. "Seems we received y'all's mail by accident." He'd passed the bundle up with a shrug.

How different he now seemed. I wondered if Trish's flintiness had rubbed off on him, some sort of marital osmosis that took place over the decades. Or maybe he was just having a bad day.

Then again, in June on Cattail Island, bad days were few and far between, even for people who lived and worked here. The tragedy with Eva was a dramatic exception, of course.

I thought of Trish cracking her pretend whip, and I felt sorry for him.

Two women strolled past, their gray heads bent close as they raised their voices over the music. *Lighthouse curse . . . don't you remember the seamstress, Teri Padget? . . . twenty-six years . . .*

The lighthouse curse. It wasn't just for tourists, apparently. The locals were getting into it too.

Sipping my water, I glimpsed the belle of the ball herself, clutching the forearm of her formidable grandson. A gold cross sparkled from the wattles of Pearleen Standish's neck. She'd donned a bubblegum-pink suit, likely Chanel or some brand that would have met the approval of rich people, even though Pearleen was the richest person by far to ever totter through Cattail Heritage Garden, and none of the guests at her own party would have known Versace from last year's crab derby T-shirt.

Next to Pearleen, Whitman Standish towered, an inverted triangle of seersucker-covered muscle. Even his face, pinned by steely eyes, seemed capable of carrying ten times its weight.

"Cattail royalty," I said to Jeff. "Two o'clock."

"I've already had the pleasure. They're all yours."

~

I approached the royalty. "Happy Birthday, Ms. Pearleen. Lovely day for a party."

"You mean lovely party, of course," she said. Her voice was surprisingly gruff.

"Delivery from the MotherVine." I presented the bodice ripper.

"How nice." She gave the paperback an appraising glance before passing it to her grandson.

Whitman pinched it between thumb and forefinger and slipped it into his jacket pocket. "Grandmother," he breathed. "Honestly."

"Photo?" Pearleen angled her elbows and hips like she was on a Hollywood red carpet and showed her not-so-pearly whites. When you're as rich as Pearleen Standish, you assume everyone wants a photograph of you. Even—perhaps especially—the ragamuffin from the bookshop. I got out my phone and snapped a pic while some dark, petty part of me delighted in the smear of lipstick on her front chomper. "Can you believe Cattail Heritage Garden took away my naming rights?" she asked. "And they had the *effrontery* to inform me about the switch just now, on my milestone birthday."

I lowered my phone. "Naming rights?"

"Standish Butterfly Sanctuary is now going to be called *Meeks* Butterfly Sanctuary." Pearleen actually rolled her eyes. "That Eva was starting to fancy herself quite the philanthropist."

Something heavy sank through me. An anchor thudding to rest inside my stomach. "You mustn't have heard. About Eva. She had a terrible accident. She passed away. Just yester—"

"Oh, I've heard."

I froze, my mouth half-open.

A man carrying a beribboned gift sashayed over. "Yoo-hoo, birthday girl. Why, you don't look a day over fifty-five."

With Whitman bracing her, Pearleen teetered toward the man.

"Would it be okay if I followed up with you later, then?" I called.

Whitman flicked a business card at me and said, "God bless."

21

After Pearleen's party, I stayed at the MotherVine until closing. Mostly I worked on the bay window display. Consulting a book on origami from the arts and crafts shelf, I created some paper fish, which I tucked into the satin folds representing the ocean. I also made paper seagulls, suspending them from the ceiling with clear fishing wire. Then I tossed glitter over the whole thing.

"What do you think?" I asked Antoinette, who'd wandered over to check on my progress.

"The real question is, *What do the window-shoppers think?*"

I went outside, crossed Queen Street, and stood in front of the pirate ship. My miniature beach scene sparkled in the afternoon sun. The air-conditioning made the origami seagulls twist, and the glitter made the beach reads twinkle like stars. Best of all was the twenty-something couple pushing a baby stroller past the MotherVine. Pointing, they paused in front of the window. After some conversation, the woman pecked the man on the cheek and dashed inside the bookshop.

I couldn't deny the swell of pride that crested inside my chest.

A ghost hovered at the end of Hudson's driveway. At least it looked like a ghost, or like a kid had thrown a sheet over herself for a last-minute Halloween costume.

I was slowing from a run to a walk. I'd only gone a couple of miles, setting out after work.

Hudson, Antoinette, and Ronnie, my uncle and his best friends—the three of them called themselves the Gang—gathered around the ghost. I wondered how long they'd been lingering, waiting for me to return.

"Trick-or-treating's not for another four months, you know," I said.

My uncle's hand looked enormous around the can of Mountain Dew he was holding. With his free hand, he patted the ghost. "We know your first couple days back in Cattail have been . . ."

"Eventful." Ronnie's voice was scratchier than sandpaper. He wore a five-o'clock shadow and a half-unbuttoned Hawaiian shirt. He whipped off the sheet, saying, "Ta-da. A registered and official bookcase on a stick."

It was painted like Hudson's house, yellow with white trim. The plexiglass door had a long handle shaped like a cattail, shellacked to within an inch of its life. Inside, two shelves were lined with books.

A Little Free Library.

A smile spread across my face.

"I remembered that article you wrote not long ago," Antoinette said. "For the *Charlotte Times*. Hudson shows me everything you write. And this one was a fun piece about the Little Free Libraries popping up all over the city. About the sense of sharing and community they bring. Not to mention the championing of literacy. And I thought, Cattail should have one of those. And who better to steward it than our island's latest bookseller? I got you started with some books."

I laughed. "The ones that were too odious to sell in the Mother-Vine?"

"Not so odious that people won't trade for them. There's a good mix of genres. Hardbacks as well as paperbacks."

"You're seeding the competition," I said.

"You were such a bookworm as a teen," Hudson said, his mind no doubt casting back to all those afternoons and evenings I'd spent in the MotherVine, my nose stuck in a Mary Higgins Clark book, because doing homework after your mother died had seemed impossible. I'd wanted to feel close to Mom, and as much as I loved holing up in Hudson's loft, it didn't evoke her. At the same time, I craved escape, and MHC's heroines invariably ended up risking their lives for the sake of justice, and that was a pretty good escape.

"I supplied the post-hole digger," Ronnie said. "And I mixed the cement." He stressed the first syllable: *ce*-ment. A fishing hook clung unironically to the Evinrude baseball cap perched on his head.

"I might have another go at that handle," Hudson said. "Looks more like a corn dog than a cattail. At any rate, we'll find out just how quality the construction is when hurricane season rolls around." He patted the shingled roof. A little red-lettered sign was pitched at an angle. CATTALE QUEEN.

"Get it?" Ronnie asked. "Because you're back on Queen Street. And *tale* is spelled—"

"I love it," I said. "Thank you. It's very sweet."

"It's too hokey." My uncle shook his head. "I knew it."

"I love hokey. I *need* hokey. But I'm not staying here. I don't *live* here now—"

"Of course," Hudson said. "I'll become steward if you move out."

"*When* I move out."

"Just as soon as you get back on your feet," Antoinette said.

I sighed. "Right."

22

You look more tired than a sloth in a hammock," Hudson said.

"Just what every woman longs to hear." It was later that night, and I was sitting cross-legged at his backyard table, scanning the news headlines on my laptop for anything about the lighthouse.

"Sloths are kinda cute, you know." My uncle flicked his old Zippo lighter. *Click-zip-hiss. Click-zip-hiss.* It helped calm him, he claimed. He'd quit smoking cigarettes, but he'd be damned if he was going to quit fiddling with his trusty Zippo.

"Thanks for replenishing your supply," I said, in reference to the bottle of Cattail Island Blonde sweating before me. The brew tasted crisp, with hints of grapefruit.

"I walked all the way up to the Piggly Wiggly and back for that six-pack. That's almost one and three-quarter miles."

"Good. Walking's good exercise." I clicked on an article out of a daily paper in Virginia. It mentioned the lighthouse-fall death but didn't identify the deceased.

Also good. For Summer's sake. For Georgia's.

Click-zip-hiss. "Bless her heart," Hudson said. "Eva Meeks."

I closed my laptop, knowing I wasn't going to get much reading done with my uncle in a talkative mood. "Yeah," I said.

"You know. I've been thinking."

"Uh-oh."

"She lives on Muscadine Street, right?"

"Lived. Past tense."

"That house around the corner from the hardware store?"

"As far as I know."

"Where her house is now, there used to be a park. For the apartments, which were across the street."

"There were apartments on Muscadine Street?"

"Long time ago. For the folks who worked in the furniture factory."

The factory had been converted into condominiums. But I didn't remember any apartments, or any park. "When did the apartments come down?" I asked.

"Early nineties. Soon after your mother. The commotion was really something. Don't you remember? Wrecking balls, barricaded streets. They tore it all down right before a big storm hit. Big, *big* storm. Hurricane something or other."

I shook my head. What I did recall of that time was my own internal hurricane, a whir of headaches, stomachaches, and attacks of sadness. "You think the riddle Eva found had something to do with those apartments?"

"What I'm saying is—whoever planted that glass vial might have done so when there was nothing around there but parkland. And years went by and houses were built and no one was the wiser. It's as reasonable as any other theory."

"I don't have any other theory." I pressed the heels of my palms to my eyes. My head felt as heavy as a bowling ball. But Eva's neighborhood was only a couple of miles from there. What if a quick visit could reveal something? Shake something loose? A clue. An answer.

I looked over at my uncle. He was watching me. *Click-zip-hiss.* "I'll drive," he said.

23

The Old Fart Van—OFV for short—was a 1984 Chevy G-Series G20. It made the road rumble like a cyclone was coming. I braced myself against the dashboard as Hudson swerved to avoid potholes. The saggy seat belt was pretty much useless, but I'd buckled it anyway.

Muscadine Street was dark except for two streetlights. It dead-ended at some skinny-trunked ash trees. Hudson aimed the headlights into them, giving them a ghostly underwater quality, like we'd come upon a sunken shipwreck. "That's where the apartments were," he said, braking.

"Did you know anybody who lived there?"

"I don't think so."

"What about Ronnie? Or Antoinette?"

"Worth asking. I'll text them."

To our left sat a modest, late-nineties-era brick ranch. A carport covered a red SUV. I recognized it, and its decals—bigger versions of the logo on the sweatshirt Eva Meeks wore the night she died. I wondered who'd driven her vehicle back home. "There's Eva's place," I said.

"Where the park used to be." He swung the OFV in front of her house, more or less identical to the others on the street.

"Give me a sec?"

"Take your time. I'm not going anywhere."

The passenger door creaked like fifty pounds of pure rust as I shut it behind me. I followed the path of crushed oyster shells that led to Eva's house. No one was home. Any off-island mourners must have been staying with Georgia or other relatives.

Begonias lined the south side of the path but stopped halfway to the house, just as Summer had described. A yellow-handled cultivator lay in the grass, marking a fist-size hole. A wagon held trays of begonia flats, the waxy leaves dotted with moisture.

The last person to touch the cultivator must have been Eva herself. She'd hacked into the grass, then heard a clink—and there was the thick-glassed vial. So she brushed it off. Broke the wax seal. Coaxed out the scroll. I imagined her getting to her feet, cradling her discovery.

I knelt in the grass before the fateful last hole she'd dug. I scooped some dirt and let it sift through my fingers. Then I did it again. Some fantastical side of me was hoping to find another vial. One containing the whole truth of what had happened Saturday night.

I eased a begonia out of its plastic casing, massaged the roots, and placed it in the hole. I mounded the earth against the stem.

Back in the van, Hudson had rolled down the windows and popped a Willie Nelson cassette into the tape deck. As he whistled and tapped the steering wheel, I whacked the grass with the cultivator. Dug another hole. Planted another begonia. Repeated and repeated, dragging the wagon with me when necessary.

It was an activity wholly different from running. Still, in the five minutes it took to finish the plantings, I'd obtained a similar mental quiet. Eva had known exactly how many flowers would take her to the end of the path; the wagon contained only empty flats by the time I reached the steps leading to the front door of her home.

I stood and stretched and noticed a concrete tray poking from a hedge underneath the windows. A tray exactly like the one in Gwen's trunk. On the other side of the steps, a gutter spouted over a patch of dirt. The patch had the shape of the tray.

Its match had been there.

Up on Eva's porch, I peeked through the window. Pots and pans hung over a kitchen island. A greenish light glinted from the oven's digital clock. Tucked between floor-to-ceiling cabinets, the back of a chair curved before a narrow built-in desk. The ideal place to do your bills or prop your iPad while you were cooking.

Eva had sat there Saturday afternoon. Sat and puzzled over the riddle. And then she'd come to the MotherVine Bookshop, desperate for help.

I stepped to the front door and tried the knob. Locked. In the wake of Eva's death, someone had decided to secure things.

With my toe I lifted a corner of the welcome mat. A house key gleamed up at me.

I glanced back at Hudson. He had reclined the seat and closed his eyes, arms crossed over his chest.

Stooping, I snatched the key and let myself in. I replaced the key where I'd found it.

I stepped into a small foyer. Somewhere close by, a timepiece ticked a soothing rhythm. My eyes adjusted to the dark, my nose to the leftover tinge of sautéed onions. The green bean casserole Eva had been experimenting with.

Turns out trespassing comes easier the second time. I experienced none of the anxiety that had overcome me when entering the keeper's cottage. In fact, a jab of focus sharpened my senses.

Then a gong practically deafened my right ear. I jumped and slapped my hands over my mouth, sucking air.

Next to me, a grandfather clock bonged out ten o'clock.

Who was I kidding? Hadn't I done enough snooping?

But the desk, awash in that ghoulish light, sat just past the kitchen island. Straightening, I took a few chest-expanding inhalations.

Let's face it. I hadn't come here to plant flowers.

Turning on lights might have aroused the neighbors, if the OFV hadn't already. I patted my side, but I'd left my phone in the van. No flashlight app.

Cursing under my breath, I made my way toward the desk. It was rustic wood, like the cabinetry. Shadowing the desk's far corner was a rectangle. A book. The book she'd bought from me on Saturday, about pirates and the Outer Banks. Something was tucked between the pages. I slipped it out: a booklet with a stapled binding. The musty odor suggested it had spent time in storage, perhaps underneath heavier objects that kept it flattened for many years. It was stiff, reluctant to open.

A voice inside told me to hurry. Get out of there. I was pushing my luck.

Another voice told me this booklet might make interesting reading.

A soft creak sounded from an adjacent room. Clutching the booklet, I twisted around, scanning the darkness. "Hello?"

Silence.

It's just the wood settling, my mother used to say of our old house, when I'd wake up in the night, imagination rampant due to unexplained noises.

That was when the OFV's horn started blaring.

I sprinted from the house and ran down the path. I yanked open the driver's-side door.

Hudson reached for me. His face was panicked, the color of paste.

"What's wrong?" I asked. "Why were you beeping the horn?"

"Where were you? Where'd you go?"

"I just went inside Eva's house for a second."

"I looked over at the yard. You weren't there. And I tried calling you but your phone was right next to me. And out of nowhere

I started thinking—what if I'd lost you? What if something happened to you? Something bad—and then my chest—my lungs—I tried getting out of the van but my hands felt numb, and then—"

"Uncle Hudson, I'm right here."

"You're okay. Thank God."

"Of course I'm okay. Why wouldn't I be okay?"

"It doesn't make any sense. I don't know why I got so scared. Hit me like a half ton of hydrogen." His hand flew to his chest. "My heart."

"What is it?"

"Can't breathe—"

"I'm calling 911." I reached over him.

"Can't—can't breathe—"

I grabbed my phone. Dialed.

"What is your location?" came the operator's nasally voice.

"Muscadine Street," I said.

"Ma'am, I'll need the house number."

I craned my neck, searching. Willie Nelson sang about lonely, lonely times.

Inside the neighboring home, a light turned on.

"Sixty-one Muscadine Street," I said.

"Callie," Hudson said. "My heart . . ."

Panic surged inside me, sucking like a whirlpool. *Don't you leave me, Hudson. Don't you leave me too.*

24

I jabbed the elevator button. Up. Up. Up.

"Got you some jitter juice." Officer Fusco ambled toward me.

I took her in with my bleary eyes. A tall midnight-blue figure outlined by the harsh hospital lighting. In each of her freckled hands, a disposable cup steamed.

I didn't want coffee. It smelled stale, as if it had been sitting on a burner since breakfast. Plus, coffee was for morning, and I didn't hear any roosters crowing.

Fusco had been behind the wheel of the cruiser that purred into Eva's driveway. Lights twirling, no sirens. The ambulance followed.

I'd sat for an hour in Cattail Island Hospital's tiny ER waiting room. I'd called Ronnie and Antoinette and told them what happened, told them not to worry, that Hudson was out of it but going to be okay. It took some insisting, but I convinced each of them to stay home. Then Hudson had been moved to a private room. I'd just been informed of the location.

The elevator doors slid open. Fusco and I stepped inside. I jabbed another button. Three. Three. Three.

"That a negative on the coffee, then?" she asked.

I took a cup. "Thank you."

"What you got there?"

My other hand grasped the booklet I'd swiped from Eva Meeks's desk. I'd tried to read it but had been too numb. Why had I taken it? It rightly belonged in Summer's hands, not mine.

The title was legible now: *Camp Cottontown Funbook: 1988.* Three Latin words scrolled along the bottom. I'd seen them before somewhere.

"It's nothing." Forcing an exhalation, I slipped the booklet into my bag.

Fusco walked with me to Hudson's room, which wasn't far from the elevator. Not wanting to disturb him, I stood in the doorway. His eyes were closed, his mouth slack. His breathing came in soft whistles, and his face blended with the pale pillowcase. He seemed to have aged thirty years in as many minutes.

"He looks better," Fusco said.

"He looks like he's circling the drain."

"Better than going down it." She slurped her coffee. Smacked her lips. "Eva Meeks's front door was wide open. But you wouldn't know anything about that, would you?"

I half lifted a shoulder. A proper shrug was out of the question. I was blasted, emotionally and physically.

"How about your uncle?" she asked. "Would he know anything about it?"

"He's practically unconscious, Officer. Cut us some slack."

"Would either of you know anything about being outside—or *inside*—the deceased's home at ten o'clock at night?"

The hot coffee cup was itching my palm. I switched hands. "Have you ever handled a murder?"

If the question surprised her, she didn't show it. "My first job down in New Bern? There was a murder-suicide. Old nutter poisoned her husband, then herself. Crushed up a whole bunch of apple seeds and stirred them into his grits. That was how I learned apple seeds have cyanide in 'em. The question flying around the station was, 'Don't you think you'd notice there was something in your grits?'" She nodded toward the bed, as if my uncle was somehow involved. "Best I figured was, when you get up there in age—when you get round to your zillionth lifetime bowl of grits—you just suck 'em right down."

"Nothing like that since then? Murders, I mean."

"Naw. Hit-and-run a few years back. Who wants to know?"

"What would you tell someone who believes there may have been a suspicious death?"

"Go to the police."

"And—hypothetically speaking—what if the police were not the best people for the job?"

Fusco's carrot-stick eyebrows lifted. "The police are always the best people for the job. The police. *Not* the press. Or booksellers. Or whatever you are." She held out her free hand. "Why don't I give you my number? That way, you can get ahold of me. Any time, day or night." I produced my phone, and she punched in her info. "Remember," she said. "The *police*."

25

Dr. Rudd-Ortiz had coral lipstick that matched her blouse and a mane of hair that matched her lab coat. She didn't waste any time. "Your uncle had a panic attack," she said while I was still shaking her hand at the foot of Hudson's hospital bed.

"That's it?" I said. "I mean, it's nothing physical?"

"Anxiety manifests physically. But medically speaking? There's nothing wrong with him. Aside from high blood pressure and a cholesterol count that's through the proverbial roof. Ticker's working properly, at least according to preliminary evaluation. No neurological issues. But if he wants to avoid future ambulance rides, some lifestyle changes are in order." She rifled through the pages of her clipboard. "He could stand to lose a few pounds. By a few, I mean fifty to seventy. I recommend daily exercise and a low-fat diet emphasizing leafy vegetables, whole grains, and lean proteins. No salt. No alcohol. No sugar. No—"

"No fun." Hudson's eyes were open. A duskier green than I was used to.

I rushed to the bedside and laced my fingers through his. "Hi."

"Don't fuss, now." His voice wasn't thundering out of him like normal, but at least each word sounded whole.

"How are you feeling, Mr. Padget?" asked the doctor.

"Aces. I'm ready to go home, so let's get this show on the road. First get this tube outta my nose. And it feels like there's another tube up my—"

"No stress." The doctor placed her manicured fingertips on

the bedrail. "That was the next item on my list, Mr. Padget. You really need to put some effort into relaxing."

His head lifted. I knew what was coming. *Put some effort into relaxing? That's an oxymoron if I ever heard one.* I rested a hand on his clammy forehead, where a vein was throbbing. Sedatives didn't have much effect on a guy like my uncle. Grumbling, he let his head drop onto the pillow.

Dr. Rudd-Ortiz clicked her pen and made a few notations. "The EKG revealed normal cardiac rhythms. Just to be sure, I'm ordering a stress test for him tomorrow."

"I'm not running on any stupid hamster wheel, if that's what you have in mind."

She gave me a look—the treadmill test was exactly what she had in mind. "If all goes well, he'll be home by tomorrow evening. But he needs to take it easy. And he really needs to start taking care of himself. I'll give him a prescription for blood pressure medication—"

"He won't take it," I said.

"Very well. How about a script for something to help you relax, Mr. Padget? Something you can take as needed."

"No pills," he said.

She blinked. She was startled, but not necessarily impressed. "With most patients, that's the first thing they ask for. Pills. Are you sure?"

"No. Pills."

"Doctor," I said. "Wouldn't it be a good idea for him to cut back on caffeine?"

"Certainly. Google it. I suggest tapering, rather than quitting cold turkey."

"Thanks," I said as she turned to go.

"Tapering." Hudson wheezed. "*Tapering*, for the love of lizards."

I stood there awhile, squeezing his hand. Stroking his puffy hair.

The foody odor of Eva's home was still in my nostrils. Not even antiseptic hospital smells could expunge it. Green bean casserole. One holiday when I was six or seven—Thanksgiving or Easter—green bean casserole had been Hudson's assigned dish. His version involved Ritz crackers and Funyuns and Green Giant cans—far from the from-scratch, garden-fresh effort Eva had been putting forth. At the table, I'd made a face. Mom nudged me with her foot. "It's more than you made," she'd said. "Eat it." Then she'd winked and spit something into a napkin.

"You should go home," Hudson said. "I'll call the Gang in the morning."

"I'll stay."

"You'll go home and get some shut-eye. And tomorrow you'll go to work. Business as usual." He gave my hand a squeeze. It felt weak. Quarter-strength. "There's nothing wrong with me," he said. "Dr. Google said it herself. I just got nervous."

"So nervous you thought you were dying?"

"What we both need to get through our skulls, Callie, is that no one gets to stick around forever."

I sucked in air. It lodged in my throat, a painful pocket I couldn't swallow.

"Antoinette told me you went to see Trish Berryman," Hudson said.

"Only because I had to deliver a book."

"It's a good thing. She isn't a demon, you know. She's really not to blame."

Tears jabbed my eyes, threatening to spill. "I'm gonna go," I said, and released his hand.

Five minutes later I sat behind the wheel of the OFV, which was idling in the hospital parking lot. On the radio, a reporter described a future of driverless cars. I wasn't sure I wanted to imagine that. What American didn't love driving? The control coupled with the risk? If there was a better metaphor for living, I didn't know it.

This van had known some good times. Years ago, before dawn on weekend mornings, if the wind was light and offshore, my uncle, Ronnie, Antoinette, and her husband, Alfred, who died ten years ago, would all pile their surfboards into the OFV. I'd tag along. One of the adults would take turns playing heads-up poker for nickels and dimes with me, hanging out in the back of the van, doors thrown open to receive the ocean breeze, while the others surfed. Eventually, they'd emerge from the waves, dripping and calling for towels. They'd been in their late forties—before my uncle started looking like a woodshop-themed Santa, before Ronnie's spine became C-shaped. They had joked about being old farts.

Now, Antoinette liked to say, it wasn't a joke.

I snapped off the radio. Gave my cheek a few small slaps.

Then I peeled out of the parking lot, heading for home.

Not *home*. Hudson's house.

26

No sooner did I pull down the Murphy bed than Scupper jumped onto it, turned around a few times, and curled into a ball the circumference of a dinner plate. I'd carried him up the ladder. No easy feat, since he'd wiggled the whole way.

He was asleep within minutes.

Couldn't say the same for myself.

I still hadn't unpacked very much. I probably should have tackled a few boxes. Instead, I sat on the edge of the mattress and opened Eva's booklet from Camp Cottontown. The binding crackled like a new wick. Poor-quality black-and-white photographs of children potato-sack racing, aiming BB guns at paper targets, paddling canoes. Mountains rose in the background. The place must have been well inland. In the captions, no one was identified by name, but I recognized Eva in more than a few. She looked to be in her early teens. A counselor. Her cheeks were fuller back then, her hair shorter, her legs plumper. In one shot, out of focus and grainy, a teenaged boy dangled an arm over her shoulder. *Getting cozy*, read the caption. In another she proudly held up an in-progress macaroni necklace she and a younger camper were stringing.

I didn't notice Georgia in any of the photos.

I examined the cover again, unadorned except for the lettering. The Latin words rolled across the bottom: *Esse quam videri*. I typed the phrase into my laptop's search window. A common motto that appeared in scores of places, from school charters to whiskey labels to the official state seal of North Carolina, which must have been where I'd seen it before.

Esse quam videri. To be, rather than to seem.

I tucked the booklet safely away inside my cardboard chest of drawers, alongside the vial Summer had given to me. The vial containing the riddle. *Spiraling upward toward the light / Pass through blue and into white. / Then hold on. Hold on tight / and you'll spy the hidden sight.*

I took my mother's crown of cattail leaves from the drawer and set it on the pillow next to me, the one I wasn't using. I laid a hand on the crown and traced its valleys and peaks.

The whisper of my skin sounded like the breeze through cattails.

I thought about Eva Meeks. About Mr. and Mrs. Meeks driving little Eva inland for summer camp, while vacationers by the thousands headed in the opposite direction, to descend upon her hometown.

And what about adult Eva? If she'd found anything at the top of Cattail Lighthouse on Saturday night, she didn't take it with her.

And what could *it* be? A treasure of some sort? Another tantalizing clue?

I'd been to the top of Cattail Lighthouse countless times before the age of twelve. One winter Sunday when I complained about being bored, my mother set aside the project she was working on—fixing the zipper on a Carhartt jacket belonging to a fisherman. She grabbed my hand, pulled me out the door, and tossed me into the car. Twenty minutes later, panting at the top of the lighthouse, I wasn't frightened by the dizzying views of the ocean, the Pamlico, Albemarle, and Currituck Sounds, and the string bean–shaped barrier islands that were the Outer Banks. Instead, I was awed. Mom commented on just how vulnerably we lived, saying something like, *A teensy bit of land and a whole lot of water.* Then she noticed mustangs, a mare and a yearling, galloping down one of the beaches. She pointed them out, the bare skin of her hand turning red in the icy wind. The horses had looked like tiny plastic toys.

Anyway, one thing was certain: the top of the lighthouse was hardly more than an iron railing circling a parapet. It wasn't exactly bursting with secret hiding places, which presented three outcomes:

Outcome A: nothing was there to be found.
Outcome B: someone else took it.
Outcome C: it was still there.

27

The next day dawned hot and hazy. I walked to work, flip-flops smacking my heels, the scents of fudge from the candy shop floating on the breeze. Underneath the wipers on every parked car, Cattaillion flyers rippled. They showed the old Smile Beach fishing pier when it was first built, shining and sturdy. *This year, when you support the Cattaillion, you support the restoration of a favorite local landmark!*

I slowed to a stroll so I could make some phone calls. With earbuds fitted into place, my first call was to Hudson. When I heard that his voice had regained its normal deafening volume, I smiled.

"Ronnie's on the way with a fresh pack of cigs," he said.

"Aren't you the comedian."

"He's bringing a deck of cards, a phone charger, and a few issues of *WoodenBoat*. And Antoinette might come later." So that was why my uncle sounded so chipper. "You just wait," he said. "I'm turning a new leaf. No more Mountain Dew."

"I'll believe it when I see it. Or stop seeing it, really." Hanging up, I savored the rich aroma of freshly baked muffins wafting from Cattail Café. I passed the kiosk for dolphin-watch cruises and the purple-and-cream-painted bed-and-breakfast, the Casa Coquina. I dialed Whitman Standish, entering his number from the business card he'd given me. Voicemail. "I'd like to sit down with your grandmother, if possible," I said. "I know she's a busy woman, but I have a, um—a unique publicity opportunity for her and promise to be fast and professional."

As I was hanging up, a man bumped into me. He'd been reading something on his phone while walking. "Pardon me, ma'am," he said.

"That's all right."

Continuing down the sidewalk, he made a call. "You see this week's *Crier*?" he said into his phone. "Just came out this morning . . . The *Crier*? No, I wouldn't wrap my fish in it either. But you'd better check it out. And get your cash-counting fingers ready . . ."

He kept on walking, out of earshot. *Cash-counting fingers?* What was that about? A dark foreboding rolled through me. I scraped my teeth against my lip, an old anxious habit.

To my right, a storefront was changing over. Butcher paper covered the windows, blocking any chance of a glimpse inside. I looked around for clues as to what this mystery business was going to be, but nothing stood out—except a Jeep Grand Wagoneer parked directly out front. Mint green with wood paneling. The same Wagoneer that came too close to Tin Man as he'd dined on a fish taco in the crosswalk.

My cheeks grew hot as I remembered the cat trembling in my arms. The driver had apologized, but still.

I rapped my knuckles on the red door of the papered-up shop. No answer.

I lifted my hand, about to knock again and harder, when the door swung open. Standing there was a man about my age, a head and a half taller than me. His dark hair was gathered back, and his eager, alert face made me think of a hunting dog. A sleek shirt stretched over his taut chest, but not in a show-offy or macho way. It was just what he looked like in workout clothes.

Silent seconds passed before I realized I was staring.

"Can I help you?" His voice was musical, like if an upright bass could speak.

Coming back to earth, I blinked a few times. "Is this your Wagoneer?" I asked.

He grinned. "You mean my pride and joy? Saved up for six years to buy that beauty. Restored it myself. Just put in a diesel conversion kit, so it runs on vegetable oil. Isn't that cool? No noxious emissions here."

I did some more blinking. The almost cat killer was concerned about the environment? What was going on here?

I suddenly regretted my spur-of-the-moment decision to knock. It was turning out to be the hottest morning of the summer so far. No doubt sweat stains were darkening the armpits of my dress. But this guy was regarding me with a kind expression, as if he didn't care one way or the other. Or maybe he was simply polite.

"I just wanted to introduce myself," I said. "I'm working at the bookshop. The MotherVine. It's just down the sidewalk a ways."

"Of course." He shook my hand. His grip was strong, and I felt a little sad when he let go. "Toby Dodge," he said. "Got something cooking here. Should be going live any day now." He grinned again. "Hey, I know you. You're the one who scooped the cat out of the street. I'm afraid you caught me in a momentary lapse of good judgment that day. Happens to the best of us, I guess. Summer traffic just gets to you sometimes, doesn't it? Anyway, is the cat okay?"

I found myself smiling. "He works in the bookstore, actually."

Toby chuckled.

"It's a tough job," I added.

"I didn't catch your name."

"Oh. Right. I'm Callie. Padget." I extended my hand, then quickly pulled it away when I remembered we'd already shook. "I actually have to get going," I said. "Thank you."

"What for?"

"Bye!" I called over my shoulder, hoping he'd believe I was importantly busy instead of blindsided by attraction. Only when I'd reached the end of the block did I realize I hadn't asked about his business—what the something was that he had cooking.

Wait. What was wrong with me? How could I be attracted to Tin Man's would-be murderer?

I whacked my phone against my forehead a couple of times. *Business as usual, Padget. Come on. Pull yourself together.*

28

The MotherVine sign hung over the sidewalk, a rose-gold oval with deep green lettering. Quickening my pace, I headed toward it. The red door flung open and Antoinette emerged, sweeping the bricks with caffeine-fueled intensity.

The smell of books floated out, and I inhaled deeply.

She handed me the broom. "Gets the blood flowing."

A minute later, after I'd brushed away sand and leaves and flower petals, I joined her behind the checkout counter, which she'd cleared for a workspace. On it were rolls of plain brown paper, skeins of green and rose-gold raffia, and stacks of books, both used and new, representing every genre she sold, from science fiction to historical accounts to poetry.

"Let me guess," I said. "An assembly line is in my immediate future."

She tore off a sheet of paper. "Got to get ready for the Cattaillion. Bidders make donations for a surprise read. They might pay fifty bucks for a clobbered ten-cent copy of *Les Mis*, or five bucks for a pristine first-edition hardback of the latest Nicholas Sparks. It's all in the spirit of the Cattaillion." She wrapped a book and passed it, and I finished it off with raffia bows as fluffy as I could make them. Soon the end of the counter was crowded with enticing book-shaped mystery packages. I admitted to Antoinette that I had a ridiculous urge to tear them all open like a kid on Christmas morning.

She laughed. "I can relate."

"Is there a way we could attach grapes?" I asked. "Kind of like as a decoration? Or a garnish."

Her hands hovered over the brown paper. "Interesting. Say more."

"Well, obviously there's a squishing risk, but—"

"Let's try it." She reached into a cubby underneath the cash register and produced a pair of shears, which she slapped into my palm, and an apron, which she tossed over my head. "Go snip some test subjects."

"You got it."

Out back, I stepped from the pavers onto the soft dirt. Like Antoinette, I was lucky enough to just fit underneath the vine. An inch taller, and I'd have been ducking. The air was cooler here, and perfumed with grapes. I saw some that looked overripe, the fruit about to separate from the stem. Carefully, I snipped away. Somewhere nearby, birds were chirping, and I wondered what they were. Cardinals? Sparrows? Something about Cattail Island made you want to know more about nature. I'd have to study some of the bird books Antoinette sold, brush up on my identification skills.

I had snipped a few bunches and placed them inside the apron pocket when I heard Antoinette's voice. But it wasn't her usual sparkling tone.

"No, thank you," she was saying. "And no offense, either. But it doesn't do enough for my business to justify the cost. You know that."

I bustled back inside. Jeff Berryman was standing in the doorway, a bundle of newspapers under one arm. "People are buying this week's issue," he said.

"What's so special about this week's issue, anyway?" I stepped behind the counter, taking my place beside Antoinette.

"Once word starts spreading," he said, "our ad rates will go up.

I'd like to lock in the MotherVine, right now, at a discounted rate. As a favor for being the *Crier*'s good neighbors here on the waterfront for so many years."

I cringed. Jeff just wasn't a salesman. He sounded about as sincere as a ventriloquist's dummy. I placed the grapes on the tea towels Antoinette had spread out. "Once word starts spreading about what, Jeff?" I asked.

"There's a reason I stopped advertising in the *Crier*," Antoinette said. "I couldn't afford it any longer. Meanwhile, social media is free. And it reaches people far beyond Cattail."

"The *Crier* does that too, these days," he said. "Why don't you want to support us? It's because we're mainlanders, Trish and I. Isn't it? That's why the locally owned businesses have been withdrawing their advertising dollars—"

"Oh, of course not."

"My wife and I moved here, saw a need for print news, and satisfied that need. But we'll never be true Cattailers, will we? In your eyes, we'll always be dingbatters."

"Now, Jeff." She patted the air. "Please understand—"

He gestured around the bookshop. "I see a lot of paper in here, and a lot of ink. It won't be long before time catches up with the MotherVine too, like it did the *Crier*." He turned to go, then paused. "Know this. I didn't think it was in good taste, but Trish insisted. And she always gets her way, doesn't she?" With that, he left.

Antoinette and I watched him hoof it across Queen Street and enter the pottery shop, his next target.

"Not in good taste?" I said. "What's he talking about?"

She frowned. "I don't want to know."

"Yeah. Neither do I."

But a few seconds later we were side by side in front of the computer screen, reading the article on the *Crier* website's homepage.

CURSE OF CATTAIL LIGHTHOUSE?

Submitted by Trish Berryman, Editor in Chief

CATTAIL, June 27—In more than a few travel guidebooks, Cattailers have been described as "down to earth." And yet we Cattailers love our lore. To date, two local women have plunged to their deaths from the top of Cattail Lighthouse. Both were forty-one years old. Both were local business owners. And both died on or very near the twenty-third of June, twenty-six years apart. These curious coincidences are prompting many to wonder: Is Cattail Lighthouse cursed?

Fury volcanoed inside me. Heat spiked my eyes. I clicked off the website and looked away—and noticed two books in the delivery cubby. The top one showed a woman on horseback. *Flying Changes.*

"Why don't I take care of those for you?" Antoinette asked.

"Nah," I said. "I'm on it."

Books have a way of pointing you exactly where you need to go.

29

"'The Outer Banks boasts more than a few curses.'" I glanced up from my phone. I had just stepped inside the *Crier* office and, without pleasantries or preamble, begun my recitation of Trish's article.

She spun her chair around and was staring at me so hard it felt like two hot needles searing into my face. "Please," she said, crossing one leg over the other. "Do go on."

"'The centuries-old curse of the Currituck Lighthouse Keeper's Home, for example, is legendary, with tragedy—ranging from sudden illness to sudden death—befalling many who sleep in a certain third-story bedroom.

"'Even more legendary is the curse of Virginia Dare, the first English child born in the New World. As a young woman, she was transformed by a scorned suitor into a white doe and damned to endlessly roam the forests of Roanoke Island.

"'Closer to home, Cattail Island might have a curse all its own . . . '"

Trish's phone rang. "Would you excuse me?" she said. "We've been ringing off the hook." She put her back to me. "Yes, I can help you with that . . . The rest of the summer? Fantastic . . . You won't regret it. I'll have Jeff call you to firm up details." She hung up. "That was Cattail Sand and Gravel calling to reopen their advertising account. Which makes three."

"Three what?" I asked.

"Ads sold this morning. Cattail Funeral Home's in the bag for a quarter-pager to run for four weeks. The florist also. You see? People like curses."

"People deserve the truth."

"Well, they get that too. Because the truth is, this island is buzzing about a curse."

"I can't believe you printed this garbage."

"A lot of that *garbage* came from a book. A book I got at the MotherVine, by the way." She held up a paperback. *Hauntings of the Outer Banks.* "If you haven't noticed, this place *loves* its lore. Also, the article you were just reading? It went live approximately fifty-two minutes ago. And you know how many hits the *Crier* website has gotten in that brief time? I'll give you a hint: it's more than we've received in an entire month. Just like that"—she snapped her fingers—"the local rag is relevant again. I have you to thank. You're the one who suggested a different angle."

"This is *not* what I had in mind." I fished *Flying Changes* out of my bag and tossed it onto her desk.

"I'm surprised by your attitude, Callie. I thought you'd gone grassroots like the rest of us. Working for the indy bookshop and all." She stood and dragged a hand over her face as if trying to calm herself. When she spoke again, her tone gentled. "I said it to Hudson, way back when. But I never said it to you, did I? You were so young, Callie. So vulnerable . . ."

"What? What are you talking about?"

"I'm sorry. About your mother. That's a long-overdue apology. But it doesn't mean you get to storm in here and—"

A sound of static interrupted her, whooshing from the corner of the room. The police scanner, a walkie-talkie-like device, was mounted on the table next to the printer. A high-pitched tone whined, followed by several lower bursts and another swish of static. Then the dispatcher's dispassionate voice said, "Caller reporting an unusually large number of guinea fowls blocking traffic. Anyone in the vicinity of Soundside Road?"

"En route," came Officer Fusco's voice. "I'm just around the corner. Maybe they're upset about the Cattail curse."

"There," Trish said, triumphant once again. "Even the cops are chittering about it."

"They're making fun of your article. Can't you see that?"

She flopped back into her chair. "That scanner is prime entertainment. Though I have to admit, sometimes it does feel a little creepy, listening in."

Her phone rang again, and she took another call that sounded a lot like the first. When she hung up, she didn't turn back around.

"Just one more thing, Trish," I said, my hand on the doorknob. "There *is* no curse. You of all people know that."

30

A block away from the *Crier* office, I sat on a bench. About five minutes had passed since I'd stormed out on Trish, my hands balled into fists. Now, after some people watching, I felt calmer. Nearby, a man snapped a photograph of a brown pelican preening on top of the seawall. A young girl jumped and squealed and ran for the pirate ship after her mother finally acquiesced to her pleas.

The book in my hands, my next delivery, was for Georgia Meeks. *Hardware store okay*, Antoinette had scribbled on the back of the bookmark. The prospect of stepping inside Meeks Hardware after having made zero headway in my little investigation sent a fresh ripple of anxiety through my chest. After all, the last time Georgia and I spoke, she'd sent me home.

What if I tried following up with Chief Jurecki? It was a long shot, but if I could get him on the phone, maybe I could squeeze some information out of him. There on the bench, I called the station and asked to be put through. To my surprise, my request was granted.

"I know that an event involving the lighthouse means more to you than it does the average person," he said. "I had another look around, and I spoke to the new keeper, and I'm certain this event was, tragically, a suicide. Like I've been saying. So you can stop worrying."

"Occam's razor?" I asked. "The simplest explanation is the right one?"

"The *right* explanation is the right one, Callie."

"There were a ton of people milling around the lighthouse yesterday. It's summer vacation. The crime scene's been contaminated."

"Someone's been watching *Murder, She Wrote*."

That comment shut me up. Mom and I had, in fact, watched a lot of episodes together when I was growing up.

"Let's get down to the basics," Chief Jurecki said. "In order to have a crime scene, you've got to have a crime. Simply put, we don't have a crime. There's no evidence to suggest Eva Meeks wasn't alone. And her family confirmed she'd been highly upset. She confided in multiple people about her dire illness."

I held the phone away from my face so he couldn't hear me grunt in frustration. He wasn't going to budge from the suicide decision. I had to try a different tack. "Did you recover any interesting objects around the lighthouse?"

"The usual trash. Cigarette butts. Single-use plastic bags. Nothing out of the ordinary. And nothing pertaining to this case."

"But you know about the riddle Eva found."

"The nursery rhyme her daughter was going on about?"

"Just because she's a young girl doesn't mean—"

"I appreciate what you're saying. I really do."

"But it's case closed?"

"Somebody tell that to the *Crier*," he said before hanging up.

Down the street, the Meeks Hardware awning flapped in the breeze. Amid the customers bustling in and out, a woman paused to prop a single white carnation against the side of the building.

Gathering my courage, I pushed myself off the bench and made my way toward the hardware store. A memorial had formed on the sidewalk out front. Flickering tea lights made a

U around a stuffed toy dolphin, a sign that said WE LOVE YOU EVA, and a recent photograph of her. She'd been mid-laugh, and her face was tan.

Inside, the checkout counter overflowed with baskets of fruit and trays of cookies and bouquets of flowers—sympathy gifts from locals and vacationers too, the families who rented the same cottages and patronized the same local shops summer after summer.

On the other side of the ribbons and cellophane, I spied blond hair. It belonged to Summer Meeks, slumped behind the cash register. She scribbled something in the paperback she was reading, then tucked the pencil behind her ear. She had a washed-out, haunted look, and I fought a protective urge to wrap my arms around her. "Hi, Summer," I said.

She tucked the book underneath the counter. "Aunt Georgia made me come in."

"Do you like being here?"

"When it's busy like this, it makes the day go by faster." She shrugged. "It's better than being at home alone. Or at Aunt Georgia's house. Or at the beach with all the tourists."

I made room for a woman approaching the register with an armload of plastic bottles. "This is the best stuff," she said, seemingly unaware of the sadness suffusing the atmosphere as she unloaded the organic sunscreen onto the small section of available counterspace. "I always stock up when I'm here," she added.

Summer rang up the bottles. After the customer had gone, the girl leaned closer to me and asked, "Did you find anything?"

Before I could answer, Georgia emerged from a doorway behind the counter. When she saw me, she stiffened. I didn't take offense. Grief had a way of scrambling your moods, making you unsure whether to push people away or pull them close.

"Summer, sweetie," Georgia said, her voice climbing an octave. "Why don't you go order yourself some lunch. Get whatever you want."

"All I want is French fries. With extra malt vinegar."

"Make it two."

Summer slid off the stool and disappeared into the back room. Georgia took her place. Her face was pale and lined, like it had been scribbled with a pencil. "I was going to close down the shop for a couple days," she said. "But how can I, with this action? It's that *Crier* article. It's got everybody all stirred up. You've seen it, right? I didn't read past the headline myself."

"Good idea. You really think what Trish wrote about a curse is the reason you've got so many shoppers?"

"I'm sure of it. It's only going to get worse the next few days." She rubbed her fingertips together—the *making money* gesture. "Or better, depending on your point of view. The dingbatters keep up with Cattail from their hometowns and even follow the *Crier* online. So even though the curse stuff is so god-awful, it reminds people of where they'd rather be."

"Here, on Cattail."

"That's right. Mark my words: they'll start arriving early for their vacations, filling up the motels until their rental cottages become available."

Nodding, I placed her book on the counter. *Whiskey in a Teacup* by Reese Witherspoon. The actress smiled up from the cover, her expression so adorably welcoming that for a flash I wanted to jump into her life.

"Oh," Georgia said, eyeing the book. "I've been on a celebrity memoir kick. I ordered that before—before—"

"I know."

"I won't be able to focus on it now."

"It'll be there when you're ready. That's the great thing about books." I put my elbows on the counter. "Can I ask you something? It's about Eva."

"Okay, I guess."

"What did you know about her supporting a butterfly project at Cattail Heritage Garden?"

"She mentioned it once or twice. After the diagnosis, my sister convinced herself that she should have been even *more* involved with community causes. Like she could buy her life back or something. You know, by doing good deeds. And she loved nature, so a butterfly garden made sense."

"Did she interact much with Pearleen Standish?"

"She didn't think highly of Pearleen. Said she was, and I quote, 'a witchy old broad.' And Eva didn't have many bad words to say about anybody. As you know."

"What were your sister's hobbies outside of work? Besides hunting for buried treasure."

"That was her chief pastime. Ever since summer camp on the mainland. Our parents sent her every year, and she won the big annual scavenger hunt a few years in a row."

"You didn't go to the summer camp?"

"You know how I was. Too busy painting my nails and giggling about boys."

"Eva didn't have any other interests? What about—I don't know. Knitting? Baking?"

"Callie," Georgia said. "These questions. I want to answer them. I know you think there's something strange going on, but . . ." She faltered.

I touched her arm. "I'm sorry. It's just that— No, you're right. Never mind."

"No—it's okay." Georgia's eyes flickered. "Eva was in love with her new baking blowtorch. She'd signed up for this night class at the church, and she bought the blowtorch, all ready to make crème brûlée or whatever. We laughed about it because it said *BonBlow!* down the side. With an exclamation point. Then she got sick. Lost interest. Never made it to the class and, as far as I know, never made crème brûlée."

My mind jumped with images of Eva Meeks melting a padlock with her blowtorch. It would have required less elbow grease than bolt cutters. And it sounded like something she'd do for kicks. She'd never gotten to use her spanking-new BonBlow! for its intended purpose. So she repurposed. Breaking into the lighthouse was a serious crime, especially for someone with zero criminal tendencies. But Eva was facing her own mortality. What did she have to lose?

A deliveryman lumbered up to the counter. "Mornin', Miss Georgia."

"Running early today, Hector?" She took his clipboard and checked off a few things. As they fell into conversation, Summer wandered back out. I beckoned to her, lowering my voice. "Was your mom especially friendly with anyone who works here?"

"Not really. She loved everybody."

"Say I wanted to speak with an employee who might be able to comment on your mother. Who might even *know* something. Does anyone come to mind?"

Summer didn't hesitate. "Bo," she said. "Paint."

31

A man's bald head reflected the overhead lights. Before him, the paint-shaker machine rattled insanely. When he noticed me coming, he shut it off.

I introduced myself.

"Bo Beauchamp," he said around the toothpick poking from his mouth. "You're not here to buy paint, are you?"

Bo Beauchamp. The name was familiar.

He wore a T-shirt with the sleeves torn off. Tattoos danced down his wiry arms. Flaming dice, hot rods, pinup girls. The largest tattoo was a gravestone, a name I couldn't make out arched across the top.

His beady eyes roved my chest, down to my waist, then back up to my face. "You about Georgia's age?"

"I was wondering if I could ask you a few questions about Eva Meeks."

"Not too fond of questions, Miss Padget." He tongued the toothpick to the opposite side of his mouth. "What's this all about?"

"I'm here on behalf of the family. They asked me to put something together."

"Like a tribute? To be read at the funeral or something?"

"Something like that." I winced. I wasn't a fan of skewing facts and had to remind myself that it was in service to an important cause.

"Might do me some good to talk about her," Bo said.

"Please, go right ahead."

He thought a moment. "She was salt of the earth. You probably know that. She liked to take in strays like me. The Meeks family took a chance on me. I'll be forever in their debt." Toothpick dancing, he waxed about Eva's good qualities, chief among them patience and kindness. Then he mentioned their shared enthusiasm for the Cattail Animal Shelter.

A spark flared in my mind.

Thanks to Eva's Cattail Volunteers Month, I'd spent every Monday in May of my high school career hanging out at the animal shelter, stroking the cats that would allow it and throwing catnip toys for those that wouldn't. And that's why the name Bo Beauchamp sounded familiar: he'd coordinated the shelter volunteers. Still did, from the sound of it.

Across from me now, he looked to be in his late fifties. That would have put him in his thirties when I was in high school.

"Eva's one to be missed," Bo was saying. "She was modest for real. And modesty's not a quality folks embrace anymore, is it? In this day and age of the selfie stick." He shook his shiny head. "You know she donated money for the shelter to hire a mobile veterinarian?"

My eyebrows arched. "Really?"

"Guy's got a full-blown doctor's office in the back of a cube truck. X-ray machines and everything. He's been coming every other week. Gives us medication for free. Pills to treat worms and the like. For a lowly animal shelter, it's a real dream come true. And Eva didn't want any thanks for it."

"Eva wanted to help others."

"She sure did. She was always out on the floor. Circulating. Checking in on folks. Customers and employees alike." If he'd been reluctant to talk at first, he was loosening up. Maybe even feeling proud of his work, his affiliation with Meeks Hardware.

"Can you show me her office?" I asked.

"It's right this way." He headed past the lawn and garden stuff, then past the pet supplies. "She and Georgia shared it. Here we are."

The office looked like it had just gotten over a launched grenade. A metal detector lay across the desk, next to a relic of a cordless phone, as big as a man's shoe, with a foot-long antenna. A kitten-themed calendar from last year was tacked to the hollow-core door. But what most caught my attention was the Blackbeard poster, one corner peeling from the wall. Blackbeard's eyes were crazed, he was strapped with pistols, and his beard splayed over his chest like eels.

I gestured to the image. "Did Eva ever talk to you about Blackbeard?"

"You mean her favorite historical figure?" He chuckled. "Sure."

"Recently?"

"I suppose. We never really got into specifics, Eva and I. Our relationship was of a professional nature."

"What about treasure hunting in general?" I asked.

Just then, Georgia's irritated voice bleated over the intercom system. "Customer waiting in Paint. Customer waiting. Paint."

"That's me." Bo hooked his thumbs through his belt loops. "Y'ought to come down to the shelter sometime. Mobile vet's gonna be there tomorrow, actually. Happy to make the introduction, if it'd help with your tribute."

No part of me wanted to spend more QT with Bo Beauchamp. The once-over he'd given me still had me feeling icky. But I needed to learn more. Why had Summer handpicked him for me to interview? Also, maybe the mobile veterinarian—and Eva's funding of him—would lead somewhere.

"Sounds good," I said. "See you tomorrow."

On my way out, I didn't see Georgia or Summer. They were probably eating French fries in the back room. I did, however, hold open the door for Georgia and Eva's parents, who were shuffling in as I was leaving. Wendy and Walter Meeks reminded me of a pair of screwdrivers: stiff, silvery. I considered saying hello or offering condolences but stayed mute, figuring it just wasn't a good time, and they were likely too despondent for even casual encounters. They didn't look my way anyway, which was just as well.

I strode down Queen Street, passing the alley between the hardware store and the kite shop. In front of a dumpster sat a wheelbarrow. It twinkled as if fresh off the assembly line—yet someone must have taken a sledgehammer to it. Dents the size of softballs caved in the sides. The axle was cranked at a right angle, squeezing the wheel into a ball. One broken wood handle jabbed the sky.

From the other handle, a Meeks Hardware sales tag twisted.

32

Halfway back to the MotherVine, my phone buzzed. It was Gwen Montgomery, the new lighthouse keeper, returning my call.

"The lighthouse has gotten the all clear from the safety inspectors," she said, sounding much more relaxed than when she'd slammed her cottage door in my face. She must have realized the risk of a media scandal was over, must have figured a lowly bookshop worker didn't pose many problems compared to the stress she'd already survived. She invited me to come over at sundown. A private tour.

Perfect.

That afternoon, the constant hum of the air-conditioning was an indication of the increased number of bodies in the MotherVine. The vents blew continually, just maintaining a comfortable temperature.

I worked until closing. With the window display completed and the Cattaillion books wrapped, Antoinette walked me through the computer system again. I had the quirks just about mastered, and there was no shortage of shoppers on which to practice. It seemed every ten minutes, we made a sale. I rang up many current books—a rom-com by Jenn McKinlay, a tear-jerker by Emily Giffin, a beach read by Mary Kay Andrews. I rang up a few popular classics too—*To Kill a Mockingbird*, *Pride and Prejudice*. My favorite part of each transaction was the end, when I slipped a fresh vine-patterned bookmark between the pages, then looked the reader in the eye and said simple things like "thank you," or "happy reading," or "enjoy."

Before sunset, I drove to the lighthouse. Gwen Montgomery led the way, and now I was huffing and puffing as we spiraled upward inside the 164-foot column. In front of me, the lighthouse keeper slipped into tour-guide mode, quoting statistics. Two hundred seventeen steps, eight stories, blah blah. But all I could think about was Eva and my mother. Their final climbs, their states of mind. Had their hands grabbed the railing in the very same spots? Had their feet trod heavily or lightly on each iron step?

At the top landing, I paused to catch my breath. The door that led to the parapet was small and asymmetrically shaped, like something out of *Alice in Wonderland*. Beyond it, the wind howled.

"I can't believe you make this climb every day," I said, panting. My pulse whirred against my eardrums and my thighs felt like overcooked noodles. "Multiple times per day."

Gwen was barely out of breath. "If you want to get into good shape, become a lighthouse keeper." Above us towered the lens, an obelisk of prisms about ten feet tall and six feet wide. She lifted her chin at the column of glass. "That's the original, from 1883. The actual lightbulb isn't much bigger than your garden-variety russet potato. And the beam is visible for nineteen nautical miles." She popped a piece of cinnamon chewing gum into her mouth. Her sunglasses were too big for her face. "You ready to go out there? Brace yourself. Sounds like the wind's really kicking." She wrenched open the door and ducked through.

I followed, pushing against an unbelievable gust that walled me against the bricks. My ponytail twirled like a whirligig, flicking hair across my eyes. My dress clung to my skin like it was vacuum packed.

Don't look down. Don't look down.

"Can you make sure that door is propped open?" I yelled.

"No need." To my left, Gwen burrowed her chin into a zipped Virginia Beach College windbreaker. Strands of her hair whirled like mini-cyclones. "There's a special mechanism in place that prevents the door from locking behind us. Ever since a woman got locked out up here, back in the early nineties. She fell somehow. Died. Big news at the time. That's what I've been told."

Tears stung my eyes. Must have been the wind. "Sounds familiar," I said.

"People say she was the first victim of the curse. You hear about this? The lighthouse curse? I must have gotten asked about it fifteen times today by fifteen different people."

"I don't believe in curses." The wind receded, allowing me to stretch out my arms. I took a step forward, forcing my back to leave the hard, cold comfort of the bricks. As I gripped the railing, the words of the riddle repeated in my mind. *Hold on tight and you'll spy the hidden sight.*

Hold on tight.

"What about a treasure hunt?" I asked. "Have you heard anything about that?"

"Nothing." Beside me, Gwen draped both elbows on the railing and leaned forward.

"Can you not do that?"

"Sorry." She backed up a bit, her jaw working the gum.

It occurred to me that I stood shoulder to shoulder, at a nauseating height, with the person who'd discovered Eva Meeks's body. Gwen Montgomery hadn't struck me as the dangerous type. But what if my radar was off?

"Quite the view," she said.

She was right. From our vantage point, Cattail Island resembled the slender reed it was named for. On the opposite, northernmost point, the sands of Smile Beach stretched all the way to the old fishing pier, drooping over the Pamlico Sound. In every direction, water seemed to curve around us like a panoramic postcard. Early stars studded the horizon, and the sky dripped lavender into gold into a color I didn't have a name for.

If you could relax enough to take it all in, it was stunning.

"Lighthouses have to be super tall in North Carolina," she said. "No coastal cliffs. You've been up here before?"

"Not recently." My phone vibrated inside my bag, which buzzed against my hip. I kept my hands on the railing. "The lighthouse was sort of my mother's happy place," I added, a lump forming in my throat.

"Mine too. It doesn't get old."

"Good thing you feel that way." My breathing was almost back to normal. Almost. And then the wind gusted, a blast that made me step backward until I felt the solidity of bricks. Meanwhile, Gwen hooted and punched the air.

And then I got this flash—this image. Of me jumping. Of me climbing over the railing and pushing from the edge, arms spread wide.

A shock jolted through me.

What was that? What in the world was that?

"Callie?" Her voice sounded distant. "You okay?"

"I'm fine," I said.

"You don't look fine."

I scraped my teeth over my lip. Was that what my mother had experienced? Eva too? The inexplicable urge to jump? No reason, no warning, no precedent? Was that the last vision that pulsed through their minds before they obeyed it, manifested it?

Get a grip, Padget.

No one had jumped from here, and no one was going to. And I wasn't about to let some random brain cramp knock me off course.

I sucked in another deliberate breath. My goal was to find a hidden sight. "I'm fine," I said again. Then, determined, I stepped up to the railing, pressed my ribs against the iron, and lowered my chin a fraction. And then another fraction.

In the parking lot below, my Civic was as tiny as a matchbox.

If I lowered my chin another fraction still, I'd have seen Eva Meeks's crash site. The dented cattails.

A few steps to my right must have been the last place her feet felt something solid.

"Can you tell me about finding Eva?" I asked.

"What's this for again?"

"It's for the family. They just want as much information as possible."

She nodded. "I locked up at sundown. Didn't note anything unusual. Went to bed at nine. Asleep before ten. Just lying there looking at my phone in the meantime. I heard nothing. Not a thing. I didn't wake up until six forty, just as the sun was coming up. I wasn't scheduled to open until nine, so I dawdled around the cottage a bit. Then I showered and dressed and went outside for my morning rounds. And there she was." Gwen pointed to the spot. "She was obviously dead."

"You called 911 right away?"

"Right there on the boardwalk." She unwrapped another stick of gum and added it to the one already in her mouth. "Want some?"

"No, thanks." Keeping my gaze on the distant line where the sea met the sky, I bent my knees.

Crackle, crackle.

Gwen crouched beside me. "What're you doing?" she asked.

"I just need to check something."

The railing.

It must have been painted a hundred times since 1883. Every

four inches, spindles twisted up to meet it. A small vial could have been hidden where a spindle met the railing, tucked against it somehow. But how? Superglue? And what was the likelihood that such a vulnerable object had survived thirty or forty years of harsh elements, not to mention millions of groping hands?

Then again, I was after a *hidden sight*. Not necessarily another vial.

The riddle churned through my mind. *Hidden sight.* What did it mean? What was hidden? What was I supposed to be seeing?

A gust of wind blew my dress around my waist. I let it stay there. I was somehow afraid that if I let go of the spindles, I'd get swept up, tossed over.

Goose bumps erupted on my skin.

I felt all around the section of railing within reachable distance. Then I took a crouch-step to the right and repeated the process.

She followed, squatting next to me, her forehead scrunched. "I shouldn't be allowing this. You up here. Feeling around. Does what you're looking for have something to do with *her*?"

"Her name was Eva Meeks." Feeling braver, I got on hands and knees and made a circuit of the parapet, examining each spindle from bottom to top. Sticking my hands between them, feeling underneath the bottom lip.

"For the record, I don't approve of this," Gwen said, trailing me, snapping her gum.

The wind gusted again, and the metal platform underneath me seemed to waver.

Impossible.

Unless the lighthouse was built to sway. Like bridges and skyscrapers.

She rested a hand on my shoulder. "Steady there."

"I'm swaying."

"I know. Don't close your eyes. Keep them on the horizon until the swaying passes."

"Don't say *swaying.*"

"You just did."

I breathed in deep and blew out deliberately. After a few breaths, the world stopped tilting. The horizon steadied itself. "It's gone," I said. "The vertigo."

"I think you're done here."

"One more time around."

"Suit yourself. But you're on your own this time."

I made another circuit, focusing on the lighthouse itself. The bricks tapering up. But with each crack that my fingers explored, my disappointment became more entrenched.

I didn't find anything.

Gwen first, we descended, our footfalls echoing out a steady rhythm. Eva might have made this very descent, had things turned out differently. Did she die knowing what the hidden sight was? Or did she feel as perplexed as me?

"What went on after you made the 911 call?" I asked. "Before police arrived?"

"You sound like the cops."

"It's just that—I knew her."

Turning, she removed her sunglasses. It was the first time I'd seen her eyes. Gray flecked with blue. And now I knew what the sunglasses were hiding: the whites of her eyes were bloodshot, mosaic-like. "After I hung up with 911," she said, "I did my routine check of the lighthouse, bottom to top to bottom. I didn't see any reason to abandon that duty—and had a pretty good reason to perform it as required."

"You weren't scared?"

"Sure I was."

"What exactly do you check for?" I knew she didn't control the signaling. The coast guard managed it electronically from headquarters in Elizabeth City.

"Anything out of place. Deterioration of the building. Vandalism. Power outages. That sort of thing."

"But you didn't come across anything unexpected?"

"Just the bottom door, which was open. And the padlock, which was missing. I went to the top and by the time I came back down a few minutes later, the police were here. They asked me a bunch of questions. Then I asked if I could go back inside and rest. And they let me."

"Okay," I said. "Thanks." We continued twining all the way down. I watched as she locked up. The new lock was shiny, a contrast against the lighthouse, which spoke of a bygone era. Horses hauling wagons of bricks, structures resulting from muscles and manpower rather than cranes and hydraulics.

A chill ran up my spine thinking about the old lock reduced by a blowtorch to what looked like hardened lava.

And why Gwen would hide such a thing in the trunk of her car.

And how it came into her possession.

And why she would lie about it. A lie of omission.

Back outside, it was almost dark. There were dozens more stars than there'd been just fifteen minutes earlier, at the top of the lighthouse. I felt warmer, heavier in a pinned-down-by-good-old-gravity kind of way. But I was trembling. I don't think Gwen noticed, but when I glanced down at my fingers, they were tremoring. Balling my hands into fists, I walked the boardwalk beside her.

"Please don't think that I screwed up," she said.

"What do you mean? Did you screw up?"

"No. But everyone always treats me that way."

"Who's everyone?"

She zoomed ahead, marching toward the keeper's cottage. I trotted after her until we were walking abreast. "Gwen, accidents happen. You're responsible for the lighthouse. Not people."

"Exactly," she said, punching her open palm. "They made their own choices that night."

I stopped short. "*They?*"

"Not *they*. Her. Eva Meeks. *She* made her own choices that night."

"You distinctly said *they*."

"I don't know what I'm saying these days. I've been super high-strung. All this stress, you know?"

I glanced ahead at the cottage, at the little windows on the second floor, and recalled the view from her bedroom. The lighthouse stabbing the cerulean sky. "Did you see anyone at the top of the lighthouse Saturday night?"

"I'm tired of people not trusting me."

"If you saw anything, you have to go to the police with that information."

"There *is* no information. And even if there were, I can't go changing my story now. Everyone would say I screwed up."

"What is with you and screwing up?"

Her phone jangled. "I have to take this," she said without looking at the caller. "Good night." She ran up the cottage steps, went inside, and slammed the door.

33

Night had fallen and Queen Street was quiet. I stood before the MotherVine, phone against my cheek.

"Callie?" Antoinette answered.

"Is it okay if I key into the shop?" I asked. "I need to look for something." I heard coins plinking in the background. "Are you at my uncle's house?"

"The Gang's all assembled for poker night," she said. "Hud's already down two bucks. Rough start for him. Anyway, that's fine. Just remember to turn off all the lights before you leave."

"I'll see you all soon, okay?" I hung up and keyed into the MotherVine with still-trembling fingers. Locking myself inside, I decided not to turn on any lights. The last thing I needed was Fusco or one of her fellow officers coming around to inquire about why the bookshop was ablaze after hours. The flashlight app on my phone was more than adequate, even if I shielded the little beam with my hand.

I'd told Antoinette I needed to look for something, and that was true. The only problem was, I didn't know where to begin. Though the library was closed for the night, I had access to the next best repository of information on Cattail Island: the MotherVine Bookshop. And information was what I needed. Just what had happened to me at the top of the lighthouse? Why had I seen myself climbing over the railing and leaping from the edge? Maybe Trish's article was asking the right question after all: *Was* the lighthouse cursed?

I couldn't bring myself to search that topic on my phone. I shuddered to think of the images that might pop up if I googled *Why did I get the urge to jump from the top of a lighthouse?* Books struck me as a safer, less graphic source.

I hit the section all shoppers encounter first: Local Interest. There were four books about Cattail Lighthouse, but none contained a word about jumping. Deeper into the shop, Nonfiction caught my eye. I scoured biographies, memoirs, and books of history and science. I guess I was hoping for some sort of relatable real-life story that would make sense of the grim urge I'd experienced. But if a story like that existed, it wasn't in the Nonfiction section.

Next up, Mythology/Classics. Curses were a theme in those books, of course. I found a beautiful hardbound edition of Homer's *Iliad*, cornflower blue with gold lettering. Flipping through, I remembered reading it for college, and how impassioned my professor had been about the cursed character of Cassandra. Could she have escaped her fate of no one believing anything she said?

I wandered all the way to the back door and the Mary Higgins Clark shelf. I shined my light on the sign quoting my mother.

> Good old MHC never lets you down.
>
> —Teri Padget

From somewhere in the darkness, Tin Man meowed. I found him snuggled in his bed, which Antoinette had placed on a step of the off-limits staircase. "It's okay, Tin Man," I cooed, petting him. "Go back to sleep."

It struck me then, with him purring underneath my hand, that I'd never been inside the MotherVine at night before. Wandering around the shop alone, in the darkness, provided an introverted kind of comfort, and I liked it. I liked it a lot.

Nearby, children's armchairs were set up. Picking the largest, I squeezed into it. Then I reached inside my bag and retrieved *While My Pretty One Sleeps*, the MHC paperback Antoinette insisted I take with me. "Let's see if you're right, Mom," I said.

The first time I'd read it, as a grieving twelve-year-old, had felt like a sort of rite of passage. Overnight, I'd gone from reading books about cats solving crimes to Neeve Kearny, savvy young fashion designer taking on city bigwigs. This time, as I turned the pages, a warmth settled over me, like I'd slipped into a steaming bath. The world of the story came rushing back. Neeve becomes troubled by the disappearance of her most loyal customer, a gutsy reporter named Ethel, who might have asked one too many questions. And when the police drop the ball, Neeve picks it up.

If I couldn't get answers, maybe I could at least get some inspiration.

34

An hour later, I'd parked in the street in front of Hudson's house, since the driveway was occupied by the OFV plus two trucks, one belonging to Ronnie, the other to Antoinette. I was gathering my things when my phone buzzed.

A text from Gwen.

I'd like to talk to you about something.

That simple sentence practically made me salivate. I texted back, and we solidified plans to meet at Cattail Café before work the next morning. Wondering about Gwen, I got out of my car. Then I heard a noise—wood clacking on wood.

The door of the Little Free Library was unlatched, banging. I headed for it, stepping into the yellow light spilling from a utility pole. Reaching out to close the Cattale Queen's door—I froze.

A sticky note had been slapped onto an outward-facing copy of *Where the Crawdads Sing.* Two words were stamped on the pink paper: BACK OFF.

I spun around, my head swiveling.

A possum skittered over a sewer grate. Its eyes glinted.

Behind the west-facing houses, canal water slapped against bulkheads.

Cattails whispered.

Turning back to the Cattale Queen, I peeled the paper square from the book. The message was courtesy of an honest-to-goodness typewriter, as if whoever had composed it considered handwriting too risky, and a printer too much hassle.

Was the book itself significant? No. It was chosen for its prominence and convenience. Whoever left the note wanted to be quick about it.

I shut the bookcase door, rotating the corn dog until it latched.

That was when a hoarse whisper scratched the shadows. "You going to back off?"

Electricity jolted my spine. The voice had come from a tree one driveway down. The tree hunkered in the darkness, just past the reach of the streetlight. "Who's there?" I called.

"You need to mind your business." A person-shaped shadow darted toward me. Dark, baggy clothing made it impossible to determine the body type. Gloves covered the hands while a ski mask covered the head, and makeup or shoe polish blacked out the skin around the eyes and mouth.

"Who are you? What do you want?"

The person charged, straight for me.

"Stop." Keys in hand, I cocked my fist. "*Stop.*"

The figure barreled nearer, head bent like a battering ram.

I turned and stumbled and slammed into the pavement. Pain seared my knee.

Behind me, footsteps closed in.

I sprang up and ran. Head high, arms pumping, I sprinted up the street, bag banging my hip.

Two sets of footsteps pounded in my ears: my own and those of the person chasing me. I didn't dare kick off my flip-flops or look over my shoulder. Any break in my stride might have given my chaser the advantage.

I charged through the boundary of the streetlight, surging

into darkness. The only other light was several blocks away, glowing from one of the waterfront shops. I raced for it, pumping my legs. I passed the pottery shop and the *Crier* office and Cattail Café. All dark.

The footsteps pounded closer.

35

I barged into the red door. It gave, and bells clanged overhead as I sailed inside. I crashed into a counter and collapsed onto a bamboo floor.

From another room sounded an upright bass voice. “Hello?” Seconds later, the voice was closer. “Ma’am?”

“I’m sorry,” I said inanely, drawing myself up on hands and knees.

To my left, a masculine pair of bare feet appeared. Something warmed my shoulder. A hand. Scents of clove-tinged cologne swirled. “Callie?”

“Someone was after me. Chasing m—”

The feet took off. Another flurry of bells.

“No. Hang on.” Using a bench for support, I dragged myself to standing.

My right knee was scraped and raw where pebbles had embedded themselves.

Hands quaking, I smoothed my hair from my face. I squinted as my eyes adjusted to the light.

I was alone, in a lobby. Banners featuring Japanese characters hung above benches. A watercooler hummed in the corner. Beyond it, rows of lockers stretched to the far wall. Butcher paper covered the front windows.

The owner of the upright-bass voice and the masculine bare feet had been Toby Dodge, whose attractiveness had left me breathless earlier that morning. Apparently, I'd barged into this man's shop. It wasn't a shop, though. It was a gym of some kind. The lobby opened up into an attached room, large, with high ceilings. Standup punching bags lined the walls. Japanese and American flags hung from the rafters.

I got out my phone and dialed Officer Fusco and told her, in a trembling voice, what had just happened. Where I was. "If you could come—"

"I'm good as there. Hold tight."

Toby returned. He locked the door, the deadbolt clanking. "Whoever it was, they're gone now."

"Police are coming."

"You hurt?"

"I'm okay."

"You sure? That knee of yours is scraped up pretty good."

"You didn't have to give chase. I didn't mean for— I'm okay."

He reached for my sleeve and grasped something.

The sticky note. BACK OFF.

He studied it, then my face.

I must have looked deranged. Or at least windblown and terrified. My brain felt like it was shooting off flares in a thousand directions. I couldn't shake the image of that figure charging me. Whoever it was had planted the note, then waited for an opportunity to drive the message home in person. And I'd been careless enough to provide that opportunity.

The note could only have been meant for me.

Why hadn't I just run for Hudson's house? Why did I always have to go and make things more complicated than they needed to be? Then again, it was probably a good thing I hadn't led a potentially violent person straight to my uncle's home.

A rap on the door made me jump.

Toby cracked it open. "Ma'am?"

From outside, Fusco's voice issued. "Callie Padget in there? She called the police." A pause. Then: "I'm the police, sir."

"Oh. Beg pardon." He opened the door.

Fusco stepped inside. A Cattail Bait & Tackle T-shirt engulfed her. Her spongy-looking orange hair was unbraided and blazed past her elbows. "Third day in a row for you and me," she said, striding to the counter where I stood. "That's got to be some sort of record."

"You're off duty? I should have called the station. Or—"

"An officer of the law is never off duty." She produced a leather-bound mini tablet, stylus at the ready. "Driving here, I didn't see anybody suspicious on foot. No suspicious vehicles, either. This person say anything to you? Was it a man?"

"I can't remember, but I think it was a man."

"But he did say something?"

My nostrils quivered. My throat clenched—a surge of tears threatening. I damned them up. "I think so."

"What did he look like?"

I shook my head.

"Who's mad at you?"

"What? Nobody."

"You're a reporter, aren't you?"

"Not at the moment, really."

She tucked the tablet under her arm. She hadn't written anything. "This have something to do with last night?"

Last night. Eva Meeks's house. The camp booklet. "I honestly couldn't say, Officer."

"You think of anything, you call me. Meantime, I'll patrol the area."

"That's—that's it?"

"You aren't able to provide a description, and—"

"What about this?" Toby held up the sticky note. "Can't you—I don't know. Have it analyzed or something?"

"This is Cattail, sir. Pig pickin's. Kite shows."

"*Mind your business,*" I blurted. "Whoever chased me. He said, 'You need to mind your business.'"

"He have an accent?" Fusco asked.

"Sort of Southern."

"Oh, well, *that* narrows it down." She sighed. "You sure it was a man?"

"No. Yes. I don't know." I grabbed the edge of the counter. A wave of anger crashed through me. I'd lived in a major city for years and never experienced anything like this. In Charlotte, I could walk out my door at ten o'clock at night to meet my co-workers for a pint and not even think twice about glancing behind me. But after only three days back on Cattail Island . . .

"The best I can do is keep my eyes peeled," Fusco said.

"That's the best you can do?"

"I'll do what I can, Miss Padget. It's good that you called. Now leave the police work to me."

After Fusco left, Toby locked up a second time. "Why don't you sit? We'll get you all bandaged and—"

"Oh, no. My damsel-in-distress role has been mortifying enough." That was the truth. And also, I didn't want to have anything to do with a guy who might be cruel to animals. Even if he was being kind to me at the moment.

"Not to brag," he said, "but over the years I've gotten really good at slathering people smaller than me with iodine. I used to teach PE at the middle school. I also respond to *Mr. Dodge*."

My knees were quavering. My breathing was shallow and shaky. The thought of stepping back out onto the dark street, by myself . . . Shoot. I perched on the closest bench and said, "You win, Mr. Dodge."

"Music to my ears. Hang on." He went down a corridor labeled THE HEAD and returned thirty seconds later carrying a bag of cotton balls and a first aid kit.

"I know I shouldn't complain," I said. "Officer Fusco did come out—and she wasn't even on the clock. That's not lost on me. But—*I'll keep my eyes peeled*? Really?" I had a taste of how Summer must have felt when Chief Jurecki dismissed the riddle. When someone who was positioned to help left you feeling even more impotent than you had in the first place.

Toby crouched before me. He pumped sanitizer into his hands and rubbed them together. "There's not much she *can* do, at this point."

"Right."

"She knows about it, though. It's on record. So that's good." He doused a cotton ball with antibiotic solution and pressed it to the cut on my knee. When I flinched, his hands lifted as if he'd touched a too-hot pot. "Did that hurt?"

"No. It's—I'm fine."

He resumed, gently dabbing.

All over, my skin tingled.

The last time anyone had really touched me—not counting my previous job's requisite handshaking—was during a massage last fall at this new spa back in Charlotte. I'd written a feature about it.

Before that, it had been my most recent boyfriend. He'd dumped me after a few months when his ex-fiancée, a dentist, called out of the blue wanting to get back together. He and I parted amicably enough. Our relationship wasn't all that lively, and at least he'd been up front about his ex, who happened to be crushing it professionally. Why wouldn't he have wanted to be with someone like that?

Toby's fingertips felt as warm and soothing as points of summer sunlight on my stubbly knee.

I was pathetic.

I cleared my throat, sat up straight, and looked desperately around.

Across from me hung a framed poster. Lily pads and the words BE KIND, FOR EVERYONE YOU MEET IS FIGHTING A HARD BATTLE.

"So," I said. "You train here?"

"I own it. Technically the bank owns it, but—" He pinched a section of medical tape between his teeth and tore it. Smoothed a square of padded gauze over my knee. "There were major education budget cuts last year, as you're probably aware. You used to be a reporter?"

"Back in Charlotte. Got laid off."

"I can whistle that tune."

"The school let you go?"

"The other gym teacher had seniority. I've had my black belt for years, and teaching PE didn't seem like much of a stretch from operating a dojo. So, I found this great space. I've taken on a few students but haven't had the grand opening yet. Still working out some details." He packed up the kit. "Come on. I'll drive you home."

"That's really not necessary."

"It's not. But I believe in helping bleeding people who've been chased by maniacs." He stood and extended a hand. "With their permission, that is."

My hands were still trembling.

Infuriating.

I reached out and let him tug me to a standing position.

He checked a few things in the big room, then flipped off all the lights.

"Thank you, by the way," I said, as we headed outside.

We strolled along the waterfront, then turned into a small alleyway. "Ever think of taking self-defense lessons?" he asked.

"That's not something I can afford at the moment."

"What if they were free of charge?"

"What's in it for you?"

He stopped. "When the officer mentioned *last night*—what was that?"

"Nothing. It's just that, I might have gotten myself into a bit of trouble. But I'm going to get out of it. Isn't it true that nine times out of ten, your best defense is what I just did: Run?"

"That's your plan? Run?"

"It's a work in progress." I continued walking.

"Assuming your statistic is accurate—which I'm not sure it is—but for the purposes of this conversation, *one* time out of ten, running's not going to do you any good."

"I have pepper spray. Right here in my bag."

"Did you use it?"

"Valid point."

"All I'm saying is, if you want to be prepared for that theoretical one time, let me teach you some basics. I've been thinking about offering a self-defense class for women anyway, and—"

"And you need a guinea pig."

"So do you, if you want to learn how to defend yourself."

Another valid point.

"I'll give you a free preview tip," he said. "Most cell phones have an emergency SOS feature that you can activate quickly, if you're ever in a scary situation where you can't overtly dial 911. Do you know yours?"

I nodded. "Hit the side button three times. Guess I need to practice that."

"Might not be a bad idea."

We'd reached the infamous mint-green Jeep Wagoneer gleaming under the lamplight behind the shops. Toby swung open the passenger door.

I gaped. I'd have been hard-pressed to find a single speck of dust. The inside smelled like Mentos and Armor All. Vacuum tracks striped the carpet. "So this is why you insisted on bandaging me up." I went to run my hand along the dashboard but stopped, not wanting to leave a smudge. "Did you just have it detailed? Or is it always this pristine?"

He laughed. "Hop in. I promise I'll drive completely undistractedly, obeying the speed limit, with both hands on the wheel, and absolutely zero road rage."

I hauled myself onto the tan leather seat. He got in behind the wheel and started the ignition. Heavy metal blared, symbols crashing and electric guitars screeching. His arm shot out to lower the volume. "Where to?"

"I'm staying at my uncle's place for the time being. It's just down the street."

"No problemo."

"You must be a surfer, with this kind of car."

"Used to be. Surfing's why I initially moved here. But I haven't been in ages. Got caught up in work. You surf?"

"Went to a couple camps when I was growing up. Didn't take to it. I'm not exactly coordinated."

We'd arrived at Hudson's. My car appeared to be unperturbed. And my creeper was nowhere in sight.

"I'll walk you to the door," Toby said, unclicking his seat belt.

"No, really. You've done enough. I'll be okay."

"Will I see you tomorrow night? After my last class? Guinea pigs unite?"

I hopped out. "I'll think about it."

He waited until I was through Hudson's doorway before driving off.

36

Ronnie was stooped in the kitchen, glass of water in hand. On the table behind him, cards and coins were strewn. Poker night had drawn to a close. "Who was that?" he asked.

"Nosy," I said. "Where's my uncle?"

"Hudson," Ronnie hollered into the next room. "Your girl got a boyfriend."

I fake-punched him in the chest.

"He a dingbatter?" Ronnie asked me. "Hud! Your girl datin' a dingbatter."

I punched him again, harder this time. "Living room," he said.

"How did you keep him from reporting directly to the woodshop?"

"Secret weapon. She stands about five-nine and smells like books. So do you, by the way."

"I take that as a compliment."

Scupper led the way, toenails clicking through the kitchen. I found Hudson in his La-Z-Boy. The television showed some courtroom drama with fiery defenders flashing cleavage and pencil-sharp legs. Hudson's favorite.

Antoinette sat next to him in a chair they'd dragged from the kitchen. Strange to see them holding hands. She'd spent a lot of time in this house, of course, livening poker nights when her husband was alive. But Alfred was long gone, and Hudson must have finally found the guts to let her know he'd held a torch for her all those years. Evidently, the feeling was mutual.

"There she is." Struggling up, my uncle wrapped his arms around me. His bear hug hadn't lost any vitality.

"How was the hamster wheel?" I asked when I could breathe again.

He patted his cannonball. "Fit as a fiddle. Nurse's words, not mine."

I should have been there. What kind of a niece-daughter was I, letting him go through it alone?

But he hadn't been alone. Antoinette and Ronnie were with him. Besides, if I'd been back in Charlotte . . .

But I wasn't back in Charlotte.

Hudson held me by the shoulders. "You look like you just saw a ghost. And you're all patched up. It's like you put yourself through a paper shredder. What's that bandage on your knee?"

"I tripped." Not a lie.

"Droime," he said. Another old Outer Banks word. Translation: you're full of it. He opened his mouth to say more, then shut it. Either he lacked the energy to argue or figured I'd fill him in when Ronnie and Antoinette weren't around. But the man had just experienced an ambulance ride and hospital time following a panic attack. I wasn't about to tell him some masked marauder booby-trapped the Cattale Queen and scared me half to death.

Ronnie set the water glass on the table. Harrumphing, he crashed onto the couch, knees sprawled.

"I made chicken potpie," Antoinette said. "With extra peas and carrots—lots of veggies. I'll fetch you some, Callie."

"Hudson paid you to say that part about the extra veggies." I sat on the couch cushion that wasn't taken up by Ronnie's manspread. "No, thank you. I'm not hungry." I was, in fact, ravenous. But I was also wired. Chicken potpie wouldn't sit well.

"Did you find what you needed?" Antoinette asked. "In the shop."

"Oh. Yeah. It's all good."

"At Meeks Hardware, we've got everything and *the kitchen sink!"* On the television, a small Eva Meeks was spreading her arms.

Hudson snatched the remote.

The screen went black. "What's this about a boyfriend?" he asked.

"That's just Ronnie, telling stories," I said.

Ronnie crooked an arthritic finger in my direction. "Hud tells me you were asking about the furniture factory."

"Not really the factory, but the housing," I said. "The apartments that used to be on Muscadine Street."

"Standish Apartments." Ronnie nodded with authority. "That's what they were called. And speaking of stories—I know one you won't find in your bookshop. Yours truly might be just about the only SOB who's lived to tell the tale. Not including Pearleen Standish, that is."

I settled back onto the cushions. "Sounds promising."

Ronnie seemed gleeful to have an audience. "The summer I turned seven, it was 1956," he said. "My best friend, Trip, God rest his soul, lived near the apartments. There was a swamp back there and every summer Trip and me used to spear us some frogs. Cut 'em up and sell the legs. Good eatin'."

I made a barf face. A general store in Cattail sold buckets of frog legs, skin still on, stacked in the refrigerator right next to cartons of milk and tubs of butter.

"Trip and me, we was rollin' up our pant legs one day, getting ready for a hunt, when we heard voices. Two men, talkin' hushed. So me and Trip crept closer and hid in the cattails. The two men were talking about something horrible that happened in the factory. Something horrible involving a worker. And Pearleen's daddy, Thornton Standish? He done nothing about it."

I addressed Antoinette and Hudson. "You two know about any of this? Some kind of wrongdoing at the factory?"

"I never heard of it before right now," Hudson said.

"But that doesn't mean nothing happened," Antoinette said. "People love their secrets. Including Ronnie Coot, apparently."

"It's not much to go on, Ronnie," I said. "It's sixty-something-year-old hearsay. And it's vague, at that."

"Oh, I'm not done. Get this." His eyes glistened. He tapped his temple. "All these years later? I remember a name they kept mentioning. And every time they said it, I swear they lowered their voices and looked all around. Like the devil himself was fixing to give them a beatdown. Darned if I can't come up with my own name sometimes. But that name? It's never abandoned me. Some nights I hear it in my dang sleep."

"Hold on." I got out my notepad and a pen. "Okay. Hit me."

Ronnie drew out each syllable. "Israel. Overton."

I copied it down even though I'd never forget a name like that. And with it, I actually might get somewhere. "Who was Israel Overton?"

"He may as well have been the boogeyman." Ronnie slapped his knees. "But whatever happened, you can bet your last wampum Thornton Standish went to his grave with the name Israel Overton on his lips."

Israel Overton.

I got that creepy-crawly feeling, like I'd walked into a cobweb.

"What's got you interested in all this, Callie?" Antoinette asked. Which let me know Hudson hadn't told her about my poking around.

Ronnie reached over and clamped my shoulder. "Next time you see that old bird Pearleen, ask her about Israel Overton. See if that don't get her shakin' in her gem-soled shoes."

37

Alone in my loft, I took a long slug of beer.

It had been Whitman Standish who'd called my phone while I was at the top of the lighthouse. He'd left a brief but cordial message inviting me to drop by the Standish estate the next morning, "as a favor to an old friend and fellow islander." Which was silly, because Whitman and I had never been big fans of each other. Not since first-grade recess when he purposefully splashed me with puddle water. My mother was summoned to bring me dry clothes, and she'd reamed him out in front of the other children and the teacher, and he never spoke to me after that. Well, maybe Whitman's grudge was over. Regardless, I had an in with the Standishes. And a chance to unpack Pearleen's sour attitude toward Eva.

I opened my laptop and typed *Israel Overton* into the search window. Lots of unrelated nonsense came up. The only relevant item was a map of the town cemetery, showing the location of a grave site. Ronnie's tale contained at least a portion of truth: a Cattail resident named Israel Overton had indeed died in 1956, at the age of twenty-three.

I searched *Bo Beauchamp* next and saw his profile on the Meeks Hardware page, plus a listing on the animal shelter's website. Nothing more.

Next up: *Toby Dodge.*

The first hit was from the *Crier*, a back-page feature, several years old. The photo captured him in front of floor-to-ceiling shelves lined with wooden duck decoys. Duck after duck after duck. He had his hands on his hips and a grin on his face—either embarrassed or proud as hell.

THE DECOY DUDE

Submitted by Trish Berryman, Editor in Chief

CATTAIL, September 28—Toby Dodge doesn't know exactly how many wooden waterfowl crowd the shelves of his dining room turned duck room. "I could count them for you," he says. "But get yourself good and comfortable, 'cause it might take me a while."

A physical education teacher at Cattail Middle School, Dodge admits he might have an addiction to the handmade hunting decoys, some of which are more than a century old.

Dodge grew up "in the most boondocky part of western NC." As a boy, he accompanied his father and uncles on many "bird-killing expeditions." But much to his father's chagrin, Dodge never took to the hobby.

Instead, he took up collecting antique decoys. "They're whimsical," he says. "They have undeniable appeal. Not to mention artistic and historical value. I like the wide range of styles."

When it comes to duck decoys, Cattail Island—and indeed all of the southeast coast—has a rich history. This area was, and is, known as the Atlantic flyway, the north-south route that many migratory birds follow year after year, generation after generation.

A hundred years ago, duck hunting was big business, because duck meat was considered a delicacy in high demand. Professional and recreational hunters alike wanted in on the action.

Decoys made their expeditions a lot more successful, Dodge says.

"The idea was to get a whole fake flock bobbing on the water. Those fake flocks attracted lots and lots of birds. And lots of birds meant more income for the hunters."

According to Dodge, hunters first learned to make duck decoys from Native Americans, who made them from cattails and decorated them with ash and plant-based dyes.

Then came the days of making decoys from whatever wood washed up on the beach from shipwrecks.

Nowadays most hunters use plastic decoys—cheaply constructed, readily available, and mass-produced.

"I'm not a fan of the idea of deceiving birds and then shooting them out of the sky," Dodge says. "Birds are beautiful, and they should be free to fly around as nature intended, without having to worry about bullets."

That doesn't stop him from admiring hunting decoys.

While some of his decoys were gifts, most he acquired himself, either on eBay or in antiques stores. Old decoys that have been made by well-known carvers can sell for hundreds, even thousands of dollars. But Dodge has never paid more than forty bucks for a decoy. "Simple tastes are frugal tastes," he says.

It would be impossible for him to pick a favorite. "Maybe it's the teacher in me. I like them all equally. They've each got their own personalities that make them special individuals. Just like people.

"It's a quirky thing, I'll admit," he says. "I'm a quirky guy."

38

On Wednesday morning, uniformed Officer Fusco backed out the door of Cattail Café. A pastry box was balanced on her arms. On top of the box was a tray of take-out coffees. "Nab any sleep?" she asked as I grabbed the door.

I regarded her with a strange mix of feelings—gratitude that she'd answered my call, annoyance that she hadn't done more. "Did you see anyone last night?" I asked. "You said you were going to patrol the area."

"You'll get information on a need-to-know basis, AC."

I made a confused face. "AC?"

"Agatha Callie. That's your nickname down at the station. Get it? Instead of Agatha—"

"I get it." Great. News of my interrogation of Chief Jurecki had gotten around. It would have been more analogous to mash up my name with Jane Marple, but now was not the time to be a lit-major snob. Cattail Café was bustling with vacationers and locals alike, and any one of them could have been my would-be attacker from the night before. "Did you see Gwen Montgomery in there?" I asked Fusco.

"She shot toward the restrooms faster than grass through a goose when she saw me."

"Thanks." Inside, I wended through tables and chairs. Customers' laptops were open to Trish's article on the *Crier* website. I peeked over the shoulder of one guy who was scrolling through the comments. They numbered in the hundreds.

"Unbelievable," I said to myself. I'd reached the back hallway. The ladies' room door led into a sort of antechamber, a small seating area decorated with posters of sun-drenched coffee fields.

Gwen was perched on a cushioned stool. "I was just about to text you," she whispered, toasting me with her little cup.

"Why are you whispering? And why are you hiding out in here?"

She threw back her espresso like a shot of tequila and clanked the cup against its saucer. Her hair was bobby-pinned above her ears, giving her head the appearance of shredded curtains tied back from a tired stage. A pink blob was stuck on the back of her hand. Gum. "That cop's out there, okay? You know—red braid, tall, intense. She looked at me weird."

"You should see how she looks at me. Fusco's gone now."

"You sure? You're not friends with her, are you?"

"What are you hiding, Gwen?"

She peered into her cup as if more espresso might magically appear. "I think I've changed my mind. I don't want to talk to you anymore."

"Maybe you just need a change of scenery. How about some air?"

"It's raining."

"A bit misty is all. Come on. I know where we can go."

Coffee sloshed in my thermos, which was pinched between my knees as I drove. "Have you been to Smile Beach yet?" I asked my passenger.

"The beach?" Gwen scowled. "In the rain?"

"It'll be sunnier on the other end of the island. The northwestern tip of the cattail. You'll see."

"Haven't had the chance to venture out that way yet."

"Today's your lucky day." We drove through downtown, sipping our coffee. Mist coated my car, just enough to give it a little bath and rinse off the salt. "Nature's carwash," I said, turning on the wipers.

Queen Street transitioned from quaint shops and eateries to neighborhoods to loblolly forest. When the rain stopped, Gwen and I rolled down our windows, and the warm, damp, piney air billowed our hair. I appreciated that she wasn't the kind of woman to insist on air-conditioning.

A few minutes later, we arrived at Smile Beach's parking lot, empty except for one other car. As I'd predicted, the sun was struggling to poke through the clouds and looked like it would succeed any minute. I grabbed an old quilt from my back seat and we walked over the ramp, onto the sand.

"That the famous fishing pier?" Gwen asked. "Gosh, it's even sketchier in person."

I laughed. The old Smile Beach fishing pier didn't look any sketchier than I was used to. But to someone who'd seen it only from the top of the lighthouse, miles away, the wilting structure was probably pretty alarming. "The Cattaillion's dedicated to the pier this year," I said. "Hopefully we'll raise enough money to fix it up right. Do you know about the Cattaillion? It's a summer tradition."

"That's the big fundraiser, right? All the waterfront shops get involved?"

"They close Queen Street to traffic and make it pedestrian only. Every year there's a town-wide vote about what cause to support. And this year, the pier won."

She nodded at the crooked pilings. "I can see why."

"You should come to the Cattaillion. It's fun."

"Maybe I will." We'd reached a spot halfway between the parking lot and the Elder Tree. I shook out the quilt, and we sat. "You really love this place, don't you?" she asked.

"What place?"

"Cattail Island."

"Oh. Well, I'm out of here as soon as I find work." As I spoke, I realized I hadn't applied to any journalism jobs since I'd arrived. In fact, I hadn't even job searched. I took a swallow of coffee and said, "Let's talk about you. Why are you so easily spooked? And why did you run and hide at the sight of a blue uniform?"

She looked out over the water, which was blanketed in fog. Somewhere behind it was the green, southern coast of Roanoke Island.

"You can trust me, Gwen," I said. "I think you know that. Why else would you have texted me, asking to talk?"

"I found things in the trunk of my car. Things I didn't put there. Things that have to do with that lady."

"Her name was—"

"Eva Meeks. Sorry."

"So what was in your trunk?"

She described the blowtorch and the lumps of hardened metal on the concrete tray. "I think it's the old lock that Eva—or someone—melted off the lighthouse door. After I locked up Saturday night. But why use a blowtorch when you could just use bolt cutters? Cut right through?"

"How did those things end up in the trunk of your car?"

"Someone's trying to frame me."

"For what?"

"Eva Meeks obviously didn't kill herself. You know it and I know it and somebody else knows it too—and that stuff in my trunk proves it."

Surprised, I pushed an errant strand of hair from my face. Someone else shared my convictions about Eva. "I agree," I said. "What are you going to do about it?"

"Me? Nothing. I figure it's only a matter of time before the police catch on. And if my family found out I was caught up in police business—"

"Are you guilty of any crime?"

"I can't go to the police."

"But you can come to me? Why?"

A sheepish expression came over her face. She opened her pastry bag from the café, pulled out a scone, and broke off a piece. A whiff of cinnamon mixed with the briny scent of the air. "Because my sponsor threatened to drop me if I didn't get out and talk to somebody else and make connections in my new community."

Her sponsor.

Gwen was in Alcoholics Anonymous.

Maybe that was the older man in the photograph by her bed. The silver-templed man with the sparkling eyes and sharp jawline.

"Is that who called you last night?" I asked. "Your AA sponsor?"

"Calls me all the time. I'm kind of in between friends right now. And you seem nice. Don't get me wrong—people here are super friendly. But I haven't really met anybody besides some of the conservationists, who hired me. And they're lovely . . ."

"But?"

"They're so *old*, you know?"

I smiled. When you're Gwen's age, lots of adults fall into the category of Old.

To our right, a woman emerged from the cedar trees and live oaks that lined the far side of the beach. She slid out of her sandals to stroll barefoot in the sand. As she drew nearer, I saw that her dark hair was swept into a bun, some strategically loose strands framing her cheeks. Red feather earrings brushed her neck. She had enviable posture, like a dancer.

When she spotted us, she turned and walked briskly back the way she'd come, toward the trees.

"Do you know that person?" I asked.

"Aren't you listening? I just got through telling you—I don't know anybody."

I forced my attention back to Gwen, remembering that online photograph of her standing apart from her classmates. She had a habit of lone-wolfing it.

Like me.

Small waves washed onto the sand, and a light breeze caressed my face and arms. "Do you like climbing trees?"

"You're random, you know that?"

"Come on." I led her up the beach, toward the pier and, opposite it, the Elder Tree. "They think it's about five hundred years old," I said, "but no one knows for sure." I used the old fence to pull myself up, then scooted out onto the big branch. She followed suit, climbing deftly, pastry bag clenched between her teeth.

"Nice view," she said when she was settled. She was being sarcastic. The fog was too dense to see much of anything. "Is the lighthouse visible from here?"

"Usually."

"I've got big plans for that baby, you know. Not just moonlight tours. I'm going to have stargazing nights and birdwatching events and ghost-themed climbs. Once all the craziness settles down."

"Do you attend meetings?" I asked. "AA meetings, I mean."

"I did back in Chesapeake. But now I'm working in the public sector. My first real job. And it's a good one. Okay, the salary sucks. But the job is high-profile. And coveted. And I know meetings are anonymous, but—I'm only twenty-six. That's pretty young to risk getting a bad professional reputation."

"You don't want the police knowing you have a history of alcohol abuse. Because you think that will implicate you somehow."

"They'd blame me. For Eva."

"I doubt you could be held responsible. Even if she was murdered." It was the first time I'd said that particular word aloud, in connection with Eva.

I'd covered murders in Charlotte. Gang-related shootings. Convenience store robberies gone haywire.

This was the first time I'd ever known the victim.

"Maybe I couldn't be held responsible," Gwen said. "But I'm not going to find out."

"I feel like there's something you're not telling me." Ignoring me, she peeked into the teardrop-shaped cavity next to her, in the main trunk. "When I was little," I said, "owls used to nest in there. But lately it's been empty."

She held out the scone. "Bite?"

"Gwen—"

"I fell off the wagon, okay? Friday night. I went out and bought some rum and a carton of orange juice. I dumped most of it." She looked square at me. "I swear to you, Callie, the majority of that rum got poured down my sink drain. But not before I threw back two or three sizable rumdrivers."

"What does your sponsor say about your falling off the wagon?"

"To not beat myself up." From the pained expression on her face, she'd failed to follow that advice.

I felt a stab of sympathy. Most of my adult life had featured self-flagellation of one kind or another. Plus, moving is stressful. One of the most stressful life events there is, right up there with having a baby, they say. Especially when you don't know anybody. Starting a new job on top of that, and finding a body to boot . . .

"Was Teri Padget related to you?" Gwen asked.

I looked at her, again taken by surprise. "What?"

"The white cross. The first one. Was she your mother? You said the lighthouse was your mother's happy place. That's why you care so much about all this." When I didn't answer, she added, "I shouldn't have brought that up."

I gazed into the mist rolling over the water. I just didn't want to go there with her. Or with anybody, really.

"After I dumped the rum," she said, "I put the bottles in the trunk of my car."

"Why not put them in your recycling bin?"

"Because some guy who works for the conservationists is supposed to come and empty it for me. I didn't want him to see the bottles. My struggles are none of his business. Anyway, Monday night, after work, when I finally got a breather from all the crazy going on, I got into my car. I figured I'd drive to the recycling center myself and toss the bottles into one of the big containers. But when I pulled onto the main road, I heard something thunking around in my trunk. Something a lot heavier than empty plastic bottles. That's when I found the blowtorch and the splash block."

"You're telling me you had nothing to do with those things finding their way to your trunk."

"Nothing. Not one iota."

"Go to the police, Gwen. Show them what's in your trunk. It's evidence—"

"Too late. After I pulled over, I made a U-turn. Headed for the ferry. Once I got to the mainland, I took a drive out to the landfill in West Lake."

I pounded a fist on my thigh. I should have gone to Chief Jurecki myself on Monday afternoon. Confessed to having a peek inside Gwen Montgomery's trunk, told him what I'd found. "You dumped them?" I asked. "The blowtorch? The melted lock?"

"And the rum bottles," she said. "Hurled them all right at the bucket of a bulldozer. All items are buried under a fifty-foot-high mound of trash as we speak."

"There might have been fingerprints on the blowtorch. Or some other forensic details. The police might have considered those items extremely relevant—"

"I'm gonna get the mirror image of some numbers tattooed right here." She tapped the remaining stub of scone against her left collarbone. "Six-two-two. My right collarbone's already occupied."

I stared at her, uncomprehending. "What?"

"June twenty-second. That's my *new* sobriety date. And every time I look in the mirror, I'll see it. Loud and clear."

"June twenty-second is also the date Eva Meeks died."

"Whatever happened to that poor lady is a tragedy," Gwen said. "But it had nothing to do with me."

39

On the short drive back to Cattail Café, following the gentle curves of Queen Street, Gwen and I didn't talk much. I dropped her off at her parked Jetta, and she said thank you as she got out of my car, but the words came out strained.

I drove farther south to keep my next appointment: Pearleen Standish.

I'd never been to the Standish estate before, but like all Cattailers, I knew where it was. The southeastern side of the island was where the wealthy lived. A winding driveway led to a hundred waterfront acres fifty feet above sea level, the island's highest natural point. Boxwoods and palmettos lined the private road. To access it, you had to make it past a locked iron gate, an *S* marking its center.

I pulled up to the gate, announcing myself to an intercom box mounted on the side of a faux guardhouse. After a few seconds there was a loud buzz. The *S* broke apart as the gate swung open, and I drove through, climbing the hill to a Tudor-style mansion. Abstract sculptures suggestive of giant ribbons glinted in the sunlight, separating the home from various outbuildings. According to island rumor, the carriage house had been converted into a five-thousand-square-foot bachelor pad for Whitman and featured a rock-climbing wall and an inground, Olympic-length lane pool.

Pearleen answered the door wearing diamond stud earrings the size of dimes. She was swathed in silk, a belted dress the exact shade of the roses on the bushes. "Ah yes," she said, waving me inside. Her voice echoed under the soaring ceiling. "Whit mentioned the book-delivery girl would be dropping by. I don't have a lot of time. This is something about publicity?"

"You're a great supporter of the MotherVine," I said. "So surely you know Tin Man?"

"I just adore Tin Man. And he adores me."

"He has a big following on Instagram."

"I don't understand what that is, but I do know it's very popular."

"Insanely popular. I'd love to feature you with a few words about your eightieth, your storied career, things like that. You'd get the Standish name out there, and the MotherVine Bookshop would get to brag about knowing you." I tried not to cringe at my own words. I hated buttering people up.

"What does this all entail?" Pearleen asked.

"Some quick questions and a photo or two, and I'll be out of your hair."

She patted her ice-colored French twist, as if I actually might get into it. "I never turn down publicity, as you probably know," she said. "But *quick* needs to be the operative word."

I followed her across the foyer. She was one of the few people who made me feel tall; she couldn't have stood more than five feet. We passed two cats—one white, one black—dozing nose-to-tail on a floor cushion, their bodies making a yin-yang pattern. You'd think someone like Pearleen Standish would shell out thousands of dollars for Persians or ragdolls or sphynxes. But these were run-of-the-mill barn cats.

Above their cushion hung a larger-than-life portrait of Thornton Standish, glaring at all who entered from under a straw boater. He rocked an honest-to-goodness monocle and a twirlable mustache.

Inside Pearleen's study, the first thing I noticed was a low inlaid table—and on it, in full display, an old-fashioned typewriter. Which of course made me think of the menacing pink sticky note left for me inside the Cattale Queen.

There might have been any number of typewriters in various stages of antiquity all over Cattail. Right?

"That's a very nice typewriter you have there, Miss Pearleen," I said. "Does it work?"

"Of course it works. Do I strike you as the kind of person who would surround herself with broken things?"

"I just meant—it looks vintage."

"It ought to. It belonged to my daddy." She pulled out a chair fit for royalty and sat behind a desk so large it made her look like she'd shrunk.

I took a seat opposite her. I was digging for a pen and notepad when she swept some rustling thing off her desk—a blur of pink.

Slamming a drawer, she smirked at me. Then she clasped her clawlike fingers before her. "Proceed."

I asked some generic warm-up questions, but they didn't melt Pearleen's iciness. And then something caught her attention outside the window. Two gardeners were arguing about how to trim a bush. She clicked her tongue. "Oh, for heaven's sake," she mumbled. To me she said, "Do excuse me," and whisked out of the room.

I heard the front door creak open. A moment later she came into view, her back to the window. I couldn't make out her words, but her tone sounded even more insulting than normal. Hats and shears in hand, the gardeners hung their heads. Beyond them, the ocean sparkled in the sunlight, distant sailboats like shark teeth on the water.

I looked around. At the velvety sofa opposite a matching love seat. At the surprisingly understated painting of a sailboat, like a scene glimpsed from those very windows on any given day.

Then it hit me: I was alone in Pearleen Standish's home office. I'd already rummaged around in Gwen Montgomery's place and even Eva Meeks's. Might as well go for the trifecta.

I shot up and rounded the desk. The most personal item on it was a photograph in a gilded frame. Apple-cheeked Whitman when he was six or seven, a soon-to-be orphan flanked by his parents. Holding hands, they were about to leap into a pile of raked leaves. I actually felt a jab of pity for the little guy, seeing as he was raised by Pearleen after both his parents died. Whitman had been nine or so when his mother and father embarked on their ill-fated boating trip in Tahitian waters, never to return home to Cattail. After that, Pearleen shipped Whitman off to boarding school on the mainland. Despite all the wealth, his was not a rosy upbringing.

Columns of desk drawers descended to the floor. I opened a drawer; empty. I slammed it shut. I opened another; empty except for *Very Hot Scot*. Shut the drawer. Reached for a third drawer handle—

"Enjoying the view?" Pearleen called from the hallway. From the fake-jolly tone of her voice, I could tell she suspected me.

She was closing the distance between us with alarming speed.

I acted like I *had* been enjoying the view, thank you very much. Outside the window, the lawn was kelly green; Pearleen's monthly water bill had to be more than I'd spent on rent in an entire year. "What a stunning place to work," I said.

"I'm blessed." She resumed her seat, hardly making a dent in the cushion. "I've got to be getting serious now. Let's wrap this up." She opened a wide drawer to her left, pulled out a stack of papers, and dropped them onto her desk.

"Just one last question, then." Sweat prickled my upper lip. I dabbed it away. This was it. What I'd come for. My chance to get Pearleen talking about Eva or Israel or *something*. I was risking the

MotherVine's relationship with a prominent customer. But Eva was more important. "Were you really ticked off that Eva Meeks outbid you for the naming rights to the butterfly sanctuary?" I asked. "Or was it about something else altogether?"

"I beg your pardon?"

"Israel Overton. Did you know him?" As Pearleen's lips whitened, an odd bud of satisfaction bloomed inside my chest.

"You'd best get that name out of your mouth," she said.

"Israel Overton? What did he mean to you?"

"*WHIT?*" Her holler made me leap.

Behind me, the office door swung open. Whitman Standish stuck in his brutish head. "Everything copacetic?"

I tried to imagine him dressed head to toe in formless black. Had it been him springing from the shadows last night? The sweat above my lip beaded back.

Pearleen was clutching my biceps. She marched me toward him. Her teetering frailty must have been all for show. Either that or it came and went. She felt as strong as a shark. "The delightful Callie here's got to be getting along. Would you show her out?"

40

Whitman escorted me down the driveway. He tried to do that guy thing with his palm lightly touching the small of my back, but I shirked away, and he held up both hands. "That went well for you, back in there," he said, chuckling. "I thought you'd maybe write a puff piece about my grandmother. Some nice, easy, free publicity. So much for that. Hey, I was glad to bump into you at the heritage garden. Adulthood looks good on you, Padget."

"Wait—what do you mean, a puff piece?"

"You've come back to Cattail to start a newspaper. That's the rumor, anyway."

I laughed. "Interesting."

"Isn't it true? Anyway, congratulations. As ornery as Grandmother can be, I don't believe she's ever kicked anyone out of our ancestral home before. You're the first."

"I've got some questions for you too, Whitman. What were you doing last night around nine o'clock or so?"

"Practicing my evil laugh while counting my millions." He chuckled again. "You're really ruffled, aren't you? Don't tell me you're still sore about the puddle incident."

We passed a garden sculpture curling upward from the grass. A small bird lighted on the topmost piece and began singing. "What do *you* know about this Israel Overton character?" I asked.

Sighing, Whitman opened my car door. "You're a book peddler now, right? Antoinette Redfield's little helper? That's what I heard." He made this gesture, something between a salute and a tipping of the figurative hat. Then he strode back up to the main house and went inside.

I stood alone in the driveway, just me and my crappy car and the chirping bird. "I'm a—" I was going to say *reporter*, but the word felt off.

41

Getting to the animal shelter from the Standish estate required a short drive. Along the way, I passed the wildlife center, a modern building with a beautiful entryway of glass and steel. Biologists worked there, including Daisy Kapur, the shark expert who was going to be signing copies of her book at the Mother-Vine on Friday morning.

Unlike the wildlife center, the animal shelter was far from welcoming. It consisted of kennels and low-slung buildings. The gutters needed cleaning and the shutters needed repairing. Chain-link fences segmented the yard, separating small dogs from big ones.

Scarred and scruffy, they barked as I crunched into the gravel lot. High school was the last time I'd visited, and the grounds seemed a lot smaller than I remembered. I walked to the main building. Stepping into the lobby, I was greeted by the pungent odor of ammonia, both urinary and disinfectant, and a general mood of restlessness and fear. Some things never change.

No one sat behind the greeter's desk, so I wandered down the hallway. The first door was open—a small office. Inside, Bo Beauchamp hunched over something, his back to me. His cargo shorts exposed wire-skinny legs that ended in unlaced construction boots, tongues lolling over the sides.

I knocked on the door and Bo turned. A rabbit the color of an overcast sky was cradled in his arms. "This here's Hazelnut, a Holland Lop," he said. "Her previous owner was a widow who passed on. Hazelnut's been here almost a week. But it won't be long before the next right person comes along." He gave the rabbit a few strokes before crossing the floor and gently transferring her to my arms.

I didn't protest.

Hazelnut was light, about four pounds. She was softer than silk and, except for her twitching nose, perfectly still. I half expected her to start purring.

Pets had been forbidden in my apartment building back in Charlotte, but I intended to be a pet owner someday. I'd always imagined adopting a cat. Or maybe a dog—a feisty thing that behaved as much as possible like Scupper. Scotties' independent streaks inspired me. But now, with wee Hazelnut like a furry hot-water bottle in my arms, I wondered if all I needed was a . . . what had he said? A Holland Lop.

Bo watched approvingly as I cooed at her. From a dispenser on the desk, he pinched a toothpick and stuck it into his mouth.

A forty-pound bag of dog food leaned against the wall. Above it, a bulletin board showed neatly rowed Polaroids of volunteers, from teenagers to senior citizens, labeled by task. Litterbox duty, dog let-outs, bedtime snacks, donation inventory.

"You got a soft spot for strays," Bo drawled. "I can tell."

"Yesterday when we spoke at the hardware store, you said Eva took in strays. What did you mean by that?"

"I've done my fair share of strayin', Miss Callie. But those days are long behind me."

Not exactly a helpful answer. I quickly formulated a follow-up. "Did you and Eva work well together?"

He cocked an eyebrow. His face grew taut, defensive. "Aren't you here to ask about the mobile veterinarian?" As if on cue, a grumbling came from outside—the sound of a big truck pulling up. "Doc's here." Bo grasped the dog-food bag and slung it over his shoulder like it contained only air. The man might have been autumnally aged, but he was as strong as a Percheron. "Come on. Wait 'til you see how high-tech this guy is."

After I kissed Hazelnut between the ears, I lowered her into her cage and latched the door. Then I followed Bo. Outside, we rounded the corner of the building. Parked in the dirt was a seventies-era, powder-blue El Camino. Bo gave the roof a possessive slap.

Next to a large trash bin sat a heap of mangled metal. It took me a second to recognize what it had been: a jumbo crate, fit for a Great Dane or some gigantic breed. The crate was in the same sorry shape as the destroyed wheelbarrow I'd noticed in the alleyway next to Meeks Hardware. Caved in, crushed in places, barely recognizable, as if it had survived a tornado.

"That crate looks like it's seen better days," I said as we passed it.

Bo shifted the dog-food bag higher on his shoulder. "Lost my temper. Happens from time to time. I figure—best to take it out on something that can't fight back."

42

Sunlight burned away the mist as I drove to the MotherVine in the steamy heat. Traffic had definitely thickened over the past few days. My city driving habits kicked in, tempting me to tailgate and toot the horn. I had to remember that, like many locals, most vacationers ended up driving slowly. They appreciated the glimpses of the water, the brightness of the sky.

Making an effort to do the same, I settled back into the driver's seat. My mind swam with the morning's events. First Gwen, defending her destruction of evidence. Then the dynamic Standish duo. Followed by Bo, savior of helpless animals one second, confessor to violent tendencies the next.

The veterinarian had been gregarious and enthusiastic. I explained about the bookshop and Tin Man's Instagram account, and he posed with various equipment inside the truck, alongside an easygoing hound dog Bo brought out.

Guess what, darlings? Tin Man wrote. The MotherVine Bookshop got a hot tip about Dr. Pembroke, who's devoted to helping homeless four-leggeds.

Dr. Pembroke said nothing about Eva that I didn't already know, so the meeting didn't advance my investigation. But at least we'd scored wins for his business, the bookshop, and of course the animal shelter, a cause that had been near and dear to Eva's heart.

That afternoon, the MotherVine was even busier than the day before, which got me harkening back to Georgia's prediction: in the wake of Trish's curse article, vacationers would flock to Cattail. At one point, a line formed at the cash register, stretching well past the coffee station. To the shoppers' amusement, Antoinette climbed onto the checkout counter and thanked them for their patience. "I'm training a new hire, and we've been busier than expected," she announced. "But books are worth the wait, y'all!"

As I helped her down, she said, "Next time, you can do the public speaking."

To which I replied, "Yeah, right. Never going to happen."

After work, I swung by the grocery store, then reported to Hudson's. I made a big kale salad with walnuts and even whisked together my own vinaigrette—lime juice, olive oil, honey, salt, and pepper. I got salmon fillets sizzling on the backyard barbecue while Scupper hopped after invisible vermin in the grass.

Hudson declared it too hot to eat outside. We set up in the kitchen, fan swirling overhead. "What'd you get salmon for?" he asked, sitting opposite me. "Plenty of local puppy drum this time of year. Caught fresh. Ronnie could've brought some over."

"You're welcome. It's my pleasure to cook for you."

"Just saying." He surveyed the table. "No biscuits? No butter?"

"You heard what the doctor said. Eat your dinner."

"I'll eat my *supper*, thank you very much. *Dinner* is for cityfolk and millennials." He wolfed down the salmon and ignored the salad. Then he got up, snatched something from a cabinet, and sat back down.

A Twinkie.

"You're like a child," I said. "Didn't your trip to the hospital mean anything to you?"

"I just ate pink fish. *Pink.* And if you had put a man-size serving in front of me, rather than the amount you'd feed a china doll at a tea party, I wouldn't need supplementation."

My chest grew heavy. I regretted telling Hudson as much as I

already had about my week—and I had an urge to tell him absolutely everything. But if there was one thing he didn't need, it was another reason to worry.

"What happened back in the city, anyway?" he asked, his mouth full. "Why'd you come home?"

I forked some kale, then pushed it around on my plate.

After the buyout, I'd hung around Charlotte for a week. I'd wanted to freelance, but it would have taken months to establish an income stream. And my savings wouldn't allow for months. It barely allowed for weeks, thanks to student loans I was still paying off. I'd hoisted a farewell beer at the Thirsty Beaver with my former coworkers. Sold my secondhand furniture. Packed up my car in just a few trips. After I closed the door to my apartment for the last time, I knocked on my neighbor's. More than once she'd delivered homemade dumplings, handed them to me on a paper plate as the hallway filled with aromas of sesame oil and hot cabbage. But Jin-young didn't answer, so I left my potted ivy on her half-moon table. And before I knew it, I was driving east, the columns of the city shrinking in my rearview mirror.

"You know what happened," I told Hudson. "I got laid off."

"So what? People get laid off all the time."

"I overheard my editor telling his boss that I didn't have the nerve." I could see them standing in the corner office, the blinds slicing across their white shirts. They thought the door was closed. But it hadn't latched, and when the air-conditioning blasted on, the door swung open a crack. Just as I'd been walking by.

"Didn't have the nerve?" Hudson said. "What does that mean?"

"'Padget doesn't have the kind of nerve I like to see in a reporter.' That's what I overheard."

"Whether that's true or false—so what? What's wrong with working in a bookshop, anyway? You could do a lot of good here."

"I just don't like feeling marooned."

"Marooned?"

"There's no bridge to the mainland. The *inconvenience*—"

"But that's what keeps Cattail Island unique. The isolation's what makes us *the down-home isle that's*—"

"—*worth your while*. I know, I know."

"You could settle down here. You should be with someone. Someone decent. You meet a guy? This true?"

Enough of this conversation. I held my kale-loaded fork to his mouth. "Eat," I said.

He waved it away. "Don't get your butt hairs up about your old-man uncle."

"Think of it as lettuce."

"I am. That's the problem."

"If I refilled your water glass, would you drink?"

"Fine, fine."

I got up and turned on the tap, letting the water run cold.

"Halfway is good enough," he said.

Halfway.

Pass through blue and into *white.*

My hand fell heavy on the faucet, stopping the flow. Time seemed to slow. "What did you say?" I asked.

"Nothing as earth-shattering as the look on your face suggests."

"Hudson, just—" I put the glass of water on his place mat. "Say it again. What you just said."

"Halfway is good enough?"

Snatching my bag, I planted an exaggerated kiss on his forehead. "You're a genius."

"First I'm a child, now I'm a genius. Where you off to?"

43

A single spotlight silhouetted Cattail Lighthouse against the starry sky. I got out of my car to a chorus of crickets and frogs and immediately spotted the Milky Way. The southernmost part of Cattail Island was mostly unbuildable because of the marshland—and that meant no light pollution. The thick, sparkling band of stars rising from the southeast was definitely not visible back in Charlotte.

I had parked in front of the keeper's cottage, next to another car, a Fiat. Only after I'd taken a few steps did I realize that two people stood on the porch. Gwen Montgomery and a tall boy with sun-bleached hair and leather bracelets. They were pressed against each other, more or less sucking face.

"Evening, youngsters," I said.

They broke apart. The boy murmured something to Gwen before trotting down the steps. "Ma'am," he said, flashing me a sly grin. He folded himself behind the wheel of the Fiat and took off.

Gwen narrowed her eyes at me. A cloth headband pulled her hair off her forehead, and she wore spandex-blend clothes and a sheen of sweat. I wondered if her boy toy had interrupted a living room workout of crunches and fire hydrants. "Thanks for that," she said.

"Dreamy. What's his name?"

"I'm *not* going to the police—"

"That's not why I'm here, Gwen. I need to get inside the lighthouse."

She leaned against the doorjamb. "The thing is, we already did that. You and me? Up the lighthouse?"

"We need to do it again." I pressed my hands together. "Please. You know how I was searching for something up there? Well, I was searching in the wrong place."

"I'm beginning to think *I'm* in the wrong place." She disappeared inside the cottage for a second, then returned, twirling a keyring around her index finger. "If you tell me exactly what you're searching for, I'll take you up."

I'd been afraid of that response. And I'd prepared a rebuttal. It wasn't something I looked forward to delivering, but I had to get inside that lighthouse—now, when no one else was around—and I couldn't risk sharing sensitive information with someone I'd met only a few times.

Someone I didn't entirely trust.

"If you take me up," I said, "I won't tell Chief Jurecki you lied to him."

Once again, Gwen and I wound up the metal steps. Lamps every ten feet provided murky light. We climbed steadily, not speaking. Ahead of me, her body language conveyed simmering anger. She had confided in me, and I'd used it against her. But I couldn't assuage her feelings. I had my own excitement to regulate.

Pass through blue and into white. The riddle was explicit about passing *through* the blue, bottom half of the lighthouse. But it said nothing about also passing through white—merely *into* it. What if I only needed to get to the halfway point, where blue gives way to white? *Halfway is good enough*, my uncle had said.

The inside of the lighthouse wasn't painted; the bricks were all the same uniform natural red from bottom to top. But there were eight stories total, which meant halfway was . . .

I stopped at the fourth landing.

"Breather?" Gwen's voice had a cutting edge.

"This is as far as I climb tonight."

"Whatever." She plunked down on a step, took out her phone, and ignored me.

The semicircle landing boasted six-foot-tall displays on several centuries of shipwrecks. GRAVEYARD OF THE ATLANTIC, the title declared in a font suggestive of bones. One panel chronicled African American lighthouse keepers who made daring rescues during hurricanes using only rope. Another answered the commonly uttered question, Why is there a lighthouse in the middle of a marsh? The Big Move was executed in the summer of '84, over the course of twenty days. Engineers separated the lighthouse from its base and glided it three thousand feet west to its current location, safe from the rising sea. For now.

I skimmed the displays once. Twice. Nothing stuck out. Nothing screamed *hidden sight*, or even riddles in general.

Which brought me back to *hold on tight*. The handrailing. It curved behind the displays, and I was just flat-chested enough to squeeze behind them.

There wasn't enough room for me to bend, so I simply slid my hands along the railing. I made one complete pass, then reversed direction, back to the start.

Nothing but dust and desiccated insects.

Another fail.

"Guess I was wrong," I said, reemerging.

Gwen's phone made her face glow blue. "I'm sorry, for what it's worth."

Swiping cobwebs off my arms, I crossed the landing and sat next to her on the step. "Sorry about what?" I asked.

"Tossing those things into the landfill. I can see that it was a mistake."

"Maybe. Maybe not."

"*Maybe not?* You made such a big deal about it."

"I know. But to be honest, it might not matter one way or another, in the end."

"Good, because I'm still not talking to the police. I do feel bad about things, though. Very bad, actually."

I put my elbows on the step behind me. The railing continued without a break, stretching from behind the display straight to the stairs. I crouched and began inspecting it at eye level.

"I thought you were done," she said.

"Me too."

"How long is this going to take?"

A metal knot in the handrailing caught my attention. Where it inserted into the brick, there was a gap—about the width of a fat pencil eraser. "Wait a second," I said, putting my eye to the gap.

Something was crammed inside.

"Holy . . ." I stuck in my fingertip and grazed a smooth, rounded surface. I wiggled my finger, trying to gain any kind of hold, but only succeeded in pushing the object farther in.

Gwen crouched beside me. "Is that it? You found it?"

"How do I get it out of there?"

"What is it? Let me see—"

"It's a glass vial."

Her brow furrowed. "I can't let you take anything, Callie. What if it's supposed to be there? I don't want to make any more mistakes."

"It's not supposed to be there." I huffed out a breath. There was no getting around it: I had to let her in on my secret. "It's part of a treasure hunt, okay? Eva was searching for *this* on Saturday night. Only she misinterpreted the clue, just like I did. I didn't need to go all the way to the top of the lighthouse; I needed to come right here. It might help me figure out what happened to her." I riffled through my bag for something, anything, of use. Notebook, tissues, bug spray, sunscreen. I pulled out a pair of battered sunglasses. "I could use the stem somehow. Fashion a tool of some sort."

She got to her feet. "What you need is tweezers. If I come back with a pair, you show me exactly what's inside that little hole. Yes?"

I chucked the sunglasses back inside my bag. "Yes."

Gwen panted next to me. She'd run back up the spiral steps.

I inserted her turquoise tweezers into the gap. The pincers closed around the glass. Gently, I tugged.

The vial didn't budge.

I pulled harder. No movement.

"It's being stubborn." I readjusted my grip and pinched the vial as deep as I could and squeezed and pulled—and the glass splintered. A sliver shot into my fingertip. I drew back my hand. The tweezers flew overhead, plinking off metal as they tumbled down the spiral steps. "Whoops."

Taking off after the tweezers, Gwen flew down the stairs. "Found them." As she stomped back up, I peered into the gap. The jagged edges of the vial reminded me of clear teeth. A scroll sat inside, its edges burnt, just like the first one.

I wouldn't be able to retrieve the vial itself. It was a lost cause, half-destroyed and stuck firm. But all I truly needed was the scroll.

Gwen returned, offering the tweezers. I quickly extracted the sliver from my skin and placed it into a tissue she held open.

Then, the scroll.

I gripped the tweezers, pinched the paper as softly as possible, and extracted it.

"That's it?" she asked.

"That's it." Gently, I coaxed it open.

I turned it over once, twice. Lifted it to my face. Tipped it closer to the nearest lamp.

Nothing.

The scroll was totally blank. No markings whatsoever.

Gwen peered over my shoulder. “Shouldn’t it have writing on it or something?”

Groaning, I sat back on the step.

“I take it that’s not what you were expecting,” she said.

“That’s putting it mildly.”

44

I stood at Gwen's kitchen sink, drying my just-washed hands on a clean dish towel. She passed me a box of Band-Aids. "Too bad about your little piece of paper," she said. "What are you going to do now?"

"Good question."

Humidity combined with heat was lethal for a lot of things. Updos, musical instruments, paintings. And treasure hunt clues. How long had the ink lasted before fading? Before the moisture inside the lighthouse, inside those bricks, seeped underneath the wax seal and broke down the ink's carbons and solvents until no trace remained?

"Can I help?" she asked.

"You've already been a big help." I smoothed a small bandage around my finger, where the splinter had been.

"His name's Reedley, if you still want to know."

"Reedley?" It took me a second to realize who she was talking about. And another second to remember where I'd heard that name before. "Reedley Anderson? He's the potter's apprentice, right? I dropped off a book for him the other day."

"He's on-island for the summer." Gwen sighed and smiled. "Remember how I told you someone comes to empty my trash? Well, turns out it's Reedley. Being a potter's apprentice doesn't quite pay the bills, so he also does odd jobs for the conservationists. Anyway, he came to collect my trash earlier and . . . well, let's just say he stayed on for a tour of the keeper's cottage."

Something told me the tour he got was a lot different than the one I'd given myself. "Summer fling?" I asked.

"Unclear at the moment. I shouldn't be getting involved in any kind of relationship until my sobriety's a lot more . . . sober." She glanced at her phone. "Speaking of, I hate to kick you out, but my sponsor's going to be calling any minute now."

That was fine with me. I had decided to stop by the dojo for my first self-defense date with Toby Dodge.

Not a date. A lesson.

"I thought in AA you couldn't have opposite-sex sponsors," I said, picturing the photograph I'd seen on Gwen's nightstand. Her and the handsome older man. "So that you don't risk becoming romantically attracted to each other."

"That's the general rule. But my sponsor's super old, and gay besides. Doesn't apply to us."

Making my way to the front door, I was about to thank her—but something felt suddenly off. The energy between us had shifted. "What is it?" I asked. "What's wrong?"

Casting a sidelong scowl, she folded her arms over her chest. "How did you know my sponsor was a man?"

I opened my mouth but no words came out.

"I don't think I ever mentioned that fact," she said. "No. I'm sure of it. I'm sure I never told you anything about him. How did you know? How could you possibly know? Unless you've been inside my cottage." Her eyes widened. Her nostrils flared. A horse that's just spied a snake. "Have you been inside my cottage? Inside my bedroom?"

"Gwen, I can explain."

"You've got to be kidding me. You *have* been inside my bedroom. Do you know how totally creeper that is?" Without taking her eyes off me, she sidestepped into the kitchen. "What kind of freak are you? I was actually starting to think of you as my friend. My only friend here."

"If you'd just listen for a second—"

"Get out."

"Please let me exp—"

She swiped the Band-Aid box off the counter. Bandages exploded, raining all around. "Get the hell out."

45

Rattled, I drove back toward the center of the island. Salty air gusted through the open windows and I gulped it down, trying to calm myself.

Gwen's anger had unnerved me, justified though it was. If I had to go around violating people's privacy, betraying people's trust for a just cause, then I needed to be sneakier about it. Savvier.

Moreover—how was I going to tell Summer Meeks that her mother died for a blank slip of paper?

I got out my phone, dialed Georgia, and left a message. "I found something. Something that proves the riddle Eva dug up was for real."

At least there was that.

A few minutes later, I parked outside the dojo. When I saw how the exterior had transformed, I smiled. Potted geraniums looked cheerful next to wooden benches. The red door was thrown open, and the butcher paper had been peeled from the windows. Dominating the glass was a decal, the silhouettes of a man, woman, and child striking combat poses against a background of waving cattails and red sky.

A few people were lingering out front. Parents, I realized, as I passed them and entered the lobby. I helped myself to a paper cup of water from the cooler and watched the action in the big room. Five kids ranging in age from six to nine stood in a neat row. White belts cinched their white uniforms. Their knees were bent, a horse-riding stance. They alternated punches, fists flinging in unison, left, right, left, right, timed with lively "hy-yas."

Across from them, Toby punched along. He wore a red top cinched with a black belt, and black pants.

I sat on the same bench where he'd mended my knee almost twenty-four hours earlier. Pulling out my copy of *While My Pretty One Sleeps*, I turned a few pages, reading the big flashback, where it's revealed that the heroine, Neeve Kearny, had been ten years old when her mother tragically died. No wonder I'd found Neeve so relatable. And now I was finding her relatable all over again. By insisting on justice for her friend Ethel, who'd gotten on a bad guy's bad side, Neeve sheds new light on her own mother's death, decades earlier.

Closing the book, I returned my attention to the lesson going on in the big room. "Integrity," the kids were mumbling. "Discipline. Courage. Respect."

Toby mimicked taking a powerful blow to the gut. He landed on his back, bare feet swinging over his face.

The students giggled.

"Please tell me you can do better than that," he said from the floor.

"Integrity! Discipline! Courage! Respect!"

He got to his feet and bowed. The kids bowed back. Then they charged past me, belts swinging as they zoomed for the lockers.

Toby was wiping his face with a towel. When he noticed me, he grinned big. "Wasn't sure you'd show," he said. Then he beckoned. "Enter, guinea pig."

I strolled up to him, into the odors of sweat and concentration. "Those kids really hate you," I said.

"No offense, but you look like you might need to vent some frustration."

"It's that obvious?"

"It's a good thing. When you're learning how to get somebody off your back, a little irritation goes a long way." He noticed my wounded finger. "That from last night?"

"Tonight's exploits. Just some exploding glass."

"You sure know how to party. Is it sore?"

"I'm still able to throw a punch, if that's what you're asking."

"No punching required." He walked over to a table against the wall, where a docking station was set up. "I dig music with my self-defense. What are you into?"

"Oh, I don't think—why don't you put on some of the heavy metal that you like."

"Because this is *your* lesson. I've seen you running and walking, and you're usually listening to something. Must be good if it keeps your legs moving."

"It is good. But it's also random."

"Random is my favorite."

I shrugged. "You asked for it, Mr. Dodge." On my phone, I cued up my most recent workout mix and handed it over. He fit it into the docking station and a second later, via mounted speakers, the cry of a fiddle filled the air, skidding and swirling like a swallow on the wing. A banjo and an upright bass joined in.

"Country?" he asked.

"*Country?*" I made a sour-lemon face. "No. This is bluegrass."

He listened, patting his thighs and nodding to the beat. The lead singer's voice sparked like a live wire, telling a tale of shooting stars, moonshine, and heartbreak. "I've never met anyone who listens to bluegrass," Toby said. "Not even the people where I grew up listened to bluegrass."

"I wrote about the bluegrass scene in Charlotte at my old job. Music doesn't get more salt of the earth than this." Looking down, I considered my outfit. The usual: cheap cotton dress. "I should have brought a change of clothes. Totally didn't even think of that."

"Are you gonna have time to switch outfits before you kick the ass of a potential attacker?"

I laughed—and my belly began buzzing.

It wasn't Toby. It was the fact that I felt so at ease around him. Which of course induced a fluttery nervousness.

He excused himself, saying that he was a sweaty disaster and needed to change. When he came back a minute later, he'd undone his ponytail, and his dark hair swung free, skimming his shoulders. He wore a brand-new Cattail Family Martial Arts T-shirt.

"Merch," I said. "Nice."

"You like? I'm official now." He gripped the hem, displaying the shirt. And the tattoos wrapping his wrists. A dragonfly on the right. On the left, a many-pointed buck.

"Tell me about your ink."

"My dragonfly here? Japanese symbol of agility. My mother was from Kyoto originally."

"And the other?"

He caressed his forearm where the antlers swept up. "I think that might be a story for another time. What about you? Any ink?"

"Never had the urge."

"Not having tattoos is the new having tattoos."

I joined him in the center of the room, kicking off my sandals and stepping from the hardwood onto firm, springy flooring. "So how does this work?"

"May I?" He gently took my hand and folded all but my index and middle fingers down. "Lesson One. Keep these two fingers stiff and strong. And jab straight into the eyeballs." He pulled my hand toward his face, stopping just shy of his eyes. "Will it completely incapacitate your attacker? Maybe. Will it buy you some time? Definitely." He released my hand and trotted backward. "Now, I'm going to come at you. And what are you going to do?"

"Poke the eyes."

"I like the confidence. Don't worry about me. I won't let you get close enough to hurt me. So you can really go for it. Let loose."

"Let loose. Got it."

He lunged.

I steeled my peace sign shaped hand. Just as he was about to crash into me, a small cry escaped my mouth. I darted to the side.

He sailed past.

"Do-over," I said, embarrassment churning inside me. "Can I have a do-over?"

"Do-overs are the essence of practice. The first time's always wonky. But it's okay, because energy's all around you. Use it. That's what it's there for." He went over to the docking station and turned up the volume. The high-ceilinged room reverberated with fiercely plucked mandolin strings. "Ready?" He burst toward me, arms flailing, hair flying.

I raised my hand, fingers poised. Aiming for his face, I shot out my arm like I was imitating a cobra strike.

His hands flew up and caught my hand.

We were standing very close.

I had hardly moved, but my heart was *rat-tat-tatt*ing against my ribs. "Was that right?"

He grinned. Strong jawline, flashing hazel eyes. "You're a quick study. Want to try it again?"

I absolutely wanted to try it again.

Toby jogged to the table to slug from a jug of water. He offered me some. I declined.

"When it comes to a woman defending herself against a man,"

he said, coming back over, "there's one very effective move that goes without saying. But I'll say it anyway: gonads."

"We don't need to practice that."

"Fine by me. Skipping ahead, then." He thrust up an elbow, slapped it with the opposite hand. "Elbows. Sharper than fists, and more bang for your buck. If a guy grabs you like this"—he clasped my wrist—"you chop your arm down." He moved in slow motion, demonstrating. "And as you chop down, the guy's naturally gonna lean toward you. And when he does, your other elbow swings right up under his jaw. Like so." He took my other arm, bent it, and guided my elbow to his chin.

We practiced the sequence in slow motion. Chop down the seized arm. Chop up the free arm, my elbow to his chin.

"Real time now. Don't hold back." He produced a mouthguard and fitted it onto his teeth. Then he seized my wrist.

I did the chop down masterfully. His head was there, bent and vulnerable, like we'd practiced. But my opposite elbow wouldn't move. And I had a disturbing vision of that all-in-black person, chasing me into the darkness.

Toby faux barged into me, squeezing my wrist, his shoulder shoving my hip.

I stumbled backward.

He held on tight. "Where's that elbow, Padget?"

"Can we start over?"

He sprang up and popped out the mouthguard. "You okay?"

"Yeah. Of course."

"The worst thing you can do is pause. If you hesitate—if you give him any time at all—he'll have time to dominate. You have to commit. You have to fight back. And don't stop."

Nodding, I blew air through my lips. *Fight back. Don't stop.* "Honest answer, Toby: Are you coming at me even fifty percent?"

"What I'm doing doesn't matter. And anyway, you have to start easy. Give yourself a chance to build up the muscle memory."

"You really think I could overpower someone?"

"Overpowering someone isn't your goal. Staying alive is your goal."

Staying alive. That was one thing Mary Higgins Clark's heroines always managed to do, even after ending up alone with the killer at the novel's conclusion. As long as I didn't find myself in some isolated location alongside a murderer, I wouldn't have to use all this self-defense stuff anyway.

I hopped a few times, trying to psych myself up. Fight back, don't stop. Simple. "Okay," I said. "I'm ready for more." And then my stomach rumbled—loudly—and I felt my cheeks flush. "I only had a few bites of dinner."

"I've got protein bars. Want one?"

"I'm good."

His eyes searched my face. "Maybe we should call it a night."

"No. Let's run it again."

46

Next morning, I arrived early at the MotherVine. Antoinette had picked up grilled strawberry muffins from Cattail Café, made with fruit fresh from a mainland farm just across the sound. I'd already had breakfast—a kale smoothie—but the muffins' buttery aroma convinced me to go for secondsies. I got the coffee going, and Antoinette and I ate out back underneath the pergola as sunlight climbed over the fence and waves slapped the seawalls on the western side of the island. Tin Man sat nearby, occasionally swatting at and missing a bumblebee.

Antoinette was spreading butter onto the second half of her muffin when she asked, "So, how *are* you?"

I looked at her, my coffee halfway to my mouth. For the most part, I'd been keeping my recent escapades to myself. But my boss's simple question made me aware of an internal sense of mounting pressure. And so, with a strange whoosh of relief, I explained pretty much everything. Summer Meeks giving me the glass vial. The treasure hunt that Eva had inadvertently dug up, and the second blank scroll I'd found. Didn't it prove Eva hadn't taken her own life? I talked about her late-in-life giving to local worthy causes—the butterfly sanctuary, the animal shelter. Then I recounted Bo Beauchamp and the jacked-up wheelbarrow and dog crate. And the bit about Israel Overton, which of course Antoinette already knew.

"My, you've been busy," she said.

As I spoke, it felt like an iron shawl was lifting from my shoulders, even though I kept two details to myself. I didn't mention the masked person chasing me down Queen Street—too intense. And I didn't mention what had happened on top of the lighthouse. The impulse to fling myself off had been haunting me, but it seemed too scary, too inexplicable to share.

"Which brings me to Gwen," I was saying. "Our friendly neighborhood lighthouse keeper who confessed to me that she might have come across—and then destroyed—a bit of homicidal evidence."

"*Homicidal?* You really believe Eva was murdered?"

"I haven't uncovered any evidence to suggest otherwise."

"Have you told Chief Jurecki all this?"

"Building up a stronger case before I do."

"What about your uncle?"

"He knows a little, but I'm trying not to stress him out too much."

"Devil's advocate: What if Eva found that blank slip of paper and was so disappointed, so disheartened, that she . . ."

"Come on. You knew that woman as well as I did."

"I knew she liked the idea of finding hidden treasure a whole lot. Think about things rationally for a second, Callie. You've got supposed evidence that no longer exists. You've got a seedy hardware store employee, but seedy doesn't make him a murderer. And you've got a rumor from six decades ago about a rich person—a *dead* rich person—behaving badly. What else have you got to go on?"

"But what about the riddle?"

"Well, you might have a point there. Regardless, Eva was one of us. You've got to dig even deeper. If you believe something foul's afoot, then you need to go after it."

"That's my uncle's position also."

She finished her last bite of muffin and clapped away the crumbs. "I've had something big on my mind too, related to all this."

"The *Crier*," I guessed.

She nodded. "I'm torn. Trish's article is the definition of indecent. But there's no denying that, since it came out, the local shops are getting quite the boost. One front-page story about a deadly curse, and tourists start showing up in droves."

I sipped my coffee. Jeff and Trish were monetizing a tragic death. It was tacky at best and at worst reprehensible. But along with Georgia, my boss had a point: small businesses were benefiting. "I'm torn too."

"You've only been working here a few days," Antoinette said. "So you don't really have a point of comparison. But the reality is, Queen Street usually isn't this busy until after the Fourth of July. And even then . . ." She glanced at her phone. "Well, torn or not, it's time to open shop."

We cleared the table. Inside, Antoinette flipped on the lights and ticked the thermostat a few degrees cooler. I went over to the bay window to make sure Tin Man hadn't knocked over any displayed books during the night, which he hadn't. And then my hand flew to my chest.

Outside, shoppers were queued past the window, waiting to get into the MotherVine. In fact, it was like that all up and down Queen Street: lines had formed outside every business. The pottery store, the swimsuit boutique, even the barber. The sidewalk in front of Cattail Café was crammed with patrons.

"My land," Antoinette said. Coming up beside me, she put a hand on my shoulder. "I don't believe in curses, Callie. But I do believe in selling books."

I scraped my teeth against my lip, thinking about Eva's celebrated television commercials. She'd been a businesswoman, after all. An entrepreneur. Prosperity for Cattail was something she'd have championed.

I looked into Antoinette's light brown eyes. "Let's sell some books, then," I said.

"Let's." She went over to the door, unlocked it and opened it wide. "Good morning!"

The first people to enter were Georgia and Summer Meeks.

47

Georgia was her stylish self in a stretch-lace top and flowy skirt. Summer, almost as tall as her aunt, wore a belly shirt and cutoff denim shorts, pockets peeking from the hems. Pop music hissed from her earbuds.

I wished for a moment alone with Summer, to tell her about the scroll I'd found stuffed between mortar and brick inside the lighthouse. Yes, the scroll was blank. Yes, I didn't know who planted it, or why. But I was close to finding out.

Hopefully.

Summer gave me a conspiratorial dip of the chin before taking off down the main aisle.

"I know you're slammed," Georgia said, as shoppers fanned around us. Again, I sensed her conflicted emotions; in her sorrow, she wanted me near, but also far away. "Any chance we could talk?" she asked.

Antoinette gave me a little wave that said, *I got this.* Most of the customers were wandering toward the back of the shop, so I led Georgia to the front seating area. We settled into the papasan chairs. "Did you get my voicemail?" I asked.

There was a beat of silence. "We're going to have her cremated," she said. "And then we'll have a paddle-out."

I nodded. A paddle-out is basically a funeral on the water and common practice among nonreligious Cattailers who didn't like the idea of a traditional cemetery burial. Mourners get on their surfboards or in their boats. They gather past the breakers on a calm summer morning, share some memories, maybe sing some songs. And then they sprinkle the ashes in the water.

"You know about the riddle Eva found," Georgia said. "I know you're trying to help, but when you call me wanting to talk about—it just—what I'm trying to say is, unless you can prove beyond a doubt what my sister was doing and thinking in her final moments . . ."

"I get it," I said, and left it at that. Georgia had decided to move on. It had been mere days since Eva's death, but everybody had their own style of grieving, their own timeline.

Tin Man sprang onto her lap and began kneading. As she stroked his soft silvery fur, she visibly relaxed. "My parents encouraged me to take Summer out to breakfast," she said. "Just to give us a break. But she wanted to come here. It's busier in here than I've seen it in a long time. Same at the hardware store."

"It's the *Crier*."

"Totally."

"Speaking of the hardware store," I said as casually as possible, "I've been wondering about one of your employees."

"Oh yeah?" The ring in Georgia's voice told me she was glad for the change of subject. She sank deeper into the papasan. "Who?"

"Your paint guy. Bo."

"Antoinette thinking about a new color scheme?" She looked around at the pale green paint on the walls and the deep green hue of the shelves.

"Something like that," I said. It was becoming a useful response.

"I have to admit, Bo's dependable. I don't think he's called in sick or missed a shift in ten years."

"But?"

"A few years ago, a customer complained. Someone from out of town. She said he made 'suggestive' remarks"—Georgia made air quotes, then continued stroking Tin Man—"while she was picking out paint samples. Nothing came of it, and Bo denied it up, down, and sideways. But I was more inclined to believe the customer."

So was I.

"There was another incident just the other morning," she added. "Tuesday."

I asked if the incident happened to involve a run-in with a wheelbarrow. "I noticed the aftermath out by the dumpster."

Georgia leaned toward me, lowering her voice as a shopper drifted near. "Mindy, another of our long-timers, caught Bo in the act. She was about to unlock the doors for the day when she heard a commotion in the garden supply aisle and there he was, hauling away on the wheelbarrow with a plumbing wrench. According to Mindy, he calmed down immediately. Apologized. Said he was sad about Eva. Angry. Said it would never happen again, and to dock his paycheck for the damages."

It has happened again, I thought. At the animal shelter. The dog crate around back, reduced to a jumble of wires. "Has he ever done anything like that before?" I asked, hoping to push this line of questioning as far as I could.

"Not to my knowledge. I've never had much to do with the hiring-and-firing side of the business. My parents passed that duty along to Eva. I'm the inventory person. Eva handled staffing." A cloud of worry shadowed her face. A thought to the future, perhaps. How would she keep the store viable without her sister, who contributed so much? "You know, my parents were big believers in hiring reformed prison inmates," she said. "Giving them a chance. Most of them worked a few months without incident and then went on their way."

Now it was my turn to lean in. "Bo was a convict?" I whispered. So that was what he meant when he called himself a stray.

"I honestly don't recall. It's probably in a file somewhere. He's from the *Deep* South, I think. When he first moved here, his accent was thick and strange. Nobody could understand him. You and I would have been about fifteen years old."

I heard hissing pop music. Summer had returned and was lingering next to the magazine racks.

"You know, another detail comes to mind," Georgia said. "When we first hired Bo, he spent an awful lot of time down at the town hall."

"What was his business there?" I asked.

"Beats me."

"Bo asked Mom out on a date." The quiet voice issued from beside me. Summer. She had taken out one earbud and was fiddling with it.

Tin Man leapt away as Georgia scooted to the edge of the chair. "Bo asked Eva on a date?"

"She turned him down," Summer said.

"When was this, sweetie?"

"Couple weeks ago."

"Were you there when he asked your mom out?" I asked.

Summer looked askance, as if she could read the answer on the cover of *Outer Banks Coastal Life* magazine. "They were in the office," she said. "I was just outside the door. Bo said he'd always loved her. And he invited her over for supper. He'd been practicing making lasagna or something from scratch. For her. Because she always brought pasta for lunch. He'd gotten himself a pasta maker. Spent a hundred bucks on it."

"What did your mother say to all that?" I asked.

"That she wanted to keep things professional. She was really nice to him. He didn't say anything back. I heard him moving toward the door, so I kept walking. You know, like I hadn't been listening."

Georgia and I shared a look.

I desperately wanted her to come over to my side. I wanted another ally to support my quest for a bit of sense around Eva's death. The more, the better. If Summer was telling the truth—and what reason did she have to lie?—then Bo Beauchamp had motive to hurt Eva. Wounded ego.

But Georgia's face returned to stone, as if she couldn't afford to let herself follow that train of thought. She got to her feet reluctantly, the way a lot of customers vacated the MotherVine's chairs. "We need to be getting back," she said. "Don't we, Sum?"

"Can I get a book? I brought money."

Georgia's cell phone jingled. She made to answer it. "Five minutes," she said, heading for the door. "I'll wait outside."

"Come on," I said as I steered Summer around a few shoppers, toward the back of the store and the Young Adult section. "Did you ever hear Bo and your mom talking about anything else?" I asked. "Besides work stuff."

"I don't know. I guess not really."

"Did she ever say anything to you about him?"

"Me and Mom didn't really talk much. She was a good mom, though." Summer scuffed the hardwood floor with the toe of her sandal. "She always helped me with my homework and she never got mad when I had trouble with pre-algebra. Like with inequalities? Sometimes I take a really long time listing all the different possible answers to each inequality. But she never rushed me."

"My mom was like that too. Patient."

"I really should buy a book." She scanned the young adult shelves, and I waited for her face to light up when she hit the right title. But it stayed forlorn. She didn't want to be in the world of tweens. That was her world, where she was now. And it was hell.

I led her around the corner, to the mysteries. I thought I'd introduce her to The Cat Who cozies, about a small-town reporter who solves crimes with the help of his feline companions. Before my mother died, I couldn't get enough of those books.

But Summer was pointing to the Mary Higgins Clark shelf. "These any good?"

I paused. Was it appropriate to recommend MHC to a grieving twelve-year-old? Then I remembered *I* had been a grieving twelve-year-old when I'd first read *While My Pretty One Sleeps*, and it had turned out to be the perfect paradox of escapism and true-to-life grit. "Actually, I'm reading this one now." I showed her the rain-obscured woman pushing her umbrella against the storm. "The bad guy? You'll never see him coming. It can be intense in places. Dark too. But the heroine reminds me of you."

"She does?"

"She notices things," I said. "She gets hunches about things that other people dismiss. But she doesn't ignore them. And it pays off."

"I'll try it."

As we headed for checkout, I was going to ask about her mother's *Camp Cottontown Funbook*. What Summer knew about it, if anything. I was also going to tell her about the second glass vial. But before I could get out any more words, Antoinette's voice came tinkling over the stacks. "Callie? I need you for a possible Tin Man–stagram."

After Summer and Georgia left the MotherVine, Antoinette took me out back, where a shopper was sitting in the shade, flipping through an Elin Hilderbrand hardback. The cover showed tan legs emerging from a bright yellow beach umbrella. "Excuse me, ma'am," Antoinette said to the woman. "Could you tell my assistant what you just told me?"

"Manatees," she said, rattling the ice in her coffee. "Cow and calf. They're splashing around near the old Smile Beach fishing pier. My family and I just came from there."

"Apparently, they're attracting quite a crowd," Antoinette said to me. "Better hurry. I'll hold down the fort here while you zip up north and snap some shots."

As if reinforcing her command, Tin Man appeared, slinking between my feet and meowing up at me.

Manatees.

Three weeks ago, I might have been rushing to an impromptu press conference, or a flash mob, or a multicar pileup on the freeway.

Now I was rushing to manatees.

At the behest of a cat.

48

The Hilderbrand-reading MotherVine customer hadn't been exaggerating: tourists were clustered at the end of the pier, snapping photos, trying not to lean against the wobbly railings.

One tentative step at a time, I ventured onto the rickety structure, hoping my added weight wouldn't tip the scales and send us all crashing into the water. It was only a ten-foot drop, but still.

I got some fun shots of the onlookers grinning downward. Then I elbowed my way to the railing and saw the manatees for myself: a cow about eight feet long and a calf about half that length. They weren't doing much, just floating. There was something restful about the small waves washing over their backs.

"Must be a pocket of warm water or something," an old man said as I framed them up with my phone's camera. "They've been hanging out there for a good half hour now," he added.

Manatees were a rare sight in Cattail. I'd seen one only once before, during summertime, from this very spot. I must have been eight years old or so. Mom and I were hanging around while Uncle Hudson fished for puppy drum. He had just loaded a minnow onto a hook and was about to cast out when I pointed at the whiskered, elephantine face sticking out of the water. "Look!" I swore the thing made eye contact with me.

My shots of the manatees basically amounted to two oblong

mounds, but they would have to do. I posted them to Tin Man's Instagram account.

> Cattail Island is a purrfect place to observe all sorts of animals in their natural habitats. If you missed these manatees making a splash at the old Smile Beach fishing pier, then do come and observe me, Tin Man, in my natural habitat at the MotherVine Bookshop on Queen Street. Let's paw through some books together, darlings!

I was heading off the pier when I spotted Jeff Berryman. He was staring southward, in the direction of the pirate ship and the waterfront shops. A camera was slung around his too-long neck. He held his hands in front of his face, making the shape of a square or rectangle.

Trish must have ordered him here for shots of the manatees. With that task accomplished, now he was . . . who knows.

My plan was to plow right past him. I had enough drama in my life and wasn't looking for more. But just as I was about to slip by unnoticed, he turned and said, "Hey, chum." It was what he used to call me when I was a kid. This time, though, the moniker didn't sound big brotherly. Instead, it was tinged with sarcasm.

I stopped. "Hello. What are you up to?"

"My wife's bidding. What else?" He snickered and added, "Scouting the perfect spot to shoot the fireworks for the Cattaillion. Think I found it. You know, all these years, Trish and I have been buying our books exclusively from the MotherVine. But that doesn't go very far with your boss, does it? First she cancels her advertising. And now she won't even accept a small stack of newspapers to sell at checkout. So much for loyalty."

"She's just trying to do her job to the best of her ability."

"Yeah, well—ditto."

For a second I held Jeff's gaze, but no snappy comeback sprang to mind, and I didn't want to continue standing there absorbing his unpleasantness. So I simply kept on walking.

Thirty seconds later, I'd made it off the creaky pier, and my flip-flops were kicking up sand, soft against my calves. Smile Beach worked its magic, and before long the warmth and the waves soothed away my irritation. A Frisbee spun out at my feet, and I tossed it back to a group of teenagers who shouted thanks. Their energy and ease were contagious.

Then I reached the access ramp—and saw another man I really didn't want to see.

Whitman Standish leaned against the railing, shirtsleeves rolled up to his elbows, tie flicked over his shoulder as he took the last bite of a burger. With his thumb, he wiped a bit of sauce from the corner of his mouth.

There was no getting around him.

"Aren't you going to stick around and see if the manatees put on a little show?" he asked as I got closer. "A song-and-dance routine?"

"They just did," I said. "Don't tell me you missed it."

He held up a sandwich-size bundle wrapped in foil. "Grandmother sent me out here to pick up some lunch. Couldn't wait for mine. She isn't much of an ambassador, is she? But we're real people, she and I. Not caricatures."

Pausing opposite him, I squinted in the sunlight. "I'm not sure what you're getting at."

"We have interests beyond money. And we have a proposal for you."

A proposal? I kept a cool poker face. "No," I said, and kept on walking. "I need to get back to the MotherVine."

"Just like that? You haven't even heard the terms." Whitman took the bait—he trotted to catch up with me as I marched off the ramp, into the parking lot. At my car, I stuck my key into the driver's-side door. One of these days, I'd join the twenty-first century and get a fob or even keyless ignition. "The chill thing about this proposal is—" He leaned against my car door. When he noticed the white-and-black splatter, likely from a seagull, he recoiled, checking his sleeve. "As I was saying, *you* set the terms. See, all you need to ask yourself here is, What does Callie Padget want? A nice cash bonus? A nicer, newer car? One that isn't covered in bird sh—"

"This car puts the rust in trusty, Whitman. She gets forty miles to the gallon. Can you say the same thing about your primary mode of transport?"

He gestured a few spaces down, where the Ferrari was parked, the top down. The vanity license plate read SEA-F-O.

I don't know how I managed not to roll my eyes.

"Just got her last week," he said. "Shall we go for a quick spin?"

"Does that actually work on women?"

"At least come check it out. You know you want to."

I scraped my teeth over my bottom lip. Future opportunities to sit inside a three-hundred-thousand-dollar Italian sportscar were likely scant. Plus, I was dying of curiosity to hear his proposal. And my attempt at reverse psychology hadn't worked.

A minute later, I slid into the leather passenger seat, which cradled what few contours I had. The scent was new car with a touch of black licorice. The dashboard was the very definition of minimalist. The windshield: invisibly clean.

He shut my swing-up-style door, rounded the hood, and got behind the wheel. I looked over at him, my eyes wide.

"I know," he said.

"Don't you just want to lick everything?"

"I manage to hold myself back." He flipped open the console, stuffed away Pearleen's sandwich, plucked a lemon-scented cleaning wipe, and began de-burgering his hands.

I noticed a coiled black cord tucked inside the passenger-side footwell. It attached to a black rectangular box with silver knobs and switches.

A CB radio. Hudson used to have one in the OFV.

"Seriously?" I said.

"It's an anomaly, I'll admit. An anachronism."

"Do you talk on it a lot?"

"I'm more of a lurker, to use today's parlance."

"So you just listen in? That's kind of creepy, Whitman."

"No harm in innocent entertainment. Keeps me company on my drives to and from SFI headquarters in Chesapeake. Long-haul truckers say some colorful things."

"Can you hear police scanners?"

"From time to time, sure."

"What about phone conversations?"

"Cell phones? That's impossible." He quarter-turned in his seat. "You're more interested in the CB radio than the car."

"It's more interesting. The novelty of it."

"The thing is." He lowered his voice as a woman jogged by, a spaniel at her side. "How would you like a better place to live? Get out of your uncle's place?"

"What?" The breeze stirred my hair. I tucked a strand behind my ear.

My residence was public knowledge, and I knew where Whitman lived. But this proposal, whatever it was, seemed to have taken a decidedly personal direction.

"You call the shots," he said.

I started to feel a little breathless. I was being offered hush money by the richest man in Hyde County while sitting in his convertible Ferrari. "Let me get this straight," I said. "You want to grant me some sort of special favor. A favor of my choosing."

"Now you're getting it."

"And in return?"

"That name you mentioned yesterday." He draped his arm over the steering wheel, revealing a watch likely half as valuable as the car. "You forget that name. You simply forget it."

No such thing. I'd spent almost a lifetime trying to *simply forget*. An impossible feat.

"Where's the door handle?" I looked around. "I'd like to get out now."

He reached over and pushed a button that practically blended in with the rest of the passenger door, which then glided up like a silk sheet.

I made my way back to my car.

"Hold on, now," he called, following.

"You can't buy me off." I swung into my dependable tin can on wheels and slammed the door. Pumping my arm, I rolled down the window. "You can't buy my silence."

"You've got to understand, Callie: I'm thinking of you here." He put both forearms on the roof and ducked closer. "I'm just not sure it would be worth it for you, if you went public with that name. Published it in your newspaper or your magazine or whatever you have planned. What would you get in return?"

"Look, Whitman. Despite whatever you might have heard, I'm not back in Cattail to start any sort of periodical, okay? I do have an online portfolio, which is like a résumé. When reporters are looking for work, they refer potential employers to their *previ-*

ous work." It had been days since I'd updated my portfolio, I realized. Eva and my new job had been all-consuming.

Whitman was nodding. "And editors eat this sort of thing up, don't they? The itty-bitty scrappy reporter taking down the monstrous evil corporation. Exposing injustices. Leveling out the playing field for the little guy."

I had no idea what he was talking about. But he thought I knew way more than I did. And it all sounded as juicy as hell. Had Eva found out something she shouldn't have? I turned my key in the ignition and revved my whiny Honda engine. "Let's get to the point, Whitman."

"Think of the irreparable damage you'd be doing if you shared what you know. If you put it on your little website. You'd be sending an old woman to an early grave, overcome with emotions. That big mess happened when she was a defenseless little girl." He cocked his head. "You were a defenseless little girl at one point too, you know."

"Say I stay quiet. In exchange for what? For being Pearleen's personal toadstool? Like you?" My hand flew halfway to my mouth. I hadn't meant to insult him. It just sort of came out.

"I'm CFO of Standish Furniture International," he said, trying his best to appear unruffled.

"Are you, now?" I pressed fingertips to my chest in mock reverence. "*Well*, Mr. Ferrari—"

"Okay. Fine. You don't like me. You think I'm a jerk because I recently dropped upwards of a quarter mil on a roadster that gets eleven miles to the gallon. And maybe that's fair. I don't know. What I do know is this: another offer isn't coming. You turn me down now?" His hands flew up. "You live with the consequences."

"Eva Meeks met some pretty dire consequences, didn't she? Did she turn down your hush money too?"

He bent over, his veiny forehead inches from mine.

Poke the eyes.

I wished for lightning-fast automatic windows. I'd push a button and squish his big head between glass and frame. Then I'd stomp the gas pedal. "Ready for my version of this conversation?" I said. "Where were you Saturday night?"

"Are you suggesting I harmed Eva? It's atrocious, how she ended up. I didn't know her well, but she struck me as a good, kind person. It's a shame she took her own life. Isn't that what the police determined?"

"What the police determine and what I determine are two separate beasts."

Scoffing, he shook his head. "Saturday night, I took my grandmother out for a nice meal. Along with our Bible-study group. Our treat."

"Clara's by the Waterfront, I presume?" Clara's was the most expensive restaurant in Cattail. By virtue of being the only expensive restaurant in Cattail.

"That's right, Clara's. There were ten of us. I had the mesquite-grilled prime filet. Grandmother had the rack of lamb. And then we all went our separate ways. I took her right home."

"Timetable?"

"We were seated around eight. Grandmother likes to dine late. We were home by ten, I'd guess."

"What vehicle did you take?" I knew he had a fleet, including a chauffeur-driven Bentley.

"She hadn't experienced the Ferrari yet." He crossed his arms over his chest. "You're not a cop, you know."

"I have a proposal for you, Whitman. Tell Granny that an eyewitness has come forward. This person's account has been vetted with the proper authorities. And it just so happens that I *do* plan on posting a tell-all on my *little website*. I'd love to include

Pearleen's side of the story. I'd encourage her to give me a call. But if she doesn't?" I shrugged, threw it into drive, and chirped the tires as I pulled away.

In the rearview mirror I saw Whitman kick the parking block, then grab his foot and hop a few times, his face twisted in pain.

49

Poke the eyes: lunge forward, thrust the arm, two fingers extended.

Alternating hands, I made my way down the main aisle of the MotherVine. Antoinette was running errands, taking advantage of a temporary lull. Alone with the books, I had the sense they were watching me. Maybe even rooting for me.

Out back, the only customers were regulars, a mother and two teenage daughters. The mother's hair was a pyramid of graying frizz. She snapped a few selfies with the purring Tin Man, who had sprawled on top of their table, while the daughters pored over stacks of young adult books. I'd be re-shelving them at some point soon, a task I couldn't deny looking forward to. It might have been odd, enjoying that kind of organizational chore. But I guess something inside me relished making order out of chaos, whether that chaos took the form of an unexplained death or thumbed-through books.

"Anything I can help you with, ladies?" I asked from the back doorway.

"We're fine, love," said the mother.

"Just holler if you change your mind." I turned and set in on another lap, this time practicing chop-down-right, chop-up-left.

Evil corporation, Whitman had said. *Injustices.* Sending Pearleen to an early grave.

Israel Overton must have been quite the bad boy.

Was there anyone who might shed some light on what was

going on with the Standishes? Those gardeners at the estate had looked petrified of Pearleen. But even if they did know something, they wouldn't tell me about it. They had the best-paid domestic service jobs in all of northeast North Carolina. Why risk losing that?

There was always Standish Furniture's corporate headquarters. But something told me that would be a big fat dead end. Plus, the headquarters were now in Chesapeake. Not only did I not know that area; I didn't have any contacts there whatsoever.

Guess I was staying local.

I'd elbowed my way to the front window. Pausing to catch my breath, I connected my phone to my earbuds and called the historical society. A mellow-voiced woman was happy to look through the archives on my behalf. But she didn't find any accounts whatsoever of anyone named Israel Overton, aside from his final resting place in the town cemetery. Next, I called the town hall. Same gig. No record.

Thornton Standish must have wiped Israel Overton clean off the map.

I elbow-chopped my way down another aisle, past Fantasy, into Popular Psychology / Self-Improvement, where I paused. My fingertips started tingling. Maybe here was where I needed to look. Maybe here was where I'd find an explanation for what had happened to me on top of the lighthouse.

I ran my fingers along the spines, recognizing many of the genre's big-time authors. Malcolm Gladwell, Wayne Dyer, Cheryl Strayed, Gretchen Rubin. Nothing popped out at me—until I stooped a little lower, and a title caught my eye. *Human Wiring.* I didn't recognize the author. The book was all about neurological impulses and had an illustration of the brain on the cover. Flipping through, I saw a heading: "High Places Phenomenon." That eerie thing where you're in a high place—on a mountaintop, say, or a bridge—and you get the urge to jump. It's caused by misfiring neurological signals. Instead of getting the urge to back away, the opposite occurs.

High places phenomenon.

I had a name for the vision that had played before my eyes, the impulse to fling myself over the railing. I wasn't a freak, all alone in the world. This was more than a *thing*. It was a phenomenon.

Now my whole body was tingling. I wanted to sit cross-legged on the floor in the middle of the MotherVine and read the whole darn book. But I settled for standing there, skimming. Searching. Does the high places phenomenon ever win? Does it ever take lives? Maybe sometimes the wiring gets so tripped up, the events in a person's life are so tumultuous, the perfect storm is created, and . . .

Human Wiring didn't offer much discussion on a person's social situation or frame of mind or personal history. It stuck instead to the operational. Cold, clinical facts.

But it was enough for me to know that *I'd* beaten it. I'd defeated the impulse, which meant anyone could. Eva, my mother—anyone. No one had been cursed. And the lighthouse hadn't been either.

Flooded with a sense of power and possibility, I whispered a thank-you to the MotherVine, then returned the book to its home on the shelf.

"Find anything you like?" Suddenly, Antoinette was next to me. I'd been so absorbed I hadn't heard her returning—from Meeks Hardware, by the looks of it; a canvas tote filled with cat food was slung over her shoulder.

Shaking my head, I said, "I shouldn't be manhandling the

merchandise, Antoinette. As you always used to tell my mom, 'This isn't a library. It's a bookshop.'"

She shrugged. "As far as I'm concerned, the number one perk of working here is being intimate with books."

I walked with her to the small room that served as her office. Tin Man followed, mewling with the volume of thirty felines as she stored his food in a cupboard. "You know all that stuff Ronnie was talking about the other night?" I asked. "About the hushed-up Standish factory accident in the 1950s involving a real-life boogeyman named Israel Overton?"

"What about it?"

"Whitman was at the manatee hullabaloo just now—"

"Cute post, by the way."

"Glad you liked it. Anyway, he offered me anything I wanted in exchange for *not* pursuing this Israel Overton business."

"Whitman Standish? He bribed you?"

"Tried to. I sort of told him that a true-blue source has come forward and condemned SFI. And that I was going to quote that person on my website."

"Is that true?"

"The point is, Whitman must think it's possible for me to put together a factually accurate and legally valid account about—well, about whatever happened. It's provable somehow. Why else would he be so afraid? He didn't even try to deny it."

"But you don't know what *it* is."

I held up a finger. "Yet."

A while later, as I was walking out to my car, I thought of someone I could lean on. One of the managers at Clara's by the Waterfront, the restaurant Whitman had mentioned, was a spiky-haired woman named Faith. She and I had worked together at the Cattail Diner back when I was a community college student. Faith wasn't exactly a friend, but waiting tables alongside someone has a way of forging a bond. It must have something to do with the peach polyester uniform.

Forgoing my car, I walked to Clara's, enjoying the late-afternoon warmth. Queen Street had begun decorating for the Cattaillion, and this year's beneficiary was a prominent theme. Adorning the shop windows were faded photographs from the fishing pier's glory days in the 1980s. Men with mullet hairdos and slim-fit swim trunks, women with poofy bangs and jelly sandals, everybody hanging over the railings or relaxing on one of the benches or posing with a big flounder they'd reeled in.

Clara's had a prime location at the end of the waterfront. Its windbeaten wood sign swung from rusted chains. I found Faith just inside, near the hostess podium, folding napkins into sailboat shapes. The restaurant was hopping with the early-bird crowd. Glassware clinked, voices made a din, and somewhere amid the many tables, a toddler shrieked.

Faith hugged me, her patchouli perfume making my eyes water.

"Are you busy?" I asked. "I have a random question."

"Spit it out. I've got a twenty-top coming in."

"Did you work Saturday night?"

"I work every night."

"Rumor has it there was a party of ten. These would have been conservatively dressed folks. Straight from a Bible-study session."

"Sure. There was one woman in a white collar. They sat by the fireplace."

"Any prominent citizens of Cattail in that party?"

"You mean the Standishes? They were there. Pearleen and that grandson of hers. I bet under all that seersucker he's got the body of an Adonis. He picked up the tab. Gave me a forty percent tip. Cash. They were here from eight until nine forty-five or so."

"That helps. Thanks a lot."

I strolled back to my car, thinking.

Okay. So Whitman's alibi sort of checked out.

But easy answers had never been my thing.

50

Fried oysters smelled like damp concrete and rotten rubber. Those odors now wafted from the platter set before Chief Jurecki.

I'd lured him to Salty Edward's for dinner. Called him and said I had important information pertaining to Eva Meeks's death.

He gestured to my small bowl. "That's all you're gonna eat?"

The Hatteras chowder steamed up at me. Crab meat, clam broth, carrots, potatoes. More suitable for a blustery winter's eve than a balmy June afternoon. But it was simple, not to mention the only item on Salty Edward's menu that wasn't deep-fried or piled high with processed meats. "It's actually quite filling," I said.

"Soup is not a meal." Jurecki popped an oyster into his mouth.

Salty Edward's booths were sticky with sea air and sopped-up beer. It was the kind of joint every restaurant owner on the Outer Banks strove for: popular with locals in the off-season, and a tourist magnet during the summer. The name was a reference to Edward Teach, also known as Blackbeard the pirate. A banner over the bar featured an old-fashioned X-marks-the-spot treasure map.

Jurecki's arms flabbed from a short-sleeve shirt. "Officer Fusco mentioned Eva Meeks's front door was open on Monday night. Not just unlocked, but wide open. What were you and your uncle doing there to begin with?"

"Begonias."

"Ma'am?"

"I was planting flowers. For the Meeks family."

Before coming here, I'd gone to Hudson's and retrieved Eva's *Camp Cottontown Funbook* from my cardboard chest. Now I nudged the booklet toward the chief. "This was on Eva's desk. It must have been important to her. But why? And why now?"

He handled it with more care than I would have believed possible from such a gruff man.

"I have a source who told me about some possible evidence," I said. "Evidence that might change your thinking about the nature of Eva's death."

Sighing, he closed the booklet. "I'd say you're barking up the wrong tree. But the fact is, there isn't even a tree."

"No tree. Okay. Never mind, then." I made to leave.

"Wait, wait. This source you mention. Is this person credible?"

I leaned back against the booth. "Define 'credible.'"

"The first quality a source must have, if police are going to treat the information seriously, is veracity."

Strike one against Gwen. "And the second quality?"

"Specificity. Who are we talking about?"

"I'm reluctant to say." I didn't want to betray Gwen's confidence any more than I already had.

"All right," Jurecki said. "Tell me about the potential evidence."

"The old lock. What was left of it. And the blowtorch used to melt it off the lighthouse door."

His eyebrows crept toward his hairline. "A blowtorch?"

"A BonBlow!-brand baking torch. It belonged to Eva."

"You know that for a fact?"

I flipped up a palm. "Not exactly."

"Assuming the blowtorch did belong to Eva—how would it prove her death wasn't a suicide?"

"If you found someone else's fingerprints on the blowtorch, it would prove she wasn't alone."

"It would prove someone else held the blowtorch. But not *when* that person held it." He polished off his oysters. "What did this source do with said blowtorch and said destroyed lock?"

I looked into my soup. The oily broth reflected my face. "Dumped them into the West Lake landfill."

A generic ringtone jingled. Jurecki produced his phone and punched out a text. "Your uncle doing okay?" he asked absently. "Heard he had a conniption or something."

"He's all better, thank you." I slid my hand inside my bag. My fingers found the second scroll. I'd put it inside a plastic baggie for safekeeping.

Which was ridiculous, because the scroll was blank. How could I possibly show the chief of police a blank slip of paper and convince him it was crucial? What I needed was proof.

"I know you mean well, Callie," Chief said, stuffing away his phone. "You want to be a good citizen. I get that. But the right thing for you to do here is plain and simple. You know what that is." He leaned slightly forward. "Leave police work to the police."

51

Tucking the booklet back inside my bag, I strolled along Queen Street. I needed to clear my head. Many cute families were out and about, taking in the quaintness, pausing to read the menu boards outside the bistros. A musician in a porkpie hat strummed a guitar and crooned "Carolina in My Mind." I tossed a few quarters into his open case, smiling at the thought of Hudson scolding me, urging me to save my coins for poker.

Around the corner, things got quieter, and so did my mind. I took a few deep breaths and let them out slowly—and then I froze.

I was standing just outside the open gate of Cattail Cemetery. Every cell in my body demanded I turn and walk away. *We don't like cemeteries*, they screamed. *We especially dislike this cemetery.*

Even from here, I could see my mother's basic headstone. A wreath of silk flowers hung from it, the ribbons swaying. That must have been Hudson's offering; he visited every few months.

I hadn't visited in years.

"Hi, Mom," I whispered.

Her funeral had been family only. Me and Hudson and the great-aunts and second cousins who'd packed Hudson's freezer with stews and chili. Halfway through the service, a dump truck had grumbled up, parked by these very gates, and sat there with the engine roaring. Everyone pretended to ignore it. Even the priest, who hadn't bothered raising his voice above the din.

Beyond my mother's headstone, a twelve-foot marble obelisk rose. The grand inscription, visible from where I stood, read:

A great man of industry and humility:
THORNTON STANDISH
1919–1991

Humility. Right.

I was about to keep on walking when I remembered Israel Overton was buried in the town cemetery too. What if I could set aside my aversion and locate his final resting place? Maybe I'd learn something. I got out my phone, found a cemetery map of the various grave sites, and enlarged it. I chose a path that would lead me away from my mother. I took a few tentative steps past the gate—and a flash of red caught my peripheral vision. That woman with the perfect posture—the one I'd seen while sitting on Smile Beach with Gwen—was strolling just ahead. Her hair was in a bun like the day before, and the same red feather earrings brushed her neck.

I approached her, getting close enough to make out a hello-my-name-is name tag stuck to her top.

She glanced over.

I raised a hand.

She whipped around as if I'd pointed a pistol at her and booked it toward a side gate.

Weird.

Making a three-sixty turn, I scanned all around. I was uncomfortable enough and didn't want any more surprises. Satisfied I was now alone among the dead, I continued along the path, arriving before long at a knee-high, moss-covered headstone. The plain script proclaimed:

ISRAEL "THE SWEEPER" OVERTON
January 1, 1933–June 16, 1956

Underneath the dates, covering the hole where bouquets can be inserted, someone had placed a can of chicken noodle soup.

52

I was walking back to my car when my phone buzzed. A text from Toby, asking if I wanted to meet for another self-defense lesson. And since he'd been inside the dojo all day, would I like to meet at Smile Beach?

Toby and I walked side by side in the warm sand, flip-flops dangling from our fingertips. It was suppertime, which meant many vacationers had gone back to their cottages to shower and get the kids fed and tucked in. But a few sun-kissed families remained, splashing in the shallow waves or making sandcastles. One father we passed was explaining to his boys—identical twins—that the likelihood of them finding buried treasure was very, very small. The boys were undaunted by this news, and dug their holes with even more determination as their mother looked on. She reminded me of my mother. It must have been the way the waning sunlight slanted off her cheekbones. "If you spot any gold coins from the seventeen hundreds lying around, let us know," she said, grinning as we strolled by.

"People really are friendly here," Toby said. "Or maybe people are just happy to be on vacation."

"What brought you to the Outer Banks, anyway?" I asked.

"Same story as every nonnative: spent summers here with my family when I was growing up. When I was fourteen or fifteen, I decided, someday I'm gonna live on the Outer Banks. At that age I didn't know my life wasn't always going to feel like one long, carefree summer filled with surfing. But that didn't stop me from dreaming about moving here, even as an adult." He lifted the edge of his shirt to wipe sweat from his face, and I couldn't help it—I snuck a peek. He was six-packing it. "After college," he said, "I worked in Asheville. Stashed away as much cash as I could. Scrimped and saved. Then, when the timing was right, I got a job down here teaching the wee ones. And eventually, a cheap house on some cheap land. No water view, but I can hear the waves crashing some nights, when the wind blows right."

"Sounds nice."

"Callie your real name?"

"It's short for something."

"You're gonna make me guess? All right. Carolyn."

"I wish."

"Cathleen?"

"That also would be an upgrade."

"What about Calamity?"

"Very funny."

Just then, a fluffy golden dog bounded up to us and dropped a tennis ball at our feet. With a laugh Toby gave her a full-body scratch, then tossed the ball toward her owners, a white-haired couple who waved their thanks.

Moisture flecked the breeze, raising goose bumps on my skin despite the warm temperature of the late afternoon. Something was shifting inside me. The Tin Man incident aside, Toby seemed like an all-round decent guy.

"Want to go onto the pier?" he asked.

"I was on it earlier. It's freakishly unstable. I kind of can't believe it hasn't been condemned or something."

"That just makes it more fun, don't you think?"

I laughed. "If you say so." We slid into our flip-flops, then stepped onto the planks. Toby didn't seem fazed by how they creaked and shifted underfoot, and his relaxed manner eased my apprehension. A dozen or so anglers lined the railings, their rods nodding. Most of them said hello as we strolled past.

At the end of the pier, he asked, "Ready to learn your next move?"

"We're going to work out right here?"

"The swaying will provide extra challenge for balance. Kidding, not kidding." He stepped behind me. "What to do if someone attacks from back here. May I?"

"May you what?"

As he wrapped his arms around me, warmth flooded my body. The clove fragrance of his cologne was everywhere. And there it was, twirling inside me: a longing to let him in. To show him who I was. To be unfolded like a blanket or the pages of a letter.

"Okay," he said. "The first thing you want to do is swing your hips to the side. Either side."

I shifted left.

"Good. Now, take your right elbow and swing it back."

I did it in slow motion until I made contact with his ribs.

"You might hit him where it hurts, or you might hit him in the gut—doesn't matter. Just keep swinging."

I slow-elbowed Toby a second time. A third. A fourth.

"Eventually he'll let go." His grip loosened. "Or he'll back away, or shift, trying to escape the battering-ram elbow. And that's when you spin around. And as you do, you're gonna seize the guy's shoulders. Or his hair. Whatever's there."

Facing Toby, I gathered two fistfuls of his shirt.

"Good," he said. "Now pull him down toward your knee, which is flying up into his bad-guy face."

I did it in slow motion, raising my knee until it gently docked against the bridge of Toby's descending nose.

"Beautiful." He straightened up. His eyes melted into mine,

two-toned irises glinting in the setting sun. Gold around the pupils shimmering outward into mossy green. The sunlight accented reddish tints in his dark hair. "Ready to put it all together?" he asked.

That fluttery feeling in my chest intensified. Butterflies striving for liftoff.

Great. In addition to everything else I wanted—answers and justice and order—I now also wanted Toby's hazel eyes, his six-pack abs, his mint-condition, veggie-powered Wagoneer, his confident first aid skills, his duck decoys, and his corny expressions. *Guinea pigs unite*, for heaven's sake.

Him. I wanted him. I wanted Toby Dodge.

53

Hidden sight.

Hold on tight and you'll spy the hidden sight.

I'd just taken a shower and was standing in Hudson's bathroom, swaddled in my bathrobe, thinking. I traced two words onto the steamed-up mirror: *hidden sight.* The letters dripped, as if melting. I wiped them with my sleeve. They faded back: *hidden sight.*

I wiped them a second time. Again they reappeared.

I stared. Blinked away a vision of Bo Beauchamp's dancing toothpick as I suddenly understood something. "Holy . . ." I dashed down the hall, through the kitchen, through the woodshop.

Hudson had started a new surfboard. He turned off his palm sander as I raced by. "No running in my woodshop," he said. "What are you, five years old again?"

"Don't say anything." I climbed into my loft and retrieved the blank scroll. "Remember Mrs. Ouellette?" I said as I half climbed, half slid down the ladder. "My Girl Scouts leader?"

"I'm allowed to speak now?"

"When spoken to."

"I remember you as a Girl Scout. That cute sash you used to wear. Pigtails like handlebars and hardly any teeth inside your head."

I darted to the lamp shining on his worktable and angled the bendable arm. "Mrs. Ouellette was really into spy stuff, you know?"

"Like James Bond? Pens that cause explosions?"

"Like *and you'll* spy *the hidden sight.*"

"Huh?"

"This one time in Girl Scouts, we did this experiment. With lemon juice. Dip a toothpick into it. Use the toothpick as a sort of writing implement, and write whatever message you want on a piece of paper. Once it dries, it's invisible." I couldn't remember the exact science behind it, just my own excitement as my name vanished.

"I'm sure this is all relevant to something," Hudson said.

I stretched out the scroll and held it an inch or two underneath the lightbulb. "To make the message visible again—"

"What in the name of spaghetti and meatb—"

"*Shh.* Just wait."

Thirty seconds passed.

A full minute.

"Is that another riddle?" he asked. "You found another one?"

"Lightbulbs are different now than thirty years ago." I held the scroll as close as I dared to the heat source. "Energy efficient and all that. Maybe they no longer have the same effect on lemon juice—"

"Should I just keep standing here while you lose your mind?"

"Shh." Marks the color of maple syrup were beginning to form.

In a matter of seconds, letters appeared.

Two legible words, then three, then four . . .

My hands tremored. I stretched the scroll before his face.

He scowled. "What the heck does that mean?"

Judging by the handwriting, whoever penned the first riddle had penned the second, but with a different instrument and different ink.

Not ink. Lemon juice.

In my hands, the slip of paper had completely transformed. I read the amber letters over and over.

The hidden sight has been revealed.
Don't give up now. Stay even-keeled.
Slipper Truman will lead you to
the next adventurous little clue.

"Slipper Truman?" I crashed onto the dust-covered futon. We swung our feet—mine bare, his in construction boots—up onto an old storage trunk. He handed me his phone, and I punched *Slipper Truman* into the search window. "Nothing comes up," I said, scrolling. "Just some corny clothing website that markets to old dudes and sells tartan footwear called Truman slippers. You know, for lounging by the fire on a cold winter's night while smoking your pipe."

"Now, that sounds like a fine time."

"Maybe Slipper Truman meant something back in the day. But it doesn't mean jack now." I tossed the phone onto Hudson's lap. "You sure it doesn't ring a bell?"

"I'll consult the gang." He composed a text to Ronnie and Antoinette. "This is real Hardy Boys–type stuff, you know."

"It's looking more and more like just a bunch of nonsense to me."

"The first riddle wasn't."

"You're right. It wasn't. Wait here?" I got up and climbed into my loft. My phone sat on top of the chest of drawers, charging. I composed a text to Gwen:

I owe you an apology. I'd like to deliver it in person, but I understand if that's not a possibility. The other reason I'm texting is, you know that blank slip of paper we found? Turns out it's not blank. Do the words "Slipper Truman" mean anything to you?

Minutes later, dressed in pajamas, laptop in hand, I climbed back down. Hudson was still resting on the futon. "Let me get this straight," he said. "You found a second scroll, but it was blank. Except it wasn't blank. The riddle had been written in invisible ink."

"I found it halfway up the lighthouse, shoved into a tiny gap near the handrailing." I explained the connection I'd made the night before, when he'd said halfway was good enough.

"Halfway." He raked his fingertips through his beard. "Aren't you a smart cookie."

"There's something I could take a closer look at. You can help if you want." Sitting next to him, I opened my laptop and positioned it so we both could see. "Articles from the *Crier*, circa 1992."

"I thought you'd never ask."

"You mentioned those apartments near Eva's place being torn down after Mom died, and before a big storm. So I figure, let's zero in on hurricane season of that year. We might get more questions than answers. But it's worth a look."

"Try October. I feel like it was October."

He was right. The issue from the second week in October chronicled the demolition of the factory apartments. As I skimmed the before-and-after coverage, part of me hoped for some mention of Slipper Truman, or even Israel Overton. But I had to settle for wondering if any of the nameless laborers staring from the old photographs had known a secret. And just how dangerous that secret was. The men were shown playing harmonicas on porches, swinging lunch pails on the way to twelve-hour shifts. The women had short hair restrained by kerchiefs. They bent over their sewing machines, the floor littered with scraps.

By contrast, there was a then-current photograph of Pearleen in heavy makeup and a shoulder-padded blazer, posing next to a wrecking ball. In a short speech she quoted her father, Thornton Standish, who in 1959 declared, "It is the humble hard work of the artisans in my employ that has given the Standish name its fine international reputation for producing furniture of the highest standard."

"There's nothing here, really," I said. "Another dead end. Dead ends all over the place."

Hudson patted my knee. "At least you're covering all your bases."

"Wait. Look." I'd advanced to the following week's issue, dominated by a big storm rolling through town. "Hurricane Gregor. A Cat 4 that nearly wiped the entire Outer Banks off the map. It churned through Cattail just a few days before Halloween."

"Gregor. That was it. Hurricane Gregor. I remember pine cones hitting the roof like missiles. Thought they'd come right through." Together we perused the photographs of the destruction. An entire house flattened. Water up to the first-floor windows of the Queen Street businesses.

Forgotten memories burst in my mind. A stronger, leaner Hudson lugging bags of sand up the driveway, shoving them against the foundation. An angry, greenish sky. Hail the size of golf balls rocketing horizontally past the windows.

"If those old factory apartments hadn't been torn down," I said, "they might have been destroyed anyway. By Gregor." Just as I was about to shut my laptop, something caught my eye. A headline in the corner of the screen.

TOURISM TASK FORCE SEEKS ORIGINAL IDEAS

"Check it out," I said, zooming in.

He rubbed his eyes. "Read it to me, would ya?"

I obliged:

> "A small but enthusiastic crowd attended the first meeting of the newly formed Tourism Task Force, which met in the Gathering Room of the Cattail Library last Monday night.
>
> "The Tourism Task Force consists of Blinky Ames, Jedidiah Novac, and the author of this article, who were appointed by the Cattail Chamber of Commerce."

"Jed Novac passed away a while ago, didn't he?" I asked.

"He did. And Blinky Ames became worm food sometime last year, sorry to say."

I continued:

> "'I believe there must be ways Cattail can draft off the tourism dollars coming on to the other islands,' said Ames at the start of the meeting. 'How do we get visitors to take the ferry over to us and check out what Cattail has to offer?'
>
> "'I agree,' said Novac. 'We don't have the budget, or the notion, to advertise on NASCAR, like the bigger islands do. So the summer hordes will horde elsewhere. And Cattail will remain a quiet island in the Outer Banks. But can't we get the hordes to turn in our direction for day trips? Can't we get them spending money in our restaurants? Admiring our wild mustangs? Visiting our beautiful lighthouse and beaches?'

> "'We want to keep Cattail quaint,' added Ames. 'But we also want to welcome people. Whether you're here for a week, a month, or your whole lifetime, Cattail should feel like home.'
>
> "Chip deSilva of Standish Apartments, Muscadine Street, suggested a treasure hunt, 'a series of puzzles or riddles leading to a final hidden prize,' for the purpose of highlighting local landmarks and points of interest both historical and natural."

"Chip deSilva." I gripped my uncle's arm. "Did you know him?"

"I don't think so." He punched another text to Ronnie and Antoinette.

> "'The puzzles would be easy enough for the novice to solve, but challenging enough to satisfy the more seasoned treasure hunter,' deSilva told the committee.
>
> "He went on to describe his ultimate vision: an annual event that would naturally grow bigger each year, attracting treasure hunters from 'neighboring states and eventually the whole country,' which would of course increase tourism dollars in Cattail. 'Let's remind people why the chamber of commerce long ago declared Cattail Island the down-home isle that's worth your while,' deSilva said.
>
> "The treasure hunt was voted down two to one. Dissenters Ames and Novac cited liability concerns. The author of this article saw major potential and encouraged deSilva to approach the task force again in the future with a more fleshed-out plan.
>
> "Respectfully submitted by Faye Grossman on the 19th of October, 1992."

"Faye Grossman," I said. "That's the old lady Antoinette used to check in on, right?"

"Passed on like the rest of them, sorry to say."

I tapped the screen. "A treasure hunt was voted down. But he did it anyway, didn't he? Whoever this Chip deSilva was. He planted his treasure hunt without the approval of the task force. The rebel. Maybe his plan was to tell a few close friends. Have them do a sort of test run. And he could iron out the kinks from there. But they never got around to it."

"Why not?"

"Hurricane Gregor. This Chip deSilva dude must have figured his test-run treasure hunt was all lost. Washed away."

"But it wasn't."

"Nope." A thrill zipped up my spine. He could still be alive. What if I could speak to the man himself? I typed *Chip deSilva* into the search window but got no promising leads.

"Chip is a nickname for Charles, right?" I asked.

"Try it. I've never known a Charles or a Chip. Knew a Chuck once, but that doesn't help you."

Scores of Charles deSilvas from all over the world popped onto the screen. But apparently none of them ever had business with Cattail, North Carolina.

My fingers drubbed the keys: *What is Chip a nickname for?*

In addition to Charles: Christopher and Richard.

"*Richard?*" said Hudson, squinting over the results. "Who knew?"

But among the dozens of hits for both Christopher deSilva and Richard deSilva, none seemed to pertain to our particular Chip deSilva, who'd lived in Cattail thirty years ago.

Hudson's phone chimed once, twice. "The Gang has spoken. Responses to your queries." He handed over his device.

From Ronnie:

???????

From Antoinette:

Slipper Truman—no idea. Chip deSilva—those factory families kept to themselves, for the most part. I might not have crossed paths with him even when Cattail was a much smaller place.

54

The morning of the book signing had arrived. The MotherVine wasn't open yet but Antoinette was zinging around like a bee on speed, feathering the duster over the shelves. "I just love summer signing season," she said. "Especially when the authors are local."

The shop's official signing table was a round oak beast stored in Antoinette's office. Together, we dragged it to the bay window. Then I hauled over a box containing copies of Daisy Kapur's seafoam-green reference book, *Sharks of the Outer Banks*.

Antoinette showed me how to flap, which is when you tuck the book's front jacket into the title page for easy signing. I set to work, flapping the whole lot and in the process learning a little about Daisy. According to her bio, she'd studied sharks all over the world, including at the prestigious Woods Hole Oceanographic Institution in Massachusetts, and was now the lead marine biologist at the Cattail Island Wildlife Center. The book itself was loaded with facts about sharks commonly seen in this area.

When the flapping was done, I stacked the copies along the table's edge, fanning them so they curved like the steps of a grand staircase. Around the stacks I placed crape myrtle blossoms that had blown off the Queen Street trees overnight and landed near the MotherVine.

With the table prepared, I helped Antoinette bring the chalkboard outside. We were setting it up when the author arrived, pedaling a bicycle. Daisy Kapur sported an infectious smile, ombre hair swept up into a puff, and hoop earrings that kissed her cheeks. "Brought my own signing implement," she said, twirling a thick glitter marker.

Antoinette opened her box of chalk. "Do you prefer daisies or sharks? Either way, they're going to look like a four-year-old drew them."

Daisy laughed. "How about both?" She dismounted and steered her bike into the rack. I invited her inside, ushering her to the signing table. "Looks beautiful," she said.

"We're excited to have you. It's not every day we get a shark expert in the store. Congratulations on your book."

Tin Man pranced over, and Daisy scooped him up and loved on him. I took an extra-cute photo for Instagram, posting it with the caption:

> I'm a bit starstruck, darlings. Look who's visiting the MotherVine today. Cattail's own bona fide resident marine connoisseur . . .

"Coffee?" I offered.

"I'd love some." She gestured to her books. "But can you serve it with a tight lid?"

I excused myself and made a fresh pot. I leaned against the counter, trying not to rub my eyes as the coffee maker gurgled and dripped. I'd stayed up too late turning the pages of the Mary Higgins Clark book and was now fighting an urge to curl up in one of the reading chairs and close my eyes. Fortunately, the fragrance of coffee brewing had a way of sharpening my mind. It was like aromatherapy.

Inspired, I went over to one of the lavender pots and broke off a few sprigs. The buds' clean scent filled my nose. I paused the coffee maker, laid the sprigs on top of the grounds, and resumed brewing.

While I waited, I made another call to the historical society. I asked the woman who answered if the phrase *Slipper Truman* held any significance. But she was stumped, even after I explained it had something to do with a dormant treasure hunt. She also wasn't familiar with anyone named Chip, Charles, Christopher, or Richard deSilva.

When the coffee maker beeped, I poured some and brought it to Daisy. Antoinette had flung open the red door to the gathering shoppers, an even bigger bunch than the day before. At the front of Daisy's signing line was a comb-over'd gentleman showing her something on his phone. "Check it out," he said as I approached. "Dorsal fin of an apex predator." The photograph he'd snapped was out of focus, and the supposed fin looked to me like a big tongue depressor bobbing in the waves. But when I glanced at Daisy, she lifted her eyebrows and nodded.

I studied the pic some more, recognizing the smile of beach in the background. "Did you take this from the old fishing pier?" I asked him.

"That's right."

"You've come to the right place," I said. "Daisy's book is a wealth of information. And Daisy herself is a professional biologist who lives right here in Cattail."

"It's kismet, then," the man said. "That's exactly what I'm after."

"When'd you take that photograph?" she asked, as she signed her name in sparkling ink.

"Just this morning," he said. "I'm not the only person who saw it. I overheard some local fellas saying that shark had to be nine feet long."

"Only one kind of big fish that could be," she said.

"A bull shark?"

She handed over the book with a nod. "The most aggressive,

territorial, and dangerous shark. Bulls are diadromous, which means they can thrive in both salt water and freshwater. They like the brackish, shallow sounds of the Outer Banks to have their pups, because other kinds of sharks are only freshwater species and they can't follow them. No predators."

As she spoke, I opened a copy of her book to the middle section, where photographs were clustered. The bull shark was particularly terrifying, with its thickset body, sharp eyes, and a throat that seemed big enough to swallow an entire person in one gulp. I read the caption:

> If you're swimming, stand-up paddle boarding, or kayaking, and you encounter a bull shark, exit the water quickly and calmly. Make a still, silent, and extremely hasty retreat.

I shuddered. If Daisy and the local old-timers were declaring this tongue depressor a bull shark, then that's definitely what it was. Growing up on the Outer Banks, I'd seen my fair share of shark fins—from the safety of the sand. I'd even come across a dead hammerhead that had washed up onto Wonder Beach one Christmas morning when I was home visiting and had taken Scupper for a romp.

I'd never encountered a living shark close-up, though. And I wanted to keep it that way.

"Everybody talks about great whites being the big baddies," Daisy was saying. "But bulls actually have a stronger bite force." My face must have blanched, because she put her hand on my arm and chuckled. "Don't worry," she said. "To date, there's never been any kind of shark attack in Cattail waters."

I brought a cup of coffee outside to Antoinette, who was crouched before the chalkboard, blue chalk smeared on her neck.

"Nice," I said, indicating her artwork. She'd drawn a cartoonish shark with a long daisy chain hooked onto its fin. The flowers framed the text in the middle of the board. "Good crowd in there," I said.

"Great crowd." She straightened up and accepted my offering. "So, who's Slipper Truman?"

"No idea. Get this, though." I told her about Chip deSilva. About the second riddle, and the invisible lemon juice, kept cool for decades inside the lighthouse bricks until heat from a lightbulb oxidized a hidden message. I also mentioned Red Feather Earrings. "I've seen her twice now, and both times, she turned and bolted. She's about my age. Yesterday she was in the cemetery all by herself wearing a hello-my-name-is name tag. I didn't get close enough to make out her name, though."

"You really do bring the weird, Callie. Or is it just that I haven't had coffee yet?"

"I'm like a weird magnet. I mean, who wears a name tag to a cemetery? Maybe it's nothing. But I've got a question for you. Were treasure hunts ever a thing in Cattail? In the nineties, or even earlier?"

"Not that I recall."

"That old lady you used to check in on, Faye Grossman. Do you remember her ever talking about a Tourism Task Force? She was on it at one point, in the early nineties."

"Oh, she talked about all sorts of things. Including racoon-aliens stealing the peanut butter from her pantry. I'm afraid poor Faye didn't have a lot of marbles left by the time I came into her life." Antoinette blew on her coffee and took a sip. "What's going on with this? It's . . . floral."

"I harvested some of your lavender."

"Lavender is difficult to keep alive. It's not the type of plant you just help yourself to."

"Sorry. I didn't know."

She tipped the cup for another sip, then raised an eyebrow. "Is this what you had in mind when you said we should up our hot beverage game?"

"Maybe. What about lavender lattes? We could look into an espresso maker. And what about lavender tea? Our own blend. Lavender hot chocolate in the winter. *Iced* lavender hot chocolate for a Christmas-in-July theme."

"Your mother always said I should do a Christmas-in-July thing," Antoinette said.

"She did?"

"She used to throw out suggestions like that all the time. Used to sit right there in that front chair with her legs tucked underneath her, a book in her lap. 'Hey, Ant. Ever think about a popcorn machine? One of those old-fashioned carnival ones, with the wheels.'" Antoinette's impression of my mother was spot-on.

We held each other's gaze, sharing a smile at the memory. And then Daisy came running outside, waving her phone. "There's been another death. The *Crier*'s live-tweeting about it—"

"What?" My vision tunneled. All I could see was Daisy's hand, holding her phone. My voice somehow sounded like it was coming from the other side of the street. "Here? In Cattail? Another body?"

"Over at the lighthouse. The keeper's cottage."

55

Arms crossed, feet spread, Officer Fusco stood on the porch of Gwen's cottage. "Beat it, AC," she said as I sprang from my car. "I just got rid of Trish Berryman, and she's press. Real, actual press."

"Where's Gwen?" I took the porch steps two at a time. "Is she okay?"

The grave look on Fusco's face confirmed my worst fear. Past her, through the threadbare curtains and beyond the open front door, I glimpsed Gwen's body stretched on the battered couch.

My knees turned to goo. I put a hand on the railing, steadying myself. "I'm here as a friend," I said. "Your friend. Gwen's friend. I might be able to help—"

"You can't go inside."

"I can't believe she blew a point-four-one," Dr. Scarboro said as she stepped onto the porch, removing exam gloves. When she saw me, she nodded a somber greeting. "There's a way to measure the blood alcohol level of a deceased person using a Breathalyzer," she said by way of explanation.

"It's a two-person job," Fusco added.

"Is that the cause of death?" I asked. "Alcohol poisoning?"

"I'll wait until I get her on the slab before I give the official word," Dr. Scarboro said.

"She was in recovery," I said.

Fusco removed her cap. "She should have stayed there."

A heavy heat pooled behind my eyes. The last time Gwen and

I had spoken, we'd stood right past that door. Band-Aids fluttering, her voice shrill. Had events transpired a little differently, we might have grown to like each other. Maybe we would have become coffee-and-scones friends, or tree-climbing friends, or friends with a shared love of Mary Higgins Clark.

Fusco took a step toward me. "I don't doubt your heart's in the right place. But you really need to head on back to work. We've got everything under control—"

"Who the hell is this guy?" Jurecki thundered out the door. He waved the photograph from the frame on Gwen's bedside table, the photo of her and the handsome middle-aged man.

Fusco took it and flipped it over. "I'd say it's Mack, sir."

"That's stellar police work. Who exactly is Mack? It's the only photograph in the whole damn house. He must be somebody important. A professor? An uncle? A sugar daddy?" Jurecki snatched the photo from Fusco. He'd been calm and cool at the scene of Eva's death. Now he seemed wound up. Nervous. He noticed me. "What are you doing here? Fusco, what is she doing here?"

"I might know who's in the photo," I said. "Could I see?"

Jurecki grumbled something, then passed me the photograph.

In the image, their arms were wrapped around each other. The man wore a puffy vest, Gwen a fleece jacket. Other people mingled, mid-conversation, holding cans of soda and semi-eaten hotdogs and cupcakes. Behind them was a picnic table. A sign, the words cut off, PEAKE the only visible letters.

On the back of the photograph was written *Me and Mack!!*

"He's her Alcoholics Anonymous sponsor," I said.

"Mack the AA sponsor got a last name?" Jurecki asked. "And any chance you know Gwen's password?" He waggled a cell phone. For the first time I noticed it was sheathed in a heavy-duty case, the kind construction workers use. Gwen probably considered herself a klutz, so she'd gone for the most protection money could buy.

I shifted to my left, craned my neck until I saw her lifeless feet dangling from the couch cushion. High arches, long toes, cotton-candy-pink nail polish. She was dressed for bed—plaid pajama pants similar to the ones I favored. Her arm was flung to the side, fingers curled above an empty plastic bottle, tipped over. Her preferred rotgut.

Scarboro went back inside and began packing up her kit.

Handing back the photo to Jurecki, I tried to swallow. My mouth felt sandpapered. "Are the two deaths related, Chief? Eva and Gwen?"

"They are emphatically unrelated. And you need to be getting back to the bookshop now."

"You aren't even going to consider the possibility that there's a connection here?"

"What connection? Eva jumped. This poor girl pickled herself." He slapped the photograph against his palm a few times. "Did Gwen talk to you about any family? Close relatives or friends?"

"Not by name," I said. "As far as I know, she most recently lived in Chesapeake. But that's not where she was from."

"We know where she was from," he said.

A car pulled up. A watermelon-shaped man practically jumped out from behind the wheel. Ralph Burrus, head of the nonprofit that oversaw the lighthouse. He marched right up to Jurecki and jabbed a finger in his face. "We're losing revenue at the height of the season, Chief. Revenue we can't afford. Another closure? Don't cast a pall over the whole town. Don't ruin summer."

Jurecki put a big hand on the back of Mr. Burrus's fuzzy neck. "You're out of line, Ralph. Let's take a walk." The two men descended the porch steps and ambled toward the lighthouse, where another officer kept a gathering of tourists and locals from approaching the structure. They must have arrived for the day's first tour, only to be turned away.

It was just me and Fusco again. "Who found Gwen?" I asked.

"A guy doing odd jobs for the conservationists. Some college kid. He's on-island for the summer."

My eyes widened. "Reedley Anderson? Is he still here?" When she didn't answer, I peeked around her, this time through the kitchen window, and spied the back of a tousled, sun-bleached head. Reedley Anderson was indeed still here. "You've got to let me talk to him, Fusco," I said. "I'll be lightning fast. And then I'll leave. Promise."

Glancing upward, she shook her head. Then she stepped aside, sweeping an arm toward the kitchen. "Two minutes."

I entered the cottage.

I wished I hadn't glimpsed Gwen's face. Wished her hair was strewn across it, blocking the miscomprehending expression, bloodshot eyes, parted lips, as if she were about to ask a question. Her pallor reminded me of the sky before a storm.

Turning away, I found Reedley Anderson in the kitchen, slumped in a vinyl-and-chrome chair, fiddling with his leather bracelets. He was dressed for his pottery gig in a clay-stained but otherwise clean T-shirt.

He half stood when I entered. He introduced himself, even though he seemed to know who I was. He must have recognized me from his make-out sesh with Gwen on Wednesday night. That Reedley had been suave and triumphant. This Reedley was anything but. His eyes were puffy and his cheeks were streaky and he didn't make eye contact.

"I'm so sorry," I said, taking a seat at the table. On it were two take-out cups stained with sloshed-over coffee and a bunch of black-eyed Susans tied with string.

He eyed the flowers and nodded.

"Gwen and I were sort of friends," I said. "If you want to talk about it, I'm a good listener."

"I parked right there." He pointed out the window at his Fiat. I must have been so anxious when I pulled up to the cottage that I didn't even notice it. "I was going to surprise her with coffee before she had to go to work," he said.

"And flowers."

"Yes, ma'am. Picked them on the side of the road. When I pulled up, something didn't feel right. The screen door was banging open. I knocked on it and when she didn't come to the door, I let myself in and . . ." He shielded his face with a hand.

"Did you see anyone else?"

His Adam's apple bobbed a few times before he said, "No, ma'am."

Behind me came the sound of someone clearing her throat. Then I heard Fusco's voice. "Time's up."

Back outside, an ambulance was pulling up. Two EMTs got out and angled a gurney up the cottage steps.

I leaned against my car, my hands shaking.

Gwen Montgomery. If there were any witnesses to what happened to Eva, who more likely than the lighthouse keeper? Gwen must have known something. Something someone didn't want her to know.

I remembered the photo of her and Mack. The letters PEAKE on the sign.

On my phone, I punched *Mack + Chesapeake* into the search window.

The first hit was a church. I tried the number. "Virginia Beach Evangelical Church of the Chesapeake," answered a chipper woman.

"I'm not sure I've got the right place, but I'm looking for someone named Mack. Could you help me?"

"Sure can. Mack's just leaving. Let me see if I can catch her."

Another woman, even more chipper, said, "This is Mack. May I help you?"

"Oh," I said. "I think I have the wrong Mack."

"This is Sally MacLennan. I go by Mack. I'm the administrative assistant."

"The Mack I need to speak with is a man, possibly in his fifties. He may have been photographed outside your church not long ago, at some sort of gathering. An Alcoholics Anonymous meeting?"

"I see. There's a local AA chapter that uses our pavilion and grounds from time to time, but beyond that, we don't have much interaction with them."

"I'm trying to inform him of—I don't suppose you could give me a contact name?"

"What is this in reference to, sweetheart? I'm not sure I caught your name."

"I'm on the Outer Banks, and there's been a death."

"I'm so sorry to hear that. I wish I could put my finger on the information you're looking for, but I'm afraid I'm not going to be much help to you." She took my number and promised to pass it along if the opportunity arose.

I scrolled through the remaining results for *Mack + Chesapeake*. Nothing caught my eye—until the fifth or sixth listing. Mack's Appliance Repair and Handyman Services. I clicked it, and right on the home page was a photograph of the owner and operator, Mack Abruzzi, posing next to a cube truck. The same square-jawed, twinkle-eyed man from Gwen's bedside photograph.

I dialed. It rang. A click, followed by a smooth male voice.

"Hello." I took a breath—and the voice continued. "Thanks for contacting Mack's. Please leave a detailed message after the beep and I'll get back to ya posthaste. Have a good one." *B-e-e-e-e-e-e-p.*

"Hello, Mr. Abruzzi. My name is Callie Padget, and I'm on the Outer Banks. I'm calling because you and I know someone in common. Gwen Montgomery? And unfortunately, I'm afraid there's some—some very awful news. Could you please call me back as soon as you get the chance?"

I hung up with a sigh, and the thought that Cattail had failed Gwen Montgomery. But she'd died believing it was the other way around—that Cattail was going to be her fresh start.

A fresh start.

Her sobriety date.

That was it. The password.

"Officer?" I called.

A second later Fusco's dark uniform filled the doorway. "Unbelievable. You're still here?"

"Six-two-two." She gave me a blank look. "The code to Gwen's phone," I said.

"It's six digits."

"Try oh-six, two-two, one-nine. And one other thing. Mack's last name is Abruzzi."

It was hard to tell if she was squinting or scowling as she gazed past me. The TV news van was crunching toward the cottage. I'd figured they would make an appearance. One death might not make for big news, but a second death, six days later, in the same location? Different story.

Fusco muttered something that sounded like *parasites* before ducking back inside. She reemerged a minute later, shaking her head and holding Gwen's still-locked phone. "Bad guess."

The television reporter—the same pastel wonder I'd seen at

the lighthouse—rushed toward the porch, cameraman in tow. Fusco blocked their path. "Hold it right there, ma'am. Sir."

The reporter lifted her microphone. "Have you identified the body? Do you suspect foul play? Does—"

"You can direct all your questions to the chief after he comes back. In the meantime, please get back inside your vehicle." When the reporter hesitated, Fusco lifted her arm. "Go." Then she turned to me. "You too. I've asked you how many times now?"

"Please just listen?" I waited until the news crew had turned away before continuing. "Gwen very well might have a tattoo. On her right collarbone. The reverse image of some numbers." On Smile Beach, Gwen had said she would get her new sobriety date tattooed in reverse image on her left collarbone, so that when she looked in the mirror . . . *My right collarbone's already occupied*, she'd said.

What if it was occupied by a tattoo of her *first* sobriety date?

Fusco stuck her free thumb through a belt loop. "And these back-asswward numbers will just so happen to be the passcode to her phone?"

Coming out of the officer's mouth, it sounded preposterous. But what if? "How long would it take to get into that phone if you had to send it away to some lab?" I asked. "Or wait around for a technician, or whatever your process is? Versus having a quick peek underneath Gwen's top, right now."

"I did notice some ink. When I was assisting the ME with the Breathalyzer."

I raised both hands. "I'm not telling you what to do, but isn't it worth a shot?"

A minute later, holding Gwen's phone, I hovered in the cramped living room. Fusco approached the gurney as a pudgy EMT with long sideburns unzipped the bag. He handed Fusco a pair of gloves, which she snapped on. Without touching her own skin or uniform, she made the sign of the cross. Her hands disappeared inside the bag.

"Well?" I said.

"There are backward numbers tattooed on the right collarbone. Looks like . . . oh-one, one-oh, one-seven."

I punched them into the phone. No go. I thought for a second. "Read them to me backward."

"Seven-one, oh-one, one-oh."

I punched them in again. Then I held up the phone. "You're in."

56

If Cattail Island had been on edge the past few days, now it was going to become downright panicked.

Driving, I couldn't stop thinking about Gwen.

And then my thoughts shifted to Summer.

I ended up at the hardware store and had to park a block away. Meeks's wasn't yet open, but the street parking was already taken, and tourists crowded the sidewalk. They were buzzing. *Did you hear someone else died? I'm not sure I feel safe here in Cattail anymore.* I made my way to the front of the line, where Georgia crouched, replacing the tea lights around Eva's memorial. She was dressed elegantly, burnout top, hi-lo skirt, looking more ready for a night at the theater than a shift at the hardware store.

"Have you heard?" I asked.

She straightened up, a lighter torch in her hands. "The *Crier*'s all over it. Listen to Trish's latest gem." She produced her phone. "'The most recent keeper of Cattail Lighthouse was young, fresh from a master's program and bursting with ideas for bringing the 140-year-old beacon into the twenty-first century. Now she's dead. Is she the latest victim of the Cattail curse?'"

I stepped closer. "Were you able to ask your parents about Bo Beauchamp?"

"They both agreed he wouldn't hurt a fly. My dad said, 'The past is the past.' And Mom said, 'Just because someone's rough around the edges doesn't make him rough around the heart.' That's my parents for you. They were unconvinced that the wheelbarrow incident was something to worry about." She stooped to light the last tea light.

"If there's anything I can do . . ." I faltered, and Georgia said nothing more. I was about to turn and go, not wanting to add to her distress. But once she got the flame flickering, she glanced up at me.

"Summer will want to see you," she said. "Wait here while I go get her."

A moment later, Summer came out. Kneepads dwarfed her skinny legs. A pencil was tucked behind her ear, and the kangaroo pocket of her sweatshirt sagged with weight. She propped the door open and shoppers filed inside. When it was just her and me on the sidewalk, she pulled out *While My Pretty One Sleeps*. "This is really good."

"I'm glad you like it." I retrieved the second scroll from my bag. "I've been hoping for a chance to tell you about this."

Studying the words, Summer was silent. Finally, she looked up. "My mom . . ."

"You were right, Summer. She was looking for something on Saturday night. But it wasn't at the top of the lighthouse. It was at the halfway point."

"'Climb through blue and into white.' Just into it. Not through it."

"Exactly."

"Slipper Truman?"

"That's the million-dollar question." I explained the lemon juice. The hidden sight. Chip deSilva, who back in the day defied the Tourism Task Force. "He probably figured the clues he planted got washed away in the storm, along with everything else in town," I said. "And that was that."

"Where is he now?"

"I'm trying to find out. I *will* find out."

"What if Slipper Truman is an anagram for something?"

Sudden understanding splashed me like ice water. An anagram! "Like when the letters in a word are all scrambled up, right?" I asked.

"Yeah. And you have to put them in the right order. Unscramble them to form a word." She reached into her pocket again, this time pulling out a grimy softcover book, which she handed to me. "They're addicting," she said.

The book contained page after page of anagrams, each one associated with a cartoonish riddle. In order to solve the riddle, you had to unscramble the letters of four words, sometimes six.

That explained the pencil perpetually resting behind Summer's ear.

I flipped through the book. She had solved about two-thirds. "Do you think you could solve Slipper Truman?" I asked.

"It's out of context. The anagrams in that book are all part of larger pieces. You have hints. Themes." Her eyes filled with tears.

My intention had been to make her feel better. Useful. To give her the *Camp Cottontown Funbook* and ask if she knew anything about it. But I'd gone and screwed that up, and now the sight of Summer's crumpling face sent a fresh ripple of determination through me.

"You don't have to solve anything," I said. "You don't have to *do* anything. I'm going to set everything straight. I promise."

57

I put in a few hours at the MotherVine. After Daisy left, only a handful of her books remained—one happy outcome in an otherwise dreadful day. I was in Antoinette's office, opening a can of chicken pâté for the drooling Tin Man when my phone buzzed. A call from Virginia Beach.

I answered. "Is this Mack Abruzzi?"

"I saw it on the news."

"I'm sorry, Mr. Abruzzi. You two must have been close."

"Call me Mack. I can't believe it. I really can't. I'm gutted. Just gutted."

"I met up with her a few times this week. We'd gotten together over a news event that's happened here."

"The death at the lighthouse. She told me all about it." From Mack's end came the slow, steady sound of footfalls. He must have been strolling. "She told you about me?" he asked.

"She had your picture in a frame beside her bed."

"Did she?"

"Mack, thanks for getting back to me. I know this is very difficult, but I was wondering if you might be able to meet me. If you're feeling up to it."

"Couldn't we just talk now, on the phone?"

We could. But I felt the strong need to behold Mack Abruzzi in the flesh. If there was one thing I knew from working as a reporter, it was that in-person interviews were dramatically more valuable than phone interviews. Nothing like soaking up someone's presence, observing their facial expressions and body language, their tics and reactions and humanness. "It's probably a conversation we should have in person," I said. "This is hard to explain, but something's not sitting right with me. Something's off. And you're one of the few people Gwen seemed to have trusted. If I could just speak with you about it all . . ." I bit my lip, hoping he would get it and relieve me of my rambling. Hoping he wouldn't consider me needy or crazy.

"I'm not about to drive to the Outer Banks on a Friday afternoon during high season," he said.

"Oh. Right. I understand—"

"But if you want to come up here, you're welcome to."

I had to wait for the next ferry.

After that, it was a ninety-minute drive to Virginia Beach.

It was going to be a long evening.

Mack Abruzzi wasn't hard to spot. The restaurant lounge was more or less empty, and the only guy at the bar reminded me of a workaday George Clooney, eating Beer Nuts and nursing Coke from a glass. For a handyman, he had an overall smooth appearance, one that matched his voice.

I had no reason to implicitly trust this man. But what was the alternative? Believing everyone I met could have killed Eva Meeks? *And* Gwen Montgomery?

Besides, we were in a public place. "Mack?" I said, approaching.

He gripped my hand in a manly shake, then gestured to a second soda fizzing on the bar. "Took the liberty."

I so seldom drank Coke that the sweetness exploded inside my mouth, coating my tongue, my palate, my brain, in chemical sugar.

"The cops from your town left me a message," he said as I tried to wrangle my face into a normal expression. "Gwen said she liked you—that is, until she didn't. But she didn't have *any* compliments for the cops down in Cattail." He drained his drink, tipping the glass until the ice crashed against his lips. "You ever just feel an instant connection to somebody? Gwen and me were like that. Am I babbling? I'm not sure it's sunk in yet. All this."

"Me neither."

"I was fond of the kid, you know? I have a son her age."

I felt suddenly restless—no doubt a result of the long drive, the Coke, and the subject matter. "Any chance you'd rather go for a walk?"

"Bars haven't been my scene since the nineties." He hopped off the stool. "And from the looks of it, Coke isn't your drink."

A light rain misted the street. We strolled past a church that had been converted into a club. A line of twenty-somethings extended out front.

"When's the last time you saw her?" Mack asked.

"Wednesday night," I said. "We'd had an argument, actually. A misunderstanding. Last night, I texted her an olive branch. But she didn't text back. And then this morning . . . How long have you known Gwen?"

"Couple years. Became her sponsor more recently. I'd never sponsored anyone before, so she had to work on me. You did know about that, right? That she was an alcoholic?"

"Yes. I'd like to know more about her background. Her family situation, for example."

"Her parents and a couple brothers are up in New Jersey. She's the youngest of five or six kids, all of them *mega successful*. That was her phrase for it. They're doctors and lawyers. One of her sisters is literally a rocket scientist in Texas. Has the highest security clearance at NASA. Gwen just didn't get those same genes. Didn't have that killer instinct. That's not to say she wasn't ambitious. Quite the contrary."

"She loved that lighthouse."

"It was more than that. It was almost like she thought of herself as its parent. She wanted to be a warden, a guardian."

"A caretaker."

At a convenience store, we rounded the corner. A bicyclist zoomed by, faster than the traffic. "She wanted to prove to her parents that you don't need to make a lot of money to be successful," Mack said.

"Did you ever meet her parents?"

"I don't have to meet them to know something about them."

"Meaning?"

"Let's just say, not a lot of alcoholics wax nostalgic about their happy childhoods." He ran a hand through his copious silver hair. "Earlier this week I told Gwen I was gonna drive down to the Outer Banks and see her. I told her we could talk in person. She sounded like she was coming undone."

"When was the last time you spoke with her?"

"Her lunch break yesterday. She said she was going to call me later. She didn't. I called her three times last night. She didn't pick up."

"She had a blood alcohol level of point-four-one."

Mack stopped. "That bastard. That monster inside. Buried deep. Deep in here." He thumped a fist against his breastbone and continued walking. "I just can't believe it got her."

"But what if it didn't? The cops, the medical examiner—*they* say she drank herself to death. And maybe she did. But what if she was *forced* to behave that way? What if she wasn't acting of her own volition?" I waited for Mack's response as a scenario played out in my mind: Gwen raising that bottle to her mouth over and over—because someone was making her. Someone who wanted to get away with murder.

"You know something?" Mack said. "Alcoholics can be very skilled liars. I know from experience. But all those times Gwen told me she really, truly wanted to get sober? Those weren't lies. So now that you mention it, I have to admit, I *am* having a hard time believing she did this to herself by choice. Even considering how upset she was about seeing those people."

"What people?"

"At the top of the lighthouse. The night that Eva woman fell."

I touched his arm. We stood face-to-face as three joggers went around us.

"You didn't know," he said. "She didn't tell you."

Tuesday night. The night Gwen and I made our first climb up the lighthouse together. We'd gone all the way, searched, found nothing. After, at ground level, she'd said *They made their own choices that night*. She'd punched her palm. I could see her, windbreaker rippling as she'd denied the slip of the tongue. Blamed it on exhaustion. She'd all but told me she'd seen people up there.

I should have pressed her when I had the chance. But maybe I'd have scared her away. "There were hints," I said. "Hints that she knew something. That she was afraid. I couldn't get many straight answers out of her. I failed to win her trust." We resumed walking. A traffic light stained the wet street yellow, then red. "How many people did she see at the top of the lighthouse?" I asked.

He held up two fingers. "One of them must have been the woman named Eva."

"What else did she tell you about the night Eva died? Anything you can think of. Anything at all."

"She thought it was around ten thirty when she saw those people. She kept talking about it. All week I kept saying, 'Go to the police, Gwen.' But she wouldn't." We'd arrived back at the restaurant. "What do you think really happened last night?" he asked.

"I intend to find out."

The truth was, I thought Gwen was forced to drink. I thought whoever killed Eva had come for Gwen. She didn't hide those things in her trunk. Eva's killer had. That's how the killer found out Gwen was concealing a drinking problem. And what brand of rum to buy.

Had it been Bo Beauchamp? Or a hitman hired by the Standishes? What if Ralph Burrus was offing people to create a perverse pop-culture interest in the lighthouse? His harassing Chief Jurecki was just part of his cover.

What if Reedley Anderson was a psychopathic serial killer? Eva and Gwen had both been single working women. Both blondes. What if he'd killed them, and his tearful lovelorn act in Gwen's kitchen was just that—an act?

Or the killer was someone else entirely. Someone who had found out about the treasure hunt. Someone who believed real, actual treasure was to be found, and murdered out of greed . . .

"Just a couple more questions," I said as Mack put a hand on his truck door. "Did Gwen ever mention anything about her boss, Mr. Burrus?"

"She said he was a nice enough guy, but old." He chuckled. "She thought everybody was old."

"What about Reedley?"

He shook his head. "Who's that?"

"Cute boy. He and Gwen were extra-friendly."

"She wouldn't have told me about that. When you're working the steps, getting involved in intimate relationships is frowned upon. Even casual ones. I would have frowned. Big-time."

I nodded. It was looking like Gwen kept all kinds of secrets from all kinds of people. "I'll be in touch if anything comes up," I said, extending my hand. "Thank you, Mack."

I'm not a hugger, least of all when it comes to people I've just met. But when Mack Abruzzi pulled me in, I didn't tense. In fact, my cheek sank into his shirt, and I closed my eyes and rested that way for an extra second or two.

I felt safe.

That must have been how he'd made Gwen feel too.

58

On the freeway, driving back to the ferry that would take me to Cattail Island, I kept thinking about Gwen's final moments. How confusion filled they must have been. Terror filled.

But that wasn't something I wanted to think about.

Steering one-handed, I got out my phone.

Two missed calls, both from Pearleen Standish.

Huh.

Had Whitman delivered my message? That I'd wanted her side of the story before going public with damning information?

I rang Pearleen, but she didn't answer. I left a generic saw-that-you-called voicemail, inviting her to try me again, anytime. Then I dialed Toby.

"I was just thinking about you," he answered. "I have something kind of funky in mind for your next lesson."

My heavy mood lifted at the playfulness in his voice. "I don't know if I like the sound of that."

"Tomorrow afternoon? My place. Wear boots."

I looked over my shoulder to change lanes, heading for the big green sign that said OUTER BANKS. "Can you talk?" I asked. "Why do people say that when what they really mean is, 'Can you listen?'"

"I can definitely listen."

I painted a vague but accurate portrait of my week. Broad strokes. How Eva Meeks had inadvertently resurrected a treasure hunt, one she'd potentially died for, and Summer had secretly recruited me to get to the bottom of it, because she wasn't satisfied the police or anyone in her family would . . .

"Wow," he said when I'd finished. "There's a lot more to you than meets the eye. You're a tempest-in-a-teacup kind of person."

I'd never heard myself described that way. It was true, I supposed. Placid exterior, tumultuous interior.

"Are you okay?" he asked.

"Keeping my head above water."

"Whoever chased you the other night. The sticky note. *Back off.* That's all tied in somehow?"

"I don't see how it couldn't be."

"And the poor lighthouse keeper?"

"Same."

"They announced her official cause of death."

"Let me guess. Alcohol poisoning."

"You don't entirely believe that, do you?"

I sighed. "I don't know what to believe."

59

In total darkness, I climbed the Elder Tree. My fingers examined the bumpy bark as if it were imparting a secret crucial message. But a sudden light transformed the tree into a whirlpool of seawater. The cattail crown my mom had made slipped from my head. I hadn't even realized I was wearing it. I reached for it, but it tumbled into the water. The spinning electric waves tore the crown apart—

I jolted upright.

A dream. Only a dream.

Switching on the bedside light, I forced a few breaths.

I'd been seven years old the very first time I slept in my tree house. Hudson had built it that fall, once the summer heat had begun to fade, using two-by-fours from our neighbor's old toolshed that had collapsed. Mom made a rug out of old beach towels, and curtains out of a tablecloth.

That first night, the owls wouldn't shut up. Mr. and Mrs. Owl, my mother had nicknamed them.

"Mom?" I called. The tree house was a stone's throw from her bedroom window. "*Mom?*"

Her face appeared behind the screen. "Can't sleep? Come inside."

"Or you could come out here."

She thought about it. "Gimme a minute."

I watched from my window as her flashlight bobbed over the

grass. She climbed up, spread out a sleeping bag next to me, collapsed on top of it, and was snoring within minutes. I woke up a few hours after that—I knew because the moonlight had shifted, and Mr. and Mrs. Owl no longer hooted—to my mom burrowing under my blanket. Spooning me, she kissed my neck. "I hate sleeping alone," she whispered, half-awake, as she pulled me close. "Give me some more pillow."

Past daybreak, I awoke to the sounds of munching and swishing. Mom stood looking out the window. I stumbled over. The mustangs were at it. Four or five of them, flicking their tails and hoofing the ground for acorns to snack on. The wild herd had lived on Cattail longer than people, having descended from the horses that survived shipwrecks off the coast. Around the time I moved to Charlotte, the herd was corralled inside the Mustang Beach area. But back when I was growing up, they wandered wherever they pleased, scratching their necks on fenceposts and telephone poles and plucking persimmons from front-yard trees.

"Aren't they relaxing?" Mom said, petting my hair. "I love when they come around."

"Me too."

The cattail crown was hanging on a nail near the corner. My mom lifted it and placed it on my head, but it was too big and slipped down over my eyes.

"Now you're a princess," she said. "The princess of the mustangs."

"If I'm the princess, you're the queen."

Her laugh made a small sadness blossom inside my chest. "Cattails are very versatile, you know," she said. "Versatile means you can use them for lots of things."

"Like what?"

"Like if you get a cut or a scrape, you can use the cattail to heal it. The Native Americans lined their moccasins with cattail seeds for warmth. Did you know that?"

"What else?"

"You can make a weatherproof shelter with dried cattails. You can even make cattail moonshine, but I've never tried it."

"What's moonshine?"

"A naughty drink for grown-ups."

We heard Hudson booming then. "Where is everybody?"

Mom went over to the cutout in the floor. "You're getting warmer. Warmer . . ."

"The one morning I decide to come over with breakfast, and you're all disappeared." Hudson passed up a box of doughnuts, a tray of take-out coffees, and a handful of sugar packets.

"Why'd you get three coffees?" Mom asked as her brother huffed up the ladder.

"Two bears, one cub."

"She's seven, Hud. Seven-year-olds don't drink coffee."

Click-zip-hiss. He lit a cigarette. "I did."

"You never."

"I'll drink it," I said.

Mom took the cup intended for me, dumped three-quarters of it out the window, and tapped in some sugar. "Here, Callie," she said, swirling the cup as she passed it. "And not another drop until you're seventeen or so."

The two adults sat cross-legged and selected their doughnuts.

I brought the cup to my lips, sipped, and gagged. "Is this a naughty drink for grown-ups?"

Hudson roared with laughter. "Next time I'll get her a hot chocolate."

"We'll make an uncle out of you yet," Mom said, taking a drag off his cigarette.

~

Coffee.

Just the thought was enough to reel in my mind.

I threw off the covers, careful not to disturb the crown on the pillow next to me. Careful, too, not to disturb *While My Pretty One Sleeps*. I thought about Neeve Kearny. How she honors her curiosity, following it to the next clue, and the next, and the next, until she pieces together the mystery and solves the disappearance of her most loyal customer, the ballsy reporter Ethel. Her body is found wearing a certain striped blouse, one Ethel didn't prefer. It's a detail the police don't think is important. But Neeve knows it is. If Ethel didn't dress herself, then someone else did. Her killer. He had good reason to change her outfit before hiding her body. And that particular blouse meant the killer could only be one man . . .

Maybe good old MHC would rub off on me after all. What had I been doing all week if not honoring my curiosity, like Neeve? And while it didn't feel as though much was working out, I *had* discovered things that might yet turn out to be useful. Like the second hidden scroll, and the name of the man who'd planted the treasure hunt Eva had unearthed. Or at least his nickname. Chip deSilva.

And that was when some eureka logic clicked, the way it sometimes does after a vivid dream. Maybe the very name deSilva was a clue. Unlike many of the old Outer Banks surnames, deSilva didn't evoke the British Isles. So maybe his first name didn't, either.

The most obvious variation of Richard, Charles, or Christopher—or at least the first one that came to me in the predawn surrealness—was Ricardo.

Ricardo deSilva. Why not?

I snatched my phone and punched in a search. Ricardo deSilva is an extremely popular name the world over, including as far away as Namibia. But deep on the third page of results, I scored a hit closer to home. An Asheville, North Carolina, newspaper obituary from ten years ago.

> WOODFIN—Ricardo "Chip" deSilva, formerly of 393 Black Bear Mountain Road, Asheville, died Saturday in Woodfin Nursing Home. He was 88. Born in Bermuda in 1922, deSilva immigrated to the United States in the 1950s and lived in coastal North Carolina until settling in Asheville in 1993. He was a retired furniture maker whose hobbies included calligraphy, sketching, and arranging treasure hunts for friends.

60

A sunrise and a cup of coffee later, I got a liquid breakfast going—a green smoothie consisting of kale, peanut butter, a banana, extra cinnamon, and ice water. While it blended, I mimicked the breakout move Toby had showed me, to use if you're grabbed from behind. Hips to the side, elbow back, spin around, grab the face, slam it into your knee. In the kitchen I practiced it ten times, till I was out of breath.

Then, with Scupper trotting alongside me, I carried my smoothie onto Hudson's dock. I sat with my feet in the brackish water, away from the whine of my uncle's saw. At 8:58 I stuck earbuds into my ears. And the second my phone showed nine a.m., I dialed the nursing home where Chip deSilva had lived out his final days. It had been renamed Woodfin Extended Care Facility.

A cranky-sounding woman answered. I introduced myself. "If possible, I'd like to speak with someone who may have known one of your former residents," I said. "This is going back at least ten years, but—a man by the name of Ricardo deSilva."

"Ricardo deSilva?" the woman exclaimed, as if her morning caffeine dosage had suddenly kicked in. "You're in luck, Miss Padget. He was one of my all-time favorites. We shouldn't have favorites, but there it is. A gal simply doesn't forget a guy like Mr. Chip."

"You knew him well?"

"I was a nurse's aide when Mr. Chip was around. Talked to

him every day. My name's Tammy. I'm an RN now, and the assistant director."

"Thanks for speaking with me, Tammy. What was it that made Chip so likable?"

"You ever hear of a glue person? The sort who wants everybody to get along. Mr. Chip was like that. A real shepherd. When he first moved here, he would knock on people's doors, get them venturing down the hallway into the common area. People who hadn't left their rooms in years. He would get them playing games. You know, checkers or Connect Four. He smiled at everyone, even the demented ones who threw their biscuits at him. We had a nickname for Mr. Chip: the Mayor."

"Did he ever talk about the past?"

"All the time. He used to go on and on about his treasure hunts. He tried to organize one here at Woodfin, but it didn't work out. Most of the other residents weren't as sharp as he was, and they couldn't figure out the riddles. We ended up calling it off when we discovered Mr. Chip had hidden chess pieces in the toilet tanks. He put on a good attitude, but it galled him, I knew."

"Do you know if his treasure hunts ever had any sort of predictable pattern?"

"Now, that, I don't recollect."

"Did Chip deSilva ever talk about Cattail?"

"He talked more about Bermuda. His childhood there. His salad days."

I wished she could tell me how Chip deSilva had felt about his work at the furniture factory here, and how he reacted when he found out the apartments were going to be torn down. Did he stay and watch the demolition, or had he already headed west, seeking a fresh start? What memories of the Outer Banks did he bring with him?

"He was something of an artist," Tammy said. "Did you know that?"

"I found an obituary that said he did some sketching."

"That's right. He sketched me once, using plain old pencil. It was uncannily accurate. Pretty impressive for an old man. I don't mean to make a saint out of him, though. I loved him to pieces, but toward the end, Mr. Chip suffered the same bitterness that a lot of our residents seem to come down with."

Bitterness? This was getting interesting. "Can you say more about that?"

She chuckled. "His roommate had been what we used to call a flight risk. Buster was his name. Any chance Buster got, he'd beeline for the exit, whether it was a door or a second-story window. And on days when it seemed Buster's wanderlust might get the best of him, the staff would chain his wrist to the safety railing in the hallway. It sounds horrible, and it's not something we do anymore. But in those days, it was common practice. Buster could walk the length of the railing, but no farther. It allowed him to move around while keeping him safe and in one place.

"Well, one day Mr. Chip decided this chaining was abominable. He left a little scroll on my supervisor's desk. It was tied up with ribbon, made to look sweet. But the message inside was mean. I can't remember the exact words, but it was a nasty rhyme threatening violence if Buster wasn't unchained immediately.

"I knew right away it was Mr. Chip's handiwork. I recognized his handwriting. He apologized. He truly did regret leaving that scary, silly rhyme, I could tell. He had no intention of hurting anyone. He was just angry. Frustrated."

"Did he ever have visitors?" I asked. "Friends? Family?"

"Nobody. He'd been an only child; he told me that once. And he never married or had kids of his own. He was all alone in the world. You'd be surprised how many of our residents end up like that."

I wasn't surprised at all. "One last thing, if you don't mind. There's a town called Cottontown out your way, isn't there?"

"Cottontown? Sure. It's not too far from here. That's where I get my Christmas tree every year. Chop it down myself."

"What about the overnight camp there? Do you know anything about it?"

"Camp Cottontown? Oh, that went out of business years ago. That land's all developed now, I'm afraid. Cookie-cutter housing. A right blight, if you ask me. What does Camp Cottontown have to do with Mr. Chip?"

"Nothing, Tammy." After thanking her again and returning her wish for a wonderful day, I hung up.

Scupper stuck his snout into my glass, lapping up the last of my smoothie. Then he put his paws on my leg and reached up to kiss my neck. It was as if he could sense my frustration. I scratched his back, and a strange feeling came over me. Like peeking outside your house when the eye of the hurricane passes over. It's eerily still, no birds flitting or cattails waving or people puttering by on their boats. Because everyone, everything, knows the second wall is coming. That more chaos is on the way.

Chip deSilva would remain, for the most part, a mystery man. A sweet old soul harboring an intolerance for unfairness. Someone who planted treasure hunts—as well as threats.

Later, in the shower, as hot water beat a soothing rhythm on my shoulders, it hit me: the only person who knew the locations of the remaining clues was dead.

61

Toby lived on the island's southeast side. Live oaks shaded the neighborhood of small, cedar-shingled homes. I parked in his gravel driveway. He'd told me to meet him in the backyard, so I strolled around the side of the house, past the screen porch lined with pots of petunias. He was waiting. He wore a slate-blue T-shirt, board shorts, and sturdy boots.

"Good morning, Mr. Dodge," I said, extricating myself from my bag. I set it on a patio table.

"Ready for this?" He gestured to a battered eye-high target nailed to the trunk of a tall loblolly pine. Blue rings encircled the bull's-eye.

As I stink-eyed the target, memories of high school gym class assaulted me. Every autumn we'd get marched down to the archery pit, behind the football field. My arrows never made contact with a target. Not once in four years.

"Toby," I said. "Trust me. You don't want me anywhere near a bow and arrow."

"What about an ax?" He strode over to a tree stump, wrenched an ax from the wood, squared himself off before the target ten feet away, and hurled. With a solid thwack, the ax blade sank just above the bull's-eye.

"This is what you do in your spare time?"

"Best stress relief I know. Better than a lot of alternatives, for sure. Whatever your history with archery, forget it. Ax throwing is far easier. Bigger projectile." Bending over, he picked up a broken branch. "This is your ax," he said, handing it to me. "Hold it fist over fist. Like a tennis racquet."

"Tennis. Another sport that hates me."

He came up behind me. His arms encircled me. Warmth radiated from his body.

It was all I could do not to spin around, throw my arms around his neck, and . . .

He put his hands over mine and drew them upward. "Right here's where you want to reverse direction," he said when our arms made a right angle. "Then, think of chopping. And when you get here"—our arms were straight, parallel to the ground—"simply let go. The ax slides straight out of your hands, nice and easy. And it tumbles beautifully, end over end, and hits that bull's-eye dead on. As if pulled by a wire."

I laughed. "You're truly an optimist."

"Visualize it. Nice and slow. Breathe in"—Toby guided my arms again, stopping when they made a right angle above my head—"then breathe out." He extended them straight. "It's all in the abs. Move from your center. Your core."

"What if I chop off my ear?"

"I'll plop it onto some ice and drive it to the hospital. You can come too." Stepping up to the target, he retrieved the ax and handed it to me. "Fist over fist."

I gripped the handle and planted my feet hip-width apart.

"Excellent form." Clapping, he put a foot on the tree stump. "All right. Let's do this. Remember to let go when your arms straighten out."

Eyeing the bull's-eye, I brought the ax overhead. Then I contracted my stomach muscles, brought it down as hard as I could, and released. It wobbled through the air, striking the tree well below the target. A piece of bark chipped off, spinning into the woods.

I covered my face with my hands. "Total whiff."

"You did hit the tree." He rebounded the ax. "Just like anything else, it takes a while to get a sense for it."

"I'm going to kill your tree."

"Nah. It's like me—it can take a beating."

I tried two more throws with similar results.

"Don't worry about your wrists," he said, stooping to pick up the ax. "Keep them straight as you can. And when you reach that release point, all you do is relax your fingers. Let the handle slip right out. Like doo-doo through a tin whistle, as the saying goes."

"I'm not sure what practical application this is ever going to have. It's not like I'm going to carry an ax around in my bag. Although it probably is big enough. Seriously, though—why don't I arm myself? Get a gun or a knife. Learn how to use it—"

"No." He shook his head. "Too dangerous. Too risky. And anyway, you're already armed with the best weapon there is. Nerve."

"I don't know about that."

"Don't you remember how we met? You charged into a busy street to save a cat."

"I was just reacting."

"Sure, but a lot of other people might have reacted differently." He offered me the ax handle. "Looked like nerve to me."

In the powder room off Toby's kitchen, I splashed cold water on my face. The week had caught up to me. My eyes were shadowed, and the fine lines on my forehead sagged. I pinched my cheeks, ran fingers through my hair, and dabbed balm on my lips.

When I came out, he wasn't in the kitchen. "Toby?"

"In here."

I followed his voice to the screen porch, passing the duck room on the way. I peeked in, taking a quick moment to admire the furnitureless room, hundreds of duck decoys lining the walls, from floor to ceiling. Some of the decoys were weatherworn, the wood grain showing under flaking paint. Others were so realistic and wet-looking they might have started quacking. The photograph in the *Crier* hadn't quite captured the magnitude.

"Impressive collection you have in there," I said, stepping onto the porch. Toby sat in a rattan chair, his bare feet propped on a matching ottoman.

"Thanks. The *Crier* wrote about my ducks a while back."

I know. Because I totally googled you.

A hammock hung in the corner. "Go for it," he said.

I hopped on, spreading the webbing around me and stretching out, my head close to where he sat. The hammock creaked slightly from my swaying.

"You hungry?" he asked. "Got some ginger ice cream in the freezer. Made it this morning."

"You made it?"

"What? A man can't have his own ice cream maker?"

"It's just that you don't strike me as the domestic type."

"Oh, I'm domestic, all right. I bake cookies every Christmas."

"You do not."

"I sure do. Nutella shortbreads shaped like mittens and Santa hats. Used to make 'em for my students. And if you want to get your own delicious dozen come December, you'd better quit giggling."

"Was I giggling?"

"Listen to you. One would think you've already got some man making you cookies."

Not taking the bait, I pushed the window frame, getting a good swing going.

"*Do* you have some man making you cookies?" he asked.

"I don't often eat sweets."

Grinning, he got up. "Wait here, sassy." When he returned, he carried two bowls, frosty spoons sticking out.

I sat up and accepted a bowl. The ice cream was perfect, not at all cloying. "Is that scuppernong wine I taste?"

"Last season's. I keep a bottle in the freezer. The sweetness offsets the kickiness of the ginger. And when you combine those two flavors with a creamy texture—on a hot summer day? Ice-cold flawlessness."

"Listen to you."

"A true martial artist is in touch with both his masculine side and his feminine side. Yin and yang. Sun and moon."

"Is ice cream going to figure into your self-defense for women class?"

He got quiet for a second, then said, "This is just for you, Callie Padget."

Outside, past the house, a family rode bicycles. The mom wore a baseball hat, the dad wore bloated cargo shorts, and the three kids wore deep tans. Vacationers, I knew from the bright green rental bikes leased by a local outfitter. Take-out containers were balanced on the parents' handlebars. They were all singing off-key, that Pharrell Williams song. *Happy, happy, happy . . .*

I gestured with my spoon. "Do you ever get jealous of them?"

"Tourists? Not really. They have to leave eventually, but I get to stay here year-round. Why did you leave Cattail, anyway?"

"It's different when you grow up here."

"Fair enough." He scraped up the last of his ice cream. "You going to the Cattaillion tonight? I'll be there, promoting Cattail Family Martial Arts. We could watch the fireworks together." I was trying to get up the guts to make some cheeky comment—*are you asking me on a date?*—when he said, "I'd like to take another shot at your real name. Carleen?"

"Total whiff."

"Hey, you want to know why nobody calls me Tobias? Cuz my name's Toby."

We both laughed. Then a silence fell, broken only by the chittering of birds. He placed his empty bowl on a little table, and I did the same. Outside, beyond the trees, the rounded tops of gravestones were white humps. One of the many family cemeteries still on the barrier islands, maintained by descendants.

"So, why your uncle?" he asked. "Why not move back in with your parents?"

"They're both gone." I shrugged. "I never knew my dad. He bolted when my mom was newly pregnant with me."

"Classy guy."

"Summer guy. My mom made the classic local girl's mistake of thinking she could turn him." She'd refused to tell me anything else about my father. I used to pump Hudson for information, back when I first started living with him. But he claimed he didn't know anything. And eventually I just stopped asking. "I never think about my father," I told Toby.

I did, though. How could I not? During idle moments, mostly. Climbing the stairs to my old apartment, or sitting on the edge of my tub as it filled with warm water. I didn't lament his absence so much as wonder—whose genetic code was I carrying around? And what was written on it?

"What happened to your mom?" Toby asked.

"Accident." For twenty-six years, I hadn't wanted to talk about it. Not with Hudson, not with anybody. What was it about Toby, sitting across from me with his earnest hunting-dog face and sympathetic hazel eyes, that changed all that? That made me want to tell him everything? "My mother fell from the top of Cattail Lighthouse," I said. "She had taken medication. Pills she had no business taking. And she mixed them with alcohol."

He knitted his hands together and leaned toward me, as if to let me know he could handle the heavy turn our conversation was taking.

"I think she had a psychotic reaction," I said. "That can happen, you know. Or she just panicked. There'd been a lightning storm, and the top door had accidentally locked behind her, and she couldn't get back inside. I think she tried to climb down to one of the upper windows, which at the time didn't have panes and were just trapezoids open to the sky."

"Was she alone? At the top of the lighthouse."

I nodded. "It had closed for the day. But the door was left unlocked. Back then, things were lax. The lighthouse wasn't really promoted as a tourist destination. It was something only the locals knew about. She was able to just climb right up."

Mom had been in a fantastic mood. She loved summertime. The late sunsets over the water, the extra cash flow thanks to the rise in destination weddings, which frequently demanded last-minute alterations or repairs. Her work projects accumulated in every room—gowns swaying from the shower rod, tossed over my bedroom door, making it impossible to close.

But the evening she died, she'd been tense. She'd been worried about falling behind. I was lying on the sunroom floor reading one of my beloved cozies—*The Cat Who Saw Red*—when my mother declared, "I'm going cross-eyed." With a scream of frustration, she tossed aside the bridal veil she'd been edging with lace.

"Come with me." I led her outside, and she followed me up into the tree house, and we spent a few minutes watching the mustangs mosey down the street.

Reaching up, I tried to put my cattail crown on her head, but she placed it back on my own. "It's good that you like to watch things," she said. "Observe things. Like the mustangs."

"Why?"

"Because someday, they'll be all gone."

Those were the last words she ever spoke to me. *Because someday, they'll be all gone.*

Soon after, Trish Berryman came striding across the yard. A dark bottle under her arm, the bob of her hair bouncing, her prominent brow casting a shadow over her face. She rang our doorbell.

Mom kissed the top of my head. She climbed down and went inside with Trish.

A minute later, Trish came out empty-handed and walked back to her own house.

I watched the mustangs for a while. Then, as darkness fell, I heard my mother's car starting up. I went over to the other tree house window and watched her back out the driveway. Behind the wheel, Mom was wearing her favorite celery-hued sundress. Elastic bodice, tiered prairie-style skirt. She'd made it herself. She'd wanted to make me a similar sundress. I'd been a tank-and-shorts kind of girl, though.

I waved, but she mustn't have seen me.

She drove off in the direction of the lighthouse. Shortly after, thunder started drumming, and lightning strobed the sky, dazzling flashes that left me momentarily blinded.

As the rain sliced, I climbed down from the tree house and ran inside. Trish's bottle was in the kitchen sink. The bottle was empty.

I called Hudson. No answer. I let it ring, sitting on the floor, cheek pressed to the phone, phone pressed to the cabinet, listening to the tone bleat and bleat. After about ten minutes he answered.

"Where were you?" I asked.

"Callie? I went out for cigs. Why—"

"Mom drove off."

"What do you mean? Are you alone?"

"I think she drank a lot of wine."

Four days later, during my mother's calling hours, Hudson stepped outside to smoke. I followed him onto the porch of the funeral home just as a tortured-looking Trish Berryman was mounting the steps. Jeff had dropped her off and was parking their car. "I killed her," she said to Hudson. "It's all my fault."

He turned to me. "Callie, go back inside."

I stayed put, my arms wrapped around a pollen-coated support column, as Trish rambled about my mother being such a small woman, and not a big drinker. My mother never even took so much as an aspirin, Trish said through tears. "And I had to go and give her booze and pills—"

"Pills too?" my uncle said.

"Something my family doctor gave me, to help me relax. I thought they would ease Teri's tension. She'd seemed so stressed, with all that work piling up. I thought, *It's summer. She should be enjoying herself.* Isn't that why people live here? To enjoy life."

Hudson pointed his cigarette at the door. "Callie."

I hugged the column tighter.

"We washed the pills down with a glass or two of wine," Trish said. "And then she sent me away. She must have finished off the bottle by herself. She'd never have jumped if she were in her right mind—"

"She didn't jump, damn it," Hudson said.

"We'll never know—"

"She *fell*—"

"—and she might not have even climbed up there to begin with if it weren't for me." Trish swayed over the railing, her face inches from a holly bush.

My uncle put a hand on her back. "We don't know that," he said. "She used to go to the lighthouse all the time . . ."

I blinked away the memories. Across from me, Toby was shaking his head. "That's horrible. I can understand wanting to leave here."

"Hudson could have pressed charges," I said. "Sharing prescription medication is a serious offense. He could have sued the lighthouse people too. Ralph Burrus and his conservationists crew. He could have launched an investigation and found out just who was responsible for that bottom door being left unlocked. But it wouldn't have changed what happened to my mother. So we just let it be. Life went on. And as soon as I had enough credits to transfer from community college, I was out of here."

"Why'd you come back?"

"Oh, no, you don't," I said. "I bared my soul. Now it's your turn. Tit for tat."

"Okay. I can do *tat*." He rested the back of his hand on my knee. "You still want to know about my stag?"

The ink on his forearm was full of rich browns and greens and blacks and reminded me of the cover of a fantasy novel. Pine trees towered from the fur on the stag's chest. Ravens flapped among the antlers, which gave the illusion of infinite depth, stretching back into a swirling fog.

Tattoos weren't really my jam, but the artwork was exquisite. And Toby's warm, strong hand was resting on my knee, like a salve that was somehow soothing all the old pain I'd just relived.

"Where'd you get that design?" I asked.

"Told the tattoo artist what I had in mind, then gave him free rein."

"Why a stag?"

"Because, after my fiancée ditched me, ripping out my heart in the process, I swore off relationships."

"Your fiancée?"

"Dated for two years. Engaged for two months. Then she took

up with a boatbuilder over in Wanchese, and literally sailed off into the sunset with him, to parts unknown."

"That's really rough. I'm sorry to hear it."

"Thanks. Once I could think clearly again, I made a vow to myself. No women for one whole year. Total stag. I wanted to give myself the gift of time, you know? To get to know just who Toby Dodge is. To learn what it means to be a man. My own man."

"Wow. How's that going?"

"Best decision I ever made. I started my own business, and I'm putting my needs first for a change. In a good way, not a selfish way."

"I get it. And . . ." I cleared my throat. "How much time . . . I mean—"

"Eleven months."

A lead ball formed inside my stomach. Eleven months.

He was just getting started.

Reality hit me then like a slap across the face. Toby was a catch, yes. But his dingbatter status notwithstanding, he was a Cattailer, through and through. A Cattailer who was going to be living like a monk for the better part of the next year.

Meanwhile, I was going to be leaving town.

62

I reported to work. Antoinette was out back, chatting with shoppers, so I took care of a man asking if we sold cookbooks for kids (we did) and another customer, a woman, who bought six beach reads, "one for every week I'm staying here in Cattail."

After I rung up those sales, I noticed a hefty tome occupying the delivery cubby. *Photographing Fireworks* was packed with shots of pyrotechnic-sprayed nighttime skies. I slipped out the bookmark and turned it over. *Jeff Berryman*, Antoinette had written. *Crier office.*

Dread dripped through me. Every interaction I'd had with Jeff had been tenser than the last.

In the *Crier* office, Trish's face was inches from her laptop screen. Her fingers worked the keys.

I knew that stance. It happened when a person of import called with a juicy lead. Sure enough, as I walked over to Jeff's desk, I heard Chief Jurecki's voice coming through the speaker on Trish's phone. She was taking notes while he gave a statement. "Police are treating Gwen Montgomery's death as a homicide," he said. "Eva's death too. We are open to the possibility that they are connected."

I stopped in my tracks.

Jeff's head popped up over his cubicle wall. "What are you doing here?"

"Delivery from the MotherVine," I said, passing him the book.

Trish waved to get our attention, then made a throat-slicing motion and mouthed, *Shut up.*

Jurecki's voice barked. "Officer Iona Fusco recovered a few bits of evidence that caused Cattail police to shift their focus."

Fusco found something? What? I waited for more details, but none came. Just Trish's typing, and Jurecki's matter-of-fact voice saying *pursuing all leads* and *making use of every resource available* and *urging folks to come forward with any information.*

"Callie?" Jeff had come around the divider and was standing inches from me, his face jutted out like a bird ready to peck. "As you can see, we're very busy."

"But I just want—"

"How many times do I have to tell you to be quiet when I'm on the phone?" Trish had hung up and was glaring at her husband as if he were a misbehaving child.

He tried not to wince, but I saw the corners of his eyes twitch. "Get out of here, Callie," he said softly. "Beat it."

63

From the *Crier* office, I ran about three blocks, straight down Queen Street toward the police station. I became a sweaty disaster in the process, thanks to the ninety-degree temperature coupled with ninety percent humidity. The spaces between my big and second toes were rubbed raw from my flip-flops by the time I pushed through the heavy glass door and stepped into the squat brick building.

I spread my hands on the counter, putting on my most pleasant face for the dispatcher, a twenty-something man hulking behind plexiglass. A rod stabbed his eyebrow, a stud pierced his chin, and gauges stretched his earlobes bigger than quarters. LOGAN, according to the stitching on his shirt.

"Is Chief Jurecki in?" I asked.

"Chief's in court."

"Not to split hairs"—I smiled sweetly—"but the chief is *not* in court. I know for a fact he was on the phone with someone from the *Crier* as recently as two minutes ago. Plus, it's Saturday. No court on Saturdays."

Logan looked close to rolling his eyes, but he held back.

"What about Fusco?" I asked. "She around?"

"Officer Fusco is out on patrol. For real."

"It's pertaining to the homicide investigations."

"If you have any information, you can leave it with me."

I laced my fingers together and held my hands to the plexiglass. "Please?"

After another near eye roll, Logan reached for the phone. "I'll try and raise him."

"Oh, thank you. Tell him it's Callie Padget. Tell him it's pressing. Could you say that?"

In his office, Jurecki was even more tight-lipped than usual. Letting the *Crier* know about the big development in the case must have been part of his strategy. A plan I didn't figure into.

Didn't he owe me, though? I could have pointed out, rightly, that I got the police into Gwen's phone a lot sooner than they might have otherwise. But I didn't want to throw Fusco under the bus, in case Jurecki didn't know about my involvement. Maybe she'd taken the credit for herself. I didn't really care either way. I just wanted justice to be done by Gwen. And Eva.

"What about the Cattaillion?" I asked him. "Is it still going on?"

"I was told you have pertinent information?"

"Aren't people in danger? There's a murderer on the loose! On a twenty-two-square-mile island, I might add."

"Vigilance is paramount. But the annual Cattaillion is scheduled to proceed this evening, up and down Queen Street, according to its normal schedule, with a fireworks display beginning at 9:25, as it has for the past seventy years." He jammed his index finger into his desk. "I said as much to Trish, and I'll say it to you: Drew Jurecki is not about to let some sick creep ruin this island's most time-honored and long-standing tradition. Especially when such a worthy cause stands to benefit. I have a lot of memories on that pier, as do we all."

"But, Chief. The wind." I'd noticed on my phone a forecast of possible strong gales.

He waved it off. "Should be blowing away from spectators. Not a concern."

"Did you find something on Gwen's phone?"

"Since you mention it, we *did*. A text message. From you. An apology. You and Gwen had an argument?"

I nodded. "Wednesday night."

"Concerning?"

Concerning the fact that I let myself into her cottage and had a good rummage. Then I did the same in the trunk of her car. "Nothing. A silly misunderstanding. Can you talk to me about persons of interest?"

"Leave police business to the police. Why am I sounding like a broken record here?"

"Listen to this. There's this guy, Bo Beauchamp? Works at Meeks Hardware. He had a crush on Eva and asked her on a date several weeks ago. She turned him down." Jurecki said nothing. "Chief?"

"Stay away from Bo Beauchamp."

"Why? Is he a suspect?"

"Trust me. Just stay away from him."

"What about the Standishes? Something *really* bad went down at the old furniture factory, back in the fifties. A nasty incident involving a guy named Israel Overton."

"The fifties? Callie, what could that possibly have to do with—"

"He was called 'the Sweeper.' Even says so on his headstone. You know what that nickname means? He must have cleaned up Thornton Standish's messes. Swept them under the rug. And seventy years later, Pearleen and Whitman are desperate to keep those messes a secret. What if Eva—"

"Speculation does not equal evidence. My job is to stay objective. Which, I might add, is also your job. Or at least it *was*, back when you were a reporter." He stood, walked to the door, and opened it. "You're a bookseller now."

"You know something, Chief?" I gathered my things and marched past him, head held high. "You're one hundred percent right. I am a bookseller now."

Outside, dusk leaked from the sky, pewter dripping into apricot. Queen Street was humming. Tourists ducked in and out of stores as shopkeepers readied for the Cattaillion, setting up tables and wares on the sidewalks. Town employees were using a bucket truck to string strands of lights over the road.

Heading back to the MotherVine, I texted Officer Fusco:

> Can you tell me what evidence you found? I want to help if I can. I'll be responsible with any info. You have my word.

I wended my way through the crowds, passing the *Crier* office. I spotted Trish, hunched over her laptop, typing furiously.

My stomach clenched. My brain fired.

On Thursday, when I'd confronted Trish about the curse article, the police scanner had gone off. *I have to admit, sometimes it does feel a little creepy, listening in*, she'd said.

Creepy. Listening in.

The same words I'd said to Whitman about the CB radio in his Ferrari.

I dialed Georgia. "Did Eva have a landline?" I blurted when she answered.

"Oh, Callie. I think I might need some space, you know? Some *time*."

"I know, and I'm so, so sorry. But—"

"No landline," Georgia said with a sigh. "All Eva had was a cell phone."

"And the last call your sister made from her cell was to me, correct?"

"Right. She called *me* around seven last Saturday night. We talked about the casserole she was experimenting with. And a while later, she called you." Her voice was tinged with exhaustion as she added, "As you know."

"Thanks. That's all I needed to hear."

64

The *S* snaked over the iron gate, blocking the way to the Standish estate. I pulled up to the guardhouse, stuck my head out my car window, and squinted at the camera. “Let me in. It’s urgent.”

The *S* didn’t break open.

I wedged the heel of my palm into the steering wheel. The horn blared, silencing the birdsong.

The S stayed put.

I dialed Whitman. Straight to voicemail. “Are you home?” I asked. “I need to speak with you and Pearleen right now. I’m coming in, whether this gate opens or not.”

Giving the camera lens one last glare, I got out of my car and strode up to the lowest part of the gate, where it sloped toward the guardhouse. The spiky tips reached about four feet above my head.

I shook the iron bars. They didn’t budge.

Gates like these might be effective at keeping out unwanted vehicles. But unwanted Callie Padgets? Different story.

I kicked off my flip-flops and flicked them through the gate, then stuffed my bag through to the other side as well. Grasping the bars as high as I could, I jumped and yanked upward, my knees bent deep. Each bare foot found a sun-warmed spindle. Inch by inch, I shimmied up. Sweat slicked my forehead. My knuckles ached. When I was head and shoulders above the top, I paused, panting. I was eight feet off the ground, clinging on like a monkey, with nothing but concrete to break my fall. I couldn’t simply swing a leg over like I'd done countless times climbing the Elder Tree. The bars ended in spear-like tips. And I had to pull a hundred-plus pounds over them—ideally without getting impaled.

I considered the roof of the guardhouse, but it was steep, and studded with iron fleur-de-lis, and too far a leap. Why hadn't I thought this through?

"Good grief, Callie." Whitman ran down the driveway, his sports coat flapping behind him like the wings of a giant albino bat. "I was just about to buzz you through but when I saw you were climbing, I didn't want to start the gate swinging, and—what are you doing *now*?"

I dragged one foot to the inch-wide crosswise bar connecting the spear tips. Slowly, using balance I didn't know I possessed, my other foot joined. Crouching like some sort of barefoot superhero, I sized up a row of boxwoods extending from the other side of the gatehouse, lining the driveway.

No way was I going to be rescued by Whitman Standish.

"Don't!" He barreled closer. "Please. Not Grandmother's boxwoods."

But I had already belly flopped for them.

I landed starfished among snapping branches and the rending of cotton. Something pierced the soft flesh of my left breast where it became armpit. Something else stung my cheek. After a few stunned seconds, I gathered myself to standing on two shaky feet. "You're more worried about the boxwoods than me," I said, brushing off leaves.

"They fared better than you did. Your face is bleeding."

I touched my cheek. My fingers came away dotted with red. My torn dress exposed slightly more cleavage than I was comfortable with. But this was no time for modesty.

I went over to my flip-flops and shoved my feet into them.

"Normally," Whitman said, "Grandmother's alarms would be going haywire, and the cops would be pulling up by now. But I disarmed the system. This'd better be good, Callie."

"You overheard something on your CB radio."

"We've covered this already. I overhear a lot of things. That's the whole fun of it."

"You said you never overhear cell phone conversations. But what about landline conversations?"

"Very occasionally, the CB radio picks up frequencies from early-model cordless phones."

"Like the one in Eva and Georgia Meeks's office at the hardware store." I could see it, the gigantic cordless phone on their shared desk, next to the metal detector.

"I wouldn't know." Whitman seemed to grow, his chest muscles expanding, his shirt stretching the buttons. "I have no idea what you're going on about. Grandmother and I are getting ready for the Cattaillion. So, if you'd please be on your way?"

"Hear me out. Last Saturday night, you and Pearleen were heading home from your meal at Clara's. What I want to know is—as you were gliding past Meeks Hardware in your Ferrari, did your CB pick up a conversation? Specifically, did you and Pearleen overhear Eva speaking on that old cordless phone of hers? Perhaps saying something about an old riddle she'd found."

A swath of beet red crept up Whitman's neck, flushing his cheeks. "Come again?"

"You see, the way I figure, Eva made one last call from her cell phone Saturday night. She'd been at home, and then she drove to the hardware store. She probably wanted to grab supplies. Her metal detector, maybe. And while she was in her office, my guess is she made a call from the landline. Actually, I'd bet my life the phone company's records would confirm it."

"And just whom did she call?"

"I don't know. I'd love to find out. But who she called isn't as important to me right now as what she *said*." I paused, needing to revisit the thoughts that had stormed through my mind during the drive here. What I couldn't get out of my head was the story told to me by Tammy the nurse, who had cared for the elderly Chip deSilva. How enraged he'd been by the inhumane treatment of his roommate. How he'd left a scary, nasty rhyme on Tammy's supervisor's desk. Maybe that wasn't the first time Chip deSilva had done that sort of thing. Wasn't it possible he had behaved in a similar way, in the aftermath of some grave injustice, while employed by Standish Furniture? And wasn't it possible that this whole Israel Overton cover-up was connected?

I swallowed. Part of me felt like I was taking too wild a leap. A quieter, deeper part of me said there was nothing wild about it.

Picking a piece of mulch out of my hair, I went on. "Here's what I'm curious about, Whitman. Did you and Pearleen overhear Eva describing a glass vial she'd dug up? It had been topped with cork. Sealed with burgundy-colored wax. Inside was a little scroll, and a mysterious message written in fancy blue ink. My theory is this: accidentally hearing about Eva's discovery reawakened an old fear inside your grandmother. Made her realize the awful truth about Israel Overton could finally come out, after all these years. Does any of this ring true?"

"Whit?" Pearleen stood in the driveway, halfway up the hill that led to the mansion. She was dressed to the hilt, looking like a life-size cake topper in an impeccably tailored brocade skirt suit, hair swirled on top of her head like icing. "Who's out there?" she called.

Whitman kept his gaze on me. His eyes narrowed. "How do you know we haven't laid some sort of trap for you? What makes you so sure you can trust us?"

"Because despite your reservations, your grandmother wants

to come clean. And you love your grandmother." I picked up my bag and threw it over my head. "She called me and didn't leave a message. Twice. I figured—one call like that might have been a butt dial. But a second, ten minutes later? That was no butt dial. It was a guilty conscience."

He stepped up to me. I could tell he was flexing his muscles by the way the seersucker seemed to twitch. His six-foot frame loomed over me, but I held my ground, even as his arm flung out. He pointed at my car. "Take your insane theory, climb that bony butt of yours back over that gate, and get lost. Unless you want me to stuff you through those bars myself—"

"Whitman." Pearleen had reached us. She placed a hand on her grandson's arm. "That's no way to speak to a lady."

"A *lady*? But, Grandmother—"

"Show Miss Padget inside."

"But—"

"Now."

I followed Whitman and Pearleen across the foyer, into Pearleen's study.

"You've got a bit of dirt on you still," Whitman said, draping a few towels over the velvety sofa. The towels were so vibrant and fleecy I felt bad sitting on them. "You were right about a lot of things," he said as he and Pearleen sat on the love seat opposite me. Behind them hung that painting I'd noticed when I was here a few days ago, the one of the sailboat.

"Tell me what I was right about," I said as I got settled. "And more importantly, tell me what I got wrong."

The two cats, white and black, slithered in. They rubbed against the old woman's shimmery stockings. She reached down and stroked them head to tail, saying, "Israel had an affinity for cats."

"You knew Israel Overton personally?"

"He was my best friend," she said. "My only friend."

"He—he was?" I couldn't see her face, just the top of her whipped-cream head and, as far as my untrained eye could tell, a diamond-encrusted barrette. She wore a jeweled ring on each bony finger, even her thumbs.

"Israel was—well, in my day we said *slow* or *simple*." Sitting back, Pearleen gazed past my head, out the window. "His job was to push a broom, twelve hours a day."

"The Sweeper," I said.

"That's right. He loved when we called him that."

I scraped my teeth over my bottom lip. Ronnie had gotten it wrong—and I had gone with the unfounded narrative. Israel Overton hadn't been a villain. He'd been a victim. He wasn't someone who cleaned up Thornton Standish's messes. He was, literally, a sweeper. One who swept. "Tell me about him," I said.

"Most days after school, I walked straight to the factory. Daddy insisted on it, because by that point in the afternoon, Mama was usually *ill*. That was their word for it. I used to sit on the stone steps leading into the factory and wait for Daddy.

"But the Sweeper would show up first, carrying his uneaten lunch: a can of chicken noodle soup. The second he sat next to me on those steps, a gang of feral cats shot out from the bushes across the road. They were meowing and drooling. Israel opened the can, dumped the contents onto the steps, and the cats licked up every last bite. The only sound louder than the purring was the growling of Israel's darned empty stomach.

"I started saving my lunch. I'd give it to him—a cheese, ham, and jam sandwich, usually. And you know what he did with it? Fed it to the cats. He and I ended our afternoons hungry. But those mangy felines were fat and full. I sometimes wonder if Antoinette's Tin Man is a descendant of them. Or these two, for that matter."

As if comprehending, her cats tucked themselves into bread loaf–like shapes at her feet.

"I talked that poor man's ear off," she said. "Prattled on about school and my enemies and my teachers. He never said much. Just listened to me go on and on. Every now and then he'd pat my knee and say, 'Yes, Miz Pearleen. That's a fine story, Miz Pearleen.' Bless his heart."

"What happened to Israel?"

"There was a small group of workers who protected him. A few men from the woodworking department, and a few women from upholstery. That's the way it was back then, the division of labor. And anyway, they were all friends, and they looked after the Sweeper. A lot of the other workers didn't treat him very well, you see. And one day—it was around this time of year—one of the bullies demanded that the Sweeper help fix some sort of great big spinning machine, deep inside the factory. I never saw this machine. That old heavy furniture-manufacturing equipment was off-limits to a young girl. But my understanding is, it went all the way up to the high ceiling. And it had malfunctioned." She smoothed her skirt, then got up and walked over to the sailboat painting. "The Sweeper, always wanting to be a good helper, reached inside it and got hold of one of the levers. And it snatched him up and flung him around and around. He was caught somehow. Despite all efforts to free him—to shut off the machine—he struck his head repeatedly on a steel beam." She placed her hands on the painting's gold frame, lifted it, and set it on the floor.

Inside the wall was a safe.

"Daddy was aghast," she said. "He immediately fired the man who'd lured Israel near the machine. He wanted to compensate Israel's family. But Israel had no family. None to speak of. Not a soul in the world. He'd been an orphan.

"Israel's protectors at the factory were furious. There were six of them. And they marched into Daddy's office demanding that more be done. That justice be served."

"This was before OSHA," I said, leaning forward. "Before workers' rights. They had no recourse."

"That's right. In response, Daddy donated a hundred thousand dollars to the orphanage on the mainland that had raised Israel. It was going to shut its doors, but that money kept it open. Until the seventies, anyway, when it finally did close." At the safe, Pearleen held her finger over a keypad. A light glowed orange to green. Beeping, the door popped open. She reached inside.

Before she closed it, I noticed a blur of pink.

She returned to the love seat, cupping something in her wrinkled hands. "Not long after Israel's accident, the uproar, and Daddy's subsequent donation to the orphanage, Daddy and I were heading home one day when he realized he'd forgotten his hat. An old straw boater he used to wear. We went back into his office. And there in the middle of his desk sat his hat. And underneath it—Lord knows why he saved it all those years." She held out her hands.

A glass vial. Cork top, cracked wax seal. Inside the vial was rolled-up paper, the edges burnt.

She uncorked the vial and tipped the scroll into my open hand.

Filling my lungs with all the air they could hold, I unfurled the tight cylinder.

Sixteen times Sweep struck his head.
One good bash does big Thorn dead.
How does big Thorn make wrong right?
Tell the world. Bring wrong to light.

“The man who wrote this was named Chip deSilva,” I said. “He was on your father’s payroll. A furniture maker.”

“Chip deSilva,” she repeated. “We never found out who left it. He must have been among the workers who were very angry.”

“If not the angriest,” Whitman said.

“Did anything ever come of this threat?” I asked.

“Not that I knew of,” she said.

Chip deSilva had been a glue person. *A real shepherd*, in Tammy the nurse’s words. My mental portrait of the man was fleshing out, taking on more contours, more shadows. At the factory, he must have been one of Israel’s self-appointed guardians. He’d have been young then, in his early thirties. He might have even tried to rescue the Sweeper, tried to loosen whatever mechanism had cinched ahold of him.

“Is he your eyewitness, Callie?” Whitman asked. “Is this Chip deSilva the same man who came forward, wanting you to write some sort of tell-all?”

I shook my head. “Chip deSilva died in 2010. He’d been all alone in the world too. What happened next?”

“Daddy had the paper and glass tested for fingerprints,” Pearleen said. “But nothing came of it. He hired bodyguards, and I was no longer allowed at the factory. After school I had to go straight home, where the housekeeper occupied me, keeping me from my drunken mother. Lonely years. I missed the Sweeper something terrible.”

“What I don’t understand,” Whitman said, “is how Eva Meeks came across *her* vial. A rhyming riddle? Handwritten ink? By the same man?”

“She dug it up in her yard,” I said.

“She lived where that park used to be, didn’t she?” Pearleen asked. “Across from the factory housing.”

I nodded. "Chip deSilva planted a treasure hunt. He must have hidden that vial underneath a park bench or something. At any rate, it was never discovered. Until last weekend, when Eva was planting flowers." I told them a few details and mentioned the hurricane. "So you overheard her on the CB radio in the Ferrari. Who was she talking to? Who did she call?"

"We couldn't make it out," Pearleen said. "We recognized her voice, but . . ."

"It was a man," Whitman offered. "But his words were garbled. His end of the conversation didn't come through."

"What was *she* saying, exactly? Besides describing the riddle." My chin trembled. Eva'd had no idea that phone call was the last she'd ever make.

Pearleen cleared her throat, a tiny noise. "There was a lot of static. The only other phrase we heard her say loud and clear was . . ."

"What?"

"*Meet me,*" Whitman said.

Meet me.

Who had met her?

I breathed in deep, dipping my chin to my chest. Then I addressed Whitman. "You've been against coming out with the truth of Israel's accident. You're not convinced it's a good idea."

"It's a public relations nightmare. But if it's what Grandmother wants, she's the boss."

"Whitman told me he offered you hush money, Callie," Pearleen said. "I want you to know that I knew nothing about that." She turned to her grandson. "Whit, dear, would you excuse us?"

After a surprised pause, he stood. Something about the ornateness of the room, along with Pearleen's dismissal of him, made him seem diminished, as if all those muscles didn't amount to much real strength. He left, softly closing the door behind him.

"I don't think your riddle was part of any treasure hunt," I said to Pearleen.

She shook her head. "When I heard that Eva talking on the CB—going on about a glass vial and red wax and a riddle—I immediately thought it was somehow going to lead back to my father's one big mistake in an otherwise stellar career."

"You could ask Trish Berryman at the *Crier* to write about Israel Overton. I'm sure she would salivate over this story. And the article might result in some sort of compensation being done. You and Trish could even solicit ideas from the community. She'd have to vet your story somehow, of course. But I have a feeling all you've said here is going to check out."

"It will, because it's the truth. I'll likely be received as a repulsive troll. Then again, this town doesn't think too well of me anyway. What would the harm be? It's only a reputation, after all."

"The donation your father made. Wasn't that enough?"

"How could anything ever be enough? He installed a safety rail around that spinning machine. But that didn't ease his conscience either." Pearleen leaned forward, her palms upturned. I hesitated, then slid my hands into hers. Her skin was satin. "My father made that donation anonymously, you know," she said. "He never took any credit for it. That's why I make my good works public knowledge. I want the Standish name on everything. When I found out Eva Meeks had beaten me to the punch over the butterfly sanctuary?" She shook her head. "I must have come off as a cruel cow. Not my finest hour. I could easily outbid her now, of course. Get those naming rights once and for all. But that seems rather a vulgar thing to do."

"You'll have to pardon me. But why are you sometimes so . . ."

"Nasty? It's quite all right, child. I've heard it before, believe you me. I guess I thought I needed to be nasty in order to make it as a woman in the business world. And then the nastiness just spilled into my other worlds."

"So it's not really you?"

"Oh, it's me. But it's not the only me."

"You put a can of chicken noodle soup on Israel's grave."

"I do every summer, to mark his passing. Much to the chagrin of my two gluttonous pussycats here." The white cat leapt onto her lap, luxuriating as she scratched it under the chin. "You don't have an eyewitness, do you?" Pearleen asked. When I didn't answer, she chuckled. "You're a little firecracker."

"How come your father didn't 'bring wrong to light'? How come he didn't come forward? Admit what happened?"

"Maybe because no one else demanded it. He never discussed the accident. Not even with me. Not even after I'd become an adult and started taking over the business."

"You never brought it up?"

"Standish Furniture was my father's whole life. And then it became my whole life. I've been doing a lot of thinking. If admitting this stain on SFI history will somehow lead to some peace around Eva's death, and now that poor young lighthouse keeper's too, then . . . it's the right thing. It's time."

"I hate to be intrusive," I said. "But I have one last question." There'd been that blur of pink inside Pearleen's safe. What if it could explain the threatening sticky note, also pink, inside my Little Free Library? A stretch, perhaps, but I was hungry for as many answers as I could get. "When you opened your safe, I saw something pink. Any chance you could show me what it is?"

Pearleen smiled. I noticed for the first time that she had apple cheeks just like boy-Whitman in the photograph on her desk.

She stood and put the vial back inside the safe. When she returned to the love seat, she held a handmade card, faded and heart-shaped. “I take it out from time to time,” she said, placing it on the table.

It was dated February 1954.

To my darling dearest wee Pearleen:

I will always protect you. Happy Valentine’s Day.

Love, Daddy

65

At Hudson's house, my shower was rushed, my makeup application even more so. There was no time to dry my hair; it clung damply to the back of my shirt. But I felt confident in a figure-hugging ivory top, swingy linen pants, and wedge sandals. On Cattail Island, there weren't many reasons to get gussied. The Cattaillion was one of them.

As night fell, I walked to the waterfront. Queen Street was transformed. Chatting Cattailers of all ages weaved among the bidding tables, pausing to sign clipboards or strike up conversations. Caterers circulated, offering cups of cattail salad. "Tastes like cucumbers," was the famous refrain. A string quartet lent the evening an air of refinement. Beyond the rising and falling of the bows, the Pamlico Sound heaved, the waves bigger than usual thanks to the wind, which was picking up.

I tried to drink it all in, the charm and camaraderie, the white lights twinkling overhead. But I couldn't ignore the undercurrent of unease. News of the police's turnabout was spreading, and words like *murder* and *nervous* peppered the bits of conversation I overheard. Plus, Pearleen's story still swarmed in my mind, along with a nagging question: If she didn't have anything to do with the threatening sticky note, then who did? And would that person strike again?

I picked my way through the crowds, heading for the Mother-Vine. Toby seemed speechless as I reached Cattail Family Martial

Arts. He was sitting out front at a table, auctioning off lesson packages.

"Hey," he said, standing. "You look—wow. I don't think I've ever seen you wearing anything other than a casual dress or running clothes."

"Thanks." I brought a fingertip to my eyelashes, unused to the gooey sensation of mascara.

"What happened to your cheek? You've got a scratch."

"Had a run-in with some shrubbery."

"Why am I not even a little surprised by that response?" He smiled, and I wanted to return it, but I also didn't want to mislead him. We were friends, and that was all. "Everything okay?" he asked.

"Yeah. I won't keep you." I moved on, not looking back despite the disappointment tearing through me.

I passed a cattail-basket-weaving demonstration, then Native American dancers preparing for a performance, waving smudge sticks that scented the air with herbs. At the Cattail Pottery table, Reedley Anderson arranged bud vases to suggest a rainbow. Beyond him, I saw Antoinette in a lacy dress, flowers in her hair. Hudson was piggybacking her section of sidewalk and had set up his gleaming surfboard on a card table. A family paused to admire it, and he stood with his hands clasped behind him, smiling proudly. His khakis were creased and a section of shirt hung untucked, but at least he'd combed his hair and, from the looks of it, even his beard.

The MotherVine table was covered with the raffia-adorned books Antoinette and I had packaged. A platter of grapes was the centerpiece. (Our experiment to attach grapes to the books hadn't worked out—no way to stack them.)

From inside the shop, Tin Man observed the festivities, his amber eyes half-closed, his tail swishing like a hypnotist's watch chain. He hadn't disturbed my window display. Not one book had been nibbled, not one cocktail umbrella upturned, not one origami seagull batted from the ceiling. It was almost like he was part of the scene, nestled among the satin.

I'd reached Hudson. "Incredible turnout," he said as he put his arm around me. "They're predicting more than adequate profits to repair the pier."

"I'm really glad to hear that."

"You know, I've been thinking."

"Again?"

"Whip me up me one of those green potions tomorrow morning, would ya?"

I laughed. "A kale smoothie? Really?"

"Gotta make some changes."

"Me too," I said. But I wasn't sure what I meant. The words had kind of just slipped out.

And then I noticed Summer, all by herself, leaning against a streetlight. She wore a black romper and appeared less washed-out than the day before. Must have been the cattail torches all around, bouncing warm light.

"Be right back." I kissed Hudson on the cheek, then made my way over to her. "Hey," I said.

"My aunt Georgia made me come here."

I wanted to say something like, *Your aunt loves you. She's trying the best she can.* Which I believed. But I didn't want to play that role in Summer's life. Didn't want to be just another adult who tried to explain things.

"I should get back," she said, indicating the other side of the street. Behind the balloon-adorned Meeks Hardware table, Georgia was handing out the gift pots she'd been assembling Monday morning in her she-shed. She wore mauve espadrilles with a jumpsuit that would have looked about as stylish as a garbageman outfit on me, but she pulled it off with characteristic trendiness.

"Before you go," I said to Summer, taking the camp booklet from my bag. "This belonged to your mother. I came across it during all my poking around. It's time I returned it."

"That was on her desk in the kitchen." She flipped through the pages. I glimpsed, upside-down, the blurry *Getting cozy* photograph: Eva and an older boy sitting side by side on a log, grinning up into the camera.

"Did she ever say anything to you about her camp days?" I asked. "Any ideas as to why she might have been reliving them?"

Summer shook her head. "Thanks anyway. I know you tried."

She thought I was quitting. She thought my giving back the *Funbook* was an admission of defeat.

"This isn't over yet, Summer," I said. "There's still a chance—"

But she was halfway across the road. I watched as she rejoined Georgia. They greeted passersby with forced smiles that did little to mask the brokenness behind their eyes.

After a moment, I turned to head back to the MotherVine table—and nearly bumped into Red Feather Earrings, that random woman I'd been noticing around town. She was standing there twisting her hair into a bun.

I wasn't about to let her get away again.

We locked eyes—hers a startling lake-water blue.

I stuck out my hand. "Hi. I'm Callie."

Her hair came tumbling down as she clasped my hand with both of hers. She pumped my arm like it was a well handle and she was mad with thirst. "It's outrageous what's happened here this past week," she said. "My group leader called two emergency meetings just to assure us that we were safe. Other than that, I haven't spoken in fourteen whole days, so you'll have to excuse me if I come off as manic. I've been avoiding people because I didn't want to be tempted to talk."

"Why haven't you spoken in two weeks?"

"Silent retreat. I'm here with my meditation group. Four of us, all told. We're from Chapel Hill. Booked up most of the rooms at the Casa Coquina. Have you ever gone that long without speaking? Woman, it's a trip. At least for someone like me." From her shoulder bag she produced a name tag pierced with a safety pin. *Hello, my name is Meredith. I'm doing my best to minimize or eliminate speaking. Thank you for understanding.*

She tilted her head, studying me with a kind smile. "I think I saw you in the cemetery the other day. Every morning we got an envelope with an assignment inside, a task to perform. And one was to read the inscriptions on the headstones." She glanced past me and waved. "There's my leader. I'm glad you introduced yourself. See you!"

Another mystery solved.

I smiled after her. But the smile quickly faded as I noticed a shiny bald head bobbing toward me. Bo Beauchamp. He and the mobile veterinarian were engrossed in conversation. Neither noticed me as they walked by, edging around some people. But I saw the tattoos parading up Bo's wrinkled arm. And one caught my eye: the gravestone, a name curved across the top.

This time I was close enough to make out the oozy gray-green letters.

STELLA RICHER

Out came my phone.

An obituary, circa 2002, from a newspaper in Louisiana. Stella Richer had left a son, Beau. A search for Beau Richer got me nowhere. Same with Bo Richer. Then I typed *Beauregard Richer*—

a hit. Another newspaper, requiring an account to see the whole article. But snippets were readable.

> Steven Beauregard Richer, 30, of Bayou Drive, Bunkford, Louisiana, was arrested and charged . . . animal cruelty . . . aggravated assault . . . breaking and entering . . . shoplifting . . . up to fifteen years in prison . . . $30,000 in fines . . .

I studied the thumbnail-size mugshot. Take away twenty-five years of sun exposure and add a helmet of black hair, and it was him. Bo Beauchamp.

"Evening, Miss Callie."

I spun around, tucking my phone behind my back. "Hi, Bo."

He produced a toothpick from a case and poked it between his lips. "Forgot my phone in my car."

"I actually have some more questions for you, if you're feeling up to it."

"More questions? Now?"

"Good a time as any." I had no idea what I would say. But we were in a crowded public space. A safe space. And maybe there was a way I could get him to admit something, even if it was small. If I'd learned anything that week, it was that small can have a way of very quickly becoming big.

"You and all your questions," Bo said. "I'd like to know what this's *really* about."

"Maybe we could get to that. I know you want to be of service to the Meeks family."

"All right. I'll just go to my car and get my phone. I'll meet you right here in a few minutes."

I watched as he strode off—and jumped when a hand touched my arm.

It was Officer Fusco. "Got your text," she said. "You know I'm not at liberty to divulge sensitive information pertinent to an ongoing investigation."

"I helped you get into Gwen's phone. I got you Mack's last name."

"Both things I would have done eventually. If you know anything, you're obligated to tell the authorities."

"Okay, listen. There's been some awkwardness between us. You think I need to stay in my lane. Right?"

"You can say that again."

"But wouldn't we both be better off in general if we threw each other a bone every now and again? I've thrown you a bone. It's your turn to throw me one."

She rocked back on her heels. I'd laid out some appealing logic. She couldn't deny it. Could she?

"We're gonna give this arrangement one shot," she said. "If it doesn't work out, then that's it. No more nicey-nice between you and me. Don't make me regret trusting you with some intel, AC."

"I get it, Fusco."

She stepped closer. "We found a photo on Gwen's cell. Taken at 10:02 Saturday night. Poor quality but when enlarged, two people can be seen on top of the lighthouse."

It wasn't anything I hadn't already heard. But proof existed, photographic proof that what Mack Abruzzi told me was true.

"And we found fur," she said. "On the armchair inside the keeper's cottage."

"Fur?"

"Chief thought it was unusual enough to send away for analysis, seeing as Gwen wasn't a pet owner, and neither was the previous keeper. Official results will take a while, but meantime, we showed the biologists at the wildlife center a sample."

"Did they say it was rabbit fur?"

Fusco's eyes narrowed. "How do you know that?"

"Gray rabbit fur?"

She gave a single nod.

I saw Gwen's tiny living room.

I saw her lying there, arm flung out, fingers curled over the rum bottle.

I saw, opposite the couch, the red armchair.

And in it, Bo Beauchamp. Whom I'd witnessed holding a gray rabbit just days earlier. In my vision he had a shotgun across his lap. Or a pistol in his hand. Or a blade that glimmered whenever the lighthouse beam swept through the curtains. *Keep drinking*, I could practically hear him sneer.

And then, in real life, over the din of the Cattaillion, came the unmistakable rumble of a souped-up 1970s Chevy engine.

I took off, dodging people, racing toward the noise.

66

I turned down a side street just in time to glimpse Bo's powder-blue El Camino peeling down the road.

My car, at Hudson's house, was a block away. I ran for it, dialing Fusco on the way. She didn't pick up. "It's Callie," I huffed into her voicemail. "I'm tailing a classic El Camino. The driver is headed north on Queen Street. His name is Bo Beauchamp. I think he's done some bad things. This isn't an emergency or anything. I know you're on duty at the Cattaillion right now. I just wanted to let you know where I am."

I'd reached my car. I hopped in and turned the key and took off. Bo was out of sight, but maybe I could catch him.

Maybe he wanted me to catch him.

My phone buzzed. Without looking I answered, one hand on the wheel. "Fusco?"

"Nope."

"Toby." Ahead of me on the road, taillights shrank. Was it Bo's car? I stomped the gas pedal.

"Where are you?" Toby asked. "They're setting up for the fireworks. It's getting pretty windy but they're saying it'll be safe."

I caught up to the car and accelerated even more, until I could make out the powder-blue color. It was definitely Bo.

His taillights swerved left.

I put my phone on speaker. Both hands on the wheel, I cut a hard left. "I'm chasing a lead."

"Callie—"

"I'm going to put an end to all this craziness once and for all."

My Civic looked puny parked next to Bo's Chevy. I exited my car to a cacophony of dogs braying, yipping, whimpering.

"Bo?" I called. The dogs drowned out my voice. "Bo! Where are you?" I marched for the animal shelter's main building. In the reception area, my eyes adjusted to the dark.

Ahead, from Bo's office, a single light shined. The door was open. I spied heaps of papers on the desk, the corner of the rabbit cage, cabinets against the far wall.

The dogs quieted.

"Bo? I know we can work this out. You don't want to hurt any more people, do you? You're a good guy at heart." I edged nearer the office. "Police are on their way. They're willing to go easy if you turn yourself in. We all know you loved Eva. You didn't mean to hurt her."

There was a massive shove against my back, a brutal impact that sent me sailing into the office. I slammed against the desk. Recovering, I lunged for the door. But it shut, and from the other side came a scraping noise.

I twisted the doorknob and shoved.

The door didn't budge. He'd jammed it.

"Let me out." I pounded my fists.

"Save your energy," came Bo's voice. "You'll only hurt yourself."

"Bo? This is really unnecessary. The cops will be here soon and—" Through the door, I heard my phone vibrate.

I patted myself down, then looked all around. My bag was gone. He'd taken it. Slipped it off me.

My head dropped, smacking the door. He had my phone, my car keys, everything.

"Who do we have here?" Bo said from the other side of the door. "A Toby Dodge is calling you. Should I answer it? Naw. I think I'll let it go to voicemail. You and me need to talk."

I filled my lungs, sipping as much air as I could, then let it out deliberately. *Calm, Padget. Calm.*

What did I know about Bo?

Jurecki must have been familiar with Bo's criminal history. That was why the chief had warned me to stay away from him. The police had let him integrate back into society. But they knew his background.

Georgia had remembered Bo making repeated visits to the town hall when he first moved here. A legal name change might have required a few tries to get all the paperwork right. Before he could go from Steven Beauregard Richer to Bo Beauchamp.

Again, I inhaled big. "Bo? When the police arrive, you'll look a lot better if you don't have a defenseless woman trapped inside a windowless room."

"If the cops were coming, they'd be here by now. It's only a five-minute drive from downtown."

So much for that tactic. I couldn't make him believe the police were on their way if I had a hard time believing it myself.

I surveyed my surroundings. There was no office phone. Hazelnut, the gray rabbit, cowered in the corner of her cage. The wood shavings rustled with her trembling. "Don't be scared," I whispered, sticking my finger through the holes. I couldn't reach her. "You're safe."

On the other side of the door, a second object scraped the floor. A chair, perhaps. I pictured Bo straddling it backward, resting his forearms on the chairback while his toothpick danced.

I rounded the desk and opened the top drawer. Pens and pencils and paper clips.

I didn't know what I was looking for. Something to help me

escape. Something to keep me occupied. "What do you want to talk about?" I asked the door.

"You think you know all about me. But you don't."

"Enlighten me, then."

"To begin with, I'd wager a bet you don't know Bunkford, Louisiana, from a hole in the ground. Place is crawling with alligators. So many they're like squirrels. What's your opinion of squirrels?"

"They're harmless enough." I opened the second drawer and rifled through more office supplies. A stapler, some envelopes and rubber bands.

"Harmless enough," he said. "That's exactly right. I kept an alligator as a pet in my bonehead stepfather's swimming pool. Captured her when she was a baby and raised her by hand. I cared for that alligator like she was my own child. And when she started to get big, I knew she needed to eat more than crickets and frogs."

I opened the bottom drawer. It appeared empty, but something bumped around in the back. I stuck in my hand and corralled a few small objects.

Stacks of sticky notes.

Pink.

It didn't necessarily mean anything. Plenty of people on this island used pink sticky notes.

"Something tells me you didn't set your illegal pet alligator free," I said. "You didn't bring her back to the bayou where she belonged. Did you?"

"I wasn't ready to part with her. I broke into a pet store and stole some things. Mice, mostly. A few gerbils. Some hamsters. I loved those critters too. But I knew they had to die if my alligator was going to live. That's simply the way of things. The circle of life, as they say. So I shoved them into an empty pillowcase."

"You stole animals. Nice."

"I didn't know the owner lived above the pet store. I didn't know that when he jumped out and yelled, he wasn't holding a *real* gun. Just a BB gun. I shot him. Knee-jerk reaction. He survived, but they got me on assault. I'd had a clean record before all that. Squeaky clean."

Bo's backstory snapped together in my brain. After serving his sentence, he moved here, where no one knew him. He changed his name. Managed to convince the animal shelter to let him get involved. It was a smaller operation back then. Understaffed. They'd have taken anyone who demonstrated commitment. The man was reborn.

He'd sullied the Richer name. He couldn't afford to sully the Beauchamp name too. He'd worked too hard to rebuild his life.

Spinning around, I opened the first cabinet door. Neatly folded blankets and towels, smelling of wet dog and laundry detergent.

"Eva could always tell that I had no bad intentions," Bo said. "She saw the good in everyone."

Second cabinet: stack after dusty stack of Fancy Feast. "Believe it or not," I said, "I don't really care about your past."

"Like hell you don't. You reporters are all the same, with your big ambitions. That's right. I know how to use Google. I'm not some simpleminded hardware store clerk like everyone wants to think. You work for a big paper out in Charlotte."

"I used to, Bo. I *was* a reporter. In my old life."

"Bull. You're fixing to write an exposé on me. About the lowlife you think I really am. It's all over town that you've come back here to start up some big website."

"That's just island gossip."

"Maybe it is. Maybe it isn't. Either way, I've got some news for you. I was just a dumb kid when I committed those senseless crimes. I've done my time. More than my share. And I've lived a good clean life since."

"Until last Saturday night. How did you know Eva was going to be at the lighthouse? Were you stalking her? If you were so devoted to Eva, so indebted to her, how could you kill her?"

A clunking noise, as if Bo had tossed aside his chair. "I told you. I done my fair share of strayin'. But I'm through with all that." He battered the door.

I felt the vibration in my ribs and jumped, bracing myself against the counter.

"I didn't kill Eva," he said. "I loved her. I was working here Saturday night. Like I do every Saturday night. That's the reason I'm here right now. I do a round of extra let-outs for all the dogs. Call the shelter director. She can confirm it."

"You're here because you wanted to lure me. To trap me. It's part of the web you're weaving. The game you're playing. You didn't mean to kill Eva. But you did. And then you killed Gwen, because you were afraid she saw something. You put the melted lock in her unlocked trunk to make the cops think Gwen was involved. And that was when you saw the rum bottles. You knew it wouldn't look like you murdered Gwen too, if you did it right. But you should have taken a lint brush to your clothing first. Because the police found rabbit fur. Gray rabbit fur. Inside the keeper's cottage."

"You think I'm the only person on-island with a gray rabbit?"

I faced the last cabinet and pulled it open. A typewriter. Its carriage was cued with a pink paper square.

An icy dread tightened my skin. "I wonder what the police will think when I tell them you tormented me. Left me a threatening note. Chased me down my own dark street—"

"Bo Beauchamp is not the type of man to stand around while some two-bit reporter goes dredging up his past."

"Let me the hell out of here, Bo."

"You're staying right where you are. And I'm keeping your bag for a while as collateral while you check out some information. Information's what makes you people tick, after all."

"Information? Why should I believe anything you say? You just admitted to chasing me. Terrorizing me."

"You don't have to believe my information. All you have to do, if you want your bag back, is verify what I'm about to say. And when you're satisfied it's the truth, you go and tell it to the cops. Simple as that."

"If you have information, why don't you go to the police yourself?"

"Are you serious? *Me?*" He laughed a raspy laugh. "You're right naïve, you know that? Look. I'm sorry about all this. The note, and the wheelbarrow. All of it. The man I used to be did those things. Not the man I have been lately. You're going to want to hear this information, Miss Callie. So, do we have a deal?"

I pounded my fist on the counter. What choice did I have? "We have a deal."

"Saturday night," he said, "I was on my way here, to do the let-outs."

"What time Saturday night?"

"Must have been before ten o'clock. I drove past the hardware store. And I saw Eva pulling out of the lot in her company car. The red SUV. I'm a curious man by nature. I followed her. To the lighthouse."

"She didn't notice? Your car's not exactly inconspicuous."

"She might have noticed. Who's to say? I kept a good distance behind her. I didn't get too close. When I hit Lighthouse Way, I came to my senses. Realized what I was doing could be perceived as inappropriate. The last thing I wanted to do was scare Eva. Make her uncomfortable. I turned around and headed here. But not before I saw something near the boardwalk."

"What did you see?"

"Buick. Silver. Eva pulled up alongside it. It had Outer Banks plates and a dented rear fender. Bumper sticker said something about horses."

My heart raced. "That's impossible. You're describing Trish Berryman's car. And Trish would never—" My hands clamped my mouth.

If Bo's story was true, if he really had seen her car at the lighthouse that night . . .

"I believe you, Bo," I said. "Don't leave. Let me out first—"

"Not a chance. What I've got to do now is lay low until the truth comes out. Don't want to give the cops any reason to come breathing down my neck. I've had enough of that hassle to last me a lifetime. They've been giving me the side-eye for decades, and I'm sick of it. Don't want to give you your phone, neither, because who knows how many people you'll call before I have a chance to get myself good and hidden? But don't you worry. You'll find a way out of there eventually. And if you want your bag back, you'll find a way to prove my innocence. And the driver of that Buick's guilt."

I heard fading footsteps. He'd left the shelter.

Reaching up, I tested the typewriter's weight. It was heavy, more than twice Tin Man's bulk. But all week I'd been getting stronger. I'd been running and walking and practicing self-defense. Carrying the typewriter, I again rounded the desk. When I reached the door, I widened my stance. With as much upper-body strength as I could muster, I brought the typewriter down on the doorknob.

It separated from the door. Just a fraction.

I lifted the typewriter again. Slammed it down.

Lifted. Slammed.

Lifted. Slammed.

The doorknob crashed to the floor.

I dropped the typewriter. Chips of floor tile went spinning.

Outside, a Chevy engine rumbled.

I threw my body against the door. Did it again. And again. Whatever blocked the door shifted, and I was through. I raced past two upturned chairs, through the lobby, and out the front door.

The El Camino roared off, gravel cyclones swirling in its wake. I strained my ears, trying to determine which direction he'd headed. North? South? The trees all around were alive with engine noise before it faded altogether.

The dirt settled. I was covered in it, my ivory shirt almost completely tan. Blinking out the grit, I found a clean patch on the inside of my sleeve and wiped it over my eyes.

The dogs were barking again. Caterwauling. The treetops swirled in the wind.

Without a key, my car sat useless.

I darted back inside, to the greeter's desk. I grabbed the phone and held it to my ear. The dial tone droned. My fingers quavered over the keypad.

I didn't know Fusco's phone number. Or anyone's, really. In fact, the only phone numbers I could think of were my own, Hudson's landline, and 911. And my current situation didn't constitute an emergency. Did it? If what Bo told me was true, he hadn't killed anyone.

But I knew who did.

I also knew that person was just a couple of miles away, on the northernmost point of Cattail Island.

67

I kicked off my sandals and started running, leaving the animal shelter and the barking behind me. I crossed Queen Street and picked up the winding path through the forest. It was dark but I knew the way by heart. Navigating the turns, I felt swift and aerodynamic, my breathing fast but steady.

My mind zoomed.

That silver Buick Bo described belonged to Trish, no doubt about it. But the Standishes had confirmed that, from the hardware store, Eva had dialed a man. *Meet me*, she'd told him.

I remembered Jeff on the pier, the day of the manatees. He'd gazed toward the waterfront, squinting through the square he'd made with his hands. *Scouting the perfect spot to shoot the fireworks for the Cattaillion*, he'd said. *Think I found it.*

It was almost fireworks time. Which meant Jeff would be setting up his shoot.

On the old Smile Beach fishing pier.

I remembered something else he'd said—angrily, bitterly—that day he came into the MotherVine: *The locally owned businesses have been withdrawing their advertising dollars.* If Eva had been among the shop owners who'd canceled their *Crier* ads . . .

After fifteen minutes of running, I couldn't feel my feet. The soles had gone numb. After another five, my lungs were aflame. I hadn't run that hard and fast in my whole life. When I glimpsed the moon through the trunks of the loblollies, I knew I was almost there. I pumped my legs harder, sprinting toward the orange slice hanging low in the sky. The path dumped me onto the grass. Without the shelter of the forest, the wind hit me like a wall.

I leaned toward it. Ran into it. Trudged past the picnic tables, onto Smile Beach. The sand stung my shins. As I rounded the point, the Elder Tree sprawled into view, its branches beckoning the dilapidated fishing pier.

Halfway up the pier hunched a man, adjusting the legs of a tripod. The waves were alarmingly big for the sound, swallowing the pilings as they swelled.

I sprinted onto the pier. The planks underfoot felt brittle and loose, a funhouse floor about to give way. The wind gusted. The pier moaned. I stopped and cupped my hands around my mouth. "Jeff!"

"Callie? What are you doing here? Why are you covered in dirt?"

Panting, I waved him over. No way I was going any farther onto the pier. Not in that wind.

He walked toward me, his camera around his neck. "Where are your shoes? What's going on?"

I mentally superimposed the boy from the blurry *Getting cozy* photograph over Jeff's face. Subtracted about thirty-five pounds and a half dozen forehead creases. Subtracted glasses. Made his chin go from froggy to sharp.

If only I'd paid more attention.

"Did you drive Trish's car at some point last weekend?" I asked.

"What? Why do you ask?"

"Humor me."

"Last weekend? No."

A lie. I knew it in my bones.

Jeff snapped a test shot. The flash fired, momentarily blinding me. "There's been a lot to take in this week, hasn't there?" he asked. "Between Eva and Gwen."

"This isn't about my stress level." I was blinking, my pupils adapting to the fading burst.

Jeff's features came back into focus. Glasses, beaky nose, drapey jaw.

"Since you brought up the word *stress*," he said, "I'm seriously thinking it's gotten to you."

"You drove the Buick last Saturday night. Didn't you? Around nine thirty or so. You couldn't find your car keys. You misplaced them. You didn't feel like turning the house upside down looking for them. So, you took the Buick instead." I remembered that day in the *Crier* office. Trish's words. *I wonder what's taking him so long. Probably lost his car keys again. Guy would lose his head if it wasn't screwed onto his neck.*

"Callie," Jeff said. "You've been working really hard at the MotherVine. You've earned a rest, don't you think? Why don't you go on home? Get some sleep."

"You knew Eva Meeks from Camp Cottontown."

"We were counselors together. So what?"

"She didn't remember you. That's why her old *Funbook* was on her desk. She hadn't opened that booklet in years. But she wanted to verify your identity. She wanted to make sure you really did know each other once."

"*Funbook*? I want to understand you here, Callie. But I'm afraid I have no idea what you're talking about." Behind him, the tripod tipped over. He scrambled after it, collapsed it, and stuffed it into his camera bag. "Silly to think I'd be able to get any shots from here tonight. There's too much wind. It really kicked up as I was leaving the Cattaillion." He seemed so chatty, so relaxed.

"You were the last person to see Eva alive," I said. "A source described Trish's car—which I think *you* were driving—parked next to Eva's company truck at the lighthouse last Saturday night."

He peered into his camera's viewfinder, then fiddled with some buttons. "We were buddies at camp, me and Eva. That one summer. I was a senior counselor and she was a junior counselor. So what?"

"Did you grow up near Camp Cottontown?"

"Couple hours southeast of there."

"When did you move here?"

"What's with the third degree? I did a few semesters of college, then quit for Cattail. I'd come to the Outer Banks on vacation with my family, and I decided I never wanted to live anywhere else. Like thousands of other people. What does that have to do with anything?"

"How long before you saw the commercial for Meeks Hardware on TV? *Everything* and *the kitchen sink!*"

"Not long. A few times that first year here, I found myself shopping at Meeks. And Eva rang me up. But she didn't seem to remember me. Either that, or she wasn't interested. And I decided to leave it be."

"And then you met Trish."

Genuine sadness came over Jeff's face. "Trish was never the same after your mother, you know. She retreated deep inside herself. The two of them had been good friends. Your mother was almost twice her age, of course. But they were close. Trish looked up to her. She *still* blames herself."

"And all the while, you never stopped thinking about Eva."

"How could I? My wife had become a shell of her former self. And by comparison, Eva was so *alive*. And I was always seeing her. On the TV screen. In the flesh, walking past the *Crier* office, or ringing me up in the hardware store. We talked on the phone a few times last fall, when she was still buying ad space."

"When did she finally realize that you'd also been at Camp Cottontown? It must have been fairly recently."

"A few weeks ago. Trish sent me to buy a birdfeeder. They have one at the stables, so she got it in her head that we needed one at home. And of course, I'm her errand boy. Anyway, Eva helped me. She said something about Camp Cottontown. 'We used to make crafts with birdseed, using toilet paper rolls and peanut butter.' And I said, 'I know, because I was actually at camp with you one summer. Nineteen eighty-eight.'"

"Were you in love with her?" I asked.

"This whole town was in love with her."

"That's not what I meant. Eva called *you* last Saturday night. From the hardware store. Now, why wouldn't she have used her cell phone to make that call? Maybe she didn't want anyone knowing you and she were a thing."

"Relax. She was there to grab her metal detector. Maybe her cell was low on batteries, and that's why she decided to use the landline. Maybe she left her phone in her SUV. I don't know. What I do know is, Eva and I weren't ever a thing. And that's that. That's all there is to it. Period, end of sentence. End of story—"

"It's just the beginning of the story, Jeff."

His eyes flicked to the water, then back to me. In that brief instant, his face had changed. Gone from cool and casual to taut. Electrified.

"What?" I asked.

"Nothing."

I didn't want to take my eyes off him, but I had to know what he'd seen. I inched sideways. My fingertips found the rotted railing. *Please let it be a manatee. Please let it be a goofy, sweet manatee floating there.* I allowed myself a quick downward peek—just as a silver-black triangle pierced the waves, and a tapered shadow muscled underneath the pier. The shadow was nine feet long. At least.

The hair on my arms frizzed.

A bull shark. The only kind that swims in brackish water. *The most aggressive, territorial, and dangerous shark.*

Another gust of wind made the pier groan and rattle. "We need to get off this thing," I said.

Jeff took a step toward me. "You want off? I can help. *Chum.*"

"What are you—"

He surged, shoving me against the railing. His arm slipped behind my knees. I was tipping up, tipping backward. I grabbed the neck of his shirt. My other elbow flew up and caught his chin.

His teeth clacked. He stumbled away.

I crashed onto the pier. Along with something else—something clattering onto the planks. His phone. I scrabbled for it and hit the side button three times. Emergency SOS.

Jeff's shoe whacked my knuckles. The phone skittered out of reach.

But it was glowing. Had my call gone through? Was 911 listening?

Jeff loomed. He was the only thing standing between me and the beach. Between me and the phone. Between me and safety.

My knuckles ached. My belly lurched. "What are you going to do, Jeff?" I said, pulling myself up. "Throw me to the shark?"

"I don't know how you figured all this out. But I never meant to hurt anyone. And I've got a paper to get out. And I can't do that from a prison cell."

"Does Trish know?"

"She thinks she knows everything." He lunged, swinging his arms.

I leapt back, out of reach, farther onto the pier. "Did Eva want the *Crier* to cover her treasure hunt exploits?" I asked. "She thought it would be good free press for the hardware store."

"She wanted me to put it on the front page. I told her below the fold. She was so happy about that. She called it a mutually beneficial arrangement. Good for both our businesses."

"You were skeptical. But you met her. Because it was Eva."

"She said it was her dying wish. How could I *not* meet her?"

"Why didn't she call Trish? She's the one who does most of the writing."

"Because Eva knew me. She trusted *me*. She bought ad space from me. Trish never goes to the hardware store. Haven't you noticed? Her Highness the editor in chief never goes anywhere except the *Crier* office and the damn stables. I'm the one who does everything. All the shopping. All the cooking. All the everything." He edged toward me, murder in his eyes.

I inched backward. "Jeff—"

"I couldn't find my damn car keys, like you said. So I hopped into the Buick. *Those* keys are always in the same spot. Perfect Trish hangs them on her perfect hook the second she steps inside our home. She was upstairs, asleep. She didn't even know I'd left. Not that I wouldn't have told her about it in the morning, had things transpired differently."

It was the most ridiculous of clichés. The killer, finally cornered, explains everything. It only happened in books. But it was happening now. In real life.

For Jeff, the prospect of living with his secret was too big a burden. If he unloaded it onto me, I could carry it to my own watery grave.

The pier creaked again, and swayed.

I needed off that decrepit structure. But I also needed to keep Jeff talking. I needed the truth, especially if someone was listening on the other end of his phone. The wind roared, and every backward step brought me farther from the phone. But if there was a chance . . .

"Eva got her blowtorch," I said, raising my voice. "She got the drainage tray from in front of her house. She drove to the hardware store. She called you. And then she drove to the lighthouse. Where you met her."

"I tried to convince her to go to the keeper's cottage first. There were lights on." He lunged again.

I hopped back, dodging him. "Eva wouldn't have sought permission from Gwen," I said. "She liked doing things her own way."

"It took about five minutes for her to torch the lock. She giggled the entire time. And then she flew up those spiral stairs. We spent at least a half hour searching up there. We were all over the spindles. The bricks. She was convinced she would find *something.* You know how she loved all that hidden treasure stuff. She figured it wasn't going to be anything serious. But she said this riddle she stumbled upon was driving her crazy, and she just had to know, and it would be a great, fun feature for the *Crier.* She kept saying, *I'm gonna get to the bottom of whatever this is.* But she found nothing up there. Nothing."

"This was never about a curse," I said. "All along, it's been about you not being able to control yourself." The wind gusted, and my body began to tremor. I remembered how excited Eva had sounded when she called me that night. How giddy she must have been as she searched the top of the lighthouse. I pictured her finally admitting defeat with a laugh or a shrug or a self-deprecating joke. She probably expected to climb back down to ground level, climb into her truck, and then climb into her own bed.

But Jeff had other ideas.

"Last weekend," I said, my voice shaking, "was the anniversary of my mother's death. And you remembered what a big deal that was. I bet you and Trish sold a lot of newspapers when my mom died. You were angry with Eva for pulling her advertising, weren't you? You were angry she never recognized you. You were angry that your wife wears the pants. You found yourself there at the top of the lighthouse thinking, *A little push might sell a lot of papers*. You can't deny it." My mind raced. My fingers twitched. All the little details were fitting into place—including the high places phenomenon, which I'd read about in that book in the MotherVine, the one with the human brain on the cover. Instead of the urge to jump, Jeff got the urge to push someone. And instead of letting the urge slide on by, he acted it out. "You did it," I said. "You killed her."

"It wasn't my fault."

My jaw dropped. "Whose fault was it?"

"I wish I could take it back—"

"But you can't. You flipped her over the railing. And then you raced down to the bottom of the lighthouse and you picked up the blowtorch and the drippings and put them inside Gwen's car, in an attempt to implicate someone else. You didn't realize how easily the police would accept the suicide explanation. And then you went home, and went to bed, and got up the next day and let your wife report to the scene of your own crime. And four nights later, you went after Gwen Montgomery."

"I couldn't stop thinking about how the light was on in the keeper's cottage when Eva and I first got there," he said. "I couldn't stop wondering whether the new keeper had seen anything. I wanted to find out what she knew." Jeff sprang. This time, I wasn't fast enough. His arms clamped around my neck, headlocking me. He shoved me toward the railing.

I kicked, planting my heel on something hard. His shin, maybe. He let out a string of profanity, and I wriggled away.

"I thought of confessing, you know," he said.

"But instead, you decided on the murder of a second innocent woman."

"That's *not* what I decided. I got my Ruger out of storage, and

I got a bottle of cheap rum as backup. The brand she liked, based on the bottles I saw in her trunk. My initial plan was simply to scare her, if it turned out she'd seen me. You know, knock her off-balance. Show her who was boss. Explain to her, if necessary, that *Crier* sales had reached an all-time low, and this whole Eva Meeks thing was just the bump we needed to boost the family business out of a dangerous rut. My gun wasn't even loaded, by the way."

"Gwen wasn't so easy to convince, was she? She wasn't so easy to scare."

"She wasn't sympathetic to my plight, so I activated Plan B. Forced her to drink. It went on for a while. I had a few swigs myself. And something came over me. Probably the booze, making me loose. Regretful. I thought better of it all. I decided to leave her alone. Decided to face my fate, whatever it might be. That girl was alive when I left the cottage, I swear it. I thought she'd just blacked out."

"The rabbit fur," I said. That photo Trish had—her holding a lamb. There were all sorts of different animals at the barn, she'd said. There must have been rabbits. Gray was a common-enough rabbit color. "The police found rabbit fur on Gwen's armchair," I said. "You had fur on your clothing. From Trish's car. She's been going to the stables all week—"

He came at me, his hands outstretched, reaching for my throat.

I stood my ground and leaned in, my arm uncoiling. *Poke the eyes.* My fingers struck the lenses of his eyeglasses. My knuckles jammed, pain shooting. I jerked back.

He clenched my arm. I chopped it down—but he held on and yanked me closer. His other arm locked around me.

I twisted, my back to him. He had both my arms pinned. I could barely move.

He picked me up and swung me toward the railing. "I don't want to do this, Callie. I'm sorry."

Overpowering someone isn't your goal. Staying alive is your goal.

I stomped my feet. I squirmed and bucked. But he pressed me against the railing. "One way or another, you're going over," he said.

Fight back. Don't stop.

I screamed. Jeff's hand clamped my mouth. I chomped down hard and tasted salt and blood.

Releasing me, he staggered away. "I'm sorry about everything. I always liked you. My sweet little across-the-street neighbor. But you're off the rails now. I can't let you live—"

A boom rattled the night.

In the southeastern sky, a bronze parachute popped open. The first Cattaillion firework. Its tendrils glittered against the moon like octopus arms.

The wind gusted again, the biggest gust yet. The fateful gust that finally did in the old Smile Beach fishing pier.

With a deafening grinding of rust on wood, the pier wrenched toward the water. I was sliding, groping, falling. Splinters pierced my heels. And then water was everywhere, briny and cold, pulling me down, flooding my throat.

I got my feet underneath me and dug my toes into the silt and shot straight up. I was barely standing. I tipped back my head and gulped air. A wave battered my face and I sputtered and swiped a hand over my stinging eyes. The pier was crumbling section by section, dropping into the water like toppled dominoes. Swimming away from the turbulence, I bumped Jeff, a limp facedown T-shape. Something must have struck his head and knocked him unconscious. A plank, a piling, a segment of railing.

"Jeff," I screamed. "Wake up. You have to swim." I grabbed a handful of his hair and yanked his face out of the water. A gash over his eyebrow spilled blood. He moaned but didn't open his eyes.

A nail-studded board was sailing toward us. I dove away, pulling Jeff with me. I resurfaced, gasping. I was kicking as hard as I could for the beach, dragging Jeff by his shirt collar, when I saw it. The dorsal fin rising from the waves, slicing straight for us.

Make a still, silent, and extremely hasty retreat.

Fear shuddered through my limbs. Jeff's body jerked away, the fabric of his shirt ripping from my hands. I got sucked after him, into a powerful wake.

That was when something hard rammed my shoulder, shooting me down, pinning me under the waves. I bucked and kicked until my lungs burned but couldn't budge whatever heavy thing had come to rest on top of me.

Stars zigzagged, and everything went black.

68

I was on my back and couldn't open my eyes. Sand coated my tongue. But I was breathing. Shallow, salty-sweet breaths.

I heard a woman's voice. A gooey accent. Officer Fusco, huffing hard. "Ambulance is en route."

Then another voice, rumbling. Hudson. "What happened?"

"A plank landed on her," Fusco said. "Caught her as it sank. I had just arrived and was running down the beach and I saw where she went down."

Me. She was talking about me.

I forced open my eyes. Fusco's arm extended over me. Water dripped from her dark sleeve. She was pointing. "Right there. Only three or four feet deep. I was able to free her. She was only under a few seconds."

"Fusco?" I tried to say through jackhammering teeth.

"She's coming to." A third voice, deep and musical, like an upright bass. A warm, strong hand was holding mine.

"Toby?" I said. "You're here?"

His face floated above mine. "Where else would I be?"

My ribs were thundering. Above Toby's head, bronze parachutes and emerald spirals and ruby streaks painted the sky. The Cattaillion fireworks grand finale.

I tried to sit up but was gently pushed back against the sand. "Jeff," I said. "Jeff Berryman killed Eva and Gwen. And then the shark—the shark—"

"Hush," my uncle said. "Just be still."

Sirens screamed, and red and blue lights twirled around us.

"Chief!" Fusco waved. "Over here."

"We got it all." It was Jurecki's voice. "It's all recorded on the 911 call. Jeff Berryman did it. He killed them both. Callie, you were outstanding." The chief had reached us. He bent over, hands on his knees, panting. "She going to be okay?"

Hudson smoothed the wet hair from my forehead. "She's going to be better than okay. She's going to be aces."

"Good," Jurecki said. "So where is he? Where's Jeff Berryman?"

69

I awoke in my Murphy bed. Sunlight streamed through a crack in the curtains. From outside came a happy chirruping, the unmistakable cries of purple martins. If I looked out the window, I'd have seen a dozen lacing the rooftops, streaking the sky purple-black. But I was too tired, too sore, to move.

The chirruping was drowned out by the whirring of helicopter blades. The coast guard, still looking for Jeff Berryman. Last night, they'd spent hours scouring the water. Boats and helicopters shined searchlights into the chop. By now the rescue mission had become a recovery mission. And Cattail Island had its first-ever shark attack on record.

I hadn't gotten much sleep thanks to leftover adrenaline making it impossible to keep my eyes closed. I'd stayed up finishing *While My Pretty One Sleeps*. Neeve pursues Ethel's killer, following him into an empty office building after hours. There's a confrontation, and of course Neeve comes out on top.

I'd closed the book cheering, just like I had when I was twelve.

Now a wave of fatigue rolled through me, and I pulled the covers to my chin. Outside, the helicopter beats faded, replaced by the purple martins' song.

And that was when, in my mind, words began pulsing. Acrobatting, like the dark swallows.

Purple martins.

Purple martins.

Sudden energy spasmed through me. I vaulted to my feet and

crossed the room to my bag, which Fusco had retrieved after tracking down Bo.

Pen and scrap paper in hand, I dashed out two rows of words.

PURPLE MARTINS

SLIPPER TRUMAN

I traced a line connecting the top *P* to one of the bottom *P*s. Drew another line connecting the top *U* to its bottom counterpart. Another line connected the *R*s, and so on.

Every letter had a match.

Summer Meeks's theory was dead-on. Slipper Truman was an anagram. For purple martins.

Purple martins will lead you to / the next adventurous little clue.

The locally famous roost under the old fishing pier. Exactly the sort of thing Chip deSilva would have picked for a Tourism Task Force treasure hunt, whose purpose was to lead folks to Cattail's places of interest.

70

I scoured the area of Smile Beach that hadn't seen the sun in almost forty years, shaded as it had been by the pier. The beach was all mine, thanks to the red NO SWIMMING flags and news of a man-eating shark. The beach was also a mess, littered with debris. I clambered over barnacled posts and hunks of concrete. I sifted through mangled nails and fishing hooks and tangles of line and seaweed-strangled crab pots.

An hour passed. I turned up nothing. I headed for a washed-up bench sticking out of the sand, detritus from the pier. The bench was a former built-in for the birdwatchers and the fishermen. It had lost its rear supports, and the back was tipped against an escarpment that had formed during last night's gales. I sat angled toward the sky, feet dangling, head on the sun-warmed sand, nothing but blue in my vision.

On the bench, I rested in the approximate spot where I'd come to the night before, after Fusco dragged me to safety. The events of the past twenty-four hours flashed in my mind like a spastic news reel. I saw Jeff on the pier, lunging for me. I saw Bo's El Camino kicking up gravel in the animal shelter parking lot. I saw Pearleen on her love seat, her hands welcoming mine.

And I heard the words I'd said to her, the scenario I'd imagined. Chip deSilva hiding a vial underneath a park bench.

Underneath a bench.

Like the one I was now sitting on.

I sprang up, then dropped to hands and knees. I scooped

sand, clearing it from the underside of the seat. And there it was: a wad stuffed between the concrete and a rusted bracket.

Excitement zipped through me. My hands were shaking so badly I could barely wriggle the thing loose. It was nesting-dolled inside about a million plastic baggies. Chip deSilva must have figured any clue stashed ten feet above the water would need extra, mega protection.

One by one I peeled away the clear layers, fishy odors making my nose crinkle. When I reached the final baggie, I shook out the bits of glass, all that remained of a pulverized vial. The swollen scroll looked about as flimsy as a Kleenex gone through the washing machine, so I didn't touch it, but instead resealed the bag. Through the plastic, the blotted blue ink of Chip DeSilva's final riddle seemed to sing up at me.

Amazing work! You're almost there.
A final treasure awaits. But where?
Look inside our queenliest tree—
a smile for all, inherently free.

71

The Elder Tree stood about fifty feet from where I knelt in the sand. I wanted nothing more than to sprint over to it, vault up it, and stick my arm into the old cavity, the one I'd sat next to countless times. I wanted to sweep my fingertips over rotten twigs and crumbled leaves until I uncovered whatever Chip deSilva had hidden.

But it wasn't just for me.

So I got out my phone, and I orchestrated.

I asked Reedley Anderson and Faith the restaurant manager and Daisy Kapur and Toby and Chief Jurecki and everyone I could think of to get the word out, however they saw fit. Georgia was all too willing to update the hardware store's social media pages. I updated Tin Man's Instagram account:

> Well-read cats are suckers for secrets, and word has it Smile Beach is gearing up to reveal a big, BIG secret. You don't want to miss this, darlings! In all seriousness though . . .

Summoning the public was a risk. Whatever was hidden inside the Elder Tree might have disintegrated, or been taken, a long time ago. But I had a feeling. That old reporter's instinct. Something was there. Something worth finding.

On any other day the *Crier* would have been an obvious resource. But Trish was likely just learning about her husband's nefarious deeds and horrific death. How does a woman get over a thing like that? I sent some compassionate thoughts her way.

Then I zipped to Hudson's house, retrieved something, and returned here, to Smile Beach. In the absence of wind, the Pamlico was waveless, mirrorlike. *Slick-cam*, the old-timers would say. Without the pier to beckon to, the Elder Tree looked even bigger, its outermost branches casting shadows on the soft sand. Strolling toward the tree, I saw clear to the opposite end of the island. The lighthouse poked from the distant treetops, and for the first time in years, at the sight of it, my chest didn't hollow out and ice over. Instead, it filled up. With light and warmth and gratitude and I don't even know what else. The side-by-side white crosses at the foot of the lighthouse were too small to see from my vantage point, of course. But it was enough to know they were there. I was going to make sure they'd always be there.

Placing a hand on the Elder Tree, I knew what I'd meant when I told Hudson that I, too, had some changes to make.

I was going to stay in Cattail. For good.

People arrived—curious vacationers and concerned locals shuffling over the sand, their voices a low murmur. Just before dusk, a soft golden light settled on Smile Beach and on the hundreds who had gathered.

The Meeks family was clustered near the Elder Tree. Not only Summer and Georgia and Walter and Wendy, but others—cousins and aunts and uncles of all ages, from babes-in-arms to walker-dependent blue-haireds. Near them lingered the law enforcement crew: Fusco, Jurecki, Logan the dispatcher, and Dr. Scarboro. Pearleen Standish wore a designer madras pantsuit. Whitman escorted her, pausing whenever she encountered someone she wanted to schmooze.

Closer to the water, Red Feather Earrings appeared to be making small talk with Mack Abruzzi, who'd driven down from Virginia. Even Bo was there, wading in the shallow surf, work boots hugged to his chest.

I spotted the Gang. Ronnie, Hudson, and Antoinette were strolling down the beach, with Scupper trailing. As I walked to meet them, I realized Antoinette was holding a thin leash attached to a harness—which was attached to Tin Man. Wide-eyed, the cat picked his way around the people.

Hudson waved me over. "If you told me even just last month that someday I'd be walking down the beach following a cat on a leash, I'd have—"

I rolled up on my toes and wrapped my arms around him and squeezed. The smell of him enveloped me. Wood shavings and Irish Spring soap.

He squeezed back, kissing the top of my head. "What was that for?" he asked when I let go. A smile made his sea-green eyes twinkle.

"We'll talk later, okay?" I said.

Antoinette patted my cheek. "I'm impressed with you, Callie. With all this."

"Look," Ronnie said. "The big guy wants to explore. He loves it here!"

Sure enough, Tin Man was straining against the harness. The three of them continued on, letting the cat lead the way, his whiskers quivering over the sand.

I noticed Toby striding toward me, weaving through the crowd. A thrill traveled up my spine. I found myself standing a bit straighter. "Hello, Mr. Dodge."

"There you are." He led me a short distance away from any listening ears. "I was so worried about you last night," he said.

"I know. But I'm fine."

"You sure? Because we've got eleven months to go. And we both need to be in peak condition—mentally, emotionally, and physically—to survive."

Eleven months. That was how much time remained on his celibacy vow.

He wanted me to wait. And *he* wanted to wait—for me.

My whole body felt like a warm, glowing smile.

In just eleven months, Toby Dodge would be a free agent.

In just eleven months, I'd have a sun-kissed tan, and I'd be a whiz in the bookshop—and there'd be a fresh new summer to savor.

"It's less than a year," I said. "Think you'll make it?"

"Oh, I'll make it. I'm the kind of guy who accomplishes whatever he sets his mind to."

"And then what?"

He brushed a strand of hair from my face. His fingertips feathered my jawline, and I nuzzled his hand. "I've got some ideas," he said. "*Calliope.*"

"Decent guess." I beckoned him closer. He bent his head toward mine, lowering his ear to my mouth. "Next time," I said, "try Calista."

Applause broke our spell; Summer Meeks had begun climbing the Elder Tree.

Georgia bustled over to me. "Someone needs to say a few words," she said, her eyes filling up. "I can't. And none of my cousins have stepped forward, and—"

"I would, Georgia. But I'm not a speaker. Especially not off-the-cuff. And there's an awful lot of people here and—what about your parents?"

"They're beside themselves. And they want you." She gestured to a footstool someone had set up. "I'll never ask you for anything else ever again. I swear."

"Okay. Of course."

"Thank you. Thank you for everything," she said before rejoining her family.

I dipped my hand inside my bag. One last time, my fingers traced the peaks and valleys of my old crown. Then I offered it up to Summer, who was straddling the Elder Tree's main branch. "I'd like you to have this," I said. "My mother made it. It's cattail weave."

"Wow." She perched the crown on her lemonade hair. "Perfect fit."

For a second I took her in—heart-shaped face, skinny legs dangling. Then, exhaling, I stepped onto the stool. The chitchat had started up again. I looked past the hundreds of faces, toward the glistening water. "Thanks for coming, everyone."

The chatter continued.

"Louder." Toby flashed me double metal-head horns—middle fingers tucked, index fingers and pinkies extended. "You got this."

I cleared my throat, drew back my shoulders, and forced myself to look directly into the front-row faces. "Good afternoon."

The crowd hushed. All eyes turned to me.

I wiped my sweating palms on my dress. "I'm Callie Padget, a bookseller at Cattail's own MotherVine Bookshop. If you're here, there's a chance you've been affected by our island's recent tragic events.

"First I'd like to say a few words about Gwen Montgomery. We didn't know her very long. But she loved the lighthouse and was working hard on becoming a better version of herself. I think Gwen would have eventually felt at home here in Cattail. Like she had ended up right where she belonged.

"Some of you might not know this, but for the past twenty-four years, every Monday during the month of May, high school students on Cattail Island are encouraged to volunteer. Offer their time and services to whatever group interests them. The animal shelter, the library, the hospital, the churches. It was Eva Meeks who started that tradition. And it's for Eva that the tradition will continue."

A few sniffles came from the direction of the Meeks family.

"Before Eva passed away," I said, "she unearthed a treasure hunt. It was planted by a man named Chip deSilva, who lived and worked here many years ago and was trying to satisfy a town committee's special request.

"Searching for hidden treasure was something Eva loved, and she died doing it. She didn't get to solve this particular puzzle. But fortunately, her daughter, Summer, now has the honor of finishing what her mother started."

A cheer and several whistles erupted as Summer stuck her arm into the Elder Tree. The crowd leaned forward, their faces pointed upward. Anticipation seemed to make the air shimmer. "I feel something," she said.

"What is it?" someone shouted.

"Pull it out!"

She crammed the crown lower on her head—assurance that it wouldn't slip. Gaining as much reach as possible, she flattened herself against the Elder Tree. From deep inside came a creak, the heartwood giving up whatever thing it had grown around. Summer leaned back. The license-plate-size object in her hand cleared the cavity. She brushed the dirt from her payload, revealing artwork inside a cheap plastic frame.

"Hold it up," a man hollered. "Let us see."

She swung her back leg over the branch and displayed the sketch. Plain old pencil, by the looks of it. A map. Chip deSilva had captured the curved-reed shape of Cattail Island and labeled many points of interest. The Elder Tree, the pirate ship, the beaches. On the northern end, purple-black birds swooped toward the cartoonish pier. From the southern end, a lighthouse beam swept outward.

Along the bottom of the sketch, I noticed deSilva's unmistakable calligraphic hand. "What's the message?" I asked.

Summer cleared her throat and enunciated. "It says, *Cattail—the down-home isle that's worth your while.*"

A couple in the front row turned away, disappointment on their faces. But Summer's voice made them halt. "Cattail really is worth your while," she said. "Don't you think?"

I had to agree. Cattail was worth it. All of it.

In essence, Chip deSilva's final treasure was an advertisement selling the virtues of Cattail Island. But his sketched map wasn't merely that. It was also simple, sweet truth.

Applause began to ripple through the crowd. A smattering at first, and then it erupted, drowning out the far-off bellow of the ferry. There were high fives and embraces. Kids jumped and dogs wagged their tails and some people even laughed and hooted and punched the air.

I looked around, wanting to remember everything. Toby's arms wrapping around me. Hudson bear-hugging Antoinette. The smells of summer in my nose: sunscreen and cedar trees and French fries.

I even wanted to remember the ache in my heart.

ACKNOWLEDGMENTS

Thank you—yes, *you!*—for reading *Smile Beach Murder.* Mercifully, there are hundreds of millions of books in the world. The fact that you selected this one is not lost on me. I'm honored.

My talented agent, Adam Chromy, saw potential in a scruffy manuscript and patiently guided me as I groomed it into a proper story. Adam, thank you for taking a chance on me, for teaching me, and for elevating my writing.

I'm thrilled to have found a home at Berkley Prime Crime and very grateful for my crackerjack editors, Michelle Vega and Mary Geren, whose sharp observations made this tale swifter and smarter. To the designers, marketing experts, and other team members I haven't yet met: thank you one and all for your hard work, creativity, and acumen. Special thanks also to Kate Seaver.

Cattail Island, its people, and its events are fictional, yet I strove to imbue these pages with authenticity; any mistakes are mine. The following fine friends helped me fine-tune the details: Jamie Anderson of the wonderful Downtown Books in Manteo, North Carolina; Matthew Huband; Emily Midgette Pharr; Jennifer Shagensky; and Sherry Thorp. I appreciate you. And EMP, I'm thankful for time spent gliding (ha!) at your side.

Gratitude to Jamie Brenner and Kat Morgan, fellow creatives and kind early cheerleaders for this project; and to my sister Ann-Marie Hanlon, Bananagrams aficionada

Most of all, my husband Matthew Quick. It's been decades, and I still don't know what I did to deserve you. I do know that m every bit the goner today as I was at seventeen, gazing into your ocean-green eyes during our first-ever conversation, which was about the Outer Banks. “What’s that?” I asked; having grown up in New England, I’d never heard of the place. You described wild mustangs and shooting stars, towering old lighthouses and break-your-heart beautiful beaches. You promised I’d love it here. You were right. Thank you.